# ᵀʰᵉ Gospel ₒf
# Santa Claus

*Inspired by the True Story of Saint Nicholas*

**Wayne A. Van Der Wal**

Published by *Five Vines Press*

For more information: TheGospelofSantaClaus.com

Print Book  ISBN 978-1-7327710-0-0
Ebook  ISBN 978-1-7327710-1-7

10 9 8 7 6 5 4 3 2

Cover Art — Brandon Swann

*Dedicated to my beautiful children, Kari and Dax,*
*may the Spirit of Christmas live in your hearts forever.*

# DISCLAIMER

This novel is historical fiction based on limited historical records about the life of St. Nicholas. This novel presents two story lines: Nicholas' history and a modern-day family's story. The basic chronology of Nicholas' story and its known historical characters reflects historical accuracy (see reference section). However, situations, incidents, and conversations concerning historical characters and non-historical fictional characters are fictional. The story concerning the modern-day family is entirely fiction. The author's name, Wayne; his children's names, Kari and Dax; and the names of two of Wayne's friends, Craig Roegner and Ekanem (Israel) Ita, are used with electronic permission. The makeup of the author's family of origin—two parents with three children, with father former military—is used as well. Beyond that, in all other aspects, the remaining content is a product of the author's imagination, and any resemblance to actual persons, living or dead, is entirely coincidental.

# ℌreface

During my childhood, life seemed to move at a slower pace. A day, a week, or a summer vacation seemed like a long time. As I have gotten older and I now have many years behind me, it feels as if time has sped up and the days, weeks, and years are flying by. I encourage you to embrace taking your time with this novel and enjoy it for what it is, especially the first third of the novel as characters develop. If your childhood was like mine, let it take you back to your leisurely childhood. Soak it in.

You can read this historical novel as a whole novel any time of the year, *or* in 30 daily readings anytime, or over the 30 days before Christmas. I call this book "*a novel for the whole family.*" My hope is that adults, such as parents, grandparents, and others, will read it to children. It contains some adult concepts and content, so I hope it fosters positive pondering, and conversations for all. The 30 chapters coincide well with the Advent season, the four Sundays before Christmas. This is when Christians around the world remember and celebrate the Savior's first coming on that first Noel long ago, while also looking forward with anticipation to the Savior's Second Coming when He will gather His people and restore His Kingdom.

This novel was a labor of love written over a period of seven years during Christmas, Easter, and summer vacations. I am a visual person; I conceived this story as a movie in my mind, and it would not go away, so I felt driven to get it out of my head and onto paper. This novel is the result. Christmas is a special time of year for me, and I felt God put it on my heart to write a story illuminating and celebrating the true meaning of Christmas.

I added devotions at the end of each chapter to go a little deeper with the content. They are optional of course

My prayer for you, the reader, is that you'll be touched, taught, and entertained: *touched* emotionally by something or someone in the story, but especially touched spiritually by God in some way; *taught* something new about Nicholas, God, Christmas, and the Christian faith; and *entertained*, so that you enjoy the read and feel satisfied after you've finished the novel. If somehow these things happen, then all the glory, honor, and praise go to our Father in Heaven.

Blessings,
Wayne

# Acknowledgements

Special thanks go to the following:

To Kimberly Craft-Parkhurst, for being the first person to embrace reading the manuscript, lifting my spirits when I was not sure if I had something worthy of print, and helping me begin the editing process.

To Pastor Terry Fred, of Destiny Center Church Reno, for reading the manuscript early on and giving me positive and constructive feedback, especially the idea to split the novel into readings for daily devotionals to read with his grandchildren.

To Pastors Bill Osgood of Midtown LifeChurch Reno, Rod Halecky of The River Christian Church, and Tom Chism of LifeChurch Reno, for taking the time to read the manuscript early on and give positive and constructive feedback.

To Christy Callahan, for assistance in the early stages of editing.

To Mel McGowan of PlainJoe Studios, for suggesting the final title of the novel.

To my sister, Lisa Compton, for giving positive and encouraging feedback.

To Kathleen Johnson, for being a listening ear and encourager through the editing and publishing process.

To Ana Hollinger, for embracing reading the manuscript, being positive and encouraging, and allowing me to bounce ideas off her toward the end of the process.

To my wonderful kiddos, Kari and Dax, for letting me bounce ideas off them when I needed another set of eyes or ears on something.

To Brandon Swann, for his patience with me and his artistic skills for the novel cover.

To Jessica Santina of Lucky Bat Press, for her patience with me and her help with the editing and publishing process. God made me smile when I realized, of all the editors in the world, the managing editor I was led to had the last name of a female Santa (Santina).

To Quantum Leap for all their marketing and publicity expertise.

Finally, ultimate thanks to God my Father, who art in Heaven. Thank You, Lord, for putting this movie in my head and then giving me, a person with an attention deficit, the perseverance to get that movie out of my head and onto paper over seven long years, during holiday breaks. Then, after finishing the writing, three years to edit and publish. I can't believe it. For me to write this novel was a "God thing," a true miracle. All glory, honor, and praise goes to You, Heavenly Father! Thank You, my Lord!

# Pronunciation Guide

Aindriú: 'ayn-dru

Amuruq: ah-ma-rük

Aria: 'ahr-ē-ə

Diocletian: dī-ə-'klē-shən

Ekanem: ē-'kăn-əm

Falon: 'fā-lən

Kari: 'kar-ē  (car-ee)

Mikros: 'mē-krōs

Nona: 'nō-nə

Pol: pōl

Prisca: 'prĭs-kə

Sandor: săn-dor

Tana: 'tah-nə

Thalassa: thə-'lah-sə

Theophanes: thē-'ah-fə-nēz

Valeria: və-'ler-ē-ə

Vida: 'vē-də

Yahya: yah-yā

# 1
# The Train Ride of Their Lives?

"HURRY UP!" It is early Christmas Eve morning and a family rushes from their car, across a parking lot, to board an olden-day, steam-engine train. They are visiting the mother's parents, who live way up north, for Christmas. It is cold, and snow flurries are fluttering in the air. The train whistle blows *WOO WOOOOO!* From the father on down to the youngest child, they bark at each other, "Hurry up!" They are carrying luggage, backpacks, bags, and wrapped Christmas presents.

They are the last passengers to board the train, and they rustle down the aisle to find their compartment. Observers, including one friendly faced stranger seated in their compartment, can see the tension on the faces of the family as they find their seats without talking to each other. The train begins to move, jolting their heads in the same direction. They have made it just in time, but they are not celebratory about it; in fact, they are quite the opposite—subdued. They do not even notice the stranger who sits among them.

After a moment to collect herself, Mary, the mother, perks up in her seat. "Well, this will be nice. A snowstorm may be coming in, and we won't have to be cramped in our car driving in the bad weather to my mom and dad's, huh, dear?" She raises her eyebrows above her black-pearl eyes and looks at her stoic husband for reassurance.

Her husband, Joe, scratches his unshaven scruff. "Yeah, sure, hon. Instead, I spent a fortune for us to ride this old train with no modern conveniences to let me catch a single football game score. If we weren't visiting your parents, I could be home watching the games in my comfy recliner on our big screen TV." He takes a deep breath and gives a long exhale, releasing pressure that has built up within him; displeasure is all over his face.

Mary's eyes tear-up. She has much more than the normal holiday stress weighing heavy on her heart and mind. "Yes, but you know my Dad isn't doing well with his heart, and it's too risky for him to travel. He might not be around next Christmas. My parents wanted the kids to experience riding this classic train. They said they'd help pay for the tickets as much as they can."

Joe's face softens; he gives her a glance and rubs her back for a moment to give some comfort. Mary dabs her eyes with a tissue she has handy and pushes her wavy, black, shoulder-length hair behind her ears. The train continues to move, and they hear released a burst of steam as the train picks up speed.

Mary looks out the window; she is determined to be positive. "Look, kids! We're really moving now! This is going to be sooo much fun riding a train for the first time together as a family and seeing the beautiful mountain scenery! And look, see how beautifully the train is decorated for Christmas! It looks magical!"

She looks at all the holiday décor—tinsel, colored Christmas lights, wrapped presents, and stuffed animals strewn on the shelving. Feeling inspired, she looks at her children. A video game entrances Thomas, who is twelve; Laura, age nine, has her nose in a book; and five-year-old Wayne is fogging the window up with his breath and drawing faces on it. Not one is paying attention to their parents.

Joe crosses his arms, leans his head back into the corner, and closes his eyes. "Whoop, whoop. Par-tayyy."

The excitement leaves Mary's face as she looks at her children, who appear to be anything but interested in the train ride. Like an air-filled balloon when slightly opened at the base letting the air slowly leak out, the excitement in Mary's voice fades with each word that comes out of her mouth. "This might be the train ride . . . of . . . our . . . lives." Deflated, she slumps back into her seat and stares at the floor.

The stranger sitting among them takes the whole scene in and his face saddens. After a sympathetic moment, he gets a twinkle in his eye and his sad expression turns into a warm smile. *Ahhh, a mission*, he thinks, *to really make this trip the train ride of their lives!* It would be a Christmas gift from him to them.

There is silence except for the train slowly chugging up to speed, then one last *WOO WOOOOO!*

A while later, Wayne, with brown hair and blue eyes, sits quietly with his face in his hands, staring, bored, at the floor. His family's eyes are all closed: they are napping. The conductor is visiting everyone, punching passengers' train tickets. With a loud call of "Tick-*ets!*" outside their door, she arouses everyone in this particular compartment to bleary-eyed awareness.

Maggie, a friendly, loud, heavyset conductor, arrives at their booth smiling. "Tickets, pleeeease, tickets!" She puts her hand out to the person closest to the door. "Merry Christmas, Kristopher! Getting back from doing some last-minute holiday shopping?"

The family notices Kristopher for the first time. This unassuming stranger is an older gentleman dressed in a nice, plain black suit with brown pinstripes, along with a red vest and tie. He has white hair and a cleanly groomed, matching white goatee.

Kristopher hands her his ticket. "And a very Merry Christmas to you, Miss Maggie! Yes, lots of preparation to do for Christmas Eve!"

Maggie punches his ticket. "I hope it was a productive trip for you."

"'Twas my dear, 'twas." He gives her a wink.

Maggie smiles at him and turns to look at the family. "Well, hello there, welcome to our humble train going to the northernmost parts of the wooorld! Tickets, pleeeease, tickets!"

They all have their tickets ready for her, and she promptly punches them—Wayne's ticket is last. He watches closely, slowly realizing she is clipping a Santa Claus face onto his ticket. He giggles as she hands it to him and he sees the finished product. He proudly holds the ticket up to show everyone. All smile at him except Thomas, who is not amused. He thinks he is too old for such childish things.

Kristopher pulls out his wallet and asks, "Miss Maggie, would you happen to have any change in gold coins available?"

Maggie plays along. "Hmm." She pats her pockets. "I'm sorry, Kristopher, I'm all out of gold coinage today, I just gave my last one away."

I wish I could help you out. Wait a minute. I think that young lady could help you out." She points to Laura. Laura looks confused, as do all the faces of the family.

Kristopher studies her. "Yes, I think you're correct. I think this fine young lady can assist." He reaches behind Laura's right ear and pulls out a gold coin. She is surprised and grins widely, as does everyone else, except for Thomas who shakes his head with annoyance.

Wayne wants to be part of the fun. "Do I have any gold coins hidden on me?"

Kristopher looks at him. "Well, let me see." Reaching behind Wayne's right ear, he pulls out another gold coin. He does it once more to Laura and Wayne's left ears, to their sheer delight. The two giggle nonstop. Now Joe cracks a slight grin and Mary is so thankful and relieved that at least some of her clan are happy and have a reason to smile.

"See if Thomas has any gold coins hidden behind his ears," Wayne says.

Thomas is about to obstinately refuse, but Kristopher beats him to the punch. "Well, it's true there appears to be a lot of empty space between those ears for gold coins to hide. However, I do not think we'd find anything so valuable in there at this time."

Thomas looks a little puzzled. He is relieved he does not have to partake in any silly magic trick, but at the same time, he is not sure how to take that remark. Joe smirks and tries to hold in a sudden laugh, enjoying the fact that his eldest son, who is too smart for his own good, has been outsmarted. Kristopher hands two gold coins to Wayne and the other two to Laura.

Joe looks at his two youngest. "What do you say?"

Laura and Wayne, in unison, say to Kristopher, "Thank youuu!"

Laura looks closely at one coin and starts peeling away an edge of what is actually a gold wrapper, with her fingernail. "Hey, chocolate coins are inside!" She opens one and takes a bite. "Mmmm!"

Wayne excitedly starts peeling one of his coins. Thomas has a regretful look on his face now because chocolate is his favorite. Wayne, with his mouth full of chocolate and a tiny piece on his upper lip, offers, "Mommy, do you want my other chocolate gold coin?"

"No thank you, Wayne," she says, "but that's very nice of you to offer!"

Laura takes her brother's cue. "Daddy, do you want my other coin?"

"No thank you, honey, I'm watching my girlish figure." He winks at her and she giggles.

Wayne offers Thomas his other gold-wrapped chocolate coin. Thomas reluctantly takes it. Humbled, he says in a soft voice, "Thanks."

"Well, you folks enjoy the trip, and we'll check in with you in a little bit!" Maggie says.

Kristopher stands up and gives her a hug. "It's so good to see you again. God bless you, my dear!"

"He does, Kris, *waaaay* more than I deserve, and especially when you're around!"

"Oh, and Maggie," Kristopher adds, "Please tell Hans I'll have his scrumptious special for lunch later. And if it is okay with my new friends, I would be privileged to take care of their lunch as well." Kristopher looks at Joe and Mary for approval.

They are both taken aback by the generous offer and are hesitant to accept, shaking their heads no. But before they can get any words out, Maggie pipes up, "Done!" and adds, as she walks away, "'Tis the season, ho, ho, hooo!" in her best Santa Claus imitation.

"That's very nice of you," Joe says to Kristopher, "but you don't have to do that; we brought some snacks with us."

"Believe me, it would be an honor, and trust me, Hans makes the most tender, juiciest steak north of the border. You will not be sorry." He winks. Joe nods his head and smiles with humble approval and thankfulness.

Mary warmly grabs Joe's arm, smiles, and nods to Kristopher. "Thank you. You're very kind."

Joe reaches out and shakes Kristopher's hand. "My name is Joe, and this is my lovely bride, Mary." She blushes and daintily shakes his hand. "And you've met Thomas, Laura, and Wayne."

Kristopher shakes Wayne's hand and makes a pained face as if Wayne's grip were so strong that it hurt him. Wayne chuckles. Kris gently takes Laura's hand and says, "Me lady." She stands up and curtsies. Kristopher then firmly takes Thomas' hand as if speaking man to man. "My dear sir." Thomas nods seriously, responding man to man.

Kristopher says, "It's a pleasure to meet you all. Please, call me Kris. You know, Wayne and Laura, it's very refreshing to see youngsters like yourselves so willing to share. It's good to share every day of the year, as if every day were Christmas, but giving has an especially sweet aroma during the Christmas season"—Kris waves the air with his hand as if smelling his favorite scent in the world—"which is what this season is based on—giving."

Wayne and Laura are enamored as they watch his hand in the air. They feel drawn to this new friend through a special, unseen connection.

Thomas, who has a curious mind and a questioning heart, asks while looking at his candy wrapper and eating his chocolate, "Who's this on the wrapper? On one side is a star shaped like a cross with 'Merry Christmas,' but there's a picture of a man with a funny hat wearing a dress on the other side."

"That, my dear sir, wearing a tunic, is St. Nicholas. St. Nicholas of Myra."

"Who's that?"

"Yeah, who's that?" Wayne asks, looking at his wrapper.

Kris looks surprised and turns to Laura to see whether she might have an answer for her brothers, but she just shrugs her shoulders.

"Does this ring a bell?" Kris asks. In dramatic fashion, he begins, "'Twas the night before Christmas, when all through the house, not a creature was stirring, not even a . . ." Kris pauses to invite a group response.

Everyone but Wayne chimes in "Mouse!" Wayne looks at his parents; Joe smiles and shrugs his shoulders, embarrassed for having joined in.

Kris continues, "The stockings were hung by the chimney with care, in hopes that . . ."

All but Wayne say, "St. Nicholas!"

Kris finishes, "Would soon be there!"

"Oh, I've probably read that poem a hundred times, but I never gave it a second thought that it says St. Nicholas, or who that is," Mary says, smiling and shaking her head in dismay.

"Yes," Kris continues, "here is a little-known, easy-to-forget fact: Santa Claus' real name is Nicholas, and every December, children around the world await the arrival of this jolly ol' gent who bears gifts to all who believe in Jesus and the Spirit of Christmas. He is known around the world by names such as Father Christmas, Sinterklaas, bearer of gifts to the Christ child, Père Noël, Noel Baba, St. Nicholas, good ol' St. Nick, and many others."

"Wow! Santa Claus' real name is Nicholas. How cool!" a surprised Wayne exclaims.

Thomas says to Kris, "Oh man, how old are you? And you're gonna tell me you still believe in—"

"Ahemmmm!" Joe gives Thomas the evil eye. The boy stops speaking and shakes his head, disgusted. Wayne looks around, confused. Laura looks unsure as well.

Kris continues, unfazed. "Yes, Wayne, Santa Claus' real name is Nicholas! He later became a saint, which means he was a Christian who lived a holy life set apart for God to help all who are in need. A calling to be a saint is for every Christian. Nicholas became known throughout the world for his generosity to those in need, as well as for his love for children, his concern for sailors and ships, his love of animals, his care for prisoners, and so much more. The Dutch called Saint Nicholas, *Sint Nicolaas*, or by his nickname Sinterklaas. Early Dutch settlers came to America and settled in New York, which was once called New Amsterdam, and they brought their traditions of Sinterklaas to America. As children from America and other countries tried to pronounce Sinterklaas, the name gradually transformed over time into what we know today: Santa Claus!" Kris pauses for a second in thought and then lights up. "Would you like to hear the *true* story of Saint Nicholas and how he became so famous?"

Wayne and Laura exclaim, "Yes, pleeease!"

Kris looks at Joe and Mary for approval. Joe gives a half-hearted smile and nod, indicating, "Not really, but go ahead." Taking Joe's lukewarm approval as a go, Mary nods an emphatic "yes!" She encourages, "Please do!"

Kris does not hesitate. "Wonderful! Okay then, here we go! Nicholas was born a *loooong* time ago, during the third century. The year was AD 270, to be exact. AD stands for *anno Domini*, which is Latin for 'year of our Lord.' He was born in a village outside the city of Patara, in a country once called Lycia, which was a Greek country then and today is the southern coast of the country called Turkey."

Laura adds, "Mmm, I *love* turkey, with stuffing and mashed potatoes and gr*aaa*-vy."

Thomas rolls his eyes and pulls out his video game. He is not interested in hearing the story of Nicholas or about Laura's love of turkey.

She catches Kris off guard. "Uh, yes, me too." He smiles and winks at her. "Nicholas was born to a very wealthy family—wealthy means they had a lot of money. Though the family had a lot of money, they lived a modest lifestyle, meaning not too fancy and not nearly as fancy as they could have lived. There, in their home . . ."

. . . Out in the beautiful countryside, in an upstairs bedroom, the daylight shone through the window in the background with a thin veil covering to soften the brightness. Theophanes bent over and kissed his wife, Nona, on her forehead. She cradled newborn Nicholas in her arms. The others in the room were the local priest, Father Absalom, and their married neighbors and best friends, Falon and Tana, who were barely tall enough to see over the bed.

Theophanes picked Nicholas up, lifted him high in the air as if giving an offering to God. He proclaimed, "Heavenly Father, on this day you gave us this gift of baby Nicholas, just as you gave the gift of baby Jesus to the world 270 years ago on that glorious First Noel. Dear Lord, Nona and I humbly dedicate Nicholas to You. We pray that, as his parents, we'll raise him in Your name, show him Your ways, teach him Your Word, and that You will mold him into Your faithful servant. We pray that in his weakness You will show your strength, and that You will bless him in the meaning of his name, Nicholas—victorious, hero to the people. We humbly thank You in the name of the Father, and of the Son, and of the Holy Spirit." Everyone made the sign of the cross and said together, "Amen."

*One year later . . .*

Theophanes, Nona, and Nicholas lingered at the dinner table, having finished eating after dusk. Candles burned all around, and Nona held Nicholas on her lap.

Theophanes stroked his beard with one hand and rubbed his belly with the other. He leaned over and kissed Nona. "Another delicious meal, my love. Shall we continue with some food for our soul? Perhaps a serving from St. Paul's letter to the saints in Philippi?"

"Sounds yummy!" Nona handed Nicholas to Theophanes and as they moved to pillows on the floor in front of the well-lit fireplace, Nona walked to a shelf on which sat numerous scrolls.

Sorting through a few, she said, "Hmm, St. Paul's letter to the Philippians is a bit intense. Persecuted for his faith and St. Paul thrown into jail, yet he still had God's joy and peace about him. It truly is amazing! And strangely it resonates with me."

She found the scroll she was looking for and joined Nicholas and Theophanes on the pillows. "To be reminded that joy is deeper than happiness and not dependent on our circumstances is comforting. That joy is found in our relationship with our Lord, and His love is bigger and stronger than the worst thing we could ever imagine in this life, even death itself, making our joy unshakeable. Now *that* is powerful."

Theophanes shared, "St. Paul says in his letter to the people of Thessalonica who were persecuted for their faith, 'Be joyful always, pray continually, give thanks in all circumstances; for this is God's will for you in Christ Jesus.' St. Paul lived what he preached, *that's* for sure. My dear, you said this resonates with you. I understand this is something we should take to heart because life has its ups and downs; good and bad happens to everyone. This is life in a fallen world, with humankind, who has freewill to choose between good or evil. Our hope, as believers, goes beyond this life on earth to our afterlife in Heaven. Is that what you mean by 'resonates' with you, or is it something more?"

"Something more. For some reason, I feel this to my core. Like we need to take this to heart. I don't know why. Call it woman's intuition." She smiled at Theophanes.

Theophanes beamed. "I will take it to heart, my dear; I will trust in the Holy Spirit speaking to you as well as trust my woman's 'woman's intuition.'" She laid her head on his shoulder. Theophanes looked at Nicholas on his lap. "And we will take our parental duties seriously, as King Solomon says in his scroll of Proverbs to 'train up a child in the way he should go, and when he is old, he will not depart from it.' We will do our best to train you up, my son, to love God, love others, and be joyful, prayerful, and thankful in all circumstances."

Nona observed Nicholas. "He sure does love to play with your beard."

"Yes, he does," Theophanes chuckled with a quiet "ho, ho, hooo."

Nona kissed Theophanes on the cheek and started to read. "Paul and Timothy, servants of Christ Jesus, to all the saints in Christ Jesus at Philippi . . ."

Laura puts her hand on Kris' shoulder. "Ohhh, so Santa Claus . . . or St. Nicholas, is a lot like his dad. His dad said 'ho, ho, ho' and had a beard like Santa does."

"Yes, young lady, you are correct!" Kris says. Laura beams proudly.

He continues, "We all tend to take on characteristics of our mothers and fathers as we grow and mature."

Thomas looks at his father. "Oh no, that means I'm gonna have a beer belly and burp and far—"

"Thomas!" his mother yells.

Joe, unamused, gives Thomas a stern look. He raises his right fist and slowly waves it as a warning to Thomas. The boy realizes he has pushed his luck and motions with his hand to zip shut an invisible zipper on his mouth, lock it with an invisible key, and toss it over his shoulder. He then looks around the room, not making eye contact with anyone, and his expression reads, "Don't mind me, I'm minding my own business, everyone can ignore me now." Joe smirks with mild amusement.

"Yes," Kris continues, "as I was saying, we all tend to take on characteristics of our mothers and fathers as we grow and mature; everyone is a role model to everyone. The question is whether each of us is a good role model or a poor role model?"

As he finishes his sentence, his eyes land on Joe—it is unclear whether he meant for this to be or not. Regardless, Joe suddenly appears uncomfortable, as if he has just realized he is sitting on the train wearing only his plaid boxers. His behavior mimics Thomas' prior act; he scans the room, clearly wishing he were somewhere else. He returns the looks the others are giving him, finally landing his gaze on Wayne. The boy looks at his father and shrugs his shoulders, clueless to what is happening.

"Yes, *everyone* can be a *gooood* or *baaaad* role model, so true," Joe announces to shift focus. "And I'll bet Nicholas' parents are going to be good role models. Let's hear more of the story and find out!" He hurriedly motions a hand for Kris to continue. If Joe was not interested in Nicholas' story before, he is now.

Now it is Kris' turn to smirk with mild amusement. He continues the story.

## **<u>Devotion 1</u>**

Joe, Mary, and the children are on a train journey north. In their train compartment is Kristopher, whom they did not notice at first because they were so absorbed in their own unhappiness.

We are all on a journey called life, and God is riding in our compartment with us. God says, "I will never leave you nor forsake you." We might not notice him because we are self-absorbed, or we *may* notice He is with us, but we ignore Him and pretend He is not there, or maybe we only interact with Him when it is convenient for us.

**Questions to consider:** Am I too self-absorbed to notice God is with me? Am I purposely ignoring Him, and if so, why? Do I only interact with Him when it is convenient for me? Alternatively, am I actively engaging with God and allowing Him to be my personal, intimate Guide on this journey called life?

## Devotion 2

Joe, Mary, and the children were in an unhappy place, personally and as a family, when they started their journey on the train going north. Mary was hoping to have a "train ride of their lives," meaning she hoped she and her family would arrive at a different place, a better place, than the one in which they currently found themselves.

Have you ever been unhappy personally? Has your family been unhappy? Have you ever hoped you and your family would get to a different place, a better place?

Our lives are one long journey broken up into 365 daily journeys per year. The better we focus on and make our daily journeys, the better we will make our life journeys. Each day we have a choice to get on the train and go "north" to be in a different and better place. Each day we have the opportunity to look to Heaven and get on board with God and His travel plans. If we do so daily, then we will be in a better place.

Our journey is important. Our destination is important. However, more important than the journey and the destination is the Person we are traveling with. If we are traveling with God, then He will guide us through the ups and downs of life's journey, and our final destination will be glorious!

**Questions to consider:** Am I journeying through this life with God, daily, and focusing on staying as close as possible to my personal, expert Guide, who not only knows the way, but is the Way?

*"Behold, the virgin shall be with child and bear a son,
and they shall name him Emmanuel," Matthew 1:23*

*Jesus said to him, "I am the way and the truth and the life. No one comes to
the Father except through me. John 14:6*

*God said, "And behold, I am with you always, until the end of the age."
Matthew 28:20*

*"You will show me the path to life, abounding joy in your presence,
the delights at your right hand forever." Psalm 16:11*

*"For I know well the plans I have in mind for you—declares the Lord—plans
for your welfare and not for woe, so as to give you a future of hope. When you
call me, and come and pray to me, I will listen to you. When you look for me,
you will find me. Yes, when you seek me with all your heart."
Jeremiah 29:11-13*

**Prayer:** "Heavenly Father, please help me recognize that I am never alone, that You are with me every second of the day, every day, and You love me so much that You want nothing more than to be with me all the time. And by being with You, You will help me in the difficult times, and you will rejoice with me in the good times. Help me cling to You every day. Thank you. Amen."

# 2
# Giving

*Years later . . .*

THEOPHANES AND NICHOLAS finish harvesting in a field. They had been working hard even while wearing tunics and outer garments of better quality than those of their hired workers. They toiled alongside their neighbors and best friends, father and son, Falon and Noll. Theophanes and Nicholas were on the short side of average height, however, Falon and his son, Noll, were noticeably smaller in stature than their friends, and, in fact, shorter than most everyone in general.

Theophanes and Falon walked toward the road. Theophanes carried his walking staff for shepherding his many animals, including sheep, goats, and cows. The staff, long and slender with a rounded hook on top, had various uses such as to reach out and catch individual sheep and draw them close to himself when needed. The staff was instrumental in the case of shy and timid sheep that typically tended to keep their distance from the shepherd.

Theophanes also used his staff to guide his sheep gently into a new path, through a gate, or along dangerous, challenging routes. He used the tip of the long, slender stick to lay gently on the animal's side, and the pressure applied, guided the sheep in the way the shepherd wanted it to go. Thus, the sheep was reassured of its proper path.

The staff also made the presence of the shepherd real to the sheep. In all of this, there was a comfort and a sense of oneness, of belonging, of being in the shepherd's care, and hence the object of Theophanes' special affection. King David wrote of God in the Psalms, "Thy rod and thy staff they comfort me." Jesus said, "I am the Good Shepherd; I know my sheep and my sheep know me just as the Father knows me and I know the Father—and I lay down my life for the sheep."

Theophanes called, "Nicholas, Noll, come! We've other business to attend!" The boys, now 10 years old, ran catching up to the men. "Have you boys been practicing the Ten Commandments?"

"Yes sir!" they answered in unison.

"Three?"

"Thou shalt not use the Lord's name in vain."

"Five?"

"Honor thy mother and father."

Falon interjected, "Ah, that's one of my favorites." He winked and asked, "Eight?"

"Thou shalt not steal."

"Excellent job!" Theophanes exclaimed. "You didn't even have to use the hand signs we taught you. Nice job. Now, look at this."

With the end of his walking staff Theophanes drew a large dot in the dirt road and said to the boys, "You see this dot?" The boys nodded. "Remember this dot as we walk."

He put his staff in the middle of the dot and started walking, dragging his staff on the dirt road, making a line behind him. Falon, who was Theophanes' business manager—small in stature but big in heart and smarts—walked beside Theophanes. Nicholas trotted behind his father and Noll behind his. They were mimicking their fathers with hands clasped behind their backs and heads held high as if they were important, discussing important business. The boys switched their attention back and forth between watching the shepherd's staff as it marked a line on the dirt road between them, and watching the workers harvesting the last of the season's crops in the fields along the road.

As Theophanes dragged his staff, he purposely spoke in a slow and deliberate teaching manner for the benefit of the boys. "Falon, my dear friend, have we collected our voluntary tithe, the first ten percent of our harvest to give back to God, from whom all blessings and good things flow?"

Falon responded in a like-mannered teaching voice, "Yes we have. Tithing is such a wonderful act. Tithing honors God by showing Him that we are thankful for all He gives us, because we do not have anything that He does not provide. And tithing blesses others because it provides for His church to do the Lord's work of ministering to those in need." The boys, while listening to their fathers, occasionally glanced back at the long line that Theophanes continued to draw with his dragging staff.

"Yes, yes, so true, so true," Theophanes said. "And also we are blessed by tithing to God because it makes us look at our own hearts to see whether we are thankful and cheerful givers or are feeling materialistic and greedy and have allowed the love of money to creep into our lives. It helps us gauge whether our hearts are in the right place spiritually with God our Heavenly Father. It shows whether our love for Him is above all else, especially more than money and material objects. He wants us to be cheerful givers, and if we are not, then we have to ask ourselves, why not? What are our minds focused on? What is going on with our hearts? Then we can ask God to help us have a right heart."

"Yes, yes, Theophanes, so true, so true."

Theophanes and Falon stopped walking and turned to the boys. "Boys, what are your thoughts?"

Nicholas and Noll, exaggerated and adult-like, both replied, "Yes, yes, so true, so true," which brought smiles to Falon and Theophanes' faces.

At this point in walking, they were near the majority of the harvesters. The sun was still high, the workday not even half over.

Theophanes took a knee next to the boys and looked back at the long line he drew; the circular dot was way out of sight by now. "Boys, do you remember the dot I drew?" The boys nodded. "Well, that little dot represents our life here on earth; it's just a tiny, little smidgeon of time. Do you know what this loooong, unending line is?" He pointed back to the line and the boys' eyes followed it as far as they could see and shook their heads. "This line is eternity, eternity in Heaven with God, if we accept God's gift of Jesus to us, surrendering our lives to Jesus for Him to be our Savior and Lord."

The boys smiled and nodded. Theophanes' face grew serious. "Or, this may sound harsh, but this line can mean eternity in hell if we choose to reject God's precious gift of Jesus to us." The boys' smiles left them and they shook their heads for an emphatic no—they did NOT want that. "Understand that God does not want people to go to hell and He does not send people to hell. We have free will, so if we choose to reject Jesus during the time we're living that tiny, little dot of time on this earth, then we are rejecting Heaven and choosing hell for eternity." The boys again emphatically shook their heads.

"The point, my dear boys—or, in this case, the dot—is that this life is short and eternity is forever. The decisions we make during this short time here on earth will affect not only how our lives will play out during our time here on earth, but our free will decisions will also affect our eternity. According to Jesus, during our short time on this earth, God's greatest commandment He wants us to obey is to . . ."

Theophanes looked to Nicholas. Nicholas responded, "Love God with all our hearts, souls, minds, and strength."

Falon joined in. "Excellent, Nicholas. As we learn how loving, caring, and amazing God is, we can't help but love Him. Then it's not really a commandment anymore, it's a privilege. That's the first part of His greatest commandment, but Jesus said two more parts to the greatest commandment. Noll?"

Noll stood up straight. "To love others, as we love ourselves."

"Excellent, Noll," Theophanes responded. "Yes, we are made in God's image and so loving ourselves is commanded, and we love ourselves by living in deep, intimate fellowship with the living God! That *is* the greatest thing a human can do for him or herself. Yet God still has a third part to His greatest commandment, loving others *as* we love ourselves. As we receive God's love, then we will *want* to share His love with others. God's love will flow from Him to them, through us. By loving God, loving others, and loving ourselves righteously, then we are obeying God's greatest commandment and we will make a positive difference in this world. Live for the line, boys, the unending line of eternity in Heaven with God, and do not selfishly live for the temporary dot of this life. Okay?" The boys nodded their heads.

"Father, may I ask a question?" Nicholas asked.

"Of course. If you don't ask, then how will you find an answer for whatever is on your mind? Just like our Heavenly Father, without judgment, He wants us to ask Him anything on our minds. I want you to feel the same freedom with me. What's on your mind, my son?"

"Well, hell is eternal and sounds like a horrible place, but God is loving and He is love. How can a loving God create such a horrible place that lasts forever?"

"Excellent question. Yes, God loves and God is love, He is sacrificial love. Additionally, we have to remember that God is a just and holy God as well. There is right and wrong in this world, and He made the rules, and He knows best; his rules are good for us to help us and protect us. In God's court, He is the ultimate Judge who is just. Therefore, He will judge us at the end of our days here on earth, and punishment is due to those who rejected Him and sinned and rebelled from His instruction. He is also a holy God, holy meaning set apart. He is so holy that in His Heaven, unholiness does not reside there. So before I answer your question about hell, do you understand that in addition to having the attribute of Love, God has the attributes of being Just and Holy as well?"

"Yes, Father," responded Nicholas. Theophanes looked at Noll for understanding and the boy nodded in agreement.

"Okay, good. Something else we have to understand is that when we sin, we may see it as something that primarily hurts other people or ourselves, but God sees it as something offensive primarily to Him, because He is the one who gives us the commands such as not to lie, steal, hate, be prideful, or murder. Think of it like this: If I lie to you, what could you do to me? Well, frankly, not much. If I lie to your mother, I'll probably be sleeping in the barn, right?" Falon vehemently nodded in the background with a frightened look on his face, as if he had been there and done that. The boys giggled at each other and nodded in agreement.

"If I lie to my customers, then they will fire me and take their business elsewhere, and I will lose money and lose my businesses. And if I lie to the Roman government, that's called treason and they will throw me in prison or have my head on a spear on the side of the road." The boys grimaced. "Now, notice in each situation my sin, or crime, was the same: I lied. What changed in the scenario?"

Nicholas answered, "The person you sinned against."

"Yes! As that person's authority, power, and stature increased, so did the punishment. Now, what should the punishment be if my lying, stealing, hate, pride and murdering are primarily crimes against God, the Creator and Sustainer of the universe?"

"Something big and bad!" exclaimed Noll.

"Yes! Because God is infinitely holy and good, then it makes sense that the punishment should be infinite and terrible. That's why in the scroll of Revelation it says about those who choose *not* to be saved by God's grace, but rather they choose to be people such as sorcerers, idolaters, liars, murderers, and the sexually immoral, that they will spend their eternity in the lake of fire. So there may be times when you or I may not think sin is that big of a deal, but God does. Does that make sense?"

Nicholas and Noll nodded their heads. "Yes, Father, thank you," said Nicholas.

"You're welcome, anytime. Again, I want to clarify one last thing boys. This is so very important. The very last thing God wants is to have one of His human creations made in His image choose to go to hell. This is where Jesus comes in, and that is where we as believers come in. For God so loved the world that he sent his Son, Jesus, not to condemn it, but to *save* it. God wants to save every single last one of us, through Jesus, if we are willing. And, God says *we*, you and I, are His hands and feet to go into the world and love His creation, not to condemn it, but to share the gospel, the good news of Jesus, so that they will have the choice to be saved or not. It is God's desire that none should perish. God gave all people freewill and it is ultimately each individual person's choice to receive God's love and salvation to be adopted into His royal family and be called sons and daughters of God. Or they can choose not to, and they will suffer the consequences of their choice. These are serious topics, are you boys okay talking about them?"

They look at each other and nod in agreement. They like being included in grown-up conversations.

"Does everything we just talked about make sense to both of you?" Both nod. "Any more questions, thoughts, or words of wisdom for us?"

Both boys shake their heads no. "Okay good, let's finish the day's business."

"But wait, the work day is only half over; how is it we are finishing the day's business now?" asked Noll.

Theophanes lit up. "Watch this! The fun begins!" He turned and walked toward the workers, who by now were gathering by the side of the road near them. Falon and Noll followed. Nicholas paused, spending an extra moment staring at the long line drawn, going over in his mind everything that he just learned and letting it sink into his mind and heart.

After a moment, he caught up to the others just as Theophanes addressed the crowd of workers. "The Lord be with you all!"

Harvesters shared back, "And also with you, sire!"

"We are blessed by you and your hard work! Thank you for all you do! We are not only fortunate to be able to work alongside all of you with

18

strong work ethics and strong moral character, but we are also proud to be able to call you friends and neighbors. We celebrate the yearly Christ-Mass during tomorrow's Sabbath Day, a day of rest from work and a time for worship and praise of God. So in honor of our annual celebration of the birth of our Lord Jesus Christ, the greatest Gift ever, with no loss of wages to you, your day is done early. Good Christ-Mass to all and to all a good day!"

The crowd gasped with a joyous exhale, and a chorus of harvesters shouted out different well wishes: "Peace be with you!" "Good Christ-Mass to you!" "Thank you!" "Mighty Christ-Mass!" They walked off in the same direction toward Theophanes' barn with their baskets of corn, picking up tools along the way. They chattered happily over the news that their day was done early, yet they will still receive a full day's wage.

Theophanes turned to Falon, Nicholas, and Noll. "Falon, you have the bags of coins?" Falon nodded. "Young men, please go with Falon to dole out to the harvesters their wages while I attend to our gleaners. Falon, as we discussed, give them double their *weekly* wages along with the nut and fruit baskets for each family that our wonderful women have kindly prepared." They nodded and started following the harvesters toward the barn. Falon led the way, and the boys followed closely behind, mimicking his upright posture and walk.

Theophanes walked across the road to address the poor and jobless whom he allowed to glean the leftovers in his fields. Nicholas peeked back to watch his father greet them, "The Lord be with you!"

Gleaners responded, "The Lord bless you, sire!" Nicholas could no longer hear as he walked farther away. He glanced back after a moment and saw his father handing out coins.

Noll glanced back also. "Your father didn't mention giving the poor gleaners money, too. He's a very generous man."

Falon slowed to walk beside the boys so he could see their faces.

"Just between us men?" Falon gave the boys a nod, making sure he had their attention. They fixed their eyes on him. "Can you keep a secret?" They nodded. "Theophanes gives away more than any man will know. As Jesus says in the scroll of the good news of Matthew, 'Thus when you give to the needy, sound no trumpet before you, as the hypocrites do in the synagogues and the streets, that they may be praised by others.'" Falon stopped walking and playfully acted out a hypocrite enjoying the praise. The boys giggled. "'Truly, I say to you, they have received their reward.'"

Falon grew serious. "But when you give to the needy . . ." Falon pulled out two coins from the bag hanging around his neck and put one in each hand, "do not let your left hand know what your right hand is doing, so that your giving may be in secret." He put his right hand with one coin behind Nicholas' right ear and his left hand with the other coin behind Noll's left ear, then pulled his hands into the open air, showing the boys that the coins had disappeared. The boys exchanged amazed looks. Falon drove the point home. "And your Father in Heaven, who sees in secret, will reward you. Okay?" The boys nodded. "Okay, now let's go have fun giving these fine people their extra wages and presents! Oh, this is glorious!"

### Devotion

Theophanes and Falon talked with their ten-year-old sons about giving, tithing, life, death, salvation, damnation, temporal, eternal, Heaven, and hell. Whew, heavy! Why did they talk with them so young about such heavy topics? And, why such heavy topics so early on in this novel, this could be a real turn off to reading further.

Let us answer those questions with some questions: What *is* the right age to talk with children about such heavy topics? How comfortable, or uncomfortable, are you with discussing such heavy topics? Did your parents ever discuss these topics with you? If so, when? If not, did you wish they had, and when would have been the right time for you?

Why such heavy topics so early on in this novel? The simple answer is because this is when it happened in the story of Nicholas' life. The less simple answer is—why wait? The future is unknown, that's how God made it, for us to be dependent on Him daily. So today may be our and our family's last day to have a chance to ponder these heavy topics and make a decision for ourselves that could impact us eternally.

Some liken these life-and-death topics to a blind person walking toward the edge of a high cliff. When is the right time to let someone know he or she is heading toward the edge? If it were you, would you rather know sooner, or later? Nicholas' parents chose sooner, when they felt Nicholas may be mature enough to understand, because no one ever knows when it will be too late, and they did not want to take any chances.

**Questions to consider:** What *is* the right age to talk with children about such heavy topics? How comfortable, or uncomfortable, am I with discussing such heavy topics? Did my parents/guardians ever discuss these topics with me? If so, when? If not, did I wish they did and when would have been the right time for me? These questions, and the answers, are between me and my life-journey Companion and Guide, God.

*"For God so loved the world that he gave his only Son, so that everyone who believes in him might not perish but might have eternal life. For God did not send his Son into the world to condemn the world, but that the world might be saved through him. John 3:16-17*

*"Call to me, and I will answer you; I will tell you great things beyond the reach of your knowledge." Jeremiah 33:3*

*"Jesus told her, 'I am the resurrection and the life; whoever believes in me, even if he dies, will live, and everyone who lives and believes in me will never die. Do you believe this?'" John 11:25-26*

**Prayer:** "Heavenly Father, thank You for being accessible for me to talk with any time, any place, and about anything. Thank You for not wanting me to walk blindly through this life ignoring serious topics and someday walking off the cliff, dying, never having considered these serious topics or answered these serious questions. You truly care about my questions, thoughts, feelings, struggles, joys, and circumstances, and You desire to be my Confidante without judgment. There is nothing I can do or say to make You love me more, and there is nothing I can do or say to make You love me less. You love me no matter what, that's just who You are, and You want me to make a decision for You, as my Lord, so I can spend the rest of eternity with You. Thank You for caring! Amen."

# 3
# ℜeceiving

AFTER HELPING GIVE most of the wages and presents away, Falon and Noll left to tend to their business and employees in the same manner, leaving Nicholas to give out the last of the wages and gift baskets. Theophanes arrived moments later. Nicholas looked happy and humbled as the last woman, whose name was Amara, thanked him repeatedly. She thanked Theophanes and he hugged her.

"Amara, how are you, how is the rebuilding from the house fire going, and how is your husband recovering from his burns?"

"I'm blessed, we are eating every day and he is on the mend and should be back to work within the month. Falon and his Mikros clan have been more than gracious helping us rebuild. Your family and theirs are such blessings."

Theophanes slid her a couple extra coins equivalent to a week's worth of wages. "Tell him I said God be with him. I wish you and your family a blessed Christ-Mass!"

Nicholas watched quietly.

"Bless you, sire!" she said. "Bless Nona and your wonderful son, Nicholas! I thank our Heavenly Father for you and your generosity." She hugged Theophanes and Nicholas.

Before she walked away, Theophanes added, "And once your new home is complete, we'll make sure Nicholas and his tiny band of chimney sweeps visit your home annually, so there will be no more fires."

"Yes, that will be a blessing, thank you, Theophanes, bless you both!" She left light-footed as if walking on air with joy.

Theophanes turned to Nicholas. "Thank you for helping, Nicholas. It was a short day, but we worked hard. How do you feel about it? What was your favorite part?" He put his arm around Nicholas, and they started walking toward the house.

"It was wonderful, Father. It feels good to work hard out in the fields and get things done. My favorite part of today was giving to the harvesters. I like to give to people, help people, and make them happy. It feels good."

"Yes, it does feel good. Giving blesses others, but it also blesses the giver. Nicholas, look around. All we own does not belong to us; it belongs to God. He has allowed us to be stewards of what is His, and hopefully wise stewards. Too many people in this world make money and belongings their idols—things they love more than God, counterfeit gods. They worship the gifts rather than the Gift Giver. God provides for our daily needs, but even more importantly, God calls us to use the resources He has given us for sharing His love for the world and to the world. He calls us to be cheerful givers. When He blesses us, He calls us to be wise stewards with what He has given us and to raise our standard of giving, not our standard of living. Giving enriches and benefits the giver. Giving is an act of worship to God."

Nicholas nodded and then asked, "Father, how do you know how much to give to the church for sharing God's love with the world and helping the world, and how much to give to help those in need ourselves?"

Theophanes smiled. "Ahhh, Nicholas that is a great question." He paused for a moment to think of how best to answer. He knelt down to be at eye level with Nicholas. "The tithe, which means ten percent, was begun a long time ago to give the first ten percent of what we make back to God and his people for various good reasons. Let us see what our Jesus says about giving. In the scroll of Mark and the scroll of Luke, Jesus teaches in the temple near the place where people make their offerings. He watches the crowd putting their money into the temple treasury. He sees many rich people throw in large amounts. However, a poor widow puts in two copper coins, called lepta—each is worth less than a penny. 'I tell you the truth,' Jesus said, 'this poor widow has put into the treasury more than all the others. All these people gave their gifts out of their wealth, but she, out of her poverty, put in all she had to live on.'"

Nicholas quieted into contemplation. Theophanes then asked, "So, my son, what do you think Jesus is saying about how much to give?"

Nicholas responded as if finding out a secret that could change his world. "Everything."

"If that is what God is speaking to your heart on this issue, then praise be to God."

Nicholas stared across the fields, deep in thought, and nodded his head.

Theophanes continued, "It is said to give ten percent as a starting point for everyone, but truthfully, between you and me, our family, Falon's family and his Mikros clan, give far more than that amount, my son."

"Yes, Father."

"Now on the flip side of giving is receiving. It is strange because it can be easier to give than to receive. For some of us, it's hard to receive due to pride, which may be an inability to admit we need help or the belief that we can do everything on our own; for others, it may be difficult to receive because they are embarrassed and ashamed. It takes humility to be able to receive from others. Therefore, Nicholas, it's important to have a right heart when giving, to have a genuine desire to help, and to be sensitive to others because they may find it difficult to receive gifts. They are humbling themselves and allowing themselves to be a bit vulnerable, which may be difficult for all of us to do at some time." Nicholas nodded in agreement. "This is a good day, my son. Let us get washed up for lunch."

Theophanes held hands with Nicholas, and with his other arm stretched outward, he breathed in the air around him deeply and then slowly exhaled. "Thank you, Jesus." Nicholas glanced up at Theophanes and smiled, they walked toward the house.

As they arrived, they found Nona walking to the barn with a big smile on her face, holding a bucket with carrots and apples. She asked, "Nicholas, would you like to help me finish feeding the animals?"

"Oh boy would I!" he exclaimed. He ran excitedly over to her with Theophanes following. Nicholas loved animals and animals loved him. Nona reached out her arm for a hug, like a mother bird spreading her wing out to cover her chick. Nicholas fit perfectly under her arm, and he hugged her with both hands wrapped around her waist. She gave him a big squeeze back, closed her eyes and smiled broadly, enjoying the moment.

"Mmm, I love my Nicholas hugs!" Nona kissed the boy on his forehead. They released their warm embrace and turned to walk toward the barn.

"So, my Nicholas, I love this time of year when we celebrate Christ Mass. There's a chill in the air nipping at my nose and I want to get cozy by the fire with my loved ones." Theophanes joined them. Nona walked between her husband and son.

"Yes and roasting chestnuts on the open fire, yum!" Nicholas exclaimed.

"Mmmmm," Nona and Theophanes both responded.

Nona sighed, "Ahhh, there's no place like home for this holy day season."

By this time, they had arrived at the barn door. When stopped, Theophanes and Nona turned to Nicholas.

Theophanes remarked, "Son, this season can be the most wonderful time of the year."

Nicholas gushed, "Yes, Father, absolutely! It's my favorite time of year!"

"There is a difference between happiness and joy. Happiness is happening in the moment. You feel good when something good happens, and happiness comes from something outside yourself such as getting what you want, doing something you like, or getting your way. It makes you happy, but it is fleeting, temporary, and it will fade away. There are people in this world who make being happy their goal, their idol, their counterfeit god, and they are never fulfilled. They are seeking and searching for happiness in all the wrong places. They lust for more money, more possessions, more status, or whatever it is that they think will make them happy, and it is a never-ending pursuit. Seeking only happiness only satisfies for a moment, but it does not last. Does that make sense?"

"Yes, Father, I understand about happiness, and I understand how it is different from joy."

Theophanes raised his eyebrows. "Oh, you do? Then please enlighten us, how is joy different?"

Nona is curious as well. "Yes, Nicholas, please tell us, my son."

"Well, you know how when I make a mistake you both tell me, 'Wise men learn from their mistakes.'?" His parents nodded. "Well, several months ago, when I was reading scripture and talking with God, He said to me, 'Nicholas, wise men learn from their mistakes, but wiser men learn from their own mistakes *and* from other people's mistakes. Be wiser than wise.' Ever since then, I have been watching and listening to others more carefully. One thing I have seen is that there are people, who have a lot, but they do not seem happy. Or they are only happy when they get what they want and then it slowly fades away, as you just described. Then I have seen people, who do not have much, yet they seem very happy, but their happiness is deeper than just being happy. Even when something bad happens to them, like Amara, they still seem to have something like happiness, but it's deeper. It is joy; they have a peace about them. The people who seek happiness seem to be focused on the gift, but the people with joy seem to focus on the Gift Giver and have thankful hearts and attitudes for all things great and small, in good times and bad."

"You're so right, my son! Joyful people have an attitude of gratitude. We are so proud of you. As for us, we believe the meaning of this season is Jesus as our Savior, our Lord, and our Servant-King. Jesus is the reason for this Christ-Mass season, and it's because of our faith in Him that we receive the fruits of the Holy Spirit that include love, joy, and peace." Theophanes said.

Nona added, "Nicholas, we're so thankful to God that you don't just know about God, but that you know God, that you have a personal relationship with Him and talk with Him intimately. God has so graciously given us His son, Jesus, for whom we celebrate Christ-Mass. There is nothing greater or more important than that. It's because God has been so giving to us that we want to be giving as well. Your father and I cannot help but want to give to you graciously during this holy day season. We have a gift for you, and since we believe everything we have is from God and we are to be Godly stewards of what He gives us, great or small, then you can say truly this is a gift of love from God."

Nicholas started to get excited but was humbled at the same time. "A gift for me? But I don't have a need or a want. You already provide all I could ever want or need. You don't have to give me anything."

Theophanes shared, "We realize we don't have to give you anything. We want to give you something. And by God's grace, we can do this for you at this time. We're thankful that you are mature enough to appreciate the gift, have an attitude of gratitude, and, most importantly, are thankful to the Gift Giver, our Heavenly Father."

At that, Theophanes unlatched the two barn doors that were connected. He grasped one door while Nona held the other. They swung both barn doors wide open and said in unison, "Merry Christ-Mass, Nicholas!" They revealed a beautiful, pure white colt standing in the back of the barn, shimmering in a ray of sunlight from an open window above.

Nicholas lit up, speechless. He had always wanted a horse of his very own. Stunned and wearing a grin a mile wide, he walked toward the colt with his hands reaching out. Halfway through the barn, he let out a gasp as if he had not taken a breath since the barn doors had opened. "Oh my goodness! Thank you! I never imagined such a gift!" Then he turned and hugged both parents, who stood close at either side, watching his reaction, as parents love to do when they see their children happy.

Looking up, raising his hands, Nicholas said, "Thank you, Lord, thank you, thank you, thank you!" Nicholas walked up to the colt, put his hand out, and the colt licked it. Nona gave her son a carrot from the bucket and Nicholas fed his new foal. The boy was in awe and whispered, "Beautiful."

He took a step back to get a better look and said, "He shimmers in the light like jewels, or, better yet, like an angel from God. My shimmering angel . . . that's it!"

Nona startled, "What?! What's it?!"

"His name!" Nicholas responded with a hop. "He is my shimmering angel. Shimmel!"

## Devotion

Nicholas had an attitude of gratitude for all things, great and small, even before he received his Christmas present. Regularly practicing thankfulness in his life made receiving this gift even that much more special!

There are many studies today that show how being thankful can change a person's negative mood to positive in no time at all. It can be so easy for us to focus on what we do not have rather than on the good we do have. It takes regular practice for us to look for things to be thankful for and to transform our patterns of thinking to an attitude of gratitude.

Additionally, Nicholas acknowledged all good things originate with God, the Gift-Giver.

**Questions to consider:** Is my focus on all the good in my life, even in difficult times, when it does not feel like there is any good? And, when I do recognize good in my life to be thankful for, do I thank God for it? In this moment, what is something, or who is someone, that I can thank God for?

*"All good giving and every perfect gift is from above, coming down from the Father of lights, with whom there is no alteration or shadow caused by change. James 1:17*

*"Give thanks to the Lord, who is good, whose mercy endures forever."*
*Psalm 136:1*

**Prayer:** "Heavenly Father, thank You for all the good in my life. Help me look for good daily, find good daily, and give You the glory for it. Open my eyes to see all the blessings in my life, even during the dark times. Thank You for You, the light of the world! Amen."

# 4
# Christ-Mass Celebration

*The next day . . .*

A CHRIST-MASS dinner celebration was prepared outside Nicholas' home with tables displaying a feast of tasty food: ham, fish, soup, potatoes, carrots, bread with honey butter, cider, wine, and more, plus desserts like baklava. Yum! Children and adults stood around the table drooling, waiting for the last of the tables to be set for the celebration dinner to begin.

Bishop Nicholas from Patara, Nicholas' uncle and namesake, and two neighbor families attended. Noll was there with his parents and his six-year-old, impulsive and energetic twin siblings, Kari and Dax, as well as their toddler brother, John, and baby sister, Leila. Lastly, next-door neighbor Brodin, his wife, Madelyn, and their three daughters—Wren, age ten; Kyla, eight; and Kalista, six.

Theophanes greeted everyone. "Thank you all for being here as we celebrate the birth day of Jesus, our Lord and Savior, for a worshipful Christ Mass. Thank you for bringing the wonderful food. I am famished and cannot wait to enjoy what God has provided through your hands this day. I must say I am already fighting the temptation of being a glutton and eating more than my fair share." He smiled and laughed a little "ho, ho, ho," and everyone chuckled with him. "We are blessed to have my brother, Nicholas, joining us for our celebration. Bishop Nicholas, will you please lead us in giving thanks to our Lord?"

Young Nicholas and Wren's eyes met, and they both played shy. Noll witnessed it and raised his eyebrows at his friend, teasing him with a mock kissy face.

Bishop Nicholas spoke. "Yes, thank you, Theophanes. And, I too, am fighting off the temptation of gluttony. Thank you for having me this day as well, all of you." He looked around, acknowledging everyone. He looked down at the ground in front of him. "Here is an anthill!"

"Ew!" Kari yelled and moved toward him to stomp on the anthill, but just as quickly, Dax jumped in front of her and held her back. "Nooooo!"

Bishop Nicholas wore a surprised but amused look on his face as he watched Falon grab both children by the scruffs of their necks and pull them back to his place in the circle, embarrassment on his face. "Forgive us, Bishop Nicholas," Falon said. "Children?"

Kari and Dax responded together as twins sometimes do, "Sorry."

"I forgive you both. Dax, come over here."

Dax cautiously approached, as if in trouble, and Bishop Nicholas turned Dax around before him to face the crowd and put his hands on Dax's shoulders. "Dax, you must love ants to want to protect them like that." Dax nodded. "Why do you love them?"

"Because they're God's creatures . . . and they are small, but they are mighty for their size, like me!" He flexed his muscles, "They can carry things ten times their size!"

Kari jumped in, "Me toooo!" and tried to flex even bigger. Falon pulled her back, shaking his head.

Dax continued, "I have an anthill by my house that I visit every day and watch over and feed crumbs to."

"Do the ants at your anthill know you love them and that you are there watching over them and providing 'daily bread,' or 'manna,' for them?" Bishop Nicholas thought himself clever and chuckled at his own joke, connecting the Lord's Prayer of giving us daily bread, with God providing manna for the Jews wandering in the desert for forty years.

Dax replied, "I don't think so; they just do what they do. They don't pay any attention to me."

"Let us try something. Tell these ants you love them. Go ahead, it's okay, do it now." Dax looked at Bishop Nicholas, a little perplexed, but obediently leaned over the anthill.

"I love you ants." All the adults smiled at the cuteness of this act, but there was no reaction from the ants.

"Hmm, you are correct; they didn't even notice you. They didn't stop doing what they were doing; they just went about their business, huh?" Dax nodded. "They don't understand you nor do they even notice you. They have very small brains, so they are not smart enough to fully understand you nor comprehend who or what you are, or what this big world is all about, huh?"

Dax nodded.

"How could you communicate your love to the ants? If you had special powers, what would you do?" Dax shrugged.

Bishop Nicholas spoke with wonder and awe. "What if you became an ant? What if you became an ant and you were still one hundred percent Dax, but you were also one hundred percent ant, and you looked like them, and walked like them, and worked like they do, and talked like them? Then you would be in a family of ants, with ant friends. Right?" Dax nodded excitedly at the idea. "Then do you think you would be able to tell the ants you love them and help them understand how the best way for them to live is?"

Dax nodded, convinced.

"Thank you, Dax."

Dax walked back over to Falon, where Kari whispered, "Ha, you love ants, smoochy smooch." He motioned as if he were about to hit her, she flinched and put her fist up. Falon grabbed both by their ears to settle them down.

Bishop Nicholas addressed the group. "This table exists because it has a creator who made it with a purpose. That beautiful home exists because it has a creator who made it with a purpose. The wondrous, creative world in which we live exists because it has a Creator who made it with a purpose! I cannot look at a beautiful sunrise or sunset, with colors even a master artist cannot recreate, and not know there is a true Master Artist that created the beauty my eyes behold. We have a Creator and we have a purpose. This Creator is our Lord God Almighty, Creator of Heaven and earth. Our purpose is to be in a personal relationship with our Maker. Who are we to be so arrogant, to think that we can comprehend God, understand all His ways, His nature, and His love for us? If we, with our small brains could understand everything about God, then he would be a small god. However,

He's not. He's a great BIG God. Thankfully. We can only understand what He is willing to reveal to us, in His time. Amen?" "Amen," the group responded.

He reflected. "It is the year AD 280. History, as was prophesied, changed forever two hundred eighty years ago. God our Creator loved this world and loved every one of us so much that he left His Heavenly realm, humbled Himself and became a tiny, vulnerable baby, in the form of His Son, born in a dirty barn with smelly animals all around. The Word became flesh and made his dwelling among us, and we saw his glory, the glory as of the Father's only Son, full of grace and truth. Given the name Jesus, he was the Christ Child, being fully human and fully God Himself. Why? To show us how much He loves us and to show us the best way to live, which is having an intimate relationship with our Heavenly Father. To make us aware of what is important in this temporary life, and then to die on the cross, take our punishment, and be the sacrificial Passover Lamb of God who takes away the sins of the world and saves every one of us. To cleanse us from our sins and sinful nature—that is, if we choose this gift of salvation, for He gave us free will. Oh that Noel, that first Christ-Mass day. What a beautiful day that was, and oh what a beautiful day this is to celebrate the day Jesus was born, the greatest Gift ever. It is my prayer we all choose to receive this awesome Gift."

Bishop Nicholas reached out for the hands of those next to him and everyone around the circle held hands, closed their eyes, and bowed their heads. "Heavenly Father, we thank You for this day to celebrate Your ultimate gift to us, Jesus Christ, in a mass service. This season of giving is because of Your wondrous gift to us, Your birth day, when You became human to show us Your love and later to sacrifice Your life for our sins on that holy Easter, to reunite us with our Heavenly Father. We do not deserve You or Your priceless gift, but we thank you from the bottom of our hearts. You love us even when we're unlovable. Thank You and happy birthday, Jesus." Everyone repeated in unison, "Happy birthday, Jesus!"

Bishop Nicholas continued, "Holy Spirit, we invite you to dwell within us and have fellowship with us, and transform our hearts and minds to be Christ-like. We love You." Everyone whispered affirmations around the table. "Heavenly Father, thank You for the delicious food You have provided to us this day, and we pray that You will bless it to our bodies and nourish us. Thank You for the hands that prepared our meal; bless them all. I pray that I will not be a glutton, eating everything in sight. Amen." Everyone chuckled in addition to amen-ing. Everyone followed the bishop, making the sign of the cross by touching their foreheads, then their hearts, then their left and right shoulders, saying, "In the name of the Father, and of the Son, and of the Holy Spirit. Amen!"

They then partook in Holy Communion, with repenting hearts, eating bread as Jesus' body broken for humankind and healing, and drinking wine or grape juice as Jesus' atoning blood for the forgiveness of their sins.

The group exchanged hugs and well wishes. "Good Christ-Mass!" "Happy Christ-Mass!" "Mighty Christ-Mass" "Merry Christ-Mass!"

Kari yelled, "Quick to the food before Bishop Nicholas eats it all!" The kids raced to the food. The feast began!


After dinner, the adults and older children sat around the campfire, relaxing into conversation. The sun was setting, and it was a beautiful evening. The days were getting colder and shorter with the winter season upon them, but the trees were still losing their leaves in this place situated between the warmer coastal city of Patara in the south, and the higher, colder mountains to the north. The fire provided warmth for those who wanted it. Everyone felt stuffed and satisfied to sit and relax, except for the younger children who ran around playing Roman gladiators with sticks as swords, led by Kari and Dax.

Bishop Nicholas sighed. "Thank you so much, ladies and gentlemen, for your hospitality. You have been more than gracious, and I had more than my fair share."

All the adults gave him nods of agreement.

"Brother Nicholas, you are welcome anytime," Theophanes said. "We wish we could see you more."

"Thank you, Brother. I wish I could visit more often, but as our Lord says, 'The harvest is plentiful but the workers are few.' There are still many nonbelievers needing to hear the gospel, the good news of salvation, so as bishop of Patara, I stay very busy."

Brodin shared, "I wish I could say the same. My harvest is not plentiful, as I cannot afford workers, and now I have three daughters coming of age for whom I will need dowries to get them married. I do not have the money of Theophanes, nor the many hands of Falon's Mikros clan to help produce an abundant harvest."

Falon remarked, trying to be patient, "Ah, my good neighbor, now, you know Theophanes and I have both offered and given assistance with your crops. Either your pride has caused you to tell us no, or when you have accepted our aid, then as we helped you more, your hands became more idle. You cannot expect to get something and give nothing. A slack hand causes poverty, but the hand of the diligent makes rich. Theophanes has worked as diligently as any person has, and still does, even after success. He is also as gracious as they come. Yes, my Mikros clan are many in number, but we instill a strong work ethic and value education as well. Commanded it is, that if someone is not willing to work, he or she will not eat. Whatever we do, we work heartily, as for the Lord and not for people. We work, therefore we eat."

"How dare you! We work and we eat."

"Then you have nothing to grieve about."

Brodin, knowing he could not argue with Falon's logic and being too full of pride to confess his shortcomings, decided to point the finger of blame for his lack of success elsewhere. "It does not help that we are taxed more than ever by Emperor Probus, who takes and takes."

Theophanes joined in. "Brodin, I'm in agreement with Falon about how you handle your business affairs, but I have to agree with you there, neighbor. Probus is very good at taking, but what is even more worrisome is that he seems to be becoming more and more hateful toward Christians. What is the talk in Patara, my brother?" All eyes turned to the bishop.

"Yes, Probus and his leaders are speaking out more and more against us. Persecution has started to become violent. Because we do not believe as they do they will target and physically attack Christians. They think themselves gods and indulge in all kinds of sinful acts. These actions are becoming commonplace." The bishop looked at Nicholas, Noll, and Wren, who had been sitting and listening to the adults. "Children, always remember what is right may not always be popular, and what is popular may not always be right. Our Lord Jesus said, 'I have said these things to you, that in Me you may have peace. In the world, you will have tribulation. But take heart; I have overcome the world.'" At that, a few amens arose from the group, and the bishop smiled and winked at the children.

Theophanes declared, "All right, enough of the serious talk. There are times to work, weep, and mourn, and other times to rest, laugh, and dance.

This is a Christ-Mass celebration, so let us go back to celebrating!" The group cheered. Some stretched after sitting for a while; others embraced and smiled and giggled; while still others clinked steins together, toasting the day of celebration. The solemn atmosphere dissipated and a lighter spirit took over.

Kari and Dax appeared out of nowhere, jumping up on a table and yelling, "Keeyiiiiiii!" The onlookers laughed as the two stood in fighting positions, as if ready to go to battle. They looked at the bishop, and Kari asked, "Bishop Nicholas, will you play David and Goliath with us?"

Bishop Nicholas was amused and asked, "And how do we play David and Goliath?"

"Well, you're Goliath," Kari explained.

"And we're David," Dax added.

"And then we sling stones at your head!" Kari finished. They both pulled out slings and several smooth, hand-sized stones hidden in their tunics.

Bishop Nicholas, having known the children since they were born and knowing their impulsive tendency to act before thinking, grew wide-eyed and weak-kneed and bit his bottom lip. He took a step away from these two tiny, but potentially dangerous warriors, and sat down for self-preservation.

Tana, their mother, quickly intervened, "Kari and Dax, don't you dare sling those stones at the bishop's head!"

"But why?" Dax asked. "Doesn't he know the story?"

Bishop Nicholas responded, "Oh, I know the story all too well, and I know how it ends—not good for Goliath."

Kari added, "Well, yeah, the ending is the best part!" At that, she put a stone in her sling and began to swing it over her head. Dax followed suit.

Falon stepped in front of the bishop, his full height only coming up to the man's neck—not much protection for his head from a slung rock. "Kari and Dax put those rocks down right now!"

"Aw, but Daddy," Dax whined, "we found these smooth stones at the stream, like David did, and they are perfect for slinging at Goliath's head!"

"I said no," Falon replied. "Put all the rocks down now." He motioned with his hand pointing down.

Kari and Dax reluctantly complied, dropping six smooth stones to the ground, all the while grumbling under their breath and stomping their feet. "Okay, okaaaay, we'll be good," Dax said. "We won't play David and Goliath and sling our rocks at Goliath's, er, I mean, Bishop Nicholas' head."

At this, the crowd let out a collective sigh of relief, especially the bishop, who was still sitting near the table Kari and Dax stood on. Recognizing that Kari and Dax were tough but playful souls, and loving children as Jesus did, he offered, "Kari and Dax, I have a game for us to play that may be less painful for me. Let's play professional Greco-Roman wrestling. Are you familiar with it?"

Kari and Dax both lit up with excitement. Greco-Roman wrestling was one of their favorite games to play. They followed some of the stories of the most famous, professional wrestlers in the region, like Sandor the Great, Craigory the Courageous, and Ekanem the Nigerian Terror. Sandor was the most famous of all because not only was he undefeated as a wrestler, but also he was undefeated as a gladiator, more skilled than anyone was in all the land. He had a reputation for being merciful as well; defeating his opponents with ease but not killing them, as most other fighters would do, thus making him very popular with the common people. Some thought he might have been a Christian.

"Yes!" Dax yelled. "We love professional wrestling!" He leaped from the table onto the ground before the bishop and, in his best, deepest voice, he said, "I am Dax the Destroyerrrr!" He flexed his muscles.

Kari just as excitedly jumped from the table, and in her toughest, deepest voice, she said, "I am Kari the Killerrrr!" She lifted up her right elbow and slammed it into her left hand, making a loud slap, as if driving it into someone's head to do some serious damage.

Suddenly Bishop Nicholas had some regret, or maybe it was more like fear and trepidation. *Oh well, I may as well go for it.* With that, he looked them straight in the eyes and said in a calm but serious voice, "Oh yeah? Well I am Hugh."

Kari and Dax looked at each other, then at the bishop, and then at each other again and began laughing. Kari chuckled, "Hugh? That's it? You're Hugh?"

Dax mocked, "Ohhhh, scaaaary. Hugh is a really tough name. I'm really scared of . . . Huuugh," he snickered.

Bishop Nicholas, in his deepest, most ominous voice, said, "Yes, I am Hugh . . ." and then, exploding to his feet, "MONGOUUUUUUS!!!" he roared, standing in a mighty, strongman pose, towering over little Kari and Dax. Caught by surprise, the twins shrieked and scurried away like little mice from a giant cat.

Those watching the scene dissolved into laughter.

Bishop Nicholas smirked confidently as he watched the little warriors run away shrieking, and at the same time, he felt relief because he no longer had to wrestle. Proud of himself, he turned to the amused onlookers and said in his tough voice, "Hughmongous is victorious agaaain!" and he flexed his muscles. At that moment, some commotion stirred behind him. Before he had time to turn around and see what was happening, the very nimble Mikros professional wrestling tag team of Kari the Killer and Dax the Destroyer bounced onto the table and flung themselves into the air. They landed on the bishop's back, and all the while Kari shrieked, "Killlllll!" and Dax shouted, "Destrooooooy!"

### Devotion

Nicholas and his family celebrated Christmas with a Christ-Mass celebration that included family, friends, food, and fun. However, it was centered around the birth of Christ. Exchanging presents was not a tradition in their day. That tradition came years later. Not to give anything away, but young Nicholas will have a little something to do with that tradition, wink, wink.

Instead of having presents to focus on, they focused on only one gift, the greatest Gift ever, the coming of the Christ (Greek), the Messiah (Hebrew), which means the Anointed One—Jesus, also called Immanuel—God with us. Nicholas' uncle, Bishop Nicholas, explained the significance of Jesus' birth.

**Questions to consider:** Today, and during the Christmas season, and on Christmas day, what is my main focus?

*"Now there were shepherds in that region living in the fields and keeping the night watch over their flock. The angel of the Lord appeared to them and the glory of the Lord shone around them, and they were struck with great fear. The angel said to them, 'Do not be afraid; for behold, I proclaim to you good news of great joy that will be for all the people. 11 [b]For today in the city of David a savior has been born for you who is Messiah and Lord. 12 And this will be a sign for you: you will find an infant wrapped in swaddling clothes and lying in a manger."Luke 2:8-12*

**Prayer:** "Heavenly Father, thank you for the gift of Jesus, our Savior and Lord. I cannot fully comprehend how You came to earth in human flesh to implement Your holy plan to make it possible for us to have an intimate, personal relationship with You, but I am ever so grateful. Please help me remember that you are the reason for the Christmas season and Christmas day. I don't ever want anything to interfere with me remembering the "good news of great joy" for me. Thank You! Amen."

# 5
# Friends

*Several years later . . .*

ON A WARM summer day, Nicholas, Noll, and Wren, now young teenagers were out in the woods riding their horses to one of their favorite spots. They arrived at a place where boulders sat beside a flowing stream. It was peaceful and beautiful. The three all sat, relaxing in the sun, and pulled from their pouches blocks of wood and knives for carving. Nicholas reported he would create a wagon; Noll would carve a horse to pull the wagon, and Wren would make a girl to be the wagon master and steer the horse.

"So," Noll began, "we'll be celebrating our entrance to adulthood with the sacrament of confirmation in a few weeks. What do you think will happen to us? Where will we all be in one, five, ten years from now? If these moments end, I'll miss them. I'll miss the two of you."

"Yeah, we've been blessed with good friends and good memories," reflected Nicholas.

"Well, I would hope after confirmation that we'll still be friends and still get to spend time together like this," Wren said. "Right?" She glanced at Nicholas for a reaction, with a longing in her eyes for something more than a friendship. Nicholas looked at her and then down, unsure of how to respond. He had an inner struggle going on.

Nicholas acknowledged and deflected. "I hope we stay close. What are your plans, Noll?"

"The usual for me being in the Mikros clan. I'll go into the family businesses of art, ..." He raised his carving. "... farming and ranching. Being a businessman in general. Then get married and, as all the Mikroses do, have lots of kids." He laughed aloud.

"You all do have lots of kids! Why is that?" Nicholas asked.

"I asked my dad that once, and he just said, when I hit a certain age I'll understand. I guess I haven't hit that age yet because I don't understand. He said something about Mikros women and we Mikros men are a lot like the land we till—very fertile. Whatever that means."

Nicholas and Wren shrugged their shoulders, but when they looked at each other a sudden spark ignited inside them both. Maybe they did know. Wren gave Nicholas a wry smile. Within both of them, a stirring arose, like butterflies flying around in their stomachs. This stirring also reached their hearts and various other parts of their bodies as well. This urge seemed to happen when they were together or thought about each other. It was a strange, new, good feeling.

Nicholas was uncomfortable with these unknown urges developing within him, despite the undeniable pleasure they brought him. He looked back at Noll, clearing his throat. "Well, I know my parents have all the respect in the world for your parents and the Mikroses in general. They speak often of how much you all love God, love others, and try to make a positive difference in the world. And they say you all have a work ethic like no other, knowledge of business like no other, craftsmen skills like no other, and your love for learning is surpassed by none."

"Well, thanks! I knew I always liked your parents for a reason. They have brilliant skills of observation!" Noll laughed.

"Yeah, well, I don't think humility was ever mentioned in your case," Nicholas quipped.

"Whatever," Noll responded. "Anyway, we're driven to do our best for the Lord. I think it's also because we, as a people, tend to be smaller. I don't know if you all have ever noticed that. Our height tends to be lacking in some instances." Nicholas and Wren knew the reality was that this was the case in all instances; however, they shook their heads as if they had never noticed. "So sometimes we're not taken as seriously as we should be. Therefore, we have to work twice as hard to receive half the credit we do get. We've never had too many problems because we have been around here for so long. But now with the region growing, commerce is growing, and more new people are coming into the area from other countries, they don't know us, and when we go into town we sometimes get teased. Hopefully, it doesn't get any worse than it is."

"I'm sorry that's happening to you. That's why the world needs the love of Jesus. When we experience His love and grace, then we can't help but want to share that love and grace with others and respect them for their differences. I wish that for you and your family."

Wren agreed. "Yes, Noll, if there's anything we can do to help, please let us know. It's a shame people will judge someone by what's on the outside rather than what's on the inside, as God does. There's a lot of good in your heart and the heart of the Mikroses."

"Thank you both for understanding," Noll said. "And you two are such liars, acting like you never noticed I am shorter than you all. Lying! God is making that list and checking it twice. You lying dogs," he laughed. Being caught, Nicholas and Wren laughed along and were a bit embarrassed.

"It's not that we didn't notice, we just don't care," Wren said. "We know the real you. We love the real you."

Nicholas added, "Yes, agreed." They all smiled at each other, and Noll was now the one a little embarrassed.

"Plus, truth be told, I'm not much taller than you. I think that's why many people think we're related," Nicholas said.

"'Tis true, 'tis true," Noll said. "Okay, Wren, how about you? What are your plans for after confirmation?"

Wren's smile turned into a frown as she looked down at the carving and knife in her hands. "I don't know. My family doesn't have much. As everyone knows, my father doesn't have a strong work ethic like your families. He's very prideful, thinking he can do everything on his own, and he doesn't ask for help. He doesn't have a good business sense, and he spends what little we have getting drunk. He doesn't have a relationship with God. My mother and sisters do, and we help each other. Your families have been very helpful to us in our times of need."

Nicholas and Noll sat quietly, carving, listening intently.

Wren continued, gaining a slight smile. "If you're asking me what I would like to have happen after confirmation, it's what most girls my age want. I want to fall in love and betroth a good man who loves God, and is from a good family who loves God. Then eventually get married and have his children and serve the Lord together as husband and wife." She looked at Nicholas, who glanced up and then back down to his carving. "That's what I would like. The problem is, because of my father squandering everything we've had over the years, I have no dowry, no extra money or goods, nor any land. Without a dowry, I won't be desirable as a wife. I'll have nothing to bring with me into a marriage for my protection against abuse or to help us get started financially as a couple. Without a dowry, my future is unknown." Her frown returned.

Noll, having seen the attraction between Nicholas and Wren that bespoke more than friendship, said, "Wren, you have everything a Godly man would want. As I have heard my parents and Nicholas' parents say." Noll looked at Nicholas, who quickly glanced at Wren with a nervous smile and then just as quickly turned away, "You, your mother and your sisters are all Proverbs 31 women, in spite of your father. No offense." Wren nodded, understanding. "All of you are women of noble character, worth far more than rubies, lacking nothing in value, bringing good all the days of your lives. You will have no problem finding a good man."

"Thank you, Noll."

Noll looked at Nicholas. "Right, Nicholas? That's what your parents have said?"

Nicholas, put on the spot, kept carving. "Yes, it's true. That's what they say. That's what everyone says."

Wren, emboldened, pressed, "Even you, Nicholas?"

Nicholas stopped carving and locked eyes with Wren. "Yes, even me." They smiled, drawn to each other.

"Somehow, some way, God will honor you and give you what you want," Noll said. "His will be done. Awww, this is so nice! We're having a little friend lovefest! Let's bring it in for a group hug." Noll set his knife and carving down and leaned in with both arms spread. Nicholas and Wren reluctantly but receptively put their knives and carvings down and leaned in. The group hugged each other with Noll giving both his friends, who were a bit reserved and rigid, a strong embrace. They sat back down, picked up their carvings and went back to whittling.

"Nicholas, young man of God, what say you? What are your plans?" Noll asked.

Now Nicholas was the one slow to speak, with a disappearing smile. "I was hoping you wouldn't ask me. Luckily, I don't have to decide right away, and I'm still praying about it, asking God for direction."

Noll prodded, "Do tell."

Wren studied Nicholas, wishing inside that Nicholas' plans were as clear as hers were and included her in it. Both Noll and Wren had known for a long time that Nicholas had a special calling over his life, that God had something different planned for him. This would be the first time that Nicholas would verbalize it to anyone.

"I love my life. I would like to be like you, Noll, and take over the family businesses. I enjoy farming, ranching, buying and selling goods, and working with my animals. I would like to be successful like my parents and, like them, raise my standard of giving, not my standard of living so that I can bless others with jobs and resources. I would like to have a family; a big family with lots of kids, like your family, Noll, which I think is a lot of fun. I know my parents would be wonderful grandparents." Noll and Wren nodded their heads in agreement. "Living this life, I could easily love God, love others, and, like our families, make a positive difference in the world ministering to those who are hurting or in need."

"That sounds good. But, I have a feeling you are about to add a 'but,'" Noll said.

"But," Nicholas replied.

"I knew it. I don't like when you throw a big 'but' at us." Wren tried to giggle, but it quickly faded, sensing what was about to be said.

"But, I feel God calling me into full-time ministry. Maybe the priesthood. Maybe missionary work in a far-off land. I don't know. I'm not sure at this time. But, I'm praying about it."

They became quiet, and all three went back to whittling. After a moment, Wren broke the silence, "Nicholas, selfishly, as your friend, I hope your first scenario happens and you live and work and minister to people in this area, but . . ."

"Oh no, here comes another 'but,'" Noll said.

"But, you are a very loving, caring, giving person, more than anyone I know, and if God wants to use you and your gifts to touch people across this region or this country, or even around the whole world, then I pray the very best for you," Wren said.

These were the hardest words Wren ever had to utter. She meant it sincerely, as a girl who loved God and understood His will be done, not hers. It stung nevertheless. Being selfless was not always easy. Nicholas, having known her all her life and having an idea of her feelings for him, knew it was not easy for her to say. Putting others before herself was one of Wren's many virtuous qualities that caused Nicholas to feel more deeply for her. This hurt not only Wren, but both of them to the core.

"Thank you, Wren, Proverbs 31 woman." Nicholas smiled, meaning the words as the highest compliment, but he knew it was not what she wanted to hear from him at that moment.

"You're welcome." She responded, wanting to hear something different from him at that moment.

There was a pause of heaviness in the conversation. Noll broke the silence, trying to lighten the mood. "Hey, I have a big 'but'!" This got Nicholas and Wren's attention. "But, Nicholas is still praying about it, and we're not sure how things are going to turn out. Do not worry about tomorrow, for tomorrow will worry about itself. Each day has its trouble, so let us just focus on today, okay?"

"Sounds good to me," Nicholas said.

"Perfect," Wren added.

"Good," Noll said. "Speaking of today, by tonight my parents want me to pick out the colors for my formal dress robe to have for special occasions such as our upcoming confirmation. What do you all think? I was thinking emerald green with white trim—the green to match my amazing eyes, of course." He pointed to his emerald green eyes and fluttered his eyelashes.

"Hmm, that's good. It sounds so you, Noll," Nicholas said.

"Yes! Er, what's that supposed to mean?"

"Oh, nothing." Nicholas smiled and looked at Wren, who returned the smile at the inside joke—Noll was smitten with himself.

Nicholas continued, "I've given my robe a little thought, too. I was thinking red with white trim. Red as a symbol of Jesus' blood, which He shed on the cross for my sins. White trim as a symbol of purity, being spotless. It is by Jesus' shed blood that I'm cleansed and my sins are washed away, and I'm blameless and holy in Father God's eyes thanks to Jesus dying on the cross for my salvation. White as snow."

Noll glared at Nicholas with a look of disgust. "There you go again. You always have to show me up in front of God every chance you get, don't you?" Nicholas smiled mischievously, looking at Wren, who giggled. Noll mocked, "Look at me. I'm Nicholas, I'm white as snow, God loves me. Me, me, meeeee. Blah!" Nicholas and Wren laughed even more, and Noll cracked a smile and shook his head at Nicholas.

"Okay, it's getting close to lunchtime," Noll changed the subject. "I may be small, but I have a high metabolism, so I need to feed this work of art." He struck a sitting model's pose. "Speaking of art." Noll reached down to show his carving. He presented a horse so beautifully detailed and accurate, so defined and polished, that it looked professionally made.

"That's niiice," Nicholas said. "The nose is a little big, though." He tried to take Noll's ego down a notch, though he truly was amazed at Noll's artistic skills.

"Whatever."

"That's wonderful, Noll, as usual. You are so talented!" Wren said and she presented her carving of the girl wagon driver, decently made but not nearly refined as Noll's, but still made with care and by someone with some whittling skills.

"Nice, Wren, you've really come a long way! Good job! Keep practicing. You keep getting better every time!" Noll said. Wren smiled, proud of her work. Noll looked at Nicholas who was sitting cross-legged with his carving inside his legs, out of sight. "Okay, Nicholas, let's see your wagon. Let's see if you've learned anything I've taught you, like Wren here." Wren proudly held her piece of art up for display.

"Well, you kept distracting me and interrupting me with all the talking. It's not finished," Nicholas said. "I still have to finish. I also couldn't decide if I wanted to do a hay wagon or a carriage wagon or a chariot wagon."

"Enough with the excuses, just show us the wagon, Nicholas." Noll demanded.

With an embarrassed smile, Nicholas pulled out a wagon that looked pretty much like the block of wood he had started with, except for four bulges on the sides meant to be wheels, which were not quite round, and a shallow hole dug on top that was meant to be the inside of the wagon.

Noll was dismayed. "Oy. Are those wheels? Where's the seat for Wren's driver to sit? Where's the shaft that hitches my horse to the wagon?"

Nicholas laughed, recognizing he was not very good at whittling, but he still tried to defend a hopeless cause. "I told you, it's still a work in progress!" They all had a good laugh at Nicholas' expense and Noll shook his head in mock embarrassment. "Lord help him."

They began to pack up their belongings and get ready to mount their horses, which they had tied to a low tree branch next to them.

Noll announced, "Okay, my brother from another mother and my sister from another mister, next time I see you, which will probably be at church in a few days, I may have my new formal, green dress robe. I'll be looking gooood. Look out, ladies!"

"Okay, my brothers from other mothers . . ."

"Yes, you got it!" exclaimed Noll, pumping a fist in the air excited Wren had copied his rhyme.

"Thanks for the nice morning and relaxing time away from work." She finished.

Nicholas mounted Shimmel, now fully grown. He grabbed the bridle and looked at Wren, "Until church, I wish you well, my sister from another mister." She curtsied before mounting her gray beauty, Aria.

Nicholas then turned to Noll, who was prepared to mount his black beauty, Vida. Vida was as big as the other horses, causing Noll to have to stand on a rock. "And to you, Noll, I look forward to seeing you in your beautiful eye-matching formal dress robe, my sister from another mister." At that Nicholas rode away, adding under his breath, "I make myself laugh, ho, ho, hooo," allowing Noll to have the last word.

Noll nimbly jumped on his horse and realizing what Nicholas had said to him, he shouted, "Real funny, court jester! Nicholas, you're no saint! I know you and God knows you even better! And you're no saint, Nicholas!" Wren giggled as she watched the scene.

Noll looked at Wren on her horse and shook his head in slight annoyance. She gave him a smile and a shoulder shrug as if to say, "You know Nicholas." He smirked, and they rode off together.

### Devotion

Nicholas, Wren, and Noll have a major life transition coming up soon. They will be confirmed in the church, which means they will be committing their lives to God. After confirmation, they will be considered adults, with expectations and responsibilities increasing greatly for them.

Noll is someone who knows where God is taking him and his plan is simple and straightforward. Wren knows where God is leading her, and she knows what she would like, but there are many obstacles in her way, so her future is uncertain. Then there is Nicholas, who has many interests and all kinds of possibilities to choose from; however, he feels a prompting from

God to go in an unconventional direction. It is not that he does not want what God wants, he does, but there are other desires of his heart pulling on him as well.

**Questions to consider:** Do I relate to any of these three teenagers? To any one more than the others? We all face major life decisions at some point in our lives. Nicholas is in the process of praying and consulting with God. When faced with a decision, do I consult with God, my life-journey Companion and Guide, who is always in my train compartment with me?

*Trust in the Lord with all your heart, on your own intelligence do not rely;*
*In all your ways be mindful of him, and he will make straight your paths.*
*Proverbs 3:5-6*

*"Be still, and know that I am God!" Psalm 46:11*

**Prayer:** "Heavenly Father, when I come to a crossroad in life, I pray that I will seek out Your divine Guidance, that I will have patience to wait for an answer, and that You will open and close doors to guide me. Please give me eyes to see what You are showing me, and ears to hear what You are saying to me. Thank You. Amen."

# 6
# 𝔜ou 𝔑ever 𝔎now

*After leaving Wren and Noll...*

NICHOLAS RODE BACK to his home in anticipation of seeing his parents. They had traveled to Patara, the nearby city on the coast of the Mediterranean Sea, to do business, which they do thrice monthly—buying, selling, and trading goods. His mother liked to go once per month to help with the business, do some shopping, and see friends and family. She and Theophanes usually took an extra day after all the business and visiting was done to have time alone together at an inn on the coast, one of their favorite places to visit. Sometimes Nicholas would join them, but usually Nicholas went alone with his father and they traveled with Falon and Noll and some of the Mikros clan who traveled in many of the same business circles.

Nicholas enjoyed the whole experience as his mother did. He had a special affection for the Mediterranean Sea and all the ships that were coming and going, traveling the world on great adventures, and visiting new and exotic places. He loved to visit the docks and meet sailors from other nations, see what they were loading and unloading, and learn about new and exciting things they found to bring back and sell.

He had seen exotic animals like lions and tigers. He had seen and smelled exotic spices like frankincense and myrrh. He had tasted exotic treats such as the candy from Egypt that was made out of fruit, nuts, and honey, in addition to date candy, one of his favorite treats made of dates, cinnamon, cardamom seeds, walnuts, almonds, and honey. Another favorite of Nicholas' was a sugar cane candy from India, called khanda, which many consider the original candy. You could say Nicholas had a serious, sweet tooth.

Nicholas loved to visit the city, meet interesting people, and hear stories of their journeys. He wanted to travel around the world someday to see as many places and meet as many people as he could. Theophanes and Nona never shied away from allowing Nicholas to see the good and the bad sides of the city and people. They wanted him to learn right from wrong, what godly choices were, and were not, and the consequences of those choices. Being a farmer, Nicholas learned early what it meant to sow and reap in farming, and in life. People reap what they sow. If a person sows corn, they reap corn. If a person sows good choices, eventually that person reaps good things. If a person sows bad choices, eventually they reap bad things.

His parents took him in the area of the bars near the ports where sailors would gather. Nicholas grew up understanding that wine and other fermented drinks were neither good nor bad in and of themselves, but rather, it was what a person did with the drink, which resulted in good or bad. He understood that there are people who did not drink alcohol, some drank in moderation, and others overused and abused alcohol to try to fill a void in their lives and numb personal, unresolved pain.

He saw many people who started out drinking moderately with just one or two, but over time, they drank more and more, overusing and abusing alcohol, thus reaping negative consequences. Nicholas saw firsthand why St. Paul wrote in his letter to the Ephesians, "Do not get drunk on wine which leads to debauchery. Instead, be filled with the Holy Spirit."

As much as he loved the city with its hustle and bustle, its diversity and education, he also enjoyed the quiet of the countryside, working the fields and watching the crops grow, taking care of his animals, and enjoying his family and friends and the people in the area.

As he rode up to his home, he noticed it was quieter than he expected. He thought his parents would be back by then and that the workers would be helping unload the goods that his parents had brought back. He opened the barn door to put Shimmel in his stall, and his parent's horses and wagon were not there.

Nicholas was hungry, so he went in and made some lunch, then sat on the front step to wait for his parents and continue to enjoy this beautiful day. He was so excited to see his parents. It had been over three days since they had left, which was the usual amount of time for them to be gone, but every time they left, Nicholas missed them dearly. He was also very excited to see what goods and goodies they would bring back!

As Nicholas finished his last bite of lunch and washed it down with his last drink of apple cider, he noticed movement on the road in the far distance. "Yes! They're here!" He ran into the house, rinsed off his dishes quickly, and ran back outside to greet them as they arrived. Trotting down the porch stairs and across the front yard, he looked up the road and realized that it was not his parents after all but rather Falon, riding his horse alone toward Nicholas' house. Nicholas stayed with Falon and Noll's family when his parents were away, and Falon helped Nicholas run their estate just as Nicholas' father and family did for the Mikroses when they were away. It was not unusual to see Falon coming here, but Nicholas was still disappointed.

As Falon grew closer, Nicholas said, "Mother and Father aren't back yet. I wish they would hurry." Falon didn't answer, but rather he rode up to Nicholas and slid off his horse. Nicholas was now as tall as, if not taller than, Falon. Falon remained silent and looked at Nicholas with a serious expression.

"Falon, what's wrong?"

"I have a message from your parents, Nicholas. They're going to be late. They're stopping by their cabin in the woods." Their small cabin in the woods, with a barn, was where they sometimes stayed and stored crops they harvested on their lands farther away.

"Why are they stopping by there? That's quite a bit out of their way. Do they have some goods to drop off out there?"

"Um, something like that, and they said they are tired from their trip and for you to stay with us tonight. After they rest there for the night, they'll come here tomorrow."

"I've no work to do, and all our business is caught up. I'll ride my horse to the cabin and make it there by dark and come back with them tomorrow!" Nicholas became excited at the idea.

"No!" Falon snapped. Nicholas hardly ever heard this sharp tone come out of the usually mild-mannered Falon, except of course when he had to use it with Kari and Dax.

"Falon, what's going on? What's wrong?"

The Mikroses, known to be hard workers and assertive but fair business people, were as honest as they came. For Falon to keep the truth from

Nicholas was difficult, especially now that Nicholas knew something was wrong.

"Your parents are not feeling well. They're sick, and they don't want to bring the sickness back here. They want to stay at the cabin for the night to rest and see if they feel better tomorrow."

The concern released from Nicholas' face. His parents had been sick before, so it made sense they would not want to spread any sickness to others. Suddenly, a violent feeling hit Nicholas in the pit of his stomach as if punched in the gut by Goliath. "Falon?"

"Yes."

"Two weeks ago, when we all went to the city, one of your family members met us upon our arrival, and he talked with you and my father privately."

"Yes."

"And then after that, we didn't do any business at the docks nor did we visit the coastline. We stayed in one particular area, took care of all our business there, and then returned promptly."

"Yes."

"At one point, Noll and I were at the market buying candy, and we overheard two merchants talking about leaving the city after the business day because there were rumors of a plague that had been brought to Patara on a ship from a foreign land." Falon was silent.

"Is it not a rumor? Is it true? Is there a plague, and do my parents think they have it?"

Falon looked Nicholas in the eyes and slowly nodded his head.

The breath left Nicholas. "Jesus help them." After a moment, he said, "I'm going to get my horse."

"Nicholas." Falon warned, prepared to pounce on Nicholas if he disobeyed his parents' request. The Mikroses may have been small, but they were strong, quick, and nimble, and he would have no problem subduing the young lad.

"I'm going to get my horse, and I'm going to honor my parents' request to stay with you tonight. But tomorrow I'm riding to the cabin," said Nicholas in an even tone, devoid of emotion.

Falon placed his hand on Nicholas' shoulder with all the empathy in the world. "Agreed."

The next day, Falon and Nicholas rode their horses on a thin dirt road through the woods rarely used, as indicated by some overgrown brush. In the distance, they spotted the small cabin and barn. As they approached, the morning sun shone through the trees. They noticed there was no movement, no stirring, not even a mouse. It was peaceful but at the same time, ominous—even birds did not sing. As they approached the cabin door, Nicholas' heart raced. His palms became sweaty, and his eyes grew big in wonder over the state of his parents. He got to the door and heard some movement inside the cabin that sounded like the sliding of a wooden chair across the wooden floor. Relief!

"Good morning, Nicholas," said Nona through the door, staying separated inside the cabin.

Nicholas gushed, "Good morning, Mother! And Father?"

"Good morning, my son," his father said.

Nicholas exhaled and his heart calmed immediately as he heard their voices from within. "How are you feeling? Are you feeling better this morning?"

The cabin door stayed closed. "Our spirits are strong, my son, but our flesh is weak," Theophanes said. "We have been honest with you all of our lives, and we will be honest with you now. Nicholas, your mother and I don't have long. We thought we would be safe doing business in some regions of the city and avoiding certain areas, but the plague is more rampant than was believed. By the second night, we had symptoms. We stayed at an inn for another night, hoping we only needed time to rest, but the sickness got worse. When we realized the inevitable, we packed up and came here to end our days close to you, close to our family, friends, and home."

A tear rolled down Nicholas' face. "This can't be happening. This isn't supposed to happen this way."

"I'm sorry, my son," Theophanes said to him through the closed door with strength in his voice. "Who is to say what is or isn't supposed to happen? Only God. Of course, we have prayed for healing. God is in control, and we have to trust Him. He has allowed this to happen in the fallen world we live in. We know one thing for sure. That in all things, God works for the good of those who love Him and are called according to His purpose. Nicholas, right now, we need to go to Him with positive expectations, knowing there is no limit to what He can accomplish. You need to allow the Holy Spirit to control your mind so that you can think great thoughts of Him. Do not be discouraged. Time is a trainer, teaching us to wait upon God, to trust Him in the dark times. The worse our circumstances, the more likely we are to see His power and glory at work in our situation."

"I cannot think of a worse time than this."

"Instead of letting difficulties draw us into worrying, let us try to view them as setting the scene for God's glorious intervention. We are to do God's will, and what is His will, Nicholas?"

Nicholas stood quietly. He did not want to respond, as he knew the answer, but something inside him did not want to say the words. He was in shock. He was losing his parents. He grieved. He felt passing surges of disbelief. This was no time to be positive.

"Nicholas, say it. What is God's will for us? What is God's will for you? Say it," Theophanes firmly commanded.

"Love God, love others, and be joyful, prayerful, and thankful in all circumstances; for this is God's will for me in Christ Jesus."

"Yes Nicholas, yes," Nona said. "Son, every day, meditate on that, and meditate on this: 'Glory in our sufferings because we know suffering produces perseverance; perseverance, character; and character, hope. And hope does not put us to shame because God's love has been poured out into our hearts through the Holy Spirit who has been given to us.' We have hope, Nicholas. We have hope."

Theophanes added, "Remember the dot on the road? Remember the line of eternity drawn on the road? Your mother's and my dot are ending, but our eternity in Heaven is about to begin. Glory to our Abba Father in Heaven, Nicholas."

Nona, appreciating her husband's deep faith and joy, recognized her young son's pain and anguish and empathized with him. "Nicholas, my beautiful, wonderful son. I share your father's strength and focus, and our hope in things to come after we leave this life, yet we hurt with you. Along with our physical pain, we have deep emotional pain, for we, too, will lose something we dearly love: you."

"Yes, Son, your mother and I grieve deeply, but we have grown in our faith to see the big picture, and we have tried to instill that in you. You will get there. You will receive God's joy and peace that surpasses all understanding. Stay the course in good times and bad, and you too will grow in faith and learn to experience our Heavenly Father's embrace daily. It's said that we cannot store up earthly treasures in Heaven, and that is true except for one treasure: each other. Our loved ones who are believers are our treasures, and that's all of us here. We'll have each other in Heaven. For God so loved the world that he gave his one and only son, that whoever believes in Him shall not perish but have eternal life. We believe, Nicholas. We believe, therefore, we will be with each other again for eternal life. So this is not goodbye, my son, this will be until we meet again."

Theophanes and Nona repeated under their breath, "Yes, yes, yes" as they gave praise and acknowledgment to God. Nicholas could not see them, but he heard them through the door and could feel a warmth penetrate his heart that softened his mind. A sense of peace slowly invaded his body from the top of his head down to his toes. Their strength gave him strength.

Nicholas stayed on the little porch outside, being as close to his parents as he could get. Falon left to return home, and it was not too long before he brought back Tana, Noll, Kari, and Dax with food and drink. They also brought some special Mikros tonics that would help relieve some of Theophanes and Nona's symptoms and pain. The two families picnicked together like old times as best they could with Theophanes and Nona quarantined in the cabin. They talked for hours, with periods of laughter and crying and reflection and praise, reminiscing about the good times and the hard times and their friendship and faith. There were times of silence when nothing needed to be said and just being together was satisfying enough. Nicholas and the others could hear the sickness from inside the cabin's walls. Theophanes and Nona rested periodically. All, under the circumstances, had a wonderful time.

Time had flown, and before they knew it, dusk was coming upon them. All were vocally thankful to God for each other and the love they had for each other and this opportunity to spend one last time together. There were no goodbyes this day. Tana, Noll, Kari, and Dax headed toward their wagon. Falon turned to Nicholas. Nicholas expected that his parents would insist that he go home with Falon, so Nicholas quickly, firmly, and defiantly reported, "I'm not going anywhere. I'm staying here as long as I can." To which Falon responded gently, "I know."

At that, Noll, Kari, and Dax arrived at the porch with blankets, a pillow, food, and water for Nicholas to spend the night. Nicholas' tense body and rigid face softened. He kindly thanked them all, and they sympathetically smiled back as they placed their goods at his feet and walked away. They left him a fire burning nearby with a stockpile of wood. He watched these dear friends ride off into the darkness that had now come upon the land.

Nicholas laid out his bedding by the front door and sat upon it, wrapped in a blanket as the chill of the night increased. Theophanes, Nona, and Nicholas continued their evening together with laughter, tears, reflection, and praise to God late into the night. They offered Nicholas more parental encouragement of faith, hope, and love. Nicholas took his parents' wisdom to heart. The forest was quiet and still; the only sounds heard were the occasional hoot of an owl and the crackle of a dimming fire.

Theophanes and Nona had weakened even more. The sickness had grown within them and sapped much of their energy, yet they persevered to enjoy every last moment they had with their precious son. They all slowly faded, physically and emotionally drained, into a sweet slumber. Their last words to each other were, "I love you." Nicholas' last thought before dozing off was, "Jesus, help them."

Only one of the three would awaken in the morning.


In the morning, with the awareness of warmth enveloping him and the sound of chirping birds like a choir of angels singing a heavenly language, Nicholas slowly came to a semiconscious state. He lay on his left side facing the small cabin with his eyes closed. In the moment, he forgot where he was, but felt at peace. If God was for him, then who could be against him. He did not budge. He did not want to disturb this peaceful time.

He slowly became aware that the warmth he was feeling was the rising sunlight shining on him through the trees. He never heard a peep from inside the cabin and it never struck him that his parents were in the cabin, for he knew his parents were not in there anymore. They had left sometime during the night, taken to a better place. A much better place. He would miss them dearly, but he knew they were rejoicing in their new Home, and that is all that mattered to him. They were rejoicing, and he could hear his father's hearty laugh and his mother's infectious giggle amid the forest choir that now was serenading him awake. He lay there at peace.

A short while later, Falon and Noll arrived with food. They rekindled the fire and had a warm breakfast of eggs, bacon, bread, and milk. Falon said grace, thanking God for the last opportunity they all had together the day and night prior, for Theophanes and Nona being in Heaven rejoicing, and for their food. Beyond that, they did not talk; nothing needed to be said. After their breakfast, they removed the animals from the barn to take back home with them and set the small cabin and barn ablaze, destroying any remnants of disease that existed inside both structures. Watching the fire consume everything gave Nicholas a feeling of closure.

Fire refines and purifies. Watching the fire and feeling its intense heat, Nicholas felt a sense of restoration, inside and out.

Kris finishes with, "It was a Friday."

A stunned silence settles over their train compartment. Five shocked and sad faces stare at Kris. Finally, dabbing a tear from her cheek, Mary breaks the silence. "Oh, dear, that just breaks my heart." More silence.

"How old was he?" Thomas asks.

"Nicholas was around fourteen or fifteen, just a little older than you," says Kris.

Joe, a bit annoyed, says, "Good story, Kris, wasn't expecting that. Way to lift us up on Christmas Eve." Perhaps Joe is very annoyed. Laura and Wayne are sitting on Joe's lap as little puppies huddled in his arms for comfort.

"I'm sorry for the downer, but this is a pivotal event in Nicholas' life, as you can imagine," Kris says. "In fact, it was a major turning point in his life. I promise the story gets better. To know good and experience good, there has to be bad. Correct? Good cannot exist without bad; otherwise, it would not be good."

"Hey, you already have us down, now don't get all deep and philosophical on us, too," Joe says ruefully. "Our wee brains can only handle so much at a time. I guess we were just expecting a happy little elf story, not War and Peace in the life of a child. No, you're right, please continue, we'd like to hear how it gets better, right kids?" All the children nod their heads in agreement. "Right, Mare?" He looks at Mary.

She nods in agreement. "Yes, good news will be good. Nicholas losing his parents hits a little too close to home for me right now, but I get it. It's the circle of life, something that we all have to deal with at some time, and there are healthy ways to deal with it and unhealthy ways. It sounds like Nicholas and his parents had a healthy way to deal with it. They had faith in God and God's presence to comfort them and give them hope. There is hope in this life and there is hope in the life to come for those who believe." Mary manages a slight smile. Kris smiles at her and the others with reassurance.

"Well, let's hope this story gets better soon," Joe says to Kris with a "don't let us down" expression.

Kris nods and continues. "The next Sunday afternoon . . ."

## Devotion

We never know when death will happen to us, or around us. The thought is very sobering and unpleasant to think about. Theophanes and Nona did not seem afraid of death. They did not seem very fazed that it was the end of life as we know it. Instead, they seemed primed to begin new lives. Their confidence came from their spiritual faith.

For Christians, our Lord Jesus Christ conquered death and rose from the grave. If we believe in Jesus and that He is our Lord and Savior, then we share in His victory over death. Earth is not our home, we're just passing through. Heaven is our home. Therefore, death is a going Home experience.

**Questions to consider:** How am I feeling about my own life, and death, right now? How confident am I about where my eternity will be spent?

*The Apostle Paul said, "Yet we are courageous, and we would rather leave the body and go home to the Lord." 2 Corinthians 5:8*

*"Do not let your hearts be troubled. You have faith in God; have faith also in me. In my Father's house there are many dwelling places. If there were not, would I have told you that I am going to prepare a place for you? And if I go and prepare a place for you, I will come back again and take you to myself, so that where I am you also may be. Where I am going you know the way." John 14:1-4*

*"Jesus told her, 'I am the resurrection and the life; whoever believes in me, even if he dies, will live, and everyone who lives and believes in me will never die. Do you believe this?'" John 11:25-26*

**Prayer:** "Heavenly Father, death is real. Help me be honest with myself and, even more importantly, be honest with You about where my mind and heart is with You. Help me to have a heart-to-heart talk with You about what I believe and don't believe. Where I have doubt, help my unbelief. Where I have faith, strengthen it. I want my eternity to be spent with You. Thank You. Amen."

# 7
# 𝕸emorial 𝖊n 𝕸asse

*The next Sunday afternoon . . .*

NICHOLAS HOSTED A memorial mass for his dearly departed parents at their home. Hundreds of people came from the countryside to pay their respects and give their condolences to Nicholas and his uncle, Bishop Nicholas, and to the Mikros clan, whom many people knew were like family to Nicholas and his parents. Bishop Nicholas had carefully and prayerfully considered the risk of coming from the city to this rural community because he so wanted to participate in the service for his dear brother and sister-in-law, but he knew there was a risk. The authorities were consulted and it was determined he was healthy and not in danger of spreading the disease, so covered in prayer, he made the short journey.

Bishop Nicholas conducted the funeral liturgy, a public worship service on behalf of Theophanes and Nona. The community gathered en masse with the family and friends to give praise and thanks to God for Christ's victory over sin and death. They gave Theophanes and Nona to God's tender mercy and compassion. They looked forward to Jesus' Second Coming when all believers are together in the Kingdom of light.

Theophanes and Nona were well loved by all because their generosity and kindness to all had been profound and far-reaching. No one had a poor word to say about either. Many from the city also loved Theophanes and Nona for all the same reasons and sent written condolences to Nicholas.

The city folk were under quarantine due to the plague and therefore were unable to leave or chose not to, for fear of spreading the deadly disease elsewhere. To extinguish the disease, the ports shut down for the duration.

The day was sad and somber, but it also had a sense of peace about it and an element of joy. Theophanes and Nona had been a beacon of light, hope, and encouragement wherever they had gone and to whomever they had met. The day was peaceful, feeling a sense of God's presence—a feeling that everything would be all right was prevalent among all who spoke.

The day had an element of joy because everyone who had the pleasure of knowing Theophanes and Nona was honored and thankful that they had had that satisfaction. There was also joy because all the believers knew Theophanes and Nona were believers and that the lovely couple was with Jesus now in a better place, rejoicing. They would get to see the two again, someday.

There was a spirit of reflection, as there usually is when the reality of death comes so close and each person remembers that this life is temporary.

There are questions many ask themselves in times like these, and young Nicholas was no different: *Where am I with God and the afterlife? Am I loving God and in a close relationship with Him as He desires me to be, basking in His grace? Am I loving others as I am called to do and giving grace? Am I making a positive difference by serving others and reaching others in this temporary world?* Nicholas pondered these questions, but for the afternoon, he soaked in the love, friendship and outpouring of care he received from the many visitors he had at his house. He could not help but think, *Blessed were my parents by living their lives in Christ, and they were blessings in this life to many others and me. They are in a better place now with God, pain free. I am happy for them. I have them in my memory and my heart. I am glad for them and myself.*

Later that evening, after the last well-wishers had gone, Nicholas, his uncle, Falon, Tana, and Noll gathered in the living room beside the lit fireplace. Darkness had fallen outside, and they sat quietly, each lost in his or her own thoughts.

"Nicholas, my dear nephew, I must return to Patara in the early morning. So if you will, I would like to talk with you about your near and distant future while Falon, Tana, and I are here together with you," Uncle Nicholas sat down next to his nephew. "Your parents had a will to let us know their wishes for you and their estate. As far as custody, your parents asked that Falon, Tana, and I be your co-guardians, making decisions together in your best interest. Are you aware of this?"

"Yes, they shared that with me."

"What are your thoughts about us being your guardians?"

"I feel lucky to have the people I trust more than anyone, after my parents, and whom my parents trusted more than anyone, to have me. I believe in whatever guidance you all agree I should have."

"Good, because, Nicholas, we love you as our very own and we want the best for you," Bishop Nicholas said.

"You're my family. You've always been there for me," Nicholas said to his uncle, and then, turning to the Mikroses, added, "and I love you all as well. I'm very blessed to have you all."

Falon stood up from the table and walked to the fireplace to add a log. "Your parents made this will a long time ago when you were small. You are now becoming a young adult with the rite of confirmation around the corner. Your uncle, Tana and I have discussed this, and we believe that you are a very mature and responsible young man. You have a good head on your shoulders, and, most importantly, you have a deep relationship with God that many at your young age do not have. Therefore, we firmly agree that you should be a part of the decision-making process for your life. The timing of your parents' passing is interesting in that you're coming to the age at which you'll be choosing your path anyway. Are you good with that?"

Nicholas affirms, "Yes."

Bishop Nicholas pats Nicholas on the knee. "Being the sole heir to your parents' fortune, all this is yours: the lands, the many fields, the many herds of animals, the many structures upon the lands, and the many businesses they have built between here and the sea. You've learned your parents' work ethic, and you've displayed strong business acumen. You could enter into an apprenticeship with the Mikroses to continue to navigate the world of your parents' businesses. Or you could branch out and be educated in an area of business in which you may be more interested. You could go away to a university and become educated; you have the intelligence for it and a wonder and awe and curiosity for everything on God's green earth. You are a sponge absorbing all the knowledge you can. You are excellent with people, maybe politics is in your future. Since you were very young, you have had a special connection with God, hungering and thirsting for Him and His righteousness. Maybe the priesthood is something to consider. Nicholas, you have the whole world at your hands. Do you feel you are being led to anything more than another at this time? Do you know which direction God is leading you?"

Nicholas stared at the floor, concentrating, while he listened to his uncle. Everyone in the room waited in patient silence for Nicholas to answer. Finally, Nicholas spoke. "Uncle, do I have to answer that right now?"

"Of course not, my dear nephew. There is no hurry. We know you'll let us know when you know. You take all the time you need."

Tana added, "No hurry, no worry, Nicholas. We've got everything covered. We've room for you at our house. We don't want you staying here alone during this time of change. Falon already manages many of your parents' financial affairs and businesses, so you can continue to help in all the ways you already do. You have the rite of confirmation coming up on which to turn your focus. And, of course, you know you have all of us to talk to and support you as long as you need. Okay?" Falon and Tana gave Nicholas reassuring smiles.

"Yes, okay." He smiled, "Thank you, Uncle. Thank you, Falon and Tana."

Noll, who had been sitting quietly off to the side this whole time, spoke up. "Hello? What about thanking *me*? I'm the one that's going to have to share my bedroom with you. I'm the one that's going to have my sleep disturbed regularly by your incessant sleep-talking, blaaah, blaaah, blaaah."

"Uhhh that would be you, Noll. You're the one that sleep talks," Nicholas said, "I'm *so* handsome! Look at how my robe matches my *eyes*! Ladies, ladies, don't fuss; form an orderly straight line, there's enough of me to go *all* around.'"

Everyone erupted in deep hearty laughter, much needed after the recent days of heartache and sadness.

Noll confidently replied, "Hey, when you got it, you got it." He stood with his arms raised and turned around like a fashion model displaying a fancy outfit.

"In your dreams my son," Falon teased. "Literally, in your dreams."

Noll rolled his eyes, shrugged his shoulders, and smiled, "Whatever." He walked over to Nicholas and embraced him, which Nicholas gratefully received. The tone in the room turned to care for Nicholas and each other.

Uncle Nicholas, Falon, and Tana joined in making it a much-needed group hug for all. If tears are healing, then healing flowed for the rest of the evening.

## Devotion

Nicholas' community had a memorial in a mass, en masse—all together, to celebrate the lives of Theophanes and Nona. For Christians, a celebration of life is bittersweet—bitter because we've lost a loved one whom we will dearly miss. It is sweet because, as believers, we know our loved one is with God in Heaven and he or she is happier now, more than they ever experienced here on earth.

The celebration of life is a time for family and friends to comfort each other and share good memories of the dearly departed—in this case, Theophanes and Nona. Because they lived grace-filled lives, receiving God's grace and giving grace to those around them, many people had many great things to say about Nicholas' parents. The Christian life is meant to be lived out in community, loving and supporting one another.

**Questions to consider:** What would I like people to say about me after I die? What are people *really* going to say about me after I die? If what I want said about me, and the reality of what they *will* say about me, doesn't match up, what can I change today in how I'm living my life, to impact other people positively, while I'm alive, and for generations to come? It's never too late to change. I can start right ... now.

*"Jesus said to him, 'You shall love the Lord, your God, with all your heart, with all your soul, and with all your mind. This is the greatest and the first commandment. The second is like it: You shall love your neighbor as yourself.'"*
*Matthew 22:37-39*

*"You have been told, O mortal, what is good, and what the Lord requires of you: Only to do justice and to love goodness, and to walk humbly with your God."*
*Micah 6:8*

*"Do to others as you would have them do to you." Luke 6:31*

*"We have come to know and to believe in the love God has for us. God is love. Whoever lives in love lives in God, and God in them." 1 John 4:16*

**Prayer:** "Heavenly Father, please help me receive Your love, grace, mercy, and forgiveness, so that I may extend to others, even my enemies, love, grace, mercy, and forgiveness, to make a positive difference in my life and the people around me. Thank You. Amen."

## 8
# Rite of Confirmation

*Several weeks later . . .*

THE RITE OF confirmation had finally arrived! This was a big moment for those ages thirteen to fifteen, coming of age. This was when a child became an adult, a girl became a woman, and a boy became a man. After this ceremony, expectations will include working more, pursuing independence, and starting and supporting their own families.

More importantly, this ceremony was a time for each candidate to confirm publicly his or her own faith in God. They may have been baptized, christened, or dedicated as babies, but it was recognized that a baby could not make a conscious and informed decision to follow God, so now these young men and women would have the opportunity to consciously make that decision and publically profess their faith in Christ.

There were ten from the local area to be confirmed this evening, including Nicholas, Wren, and Noll, and they had a special guest from the city here to conduct the ceremony—Bishop Nicholas. The ceremony took place in the local church, with friends and families of all the candidates gathered.

Inside the church was quiet; considered hallowed ground, no talking occurred inside the church and a sense of awe settled over the proceedings as a crucifix, Jesus nailed to the cross, overlooked the congregation.

Eyes could not help but be drawn to this powerful, disturbing, and beautiful image, a forceful reminder of God's sacrifice for sins. Beautifully handcrafted by the Mikroses were many rows of long, wooden pews. Candles lit up the sanctuary, giving the church a warm glow. With all the seats taken, people stood in the back and on the sides. Bishop Nicholas and the local priest, Father Absalom, took their seats on the altar under the crucifix.

The candidates gathered with their adult sponsors in a side hallway, readying themselves to make their processions one by one to the altar. Noll would have Tana with him; Nicholas would have Falon as his sponsor standing in for his late parents, and Wren would have her mother, Madelyn. Nicholas, Noll, and Wren stood at the front of the line.

"Your robe is beautiful, Wren," Nicholas said, wearing his red robe with white trim. "Purple looks great on you."

"Thanks, Nicholas. My favorite color, of course!" Wren replied with a glow.

Nicholas added, "Your robe is beautiful, too, Noll. It matches your *amazing* eyes!"

"Thanks, Nicholas," Noll caressed his new, soft robe. "I knew it would!" He caught himself because at that point he noticed Nicholas smirking at Wren and realized this had been sarcasm.

Wren went along with Nicholas. "Yeah, Noll, your robe really makes your eyes pop!"

"You two are *really* funny; you should take your show on the road. A road that takes you far, far away from here."

Nicholas and Wren shared a momentary laugh at Noll's expense, and then Nicholas peeked around the corner at the congregation. He noticed Wren's sisters, Kyla and Kalista, sitting with some of the Mikroses, their father nowhere in sight. Pulling his head back into the hallway, he whispered to Wren, "I don't see your father."

Noll stood behind her and shrugged his shoulders at Nicholas.

"He hasn't stepped foot into a church in years. He says if he did, the walls would fall because of all the bad things he has done. He doesn't feel worthy," said Wren.

Nicholas replied, "How sad. We're all unworthy. We all fall short of the glory of God, and that is the whole point of what Jesus did on the cross for your dad, you, me, and everyone. Jesus' sacrifice makes us worthy." He looked up at the crucifix that they could see from the hallway. "That's what gives us a 'done' faith. There's nothing we can 'do' to be worthy of a Holy

God, but it's what God has 'done' for us on the cross, paying our debts, wiping our slates clean, to be worthy. We all have sick souls, and one of the roles of the church is to be a hospital for the soul, a safe place to come and heal. This is a place he should be running to, not from."

Wren spoke flatly with eyebrows furrowed and mouth tightened. "I know, Nicholas. You're preaching to the choir. You're not saying anything that my mother and I haven't said to my father many times."

"I'm sorry, Wren. I know you know. I'm sorry about your father."

"Thank you, but I have no control over my father, only myself. This day is for me and my faith. That's what I'm focusing on, and this is why I'm here. Why *we're* here." She looked into Nicholas' eyes; he gave her an affirming nod and refocused on the sacrament of confirmation. In that moment, they were not friend with friend, nor even potential romantic lovers. They were a brother and sister in the Lord, here to do what God had called them to do.

Falon came alongside Nicholas and asked if he was ready. Nicholas replied, "More than ready." Falon looked back at all the candidates and their sponsors and in a loud whisper asked if all were ready. He received nods from all. Falon looked out to the altar and gave Bishop Nicholas and Father Absalom a nod. Father Absalom stood, and the presentation of the candidates, or another name for them, celebrants, began. He called each candidate by name and he or she came into the sanctuary to stand before the altar. First to be called and walk out was Nicholas with Falon. Nicholas shuffled to the far end of the front row, reserved for the candidates, and remained standing. Falon stood directly behind him in the second row, reserved for sponsors. Second called was Noll with Tana, Wren third with Madelyn, and all the others thereafter.

Everyone sat down when all ten candidates were in place before the altar with their sponsors behind him or her; Bishop Nicholas rose to give a brief homily. He explained the readings and led the candidates, their sponsors, and the whole assembly to a deeper understanding of the mystery of confirmation.

"On the day of Pentecost, the apostles received the Holy Spirit as the Lord had promised. They learned that those who believe in the power of the name of Jesus will be saved and will receive the Holy Spirit inside of them to be their counselor, comforter, teacher, and so much more. He fills our hearts with the love of God, bringing us together in one faith but in different vocations, and He works within us to make the church one and holy. At His baptism by John, Christ was anointed by the Holy Spirit and sent out to begin His public ministry. You must be witnesses before the entire world to His suffering, death, and resurrection; your way of life should at all times reflect the goodness of Christ. Under the guidance of the Holy Spirit, give your lives completely in the service of all, as did Christ, who came not to be served, but to serve. For the renewal of baptismal promises, candidates, please rise." They stood.

"Do you reject Satan and all his works and all his empty promises?"

"I do," the candidates answered in unison.

"Do you believe in God the Father almighty, Creator of Heaven and earth?"

"I do."

"Do you believe in Jesus Christ, His only son, our Lord, who was born of the Virgin Mary, was crucified, died, and was buried, rose from the dead, and is now seated at the right hand of the Father?"

"I do."

"Do you believe in the Holy Spirit, the Lord, the giver of life, who came upon the apostles at Pentecost and today is given to you sacramentally in confirmation?"

"I do."

"Do you believe in the holy church, the communion of saints, the forgiveness of sins, the resurrection of the body, and life everlasting?"

"I do."

"This is our faith. This is the faith of the church. We are proud to profess it in Christ Jesus our Lord."

"Amen."

Father Absalom prayed, "All-powerful God, Father of our Lord Jesus Christ, by water and the Holy Spirit, You freed your sons and daughters from sin and gave them new life. Send Your Holy Spirit upon them to be their Helper and Guide. Give them the Spirit of wisdom and understanding, the Spirit of right judgment and courage, the Spirit of knowledge and reverence. Fill them with the Spirit of wonder and awe in Your presence. We ask this through Christ our Lord."

"Amen." All sang out.

To anoint the celebrants, holy chrism—a mixture of olive oil and balm, blessed by the bishop on Holy Thursday—was used. The anointing on the forehead with chrism, in the sign of a cross, signified that the confirmed Christian must always be ready to profess his or her faith openly and to practice it fearlessly.

As Bishop Nicholas made his way off the altar and down to the end of the row starting with Nicholas, all candidates knelt, and their sponsors stood behind with their right hands on the candidates' right shoulders.

Falon called out, "Nicholas."

Bishop Nicholas made the sign of the cross on Nicholas' forehead with chrism and said, "Be sealed with the gift of the Holy Spirit."

"Amen." Nicholas affirmed.

The bishop then gave Nicholas a light slap on the cheek to remind him that he must be ready to suffer everything, even death, for the sake of Christ. The slap hurt a little, but the physical contact and the slap sound combined to make a thought-provoking reality check. Nicholas nodded in acceptance of this edict.

Bishop Nicholas took a step to his right standing in front of Noll. Tana called out, "Noll."

Bishop Nicholas made the sign of the cross on Noll's forehead with chrism and said, "Be sealed with the gift of the Holy Spirit."

"Amen." Noll affirmed.

The bishop then gave Noll a light slap on the cheek to remind him that he must be ready to suffer everything, even death, for the sake of Christ. Noll nodded in acceptance of this edict.

Bishop Nicholas stepped to his right to stand in front of Wren. Madelyn called out, "Wren." Bishop Nicholas made the sign of the cross on Wren's forehead with chrism and said, "Be sealed with the gift of the Holy Spirit."

"Amen." Wren affirmed.

The bishop then gave Wren a light slap on her cheek, and she too nodded in acceptance of this edict.

As the bishop continued down the line, confirming the other candidates, Nicholas, Noll, and Wren glanced at each other, giving affirming nods to one another, and then went back to private, personal reflection. As Nicholas listened to Bishop Nicholas confirming the others with "Be sealed with the Holy Spirit," he could not help but be fixated on the crucifix of Jesus hanging on the cross in front of him.

He felt as if Jesus' eyes were looking directly at him. He could not help but think that since his earliest awareness of God, Jesus had been by his side watching over him, in good times and bad. Though Nicholas had been by himself at times, and felt alone at times, he embraced the truth that God was always with him. He knew he had never been alone and knew he never will be alone, no matter what. Nicholas was at peace.

## <u>Devotion</u>

Confirmation is a time when the basics of the Christian faith are remembered and confirmed. Nicholas, Wren, and Noll confirmed their faith in God and His Word and they were serious and excited allowing themselves to be filled with the Holy Spirit. They were focused and unshaken in their faith in God. As Christians, we've all had those special times of being filled, strengthened, joy-filled, and peace-filled.

It's powerful and humbling when we experience that "come to Jesus" moment when we recognize He's God and we're not, He's Holy and we're sinful, and we need His grace, mercy, and loving kindness to be saved forever. However, most everyone experiences times in our Christian walk where we become complacent in our faith and have bouts of doubt.

This is why staying in God's Word is so important. Words are thoughts expressed. God's Word is God's thoughts written down for us to meditate on. If we want His thoughts to be our thoughts, then we have to fill our thoughts with His thoughts.

Going back to basics in our faith is important. An auto mechanic teacher used the phrase, "K-i-s-s. Keep it simple stupid." He meant, before you go tearing apart the engine to find out what is wrong, keep it simple. First, check if it has gas and oil (or these days if the battery is charged). Check for leaks and check all the hoses and wires to make sure they are connected.

Christians have to keep it simple, too. Sometimes we lose sight of what our faith is all about and we drift away from God or we start getting caught up into feeling like we have to perform to be accepted by God. That is when we have to go back to basics and remember Truth, such as our faith is dependent on the 'done' work of Jesus on the cross. His blood sacrifice for our sins is what makes us acceptable to God, not any work we do. That truly life in Christ is not cluttered, complicated, or burdensome. We make it that way, God doesn't. He says. "Be still. Come to Me and find rest." Life in Christ is actually, freeing, simple and light.

We also have to remember that all relationships take time, energy and communication. Our relationship with God is no different. If we are not spending time with God daily in His Word and prayer then we are missing out on blessings and we will feel distant and disconnected, especially if we're continually filling our minds with worldly entertainment, talk, and activities.

**Questions to consider:** Do I need a faith refresher to go back and remember the basics of my faith and the fruits of the Holy Spirit, such as love, joy, peace, patience, and kindness? Have I been backsliding, and do I need to recommit my life to my Lord and Savior and reignite that passion I felt when I first came to experience His saving grace?

*"Trust in the Lord with all your heart, on your own intelligence do not rely; In all your ways be mindful of him, and he will make straight your paths. Do not be wise in your own eyes, fear the Lord and turn away from evil; This will mean health for your flesh and vigor for your bones." Proverbs 3:5-8*

*"But without faith it is impossible to please him, for anyone who approaches God must believe that he exists and that he rewards those who seek him." Hebrews 11:6*

*"Repent, therefore, and be converted, that your sins may be wiped away, and that the Lord may grant you times of refreshment and send you the Messiah already appointed for you, Jesus," Acts 3:19*

*Jesus said, "I came so that they might have life and have it more abundantly." John 10:10*

**Prayer:** "Heavenly Father, please help me renew and refresh my faith in You, daily. And help me rededicate my life to you if need be. Thank You. Amen."

# 9
# The Big Decision

AFTER CONFIRMATION, the families gathered back at Nicholas' home. He had been staying with Noll's family, but since his uncle was visiting from the city, he and the bishop were staying at Nicholas' family house for a couple of nights until the bishop left. Nicholas felt good to be back home, and he felt happy to have his close friends and family with him on this special night.

Madelyn and Tana brought food and prepared a celebratory meal for all. Wren's and Noll's younger siblings—Kyla, Kalista, Kari, Dax, John, and Leila—were with other family members for the evening. Being confirmed, Nicholas, Wren, and Noll were now considered adults, so this was an adults-only gathering.

They finished the delicious meal of fish, cheese, corn on the cob, and of course, bread with honey butter. As stomachs grew fuller, the conversation became quiet. A bustling fire was burning in the fireplace and candles glowed everywhere, making it quite comfy and cozy for all.

After a while, Falon broke the silence. "Thank you, my beautiful wife, Tana, and thank you, wonderful Madelyn, for this delicious meal." All offered thanks and appreciative gestures to the cooks. It had been a delightful evening and everyone began to realize the lateness of the hour. However, the peaceful atmosphere had everyone entrenched in their seats, in no hurry to leave.

Nicholas announced, "I've decided what I'm going to do."

"Good," said Noll. "While you're doing whatever it is you're going to do, will you please take my plate up to the wash basin? I'm too full to get up."

Nicholas glared at Noll. "I've decided what I'm going to do . . . with the rest of my life."

"Oh, nevermind," said Noll.

"This evening I confirmed my faith in Jesus, and He confirmed to me what I am to do. I'm going to become a priest."

No one was surprised at the news. Most expected it and supported him. Noll and Wren understood but were the only ones who did not necessarily like it. Noll knew it meant his lifelong friendship with Nicholas, as he knew it, would be ending. Wren knew her imagined, lifelong future with Nicholas, as she would like to have known it, would never be, because the priesthood meant a life of celibacy.

"That's wonderful, Nicholas," said the bishop. "We are proud of you, no matter what decision God leads you to make, but I will be very proud and honored to have you as brethren in the clergy with me."

"Yes, Nicholas," Tana encouraged, "we're so proud of you. You'll make for a lovely clergy. Someday you'll have your own congregation and they will love you as much as we do."

"Yes, excellent, our dear boy," Falon said. "We will fully support you in all you do. I know you've been praying and thinking about this for quite a while now. When do you foresee beginning your new adventure, and what have you decided about your parents' estate—their money, businesses, land and everything? It's now all yours and your responsibility."

"I want to give it all away," Nicholas said without hesitation.

Noll spit out the cider he was sipping. "Huh?!"

Nicholas knew Noll would be the one to react as he did. He looked at Noll, smiled, and responded, "I know it may sound crazy to some, but that's what I feel I am to do. Jesus once said, 'If you want to be perfect, go sell your possessions and give to the poor, and you will have treasure in Heaven. Then come, follow me.'"

Noll, in debate mode, retorted, "Nicholas, you're so extreme. You know the context of Jesus' statement was to an arrogant, rich young man who didn't think he had any sin, but then Jesus exposed that the sin in his heart was love of money."

"Jesus said, 'Again I tell you, it is easier for a camel to go through the eye of a needle than for someone who is rich to enter the Kingdom of God.'"

"And again, Nicholas, you know the context of Jesus saying that was that the average rich person loves money more than God; money is their idol, the god they worship. Therefore, when they put their money, which in actuality is God's money, before God, then it will be difficult for them to enter the Kingdom of God. Did your parents put money before God? Do we Mikroses put money before God? I don't think you struggle with putting money before God."

"No. My parents put God first and were wise stewards with all that God had given them, giving much and living simply, just as the Mikros clan are wise stewards with all God has given all of you, and you all live simply. I have been fortunate that has not been me either, but I'm human; temptation is always lurking."

"You've never been tempted in this way that I've seen, Nicholas. You have never been one to love money, or materials, or possessions before God. God has given all this to you, and you can use it to bless many people just as your parents have done. 'Keep your lives free from the love of money and be content with what you have because God has said, 'Never will I leave you; never will I forsake you.' That's you, Nicholas."

"I appreciate your faith in me not to fall into temptation, Noll, and I totally agree with you that what God has given freely to my parents, and now to me, can be used to bless others. Your family is a perfect example of this as well, but I feel this is what God is calling me to do. 'For where your treasure is, there your heart will be also.' I want my treasure and my heart to be in Heaven, not on earth."

"Ugh, your treasure is in Heaven!"

Bishop Nicholas, sitting in the background patiently listening, calmly interjected, "What I am hearing from your conversation is two young men who have been diligent in reading scripture to better understand the heart of God, and your conversation is music to my ears. Kudos to your parents for instilling the importance of God's word in you." He looked at Falon and Tana and nodded. They smiled and nodded back. He continued, "And what I am also hearing is that you are both in agreement with what God says about money. Money in and of itself is not good or evil. Money is a tool to bring organization to society for a barter system, for exchange of goods. Correct?"

Nicholas and Noll nodded their heads.

"God says it's an individual's *belief* about money that makes it good or evil, it's the *love* of money that can be the cause of all kinds of evil. Many people eager for money have wandered from the faith and pierced themselves with many griefs. Whoever loves money never has enough money; whoever loves wealth is never satisfied with their income. Loving money leads people to do all kinds of evil to have money—lying, cheating, stealing, deceiving, even murdering. It is true money can give momentary happiness, but isn't that how it is with all sin? Sin can be enjoyable in the moment, but a moment of sinful pleasure can lead to pain, possibly for a lifetime. Agreed?"

Again, Nicholas and Noll nodded.

"Having money is not a sin. It is your belief about money that can be sinful. We, as Christians, try to remember that all money is God's money. Simply said, wealth is meant to advance the Kingdom of God. We are to be wise stewards of God's money. 'For of those to whom much is given, much is required.'"

Nicholas and Noll nodded.

"So, my dear young men, you both are in agreement about what role God says money should play in our lives in general, but what I do not hear from either of you is your understanding that God has a different calling for each of our lives. God's church body is not a building, it is of all of us who believe in Christ Jesus. All of us believers are one body, but we make up different parts of the body. Some are hands, some are feet, some are eyes, some ears, and some are mouths. Yes, sadly, there are some of us that I would consider rear ends, but that's a whole other conversation, and none of us is perfect. We all can be rear ends at times, amen?"

Everyone in the room humbly nodded in agreement.

"Back to the point. God calls us all to go into the world and share the good news of salvation. Our faith is to be personal, but never private. We are to be salt to the earth, a good flavoring, a preservative, a positive influence. We are to be God's light shining brightly in this dark world. However, we all have different callings, and you all have been fasting and praying during this time to hear God's guidance in your lives."

Nicholas and Noll give each other a sorrowful look.

Bishop Nicholas continued, "For me, God led me to take a vow of poverty. I do not have belongings, except for the clothes on my back. My focus is entirely on the ministry, and the church takes care of my basic needs as I am working in full-time ministry to share the gospel with my flock. Falon and Tana, and your parents, Nicholas, Theophanes and Nona, they had a calling to be farmers, ranchers, and business people. They received teaching from the clergy, studied, and knew God's word on their own, and they knew God's word as well as I do. They received ministering from the clergy and in turn ministered to others. Their outreach and giving were different from mine and touched different people than I do, by providing food and jobs to many people. Through their tithes and offerings to the church, they actually support me in my ministry to do what I and many other clergy do. Does that make sense?"

They agreed with the Bishop.

"We all need each other and have our parts to play. We clergy are no more important than the humble caretakers of the church that no one sees, but who are the ones who clean the church and make sure everything is in place. We are no more important than the workers who do the dirty jobs, such as shepherding or tending the pigs in their slop, or shoveling manure or whatever."

All agree.

"What you are is God's gift to you. What you make of yourself is your gift to God. So no matter what vocation God is calling you, whatever you do, work at it with all your heart, as though working for the Lord, not for human masters, since you know that you will receive an inheritance from the Lord as a reward. You are serving the Lord Christ. Amen?"

Everyone in the room in unison responded, "Amen."

"So rather than debating scripture, about which both of you agree, recognize you are two different children of God, just as Wren is a different child of God, and God will use all of you for His kingdom here on earth differently, but all are equally important to God."

"Nicholas," Noll said to his friend, "please know you will be in my thoughts and prayers, and I respect your faithfulness to answer God's calling on your life. I'm sorry for questioning your judgment."

"Iron sharpens iron, and that's one thing I love about our friendship, Noll. We can be real with each other and challenge each other, but after all is said and done, we can shake hands or hug and still be friends. Please don't ever stop speaking into my life because Lord knows I'm going to keep speaking into yours, whether you like it or not!"

"Nick the Lord knows I need you to keep me honest as well."

"Me too, Brother, me too."

After a pregnant pause in the conversation, Falon said, "So Nicholas, now that we know your intentions for all you have received, what is your timeline for giving it all away and entering your training for the priesthood?"

"Well, I know there is a lot to give away, and of course tithing to the church will be my first priority. It will take time to bring closure, and I am still quite young and don't feel an urgency to rush things. Additionally, I know grieving the loss of my parents will take a while. I have my good days and bad days, and God is still ministering to me in that area. So I'm thinking of giving myself at least a year to heal and get all my affairs in order."

This news immediately lifted the spirits of everyone in the room, especially Wren and Noll. They had a year to slowly transition into the next phase of their lives. Their world as they knew it, with Nicholas as a constant presence, was not going to end tomorrow as they had imagined.

"Good news!" exclaimed Noll, expressing what everyone was feeling.


The next year was a challenging year for Nicholas as he mourned the loss of his parents, but by God's grace, it was also a magnificent time because he felt the joy of the Lord while freeing himself from every earthly possession. He found it was easy to give away belongings such as furniture and knick-knacks, but the reality of giving away land, farms, ranches, and businesses was a challenge.

It made sense for Nicholas to want to give Falon and Tana everything—they were family to him. Falon had been his father's business partner, and Nicholas knew the Mikroses were wise stewards of what the Lord had given them. The Mikroses were very thankful for the proposition; however, Falon suggested they all commit it to prayer.

After some time, Falon felt the Lord was telling him to be above reproach and avoid any possible perceived inappropriateness in receiving this fortune so easily from his deceased business partner's teenaged son. Falon suggested they hire an impartial and reputable third party to come in, and assess the value of Nicholas' possessions, and then broker a purchase that was fair to both parties. That way, any questionable wrongdoing was avoided and Nicholas would have a fortune of coins to tithe to the church and disburse as he pleased. This delighted Nicholas greatly because now he could use his whole inheritance to assist the needy, the sick, and the suffering in all of Patara and the surrounding region. Nicholas gave as God instructed:

"Be careful not to do your 'acts of righteousness' before men, to be seen by them. If you do, you will have no reward from your Father in Heaven. So when you give to the needy, do not announce it with trumpets, as the hypocrites do in the synagogues and on the streets, to be honored by men. They have received their reward in full by getting all the attention they bring to themselves. When you give to the needy, do not let your left hand know what your right hand is doing, so that your giving may be in secret. Then your Father, who sees what is done in secret, will reward you."

Nicholas was filled with joy. Not only did he enjoy giving his money away, but he also enjoyed giving his time away by serving and helping others. He continued to help tend the fields and take care of the animals as his lands, farms, and ranches transitioned to the Mikros clan, however, no longer expected to be involved in matters of running the businesses, he used his free time helping neighbors with chores. Nicholas liked hard work and he liked helping people, which made them feel good. He truly had a servant's heart.

One of his favorite duties—and Noll, Kari, and Dax's as well—was being a chimney sweep. They would climb up onto a person's roof, and with hand brooms, they would slowly crawl down the inside of the chimney, sweeping as they went. Chimneys needed sweeping because burning wood had flammable emissions known as creosote, which formed when the gases condensed to a tar-like, sticky substance in the flue. When burning more fires during the colder months, creosote built up in the flues because of the amount of moisture it carried. If the creosote ignited, it would burn at extremely hot temperatures and could catch the home on fire. This is what had happened at the home of Amara, their neighbor and employee, years earlier.

It was a dirty job, but the dirtier the better for these four sweeps. They would compete to see who could be the dirtiest. They were all strong, nimble and loved running, jumping, and climbing on and off the roofs. They were all small in stature, including Nicholas, who was not really much taller than his Mikros friends, so they were made to do this job and they loved it. Chimney sweeps were considered good luck.

Nicholas continued his daily study of scripture and committed himself to daily prayer, spending precious quiet time with his Heavenly Father. Theophanes and Nona had taught him this discipline, and they had modeled it for him daily. Together as a family, they would read and pray, and they expected him to read and pray on his own as well. Talking with God came naturally for Nicholas. Most of the time when he was alone, he was chatting with God, interceding for other people, asking God questions, or sharing what was on his heart or mind no matter what it was, good or bad. He knew he could share anything with God and that God would guide him. The young man still had the awe and respect for God as the King of kings and Lord of lords and at the same time God was his safe refuge, He truly was Nicholas' best friend. What better friend to have?

Many people travel through life wondering what God's will might be for them. For Nicholas, it was simple. He had scripture memorized, written on his mind and heart. Daily, he meditated on these words from the Apostle Paul in a letter written to the church in Thessalonica: "Be joyful always, pray continually, and give thanks in all circumstances (good and bad); for this is God's will for you in Christ Jesus."

For Nicholas, loving God, loving others, rejoicing, praying, and giving thanks regularly as best he could, with the help of the Holy Spirit, was the will of God. By practicing these five things, he kept his mind away from dark places and temptation; rather, it led to holy and honorable living. Nicholas was as jolly a fellow as they come. He had learned early that holiness led to happiness and sin led to sorrow. He was able to focus on what he had rather than on what he did not have, which gave him a thankful heart. A thankful heart is a joy-filled, jolly heart.

Nicholas would go anywhere and everywhere to help people out in the countryside and in the city. He knew many people and they knew him. Even though many knew him, he was still able to travel without much attention because he was plain looking and did not stand out in a crowd. He blended in well. He liked this because then people would talk more freely around him, which would allow him to hear what was going on in their lives, the good and the bad. If he heard someone was experiencing trouble, he would do what he could to help.

If finances were an issue, he would discreetly donate a few coins to the person. This is where the skill of a chimney sweep came in handy, stealthily sneaking into people's homes at night. Up onto the rooftop he would climb, down the chimney he would go, leaving a monetary gift in a stocking hung to dry on the fireplace mantel, or in a drying shoe, and then back up the chimney and out lickety-split. Only God knew what he had done. He had so much fun!

Many were blessed by Nicholas but did not know it was he doing the blessing. Most would give God the thanks and glory for the hidden gifts they would find in their stockings or shoes, and this pleased Nicholas greatly. That was what he wanted—God getting the glory, not him. It would be a regular topic of conversation around the whole region of Patara. Who was the mystery giver? Nicholas' name would pop up occasionally, but no one knew for sure.

### Devotion

Bishop Nicholas shared the saying, "What you are is God's gift to you. What you make of yourself is your gift to God." What we are called to make of ourselves is actually us submitting our souls—our minds, wills, and emotions—to God and allowing Him to transform us into being more Christ-like, having a servant's heart. Though young Nicholas clearly had other interests and desires in his heart tugging on him, he submitted himself—his mind, will, and emotions—to God's calling, thus becoming Spirit-led and joy-filled.

God does not look for ability, but rather availability. If you make yourself available to God, He will do amazing things with you whether you have the ability or not. God will reject some people who, on the outside, look like they fit the part, then He will choose others, instead, who have the right hearts. An example is in I Samuel, Jesse had many sons that were impressive, especially one in particular named Eliab, yet God chose the youngest and the scrawniest of the sons. Why? Because he had a heart for God more than the others and his motives were righteous. That scrawny kid turned out to be King David.

God looks at our hearts. He wants us and He picks us. And He picks us for a special mission and a special purpose that only He can see because

He knit us in our mothers' wombs. He knows our hearts better than we do. We are not to be discouraged about what is happening in our lives on the outside, but, rather, we are to hear the voice of God choosing us for what He has done and is doing on our inside. God looks at our hearts, and He does have purpose for us. He chooses us. We have to surrender to Him. By surrendering, we are actually set free.

**Questions to consider:** Do I desire God in my heart? Do I have right motives? Am I humbling myself before God to transform me and change my heart to be more Christ-like? Am I making myself available to do God's will, not mine?

*"Now the Lord is the Spirit, and where the Spirit of the Lord is, there is freedom." 2 Corinthians 3:17*

*"Then I heard the voice of the Lord saying, 'Whom shall I send? And who will go for us?' And I said, 'Here am I. Send me!'" Isaiah 6:8*

*"But the Lord said to Samuel: Do not judge from his appearance ... God does not see as a mortal, who sees the appearance. The Lord looks into the heart." 1 Samuel 16:7*

*"But you are 'a chosen race, a royal priesthood, a holy nation, a people of his own, so that you may announce the praises' of him who called you out of darkness into his wonderful light." 1 Peter 2:9*

**Prayer:** "Heavenly Father, I know You look at my heart, and my heart isn't always in the right place. Help me have a right heart and be able to say, 'Not my will, but Yours be done.' Help fill me with Your Holy Spirit and empower me to be stronger and bolder in faith, more loving, patient and kind. Help me make myself available to You to use me as you wish to further your Kingdom. Thank You. Amen."

# 10
# A Royal Connection

NICHOLAS' YEAR OF transition was interesting because not only was Nicholas purging himself of all earthly possessions, but the entire Roman Empire, which included Patara, was in upheaval as a new Roman emperor was taking power. His name was Diocletian. Being emperor of Rome was a risky business in that day; in fact, Diocletian was the eighth emperor to rule since Nicholas had been born!

When Nicholas was born, the emperor was Claudius, who died of an illness. Next, Aurelian was assassinated and then Tacitus either died of illness or was assassinated (depending on whose story you believed). Probus was assassinated; Carus died either by illness or possibly a lightning strike (how unfortunate that would be). Then came Carus' sons: Numerian, who died by illness or assassination; and, lastly, Carinus, with whom Diocletian battled and who either died in battle or some of Carus' men had sided with Diocletian, and assassinated Carinus.

There was a lot of instability across the Roman Empire. It was Diocletian's turn to rule, and he was someone to watch because he was known to be against Christians as much as, if not more than, any other emperors that had preceded him. This was worrisome, but at the same time, as emperor, he had a huge job in front of him trying to bring stability back to the empire politically, economically, and militarily.

Nothing politically affected Nicholas, and he loved every moment of his year, giving away all his possessions and money, helping people in need, and spending quality time with friends and family. Coincidentally, there was a time when Nicholas crossed paths with Emperor Diocletian's wife, Prisca, and their daughter, Valeria, who was around Nicholas' age. Joining them was a young man, also around Nicholas' age, named Constantine, who was in line for the throne someday.

Emperor Diocletian had a small castle in Patara so that he could visit the beautiful coast when able, and occasionally he oversaw the very important trading port that reached to the outskirts of the Roman Empire and beyond the Mediterranean Sea. Prisca and Valeria loved to visit the coast of Patara, enjoying the Mediterranean climate and, even more, shopping at the central market with all its exotic goods from around the world.

After a short stay in Patara, Prisca, Valeria, and Constantine were heading back north to their home in Nicomedia and had just reached the countryside when their left rear carriage wheel hit a large pothole in the hard clay and rock roadway. The wheel snapped. Nicholas had been taking a shortcut from his home through the forest, riding Shimmel to the main road into Patara, when he heard a loud *snap!* He hurried quickly to the sound, and when he came out of the forest into the clearing, he saw twenty Roman soldiers on horses encircled around a beautiful, but now crippled, carriage. The soldiers stood in a defensive stance.

By the look of the carriage, it was apparent the occupants were royalty. The four horses and driver were elaborately dressed. Silken covers provided shade to the carriage, which was trimmed in gold and detailed with elaborate décor. Nicholas cautiously approached the group to offer assistance. The soldiers watched him attentively when he moved closer to the commander.

Nicholas explained he was happy to help and knew high-quality craftsmen in the area, the Mikros clan. The commander conceded and allowed Nicholas and several soldiers to remove the broken wheel and take it to some of the Mikroses' blacksmiths to fix immediately. An hour later, Nicholas and the soldiers returned with the wheel, good as new.

Prisca, Valeria, and Constantine stretched their legs outside the carriage, preparing to board for the long journey. They watched as Nicholas replaced the wheel, wearing a smile all the while.

Prisca had shiny, black hair weaved elegantly atop her head and wore a purple, full-length dress with gold trim made of the finest silk and adorned with a gold necklace and bracelets. She addressed Nicholas. "My name is Prisca. This is Valeria and Constantine. What is your name and how much will we owe you for your service? And why are you so happy while you toil? 'Tis strange."

Nicholas smiled even wider and chuckled. "Ho, ho, ho." He paused his work, stood, and faced Prisca out of respect. "My name is Nicholas, and I am at your service, dear empress." He gave a courteous head bow. "No charge. My reward awaits me in Heaven, kind lady. Does my act of kindness please you?"

"Yes, we are appreciative."

"Oh, joy! For the sake of time, may I talk with you and work simultaneously? I do not wish to be disrespectful, and you have had a long wait. I am sure you would like to be on your way as soon as possible."

"Yes, of course, please do. And thank you for your regard of our time."

Nicholas took a knee and went back to work reattaching the wheel. "I assumed you were pleased with my assistance, and this assumption that my service pleased you, in turn, pleased me, thus making me happy, therefore I am smiling. Even if you were not pleased, for whatever reason, my Father would be gratified, for He asks me to love thy neighbor as I love myself, and pleasing Him makes me happy; therefore I am smiling for that reason as well." All the while Nicholas grinned.

Valeria felt enticed by this strange, jolly, joyful young man. She was attractive and resembled her mother except she wore her sable black hair down and long. She anxiously joined the conversation. "You are a curious soul. You consider us your neighbors though we are travelers who do not live around here and you do not know us."

"My Father taught me my neighbor is anyone with whom I come into contact, especially if I may be of assistance."

Prisca inquired, "I have heard this before—love thy neighbor as thyself. Who is your father? Where did it come from?"

"I do not speak of my earthly father but of my Heavenly Father, with whom my earthly father, and my earthly mother for that matter, gloriously are this day. If you are familiar with the written good news writings, or scriptures, of Matthew, Mark, Luke, or John, or if you are familiar with someone who is familiar with these writings, then that may be how you have heard this."

"I am sorry for the loss of your parents, especially at such a young age. You must be a strong and courageous young man to have endured such hardship. I am familiar with these Christian writings; they are interesting historical documents."

Valeria, wanting to build a connection to this new acquaintance named Nicholas, said, "I have read those scriptures called Gospels also. Jesus of Nazareth was a magnetizing yet tragic figure."

Nicholas finished replacing the wheel with three last taps of his hammer. He stood and turned toward his audience and responded reflectively, "Thank you for your kind condolences. Any courage and strength I gather is from my Heavenly Father, for when I am weak, He is strong, and I have much weakness. As for the scriptures, for me those words are much more than historical documents, they are God's thoughts and life to me. That God-Man Incarnate, Jesus, is much more than an interesting figure. He *is* my life. He was the Son of God who became the son of man so that sons of man, and daughters of man if you will, can become sons and daughters of God."

"How is this so?" Prisca inquired.

"In the gospel of Matthew, he says, 'Ask and it will be given to you; seek and you will find; knock and the door will be opened to you.' I ask of God, seek, and knock daily. By doing so, I have learned to ask for forgiveness and I am forgiven. I repent and turn away from my sin and I turn toward Jesus. I have been justified by faith, redeemed by grace, the wrath I deserve propitiated, the righteousness I do not deserve imputed, thus making this wretched soul entitled to holy sanctification, for which I am indebted and grateful."

Silence. No one knew what to say in response to Nicholas.

Valeria, even more enamored with Nicholas than before, humbled herself to ask what everyone was wondering: "How have you learned this? And, what does that mean exactly?"

Nicholas, still smiling, softened his tone and spoke in awe, "I have learned this through meditating on the letters and writings of Jesus' followers, Matthew, Mark, Luke, John, James, Peter, Paul, Timothy, and others. I have many scrolls." He pointed to his bag tied to his horse. "And it means for God so loved the world that He gave his one and only Son, that whoever believes in Him shall not perish but have eternal life. He did not come to condemn us, but to save us! You ladies have read the scriptures. Faith in God comes from hearing, and hearing through the word of God, so I humbly ask you, do you believe?"

More silence. What Nicholas was asking was clear, though not ever asked of any of them before. Nicholas had asked if they believed in Jesus and were Christ-followers, Christians.

Tall, strong, and chisel-faced Constantine stood back listening to this conversation, and he studied this mystery fellow. Being Roman and becoming a young Roman soldier himself, Constantine was like most Romans believing in many gods—suspicious of these Christians with their one triune God. He resented his empress and her daughter, his dear friends who were like family, engaging this commoner. He resented even more that he sensed this working-class citizen captivated Prisca and Valeria. Though Nicholas was respectful and nonthreatening, Constantine felt threatened. He decided to chime in and put this pauper in his place. If these women were not present, he would put Nicholas down with his fist, but he had to be careful not to offend or anger Prisca and Valeria.

Constantine said sternly to Nicholas, "Servant, you call us your neighbors, yet we are anything but. We are royalty and you are a vagabond. You wear clothes that look like at one time a person of status wore them, yet you are dirty, worn, torn, and tattered. You speak as someone who is learned, yet you present as an illiterate with that unceasing grin. You ride a stallion that is as fine as any I have ever seen, and you carry yourself with confidence as someone who is somebody, but yet you are nobody. You act with no fear as a soldier would, yet you are meek. You are an anomaly, a contradiction. What say you? Explain yourself."

"I know what it is to be in need and I know what it is to have plenty. I have learned the secret of being content in any and every situation, whether well fed or hungry, whether living contentedly or in want. I can do everything through Christ who gives me strength."

Constantine, offended, said, "Are you calling us discontented?"

"I do not know you, sire, so I cannot speak to who you are or what you are feeling. I speak from my experience only. I was born of privilege, but I was humbled early, recognizing that I had done nothing to place myself there; it was not of my doing. What, may I ask, did you do to be born in your circumstance of plenty? By what task, toil, effort, exertion, trial, trouble, striving, and pains did you personally endeavor to place yourself in your high status compared with these common soldiers who protect you with their lives? What choice did you have in the matter? I know that for me there was none. However, for my parents who were born of humble means, there were plenty of choices made to achieve what they did. I had nothing to do with it. And you? What did you do?"

Constantine's face turned pale white. He did not have an answer. Just as Prisca and Valeria had never been asked the question about their belief in Jesus, Constantine had never been asked to reflect on how he had gained his life of privilege and to admit it publically.

Prisca spoke. "Valeria and Constantine, our emperor and I were born into families of low status, as it sounds like Nicholas' parents were as well. I was a maiden and Diocletian was a simple soldier at one time; he was just as these brave but unheralded soldiers who provide us safe passage now. I can tell you, Valeria and Constantine, you did nothing to be born into our families. If you believe in a God or gods then you are called blessed; if you do not believe in a deity, then your privileged circumstances are what's called plain, dumb luck. Regardless," she looked at Constantine, "you have done nothing to have all that you have, and thankfulness and humility are in order and are much more endearing characteristics to have than arrogance."

She pondered aloud, gazing at the horizon. "There are some that would look upon those who are born into plenty, who think it is not necessarily a blessing nor lucky, but maybe a curse. A curse because you know not what it means to suffer, which produces perseverance. If a person cannot persevere, that person will never succeed." She paused and continued. "I, too, understand what it means to be in need and also to have plenty, but now that I think about it, I cannot say I have found the contentment that you have, Nicholas—even now, as empress of the largest empire in the world."

Silence. A bit taken aback by her own thoughts, Prisca felt she had made herself vulnerable. It felt good in that moment to feel transparent, to feel real, but reminded of her circumstances and title, she snapped back into her status.

"Nicholas, is our carriage wheel fixed and ready for travel?"

"Yes, my lady."

"Then let us continue our journey." She put her hand out to Nicholas and he assisted her up into the carriage. Valeria followed, blushing and smiling as Nicholas took her hand. She gave his hand a tight squeeze before slowly releasing. Constantine boarded and Nicholas bowed his head out of respect.

Prisca said, "Nicholas, you refuse any payment for your troubles, but here is payment for your skilled laborers who repaired our wheel. From what I can tell, their artisanship is superior. Please give this to them along with my gratitude." She handed Nicholas several gold coins that more than covered the cost.

"It was no trouble, Empress Prisca, but an honor to serve you. I will pass the payment and message along."

"Nicholas, it was a pleasure making your acquaintance, and thank you for your time and service."

"The pleasure was all mine, Empress." He smiled and bowed. "I will pray for safe travels for you all."

"Thank you. Oh, and Nicholas, in answer to your question, I am not sure what I believe now, but I will do as you do. I'll ask, seek, and knock daily as well. Thank you for the thought- and feeling-provoking conversation."

"Me too," Valeria said. "Thank you, Nicholas! It was so nice to meet you. Maybe we will meet again? Maybe you can visit us in our castle up north? Or next time we're passing through, we can have lunch or dinner or breakfast?"

"Driver." Prisca signaled.

The carriage started moving and Valeria smiled and excitedly waved goodbye. Nicholas waved and caught Constantine's eye. Constantine nodded in his softened demeanor. Nicholas watched the carriage and all the soldiers ride away.

He walked to Shimmel, stroked his head, and said, "Well, Shimmel, did you hear what Constantine said about you? He's an heir to the empire, and he said you're as fine a stallion as he has ever seen! You should be honored; that's quite a compliment!" Shimmel shook his head up and down, and his long, soft mane made waves. "Oh, now, big fella, don't you go getting a big head." Shimmel lightly whinnied and shook his head left to right. "Oh, low blow, just because I keep you clean and well-groomed and I'm a little worse for wear, that doesn't mean you need to get personal. Oy."

Nicholas climbed on and Shimmel trotted toward Patara. Nicholas examined himself. "Hmm, there's nothing wrong with a little worn, torn, and tattered. Hey, the princess seemed to like me a lot! And I'm not even at my cleanest, so ha! She seemed nice. Okay, I guess I could be a little cleaner." Shimmel whinnied and nodded in agreement.

Nicholas smelled his armpit and grimaced. "Whew, okay, okay, I guess I let myself go a little. Give me a break, I don't have my mom around to tell me to take a bath anymore. Now I have you, eh? Mom was much nicer about it. Gee, you get one compliment and it goes right to your head." Shimmel neighed and shook his head in agreement, making Nicholas laugh aloud, "Ho, ho, hooo!"

## Devotion

Nicholas fits A.W. Tozer's quote well: "Outside the will of God, there is nothing I want. Inside the will of God, there is nothing I fear." Nicholas met royalty and Roman soldiers and was unfazed. He continued to love God, love others, be joyful always, pray continually (in his mind), and be thankful in all circumstances.

He knows God is always with him and it comforts him. He knows God's Word and stands on it as his firm foundation. He knows his identity in Christ. He is secure. To have fear, faith is not present. To have faith, fear is not present. Nicholas is clearly faith-filled.

**Questions to consider:** Am I in God's will right now, loving God, loving others, being joyful always, praying continually, and being thankful in all circumstances? Do I know my true identity in Christ? What fears do I have? On a scale of one to ten, one being with no faith and ten being with total faith, where am I?

*"For God did not give us a spirit of cowardice but rather of power and love and self-control." 2 Timothy 1:7*

*"Do not fear: I am with you; do not be anxious: I am your God. I will strengthen you, I will help you, I will uphold you with my victorious right hand." Isaiah 41:10*

*"Rejoice in the Lord always. I shall say it again: rejoice! Your kindness should be known to all. The Lord is near. Have no anxiety at all, but in everything, by prayer and petition, with thanksgiving, make your requests known to God. Then the peace of God that surpasses all understanding will guard your hearts and minds in Christ Jesus." Philippians 4:4-7*

*"God is love, and whoever remains in love remains in God and God in him. In this is love brought to perfection among us, that we have confidence on the day of judgment because as he is, so are we in this world. There is no fear in love, but perfect love drives out fear because fear has to do with punishment, and so one who fears is not yet perfect in love." 1 John 4:15-18*

**Prayer:** "Heavenly Father, I'm tired of living in fear of this and that. Help me give You my fears and please replace them with faith in You. Give me confidence that You are with me always in my train compartment of life and know that You will take care of me no matter what. Thank You. Amen."

# 11
# A Giving Dilemma

DECEMBER 5 READING

*20 days until Christmas*

NICHOLAS HAD TIMES when he felt sad, missing his parents. He had loved them so much, and he deeply missed spending time with them. He wanted his dad's encouragement and his mom's hugs. He valued giving, however, out of the whole year leading up to his departure, there was one time when Nicholas had mixed emotions about helping someone in need. It was a sad situation, and it involved someone for whom he had special feelings for.

One day, several months before he planned to leave, Nicholas was walking down the road not far from Wren's house when he heard screaming. He ran toward the house, listening closely, trying to determine whether there was danger or not. It was getting dark, so it was easy to get close to the house without being seen. He heard Wren's parents, Brodin and Madelyn, arguing. Actually, it was more like Brodin yelling and Madelyn pleading.

"Please, Brodin, you cannot! We must not! We must find a way!"

"There is no other way! We have no money! We have no dowry for Wren or any of the girls. The decision has been made. She's coming of age, she's attractive, and we can sell her for a good price."

*Sell her?* Nicholas thought as he crouched below the living room window. *Oh no! Brodin is planning to sell Wren into slavery!* His memory took him back to Wren's words when he, Wren, and Noll had been at their favorite spot by the river. Wren had said that without a dowry, her future was unknown. Nicholas remembered the moment when she said the word "unknown" a bad feeling hit him. The unknown was not good, and Wren probably knew what the unknown was back then. *How horrible for Wren!*

Nicholas was not a violent person. He had never been in a fight in his life; he could not think of a time he had ever raised his voice in anger. Yet there was a righteous fury brewing inside him as he had never felt before. It took everything in him not to enter the house and give Brodin a piece of his mind and a fistful of knuckles.

The arguing stopped. All Nicholas heard was Madelyn leaving the room, bursting into tears, and sobbing. Occasionally, glass clanged in the room—most likely Brodin drinking. Nicholas knew what he had to do, and he was thankful to God that he was able to do it. He would give Brodin the dowry money for Wren.

Then it struck Nicholas like a racing chariot. He was giving Wren a dowry to marry someone else. Nicholas trusted God to do His will in Nicholas and Wren's relationship, but he had always thought that though he was making this decision to pursue God, there would be a chance somehow, some way, for him and Wren to be together in the future. Oh, the irony! It hurt. It hurt down to his core.

The reality set in, and Nicholas planned to give Wren the dowry that would all but guarantee she would marry another man. The alternative was Brodin selling Wren into slavery, into prostitution, into a life that would be too horrible to imagine. He grimaced at the thought. The scoundrel! That would not happen if Nicholas had anything to say about it.

Nicholas went to a quiet place to pray and ask God's protection over Wren and her sisters, for God to protect them spiritually, mentally, physically, emotionally, sexually, and financially. He prayed for Madelyn to find strength and wisdom. He did not want to pray for Brodin. In fact, Nicholas was quite content with Brodin burning in hell for eternity. He talked with God about it and asked if he could help send Brodin on his way. God said no. Nicholas prayed and pleaded with God some more. God still said no.

Finally, through his hurt, hatred, and anger, the Holy Spirit convicted Nicholas, and he was finally able to hear what God was saying beyond the no. "You shall not hate your neighbor in your heart, but you shall reason frankly with your neighbor, lest you incur sin because of him. Whoever hates his neighbor is in the darkness and walks in the darkness, and does not know where he is going because the darkness has blinded his eyes. I say to you, love your enemies, and pray for those who persecute you, that you may be children of your Father in Heaven. I cause the sun to rise on the evil and the good, and send rain on the righteous and the unrighteous."

Nicholas repented to God for having judgment and hate in his heart toward Brodin. God helped Nicholas see Brodin through His eyes that Brodin was lost and did not know Jesus, therefore, he did not have the love of Jesus in his heart. Brodin had unresolved sin, unresolved generational sin, and spiritual soul ties to other sinners that had not been broken. Brodin was of the world and not of God. He had chosen the world's way rather than God's way, so Brodin was prone to making worldly decisions and not godly decisions—even more reason to pray for him. Nicholas prayed for Brodin. Nicholas did his best to rejoice, pray, and be thankful in this circumstance. It was an act of his will to do so rather than a feeling at this time, because he definitely did not feel like doing the right thing. But he knew from experience that if he was obedient to God, his feelings would eventually catch up to his will … someday; persistence and faith were required to do so.

After his wrestling match with God, which, as usual, God always won—Nicholas knew what he had to do. Brodin was a proud man, and pride cometh before the fall. God resisted the proud and gave grace to the humble. Pride was a major problem for Brodin and was the foremost reason that he and his family were in the destitute situation they were in. He would rather be irresponsible and decline assistance to the point of selling his daughters into slavery than ask for help. Nicholas knew that he could not reason frankly with a person such as this, and he did not want to bring any embarrassment to Wren.

Later that night, when all appeared to be asleep in Wren's home, Nicholas secretly made his way over to the window nearest the fireplace and knelt down. Nicholas always carried coins and extra bags with him for such an occasion; however, in this situation, Nicholas filled the bag to the brim. This was not just a dowry. This was a very generous dowry that would favor Wren to find as good a man, from as good a family, as could be found in the region. The thought of Wren being with another man pained Nicholas deeply, but there was nothing else he could do. God's calling for him could not be any clearer. After the death of his parents, this was the second worst day of his life.

Nicholas had to let go of Wren and trust God; His will be done—not Nicholas' nor even Wren's. Nicholas looked in the window. It was summer, so the window shutters were open, therefore he didn't have to go down the chimney. It was dark, but his eyes had adjusted enough to be able to see around the room. He did not see anyone. He listened for any sounds. He did not hear anything. Spotting Wren's shoes by the fireplace, he slipped in through the window and picked one of her shoes up. The bag was too big to fit inside. Overcome by a broken heart, he pressed her shoe against his face to try to, somehow, connect with her. He shed a tear and it trickled down his cheek and into her shoe. He paused and shared an anguished, private thought with God. Then after setting the shoe back down and placing the big bag of coins on top of her shoes, he slipped back out of the window. It was done.

Nicholas, by an act of his *will*, did his best to forgive Brodin for planning to sell Wren into slavery, the *feeling* of forgiveness would hopefully catch up sooner than later. Nicholas repented for having hate and judgment in his heart. He tried his best to pray for Brodin to come to know the Lord and be a better husband and father.

Nicholas also had enough wisdom to know that forgiveness and trust were two different things, and Brodin was not to be trusted. Accountability was required, so, the next morning, Nicholas confided in Falon what he had done and asked Falon to be involved to make sure Brodin did not squander the dowry. Fortunately, this was made easy because the next morning, Madelyn, out of sheer joy and praise, told all the neighbors the news of the mystery giver visiting them in the middle of the night. As Brodin slept in the next morning, word made its way around very quickly before he awoke.

This opened up the door for Falon to visit their house and offer to take care of the money until the future dowry transaction arrived. Madelyn, of course, jumped on this offer, knowing what her husband was capable of doing, and Brodin willingly agreed. Word had also gotten out about Brodin's intention to sell Wren and her sisters into slavery, to everyone's scorn. Had he not agreed, he would have received the wrath of all the decent folk for miles around.

"Whoa, whoa, whoa!" interjects Laura on the train. "This can't be right! Wren and Nicholas love each other. They're gonna get married! Wren *is* gonna be Mrs. Claus! Right?"

Silence fills the train compartment.

"Mommy, Daddy, tell Kris he made a mistake!" Laura's eyes are welling up.

Joe and Mary look at each other, stunned and unsure about what to say. They turn and look at Kris. Their deer-in-the-headlights look begin to turn into the eyes-shooting-darts look.

Joe mutters with a directive in his tone, "It's okay, dear, Kris isn't done with his story. This is another sad part to Nicholas' life, but it gets better, doesn't it, Kris? There *will* be a happy ending."

All eyes are on Kris. Kris feels the darts from Joe's and Mary's eyes, causing great discomfort. "Yes, of course, the story gets better, Laura," he says. "We have to taste the bitter to later enjoy the sweet that much more."

He forces a smile and a little chuckle, "Hee hee."

Mary consoles Laura, "See, it's going to get better, just be patient." "Yes, we'll all be patient," Joe says firmly.

Just then, Conductor Maggie pushes in a cart with lunch. The glorious scents of marinated tri-tip, along with garlic mashed potatoes, steamed carrots, and fresh, warm rolls with soft honey butter, fills the cabin with a gust of savory magnificence. The sights and smells easily lift the spirits of the cabin mates, and everyone's eyes are glued to the yummy-looking dishes. Mouths start drooling as their minds imagine how tasty the food must be if it smells so delicious. Kris is thankful for the timing of lunch being served because his audience was starting to get, shall we say, dissatisfied. This is a golden opportunity to proceed with his story while noses, taste buds, and tummies are all becoming satisfied.

Kris blesses the meal thanking God for the food and the hands that prepared it and served it. When all mouths are full with their first bites, he announces, "Yes, well, let me continue with the story."


The last month of Nicholas' time home before he left had arrived. One big change of plans he had recently discussed with his Uncle Nicholas, Falon, and Tana was that he wanted to do some traveling before entering the priesthood. It was his dream to travel far and wide. He had this yearning to go abroad for as long as he could remember, and the very first place he wanted to visit more than any other was Israel, the Holy Land. He wanted to walk where Jesus had walked and talk where Jesus had talked and see what Jesus had seen. He wanted to see where Jesus had been born and lived, taught, preached, been crucified, and resurrected on the third day! They were all in favor of that.

Noll happened to be in the room during this discussion, and he had a funny feeling inside. Not about Nicholas traveling—he was not exactly sure what the funny feeling was, but he thought it might have to do with money. Noll was a lot like his father, Falon. He had good business sense and money sense. He was organized and a planner. He had a little spontaneity in his life, but not a lot.

Nicholas used to be a lot like Noll in these same ways. They tended to bicker occasionally, like brothers, so this was not too unusual. However, since Nicholas' parents had died, he had become very carefree and footloose. Nicholas was not anxious about time. He was not worried about money. He enjoyed working still, but he did what he wanted when he wanted. Noll noticed he was different from the best friend he had known. Noll recognized that Nicholas connected with God more than ever before, which was good, of course. It seemed that, before, Nicholas had trusted his parents to take care of him, and now Nicholas was changing his life to be totally dependent on God.

"So, Nicholas, traveling is a great idea, but it can be quite expensive," Noll said. "How much have you saved from your inheritance to enable you to live your dream?" He was a direct kind of friend.

Nicholas responded in as jolly a tone as he could, "Well, that's a great question. By the end of this month, when I plan to leave, I will have … hmm … not a single penny to my name. I will have given away every cent I have."

Noll looked perplexed. "Whoa! You what? You have no money for your trip? You were one of the richest people in Patara! You were rich by empire standards, and you aren't even a Roman, you are a Christian, which they despise. It was a miracle that you and your family were wealthy to begin with, and then you gave it *all* away?!"

"Yes, isn't it glorious?! Ho, ho, hoo!"

"That was very righteous of you, Nick ol' buddy, but you didn't even think to save any money to travel abroad, which you have been planning to do for a while? That makes no sense. What were you thinking? What *are* you thinking?"

"I'm thinking God will provide," Nicholas said matter-of-factly. "I can work on the ship and travel to Israel and Egypt and Italy and wherever I want to go just as the sailors do who dock here all the time."

"Yeah, but Nicholas, you know those men work as hard as anyone and make very little money! You'll barely make enough to live."

"Yes, but even barely enough to live *is* enough to live. I'll make enough to live. God will give me a place to lay my head on a ship. Jesus taught, 'Do not worry about your life, what you will eat or drink; or about your body, what you will wear. Is not life more than food, and the body more than clothes?' Can any one of us by worrying add a single hour to our lives? And why do you worry about clothes? See how the flowers of the field grow? If that is how God clothes the grass of the field, will He not much more clothe you—you of little faith? So do not worry, saying, 'What shall we eat?' or 'What shall we drink?' or 'What shall we wear?' For the pagans run after all these things, and your Heavenly Father knows that you need them. But seek first His Kingdom and His righteousness and all these things will be given to you as well. Therefore, do not worry about tomorrow, for tomorrow will worry about itself. Each day has enough trouble of its own."

Noll was speechless and stared at Nicholas with a blank look and his mouth gaping wide open. Noll was ticked! How dare Nicholas quote scripture at him! It took everything in him not to explode, and he quoted some scripture in his mind to calm down: *"Love is patient, love is kind. Love does not envy or boast and is not prideful. Love does not dishonor others . . ."*

After calming himself, Noll finally was able to say, "Nicholas, I cannot disagree with anything you just said; you are absolutely right. And there's something to be said about wisdom. In fact, James said in *his* scroll, 'If any of you lacks wisdom, let him ask God, who gives generously to all without reproach, and it will be given him.'"

Nicholas agreed with an amen.

"So, Nicholas, you've got *a lot* of asking to do."

Nicholas agreed again with an emphatic amen. It slowly sunk in that Noll was telling him he lacked wisdom—a *lot*. He was now the one speechless.

Noll started chuckling.

Then Nicholas, who was able to laugh at himself and humble himself, joined in. "'Tis true, every day I ask for wisdom, A LOT! I cannot lie. God opposes the proud and gives grace to the humble. I need all the grace I can get, so I humbly agree with your observation. And I will covet your prayers for me to be humble and wise as I go."

"And I will include prayers for traveling mercies as you go and that God will provide all you will need as you live in total dependence of Him."

"Excellent!" Nicholas exclaimed.

## Devotion

Nicholas hated Brodin for wanting to sell Wren into slavery. Anger is a secondary emotion to another feeling of pain, hurt, embarrassment, jealousy, rudeness, uncooperativeness, etc. Anger itself is not a sin; it's what people do with anger that can be a sin. Nicholas' anger was a righteous anger, but his secondary reaction was to hate Brodin and want to hurt Brodin.

Hurting people, hurt people. Nicholas was hurting because his friend, who he loved, was hurting. He wanted to go so far as to kill Brodin. Nicholas' hurt for Wren led to righteous anger, but then he allowed his anger to turn into sinful thoughts of hate toward Brodin and wanting to hurt and kill him.

When Nicholas crossed that line of righteous anger to sinful hatred he recognized his sin for what it was, he asked God for forgiveness and he repented. The feelings did not go away immediately, but his act of obedience to God to start the process of forgiveness toward Brodin, activated the beginning process of healing in Nicholas' own life, and freedom from hatred and bitterness.

Some families consider the word "hate" a four-letter word and they do not allow it spoken in their homes. They consider it a curse word, a word of violence as other curse words are. Hate is the opposite of love, which means, it is the opposite of God. 1 John 4:8 says God *is* love. God loves people, He hates sin and unrighteousness. Jesus did not come to condemn the world, He came to save it.

When a mob of religious leaders condemned a woman and wanted to stone her to death for sinning, Jesus said, "Let any one of you who is without sin be the first to throw a stone at her." They all were honest with themselves, dropped their stones, and left the scene. Jesus told her, they do not condemn her and neither did He. He told her to go and sin no more. Jesus hated the sin, but loved the sinner. And he does that for us as well. Thankfully! Jesus did not come to condemn the world, He came to save it.

There are two kinds of "judging." We are to "judge—distinguish—between right from wrong"—and hate sin. But we are not to "judge—condemn or devalue"—a person for sinning, because we all would have to condemn and devalue ourselves because we all sin.

We are called to love as Jesus did. It does not mean that we, and all who sin, will not experience consequences for our poor choices and reap what we sow. We will all reap what we sow somehow, some way, someday. Reaping what we sow is a principle God gave all of humankind, Christian and non-Christian. But we are all called to love.

**Questions to consider:** Do I have hate in my heart for a person and/ or for a people group? Why? What is the primary emotion they are eliciting in me causing the secondary emotion of anger? Am I allowing my anger to cross over to the sin of hating someone or others?

*"Beloved, let us love one another, because love is of God; everyone who loves is begotten by God and knows God. 8 Whoever is without love does not know God, for God is love. In this way the love of God was revealed to us: God sent his only Son into the world so that we might have life through him. In this is love: not that we have loved God, but that he loved us and sent his Son as expiation for our sins. Beloved, if God so loved us, we also must love one another. No one has ever seen God. Yet, if we love one another, God remains in us, and his love is brought to perfection in us. This is how we know that we remain in him and he in us, that he has given us of his Spirit. Moreover, we have seen and testify that the Father sent his Son as savior of the world."*
*1 John 4:7-14*

*"Whoever says he is in the light, yet hates his brother, is still in the darkness. Whoever loves his brother remains in the light, and there is nothing in him to cause a fall. Whoever hates his brother is in darkness; he walks in darkness and does not know where he is going because the darkness has blinded his eyes."*
*1 John 2:9-11*

*"But to you who hear I say, love your enemies, do good to those who hate you, bless those who curse you, pray for those who mistreat you."*
*Luke 6:27-28*

*"I give you a new commandment: love one another. As I have loved you, so you also should love one another." John 13:34*

**Prayer:** "Heavenly Father, please forgive me for the hate I may be harboring in my heart. Hurt people hurt people, and if I am hurting right now, and it is in my heart to want to hurt someone or a group of people, or see them get hurt, Holy Spirit, please reveal to me what it is about this person/people that hurts me leading me to hatred. Heal my hurt. I need Your help. Help me forgive so I don't live in bitterness and darkness. Thank You for hating my sin, but loving me. Help me to do that for others, as I would have them do for me. Thank You. Amen."

## 12
# The End of the Beginning

NICHOLAS' LAST DAY arrived, the day he was to leave. It was the end of the beginning of his life, his childhood. He had given nearly all of his possessions away. He had given away all of his money from the sales of his farms, lands, ranches, and businesses. He had said his goodbyes to everyone the previous night, at the Bon Voyage feast that the Mikros clan had given him in the village in his honor. Now he felt as free as a bird.

Nicholas paid Wren's home two more visits in the night during his last couple of months at home. One night, he left a generous bag of coins for a dowry on the shoes of Wren's middle sister, Kyla, and another night, a generous bag was left on the shoes of Wren's youngest sister, Kalista. Nicholas ensured that all three sisters would not be sold into slavery and would be given a chance to marry honorable men from honorable families. Falon and Tana would help ensure this would happen, which gave Nicholas peace.

Nicholas' third-to-last possession, and his third most prized possession, was his beautiful white horse, Shimmel. This possession Nicholas was reluctant to give away, and he waited until the very last day before he left. Not only was Shimmel beautiful, smart, and fun to ride, but the horse was family to Nicholas because it had been a special gift from his parents. Shimmel reminded him of Theophanes and Nona frequently. Shimmel had also been a Christ-Mass present given ultimately by God, the Gift Giver. It was the gift of Shimmel that had reinforced Nicholas' lesson to worship the Gift Giver and not the gift. Nicholas knew exactly who should have Shimmel: his best friend, Noll. On the outside, this appeared to be a very nice gesture, but Nicholas had an ulterior motive. He knew not only that Noll would take great care of Shimmel, but he also knew that Noll would let Nicholas ride Shimmel anytime he wanted. Good thinking!

Nicholas' second-to-last possession, which he chose to keep, was his father's walking staff. Nicholas planned to do a lot of walking during his travels and in his life, so what better tool to assist than his father's favorite walking stick? It also reminded him that Jesus is the Good Shepherd, and that Nicholas is His sheep who needed His guidance.

Nicholas' last, and most prized possession, was the bundle of scrolls with scriptures on them that his parents had collected over the years. Up to that point, the Bible as we know it was still not together as one book yet. The Old Testament had been together for a while, but the New Testament was still in separate letters and scrolls, such as the four Gospels of Matthew, Mark, Luke, and John as well as all the letters written by Peter, Paul, Timothy, James, and so on.

Besides some clothes and the walking staff, this bundle of scrolls would be the only possession Nicholas would keep, and it was worth all the gold in the world to him—God's Holy Word. The Word was Holy Spirit inspired, written by over forty different authors in three different languages on three different continents, over a span of 1,500 years, with one central theme—God's plan to redeem humankind after the Fall, revealed through the prophets, and come to fruition through His Son, Jesus Christ. MIRACULOUS! Nicholas was rarely without his big bag of scrolls and he was seen regularly walking or riding Shimmel from here to there and back again, with the bag draped over his shoulder. He read from them daily and freely shared what he read with others.

The very last thing Nicholas chose to do before he left was something he had put off doing for as long as he could: saying goodbye to Wren. He had not seen her since he had anonymously given the dowry money to her. It was not just Nicholas who had not seen her, most people had not. Wren had become reclusive after that. Before the dowry incident, every week or two, Wren, Noll, and Nicholas would get together, but after the dowry incident, Wren stopped communicating with anyone outside her family.

Falon and Tana visited the house occasionally to check in on Madelyn and the girls to make sure they were all right, and they were, so it appeared to be Wren's choice not to engage with anyone, not even her best friends. Maybe she was embarrassed; maybe she was resigned to the fact that she was going to be married off; maybe she was severely depressed, but Wren had always loved socializing and being with friends and family, so this was very un-Wren-like.

Nicholas was to meet Falon, Tana, and Noll by the main road that led from their village into Patara to the docks where Nicholas had a job on a ship awaiting him. Tana made him a hearty last breakfast and sent him on his way to visit Wren as Falon and Noll loaded up the wagon to do some business while in the city. Nicholas would get to ride Shimmel this last time all the way to the docks, and then Noll would ride him back home.

Nicholas rode up to Wren's home. It was a beautiful morning with a slight chill in the air. The sun was shining, and the birds were singing. He dismounted Shimmel and walked to the front door. He was very nervous because he had not seen Wren in three months and had no idea how she was going to respond to him. Tana had arranged it with Madelyn and Brodin for Wren to talk with him this morning, and they had assured her that they would see to it that Wren talked with him. None of Wren's family had been at the goodbye feast the night before. It was not just Wren who had been reclusive, as of late; the whole family had been distant.

Nicholas knocked and Brodin answered and stepped out and onto the porch with Nicholas. Madelyn, Kyla, and Kalista followed. No Wren.

Brodin shook Nicholas' hand. "Nicholas, your parents were wonderful people, and you have followed in your parents' footsteps by becoming a wonderful young man. Good luck in your journeys and thank you." He looked at Kyla and Kalista, then back at Nicholas, as if he knew Nicholas was the one who gave the dowry money. "Thank you for being a good friend to our family, as your parents were."

Madelyn gave Nicholas a big hug. "We will miss you so much, Nicholas. You be careful out there in that big world . . . and know that we will be praying for you. I know God has great things in store for you! God bless you, dear son."

Kyla and Kalista gave Nicholas hugs as well, tears streaming down their cheeks. Profound thankfulness shone in their eyes, as if they, too, knew the dowry gifts had been from him.

Nicholas was now a bit choked up himself and humbled. "I will miss all of you as well. Thank you for being an important part of my life and like family to me. Also, thank you for your prayers. I will covet them."

Brodin, Kyla, and Kalista went back into the house. Madelyn put her hand on Nicholas' shoulder. "Wren will be okay, Nicholas. She has a swirl of emotions going on, but she is trusting in God, His will be done. She knows that He is in total control, and that either He orchestrates things to happen or He allows things to happen in this imperfect, fallen world. All things good, bad, or indifferent work for His glory and for the good of those who love Him and who are called according to His purpose. And Wren loves God. Right?" Nicholas nodded.

"And you love Him, right?"

Nicholas nodded again. He started to feel he was not going to get to see Wren, but then Madelyn pointed across their yard to a swing that hung from a grand, beautiful oak tree. Wren sat very still in the swing.

Madelyn patted him on the back and went inside. He walked over to Wren. She was wearing a long, white tunic tied with a purple rope at her waist. Her braided hair had little wavy strands hanging down each side of her face and a thin wreath of tiny white, yellow, and purple flowers encircling the top of her head like a halo. Her soft skin glowed in the morning sun. She looked like an angel. Nicholas could not take his eyes off her. She took his breath away and he could hardly speak.

"Hi," he uttered, still unsure how she would respond.

"Hi," she replied. She smiled softly. "Thank you for saying goodbye before you leave."

Oh, sweet relief. She seemed genuine, and seeing her smile lifted his spirit. "Of course, I wouldn't leave without saying goodbye. Noll and I have missed you the last few months. . . *I've* missed you the last few months."

"I'm sorry for being unsocial. I've had a lot on my mind to consider, reasons to be alone to pray."

"I heard about you getting a dowry, which was something I know you were concerned about."

"Yes, that was a concern I had, and God answered that prayer."

"I'm sure whoever gave it to you cares about you and wants the best for you."

"Yes. I'm sure whoever gave it to me cares about me and wants the best for me, too. It was an incredibly kind act, really a true act of love. Don't you think?" She looked him in the eyes as if searching his soul.

Nicholas paused. He had not been expecting that question. "Yes, I'm sure that person, whoever it is, loves you. In fact, I'm sure that person loves you deeply." They stared at each other with a twinkle in their eyes. What they thought in that private moment was only for them to know—them and God. It was a special moment that warmed their hearts as much as the sunshine warmed them in the cool of the morning, caressing their skin. They smiled and unlocked gazes, looking away bashfully.

There was a bench nearby and Wren moved over to it, gesturing for Nicholas to sit next to her. He followed.

"Eve, in the garden of Eden, had a whole garden of amazing, tasty, luscious fruit to choose from and was thankful," Wren began, "until that one fateful day when Satan tempted her by pointing out that one tree, that one fruit that was forbidden in the entire garden. He got her to question God's spoken word and doubt His goodness. He tempted her to focus on the one fruit she couldn't have, rather than looking around and focusing on the plentiful bounty that surrounded her and being thankful for what she did have. That negative focus darkened Eve's mind and she succumbed to temptation. These last few months, that has been my battle. I made the mistake of questioning God and doubting His goodness instead of focusing on, and being thankful for my friends, my mom, my sisters, food, clothes, shelter, and so on. When the dowry gift arrived that would make any girl elated, pretty much guaranteeing a safe and secure future for me, I, instead, focused on a forbidden fruit that I could not have and my mind darkened."

Nicholas had a good idea what, or whom, had been the forbidden fruit, and he figured she would say it if she wanted. Otherwise, he felt it was better to listen than to say anything.

She continued, "I went to a dark, ugly place, and instead of being thankful for this wonderful gift and for all the things I have, I became angry, bitter, ungrateful, rejecting, hard of heart, stubborn, numb, defiant, fearful, and depressed. It was a wild ride, and I wrestled with God. Oh man, did I wrestle with God." She shook her head in disbelief, appearing so deep in reflective thought that she seemed to have forgotten Nicholas was there.

After a moment of awkward silence and feeling a bit forgotten, Nicholas asked, "And?"

She smiled and exhaled as she realized she had tuned him out for a moment. "And what else happens when you wrestle with God? He won. He finally gave me a much-needed Holy Spirit head slap, er, I mean awakening, that brought me back to reality and out of my cesspool of self-pity."

"Hey, I get it, I need Him to give me a good head slap now and again as well." Nicholas gave a little ho, ho, ho. "May I ask what the Holy Spirit awakening was?"

"Yes, you may." She smiled. "One month after I found my dowry gift on my shoes, Kyla found her dowry gift on her shoes. Even after I got my gift, my father still talked about selling Kyla and Kalista, so when she received her dowry, I sat in the background and watched her response. She sobbed buckets of giant tears of joy as if she had been imprisoned her whole life and someone had just come in and set her free. Praise and thanksgiving and worship to God just flowed out of her heart and her mouth, and from that day on she has been floating on a cloud. That was the awakening I needed and I have never been so thankful. I finally saw what an ungrateful, spoiled little brat I was being. After I repented to God for my selfishness and bad attitude, and after I repented for hating my father, then I was able to have an attitude of gratitude. God's light had driven away the darkness, and I could feel God's arms around me, holding me close. He whispered, 'Wren, it's going to be all right. Everything is going to be all right.'"

She stopped as her voice cracked. She stared off into the distance while touching her bottom lip with two fingers. Blinking the moisture out of her eyes, she gently cleared her throat. She took a deep breath and continued, "After that, like Kyla, I was able to give praise and thanks for the gift God had given through a very generous donor and focus on what I had rather than on what I didn't have. I was so happy for her *and* me. Then, one month later, Kalista received her dowry gift, and she had the same reaction as Kyla. Another Holy Spirit awakening reminder for me, which I'm thankful for. I am so happy for her, too. We've been praising God all together ever since."

"Thank you for sharing, Wren. I'm sorry you went through all that, but I'm glad you're better now."

"Yes, I'm much better! Thank you for your love and friendship, Nicholas. And patience. So the first part of the last three months of my silence was because I was angry with God and the world. The last part of the last three months of my silence was because of sadness. I knew you were leaving soon, and it felt like it would be harder to say goodbye to you if we were spending time together."

Nicholas took her hand. She froze. He had never done anything like that before. He looked into her big, long-lashed eyes. "I understand now. I missed seeing you and having that time together, but I feel better knowing that you're okay."

She squeezed his hand. "I'm okay. Thank you. For everything." There was a sense that she, as well, knew that Nicholas was the dowry gift giver.

Still looking into each other's eyes, a sudden spark ignited inside them. There was that stirring, again, like butterflies in the stomach, but it blossomed in the heart and various other places of the body as well.

Nicholas' face felt a magnetic pull toward Wren's. His eyes went from her beautiful eyes to her ruby red, soft, moist lips. He thought only of the burning desire to press his lips against hers. He leaned in slowly and she mirrored his movements.

*Neiiigh!*

They both snapped away from each other, letting go of each other's hands. They saw Shimmel a few steps away watching them, expressionless, as you would expect from a horse. They both nervously composed themselves, and Nicholas looked at the sky, at the sun, and then around at the shadow of the tree. Gauging the time of the morning, he said, "Uhhh. Okay. I should probably go now. Falon, Tana, and Noll will be waiting for me soon."

Wren giggled and looked back at Shimmel with a playful disgruntled look, "Hey, where'd you come from and what are you doing scaring us like that?"

"No apple for you." Nicholas said.

Shimmel looked at them and snorts. He makes Wren and Nicholas laugh aloud, unsure of what the horse's meaning was. They shake their heads at him with embarrassed dismay.

Wren put her hand on Nicholas' and asked sweetly, "Just a few more minutes, please?" He took a breath to calm himself and nodded in agreement. "So enough about me. How about you? Did you get all of your affairs in order? Did you do everything you wanted to do over this last year at home? I heard recently that you decided to have a time of traveling before entering the priesthood. Do you still feel good about that?"

"Yes, yes, and yes." He laughed at his short answers.

"Oh, come on, Smart Aleck. Now *you're* being a brat. I just spilled my heart and guts to you about all my worries and junk, and that's all you have for me?"

"Okay, okay. Yes, I got all my affairs in order, and the Mikroses have everything under control. And yes, this last year has been magnificent! Of course, as you know, I've missed my parents often and the healing continues. I've had my moments of dealing with shock, anger, and sadness from losing them, but overall, I've come to accept my loss and I'm healing slowly, but surely. I've enjoyed the year. Minus the last few months you've been missing. *Ahem.*"

He gave her a playful evil eye, making it clear he did not like her being aloof. She curled her lips, gave puppy-dog eyes, and bowed her head.

"And yes, since I spoke with you last, God has put it on my heart to travel and experience more of life, and meet all kinds of people, and see all kinds of places, especially the Holy Land. He wants me to step out in faith and out of my comfort zone while learning how to depend on Him one hundred percent, day by day and moment by moment. I feel I need to learn how to let Him lead and for me to be better at following, if that makes sense."

"It makes perfect sense. That's something I'm learning to do as well."

"There, were those better answers for you?"

"Eh, a little better. You need to learn to put more feeling into it." She laughed.

"Whatever."

"Okay, you answered my questions to my satisfaction, now you can leave." She laughed even louder at her own wise crack.

He laughed along with her. "Oh, I see how it is, Smart Aliss. You want what you want when you want it, then use me and toss me to the side. I see how it works, I get it now." He stood and started walking to Shimmel, who was a few steps away.

She laughed and followed him taking hold of his arm. He stopped and she said, "You know I'm teasing."

He turned facing her. "Wren, I'm so thankful I got to see you one last time before I left. I'm glad you're doing better. And I'm so glad to hear your laughter one last . . . It's music to my ears that I will always carry with me."

"I'm glad we had this time together, too, Nicholas. Thank you for arranging this to happen in spite of my standoffishness."

Wren got a chill and shivered from the cool morning. Wearing a tunic underneath, Nicholas opened up his red robe with white trim and invited Wren in for a warm, covered hug. She accepted the invitation, moving into his robe and pressing her body against his. Wrapping his robe around her like a blanket he gave her a strong embrace, never wanting to let go. Their cheeks pressing against each other, almost lip to lip. Quickly came the hot sparks, the strange stirrings, the urges. It was painful to resist.

Finally, Nicholas summoned up enough courage and gave Wren a kiss on the cheek. He started to pull away, but before he could, she pulled him back in and moved her face toward his lips. She slowly passed over them and gave him a gentle, warm kiss on his opposite cheek. They stood there holding onto each other for another moment and then both simultaneously released, reluctantly letting go of each other. Nicholas closed his robe and tied it.

Wren looked up at the low oak branch hanging over their heads. It had mistletoe. She reached up, broke a little piece off, and gave it to Nicholas. "Here, mistletoe. It stays green even in the winter. It represents endurance and life, but also love and growth. May it be a blessing to you and a memory of our last moments together."

"Thank you, Wren. With its white berries, it's beautiful, another memory of the beauty my eyes behold at this moment." He stared deeply into her eyes until she blushed and broke eye contact.

Nicholas tucked the flora into a pocket, put his foot in a stirrup, and lifted himself upon Shimmel. He looked at Wren one last time. "As always, you'll be in my thoughts and prayers."

"Likewise, you in mine as well.

"Goodbye, my one and only Wren."

"Goodbye, my one and only Nicholas."

Nicholas gave Shimmel a tap with his heels and rode up the dirt driveway. He told himself not to look back. He couldn't look back. It would make it impossible to leave. What if he looked and she was gone or she was not looking at him? He would feel awful. He couldn't look back. When he reached the road he turned right, and before he was out of sight from where Wren had last been standing, the impulse was too great and overcame him. He quickly swung his head around to look back at her and take in her beauty one last time. Thank God she was still there! She was back sitting on the bench, watching him ride away. Oh, sweet relief! He gave one last wave and smiled, and she waved and smiled back. Thank God she was still there. Then he was gone.

## <u>Devotion</u>

Wren never said exactly what the forbidden fruit was that she wanted from God, but did not get, but the assumption is she wanted her future to be with Nicholas and it does not look like it will happen. God did not meet her expectation and she readily admitted that she allowed her disappointment to darken her soul—her mind, will, and emotions.

If you are alive on the planet earth, you have had this same experience, having an expectation denied—wanting what you want, when you want, and how you want, and not gotten it. Welcome to life, it happens. When this happens, we have two choices, get bitter or get better.

**Question to consider:** Is there bitterness I'm struggling with right now because I didn't get my way and now I'm experiencing anger and resentment?

*"Trust in the Lord with all your heart, on your own intelligence do not rely; In all your ways be mindful of him, and he will make straight your paths." Proverbs 3:5-6*

*"We know that all things work for good for those who love God, who are called according to his purpose." Romans 8:28*

*"For my thoughts are not your thoughts, nor are your ways my ways—declares the Lord. For as the heavens are higher than the earth, so are my ways higher than your ways, my thoughts higher than your thoughts." Isaiah 55:8-9*

*"'For I know well the plans I have in mind for you—declares the Lord—plans for your welfare and not for woe, so as to give you a future of hope. When you call me, and come and pray to me, I will listen to you. When you look for me, you will find me. Yes, when you seek me with all your heart.'"*
*Jeremiah 29:11-13*

**Prayer:** "Heavenly Father, please forgive me for being bitter when I don't get my way and my expectations are not met, rather than being thankful for what I do have and allowing You to help me be a better person. Help me trust You for my present and my future. Guide me in Your ways. Thank You. Amen."

# 13
# E-Motion Sickness

"THEN HE WAS gone." As the train keeps chugging north, Kris takes this opportunity to pause in the story and check in with his audience. All sit still, quiet, and sullen. He looks at Laura, who is now on Mary's lap, curled up in the fetal position with Mary's arms wrapped around her.

Laura looks at him, and in the saddest, most somber tone, she says, "I'm being patient."

Wayne breaks the tension-filled moment by changing the subject. "So when Nicholas gave away everything he had, that's how he started becoming Santa Claus and giving people presents. And he gave presents secretly at night like he does now with us, so no one knows he did it, except God. Right?"

"Yes, good understanding, Wayne!"

"But now we all know it's him."

"True, but maybe he *doesn't* know that everyone knows. If he doesn't know, do you want to tell him, possibly causing him to stop giving presents on Christmas Eve?"

"Uh, no, I'm good. Never mind."

"And if he *does* know, but he continues giving presents to celebrate the birth of Jesus because he enjoys it and it's a fun tradition, do you want him to stop?"

"No! Like I said, I'm good. Forget I said anything!" Wayne zips the invisible zipper on his mouth shut, locks it, and throws away the key.

"Okay, good." Kris gives Wayne a wink. "So yes, that was just the beginning of his giving, but," Kris pauses, "something happened that almost ended Nicholas' giving and. . . his life!"

Wayne's expression is both frightened and curious. "What? What happened?"

"Well," Kris begins.

"Attention, ladies and gentlemen," Conductor Maggie announces over the intercom. "Attention, ladies and gentlemen of all ages! Some Christmas elves have just radioed and informed us that we are coming up to a location where we will have a spectacular view of the aurora borealis. That's the scientific name for the northern lights. Aurora borealis was named after the Roman goddess of the dawn."

Then, in a dramatic tone, she continues as if announcing a professional wrestling match. "Displays of the northern lights occur when solar particles enter the earth's atmosphere and on impact emit burning gases that produce different-colored lights! Oxygen produces green and yellow, while nitrogen produces blue!" Back to her normal tone, "That's a fancy way of saying it makes for one bea-*uti*ful, scenic sky. So if you'd like to soak in this early Christmas gift of a view, please make your way to the left side of the train in a safe and orderly manner . . . I repeat, in a safe and orderly manner. I don't want to have to hurt anyone, and I will if I have to. We do not have a full train, so there should be plenty of space available for everyone to see, so please be kind and courteous to one another. Merry Christmas!"

"Oh, that sounds wonderful!" Mary said with her ear turned up to the loudspeaker. "Kids, would you like to see the northern lights while we have a chance? This could be a once-in-a-lifetime opportunity!" The kids all agree. "Kris, we do want to hear the rest of the story. We are patiently waiting for the happier parts. Meanwhile, this seems like a good time to take a break and lift our spirits a little. Do you mind?"

Kris says, "No, by all means, please go enjoy the view! It's one of God's most beautiful sights. I never, ever miss it when I have the chance." Other passengers are walking by to get their places by a window.

Mary waves the kids on. "Okay, let's go, in a safe and orderly manner, being kind and courteous to others."

The three kids oblige, forming a single file line from smallest to tallest. Joe and Kris stay seated, hesitating to get up. Joe seems to want to stay back for some reason and Kris notices.

"Honey, are you going to join us?" Mary asks.

"Uh, yeah babe," Joe says. "I'll catch up in a few minutes, Mare. I just wanna savor my last few bites of this amazing tri-tip while it's still warm, okay?"

"Okay, but hurry. I want to share the view with you!" She smiles lovingly, and longingly, at him for something that seems to be lost. Joe smiles back. "Yeah, me too, hon. I'll be right there." She nods and leaves.

Kris and Joe now sit directly across from each other, knees almost touching because of the tight quarters. Both sit back, taking a deep breath and sighing, enjoying some momentary quiet and roominess in the close quarters.

Joe takes the last bite of the very tender tri-tip and savors it as it melts in his mouth with every chew. He looks at his plate and sighs. "Deeelicious. So, Kris, do you have a Mrs.?"

Kris closes his eyes. "Yes, I have a Mrs." And making a face as if he has a piece of the finest chocolate in the world tantalizing his taste buds and melting in his mouth, he says, "And she is a deeelicious dish herself."

"That's great." Joe chuckles. "And now that you're making me think about it, truthfully, I'd say Mary is, um. . . a delicious dish, too. I can't believe I just said that out loud to a stranger, weird. But anyway, she's an amazing wife, mother, daughter . . . human being. I seem to forget that a lot." His eyes turn downward, struck by a turning thought. "She deserves way better than me."

"Sometimes it's easy to lose sight of the good in others, especially those close to us," Kris says. "We can take them for granted. We can become self-absorbed, and then we don't appreciate people as they should be appreciated."

"Does that happen to you?"

"Of course. I'm human, therefore, imperfect. I have my moments."

"Well, I seem to have my weeks, months, years."

"We can all change for the better, Joe. First, you have to recognize and admit you fall short, which it sounds like you're doing right now. We all fall short of the glory of God. Then you have a choice to make. Get bitter or get better. Choose better. Then talk to people, talk with the Big Man upstairs, read books, read the *Good Book*, Basic Instructions Before Leaving Earth."

"The who-ey what-ey?"

Kris gives Joe a look. Joe nods his head, figuring out what Kris means by the *Good Book*—the Holy Bible.

"It's a love letter from God to you. Our Heavenly Father, reconciling us sinful humans unto Himself. When you receive God's love, joy, and peace, then it's easy to give love, joy, and peace. I know it can be tough growing up without a father, a role model for how to be a father, husband, and leader of your family. But God is that for us. You may not have an earthly father, but you have something even better—a Heavenly Father!"

Joe nods, then pauses with a confused look on his face. "How did you know I grew up without a father?"

Kris hesitates. "Uh, when you get to be my age, you just know these things."

Joe considers the answer. Not being Kris' age, he cannot argue with it, so he goes with it and nods in agreement. Kris continues.

"We all have pain and we need someone we can go to with it. If we don't speak it, we leak it, usually in some negative way hurting ourselves and or others. Our Heavenly Father is all-knowing. He knows everything we have ever done and even our deepest, darkest thoughts. Confession is good for thy soul. I find that freeing, knowing I can be totally honest with Someone who will still like me *and* love me, even knowing the worst of the worst about me. There is nothing we can do to make our Heavenly Father love us more and there is nothing we can do to make Him love us less. He loves us no matter what. Compared with His holiness, I'm unlovely, it's Jesus' sacrifice on the cross for me, for us, that makes us lovely in His sight. There is nothing we can do, Jesus already did it for us, and we just have to receive it." Kris holds his arms out and breathes deeply as if he were a prisoner receiving his pardon. "Ah, freedom." He looks across the tiny aisle. "Does that sound freeing to you, Joe?"

"It does, but how do I get that?"

"Believe and follow. You've read John 3:16 and 17, haven't you?"

"Well, I've seen guys hold up signs saying John 3:16 during football games before, but I never bothered to look it up. I know it's in the Bible, though, Mary has taught me that much!" he is proud to say.

"'For God so loved the world,' for God so loved you, Joe, 'that He gave his one and only Son, that whoever believes in Him shall not perish but have eternal life. For God did not send his Son into the world to condemn the world, but to save the world through Him.' God doesn't want to condemn you, He wants to save you and give you His peace, rest and freedom. You receive this by believing and following Him, Joe."

Joe sits for a moment in thought. "That sounds good, but I was wild when I was young. I ran the streets and did some bad things. Then I joined the military to get out of the street life. That helped me begin on the right path."

Kris taps Joe on his knee. "Thank you for your service."

Joe acknowledges Kris' respect with a nod and continues. "Then I met Mare and, man, she rocked my world. Until then I'd never met anyone so nice and loving and caring. What she saw in me, I have no idea. We got married, and she helped me do a total one-eighty. She made me want to be the best man I could be; it just happened to be while we were in a war."

Joe chokes up, but composes himself. "The military does good things. We did humanitarian missions. That felt good. We saved people and protected them. That felt good. I learned what hard work and self-discipline are, and that was good, but that old expression rings true: War is hell." Joe's expression gets dark and he leans forward. "I saw some serious crap. I was involved in some serious crap. If you know what I mean." Kris leans across the aisle and puts his hand on Joe's shoulder.

"These days I'm angry. I'm bitter. I have fears. I have night terrors." Joe's voice cracks and his eyes tear up. Years of suppressed thoughts and feelings bubble up and are on the verge of bursting loose. "I'm different now. I used to be carefree and fun-loving. I'm not the man my wife married."

His tears start to trickle. Like a dam with a crack, the pressure eventually builds until the crack gives way and the dam bursts. Like a busted dam, Joe sits a broken man. The waters start pouring out, gushing—there's no stopping it. The deeply held, healing tears flow out of him—years' worth of tears released from their emotional dam, the dam Joe had built to protect himself and those he loves, but in reality only prolonging the pain.

In between deep, sobbing breaths, Joe whispers, "I believe, I believe, I believe."


The kids are settled in seats by the windows on the left side of the train. They kneel, looking out the window, but the only view is of a hillside with lots of pine trees and snow racing past the window. Mary stands behind them. Wayne is kneeling next to a cute little girl with blonde hair and blue eyes who is his age. She smiles at him and, without speaking, covertly offers him a chocolate coin wrapped in gold foil embossed with a picture of St. Nicholas. His eyes grow big and wide, and he gladly takes it without anyone noticing; it's their little secret in that private moment. He slips the coin into his pocket and offers her a smile of gratitude in return, which she warmly accepts.

Conductor Maggie's voice announces over the speaker, "All-righty folks, about two minutes before show time. When we get around this bend out of this valley, prepare to be *amazed*." As she's saying this, the hard snow they've watched flying by the window over the last couple hours, and which has blocked their view of the scenery, suddenly stops.

Kris walks up and stands next to Mary. "Joe will be here momentarily. He's using the lavatory."

"The who-ey what-ey?" Thomas asks.

"The restroom, Master Thomas."

"Oh. You talk funny." Thomas turns back to look out the window.

Joe arrives looking a little peaked and puts his arm around Mary. She puts her arm around his waist and studies his face. "Are you okay?"

"Yeah, Daddy, you don't look so good," Wayne chimes in. Mary and all the kids look at him.

"I'm fine, just a little motion sickness."

"Emotion sickness?" asks Laura.

Everyone chuckles at Laura's misunderstanding, except for Thomas, who just shakes his head with annoyance.

"Well, some of that, too." Joe glances at Kris.

"Motion sickness, not e-motion sickness," Thomas says. "Motion, like being car sick, but in a train."

"Yeah, yeah, I get it now," Laura says. "Daddy, did you throw up?"

Wayne gasps, "Ew, yuck!"

"I had a lot of bad stuff come up, but it was a good thing. Sometimes we gotta get all the bad stuff up and out to feel better, right?" remarks Joe.

Wayne, still with a face of disgust, repeats, "Yuck." Then immediately his face becomes one of enlightenment, "But, yeah, when I'm sick I feel better after throwing up. That's true."

"Thanks everyone for caring, but I'm getting better by the minute." Joe looks at the kids, then gives Kris a smile and a nod as if to thank him. Then he looks deeply into Mary's eyes and says again, "I'm getting better by the minute." They smile at each other and she looks at him as if she's not sure who he is. Then, out of the blue, he gives her a several-second, full-on, liplock kiss. They give each other a big squeeze.

The train brightens up and everyone's attention turns to outside. The train enters a wide-open area where the sky is aglow with greens, pinks, blues, yellows, and reds. All the colors swirl together as if a master painter has taken a giant paintbrush and made beautiful, broad strokes of color that run from the highest point in the sky to the horizon below, as far as the eyes can see. Exclamations of amazement erupt within the train.

Then over the loudspeaker, Conductor Maggie says "*Maggie*-nificent, if I do say so myself."

Everyone smiles at her play on words, mesmerized by the miracle in front of them.

Mary, soaking in the view, says with awe, "Beautiful."

"Yes." Joe says looking at Mary. She looks up at him. Staring into her eyes, he says, "And the scenery ain't bad, either." Mary melts into him. They kiss again.

"Ew, dad, I hope you brushed your teeth," Thomas says.

"I did. I'm all clean and new, from the inside out. Like I'm born again," Joe says. He smiles at Mary, and they all continue to enjoy the amazing northern lights.

Kris looks upon the family and smiles with satisfaction. He sees the little blonde girl next to Wayne looking back at him. In sign language, he asks her if everything is okay. They appear to have already made each other's acquaintance. She smiles with adoring eyes and signs back, "Everything is great! Thank you!"

He gives her a wink and slips away, walking up and down the train in the vibrant glow of the aurora borealis. Handing out gold-wrapped chocolate coins, he wishes everyone he meets a Merry Christmas in different languages as he goes: *"Feliz Navidad! I'd miilad said oua sana saida! Kung his hsin nien bing chu shen tan! Vrolijk Kerstfeest en een gelukkig nieuwjaar! Froehliche Weihnachten! Pozdrevlyayu s prazdnikom Rozhdestva is novim godom! Joyeux Noël! Buon Natale! Sung tan chuk ha!"* and so on. Oddly, he seems to have an endless supply of these special coins in his pockets.

## Devotion

For those who have experienced God's grace and mercy, there is a lot to be thankful for. Joe felt unworthy of God's grace—the gift of getting something good, when we don't deserve something good. Joe felt unworthy of God's mercy—the gift of not getting punished, when we deserve to be punished.

God's word tells us that we do not deserve the love God has for us because He is perfect and we are not, but because of Jesus' blood sacrifice on the cross for our sins, His holy blood covers us. When God looks upon us, He sees the righteousness and perfection of Jesus, His beloved Son with whom He is well-pleased. Therefore, we thankfully receive God's grace and He is well-pleased with us.

God's word tells us because of our sinful natures what we deserve is death, but Jesus took the wrath of our punishment on the cross, died, was buried, and rose again on the third day, conquering death. God says we are co-heirs with Christ and join Him in his victory over death. Therefore, we thankfully receive God's mercy.

**Questions to consider:** Do I feel unworthy of God's grace and mercy? Why? Am I ready to take the step of faith to ask God for His grace and mercy in my life? He says He is faithful to give it if I ask. Will I accept it?

*"… the righteousness of God through faith in Jesus Christ for all who believe. For there is no distinction; all have sinned and are deprived of the glory of God. They are justified freely by his grace through the redemption in Christ Jesus, whom God set forth as an expiation, through faith, by his blood, to prove his righteousness because of the forgiveness of sins previously committed, through the forbearance of God—to prove his righteousness in the present time, that he might be righteous and justify the one who has faith in Jesus."*
*Romans 3:22-25*

*"And the Word became flesh and made his dwelling among us, and we saw his glory, the glory as of the Father's only Son, full of grace and truth."*
*John 1:14*

*"All of us once lived among them in the desires of our flesh, following the wishes of the flesh and the impulses, and we were by nature children of wrath, like the rest. But God, who is rich in mercy, because of the great love he had for us, even when we were dead in our transgressions, brought us to life with Christ (by grace you have been saved)," Ephesians 2:3-5*

*"... that in the ages to come he might show the immeasurable riches of his grace in his kindness to us in Christ Jesus. For by grace you have been saved through faith, and this is not from you; it is the gift of God; it is not from works, so no one may boast." Ephesians 2:7-9*

**Prayer:** "Heavenly Father, help me embrace the truth of Your love for me and to receive the gift of Your salvation that includes Your grace and mercy. Help me walk in the freedom of that truth. Thank You. Amen"

# 14
# Believing is Not Seeing

DECEMBER 8 READING

*17 days until Christmas*

A SHORT WHILE later, the glow of the northern lights slowly dissipates, and passengers slowly start to make their way back to their compartments. Kris has given a golden chocolate coin to everyone on the train, including all the train engineers, employees, and passengers. He wanders back to his compartment, sits down, and exhales as if glad to be off his feet and satisfied that he has brought some Christmas cheer to the train. He notices he is not alone; Thomas is sitting on the bench seat against the window playing his handheld video game.

"Ah, Master Thomas, I see you're playing *TimeCraft 3.0*. Much better graphics than 2.0. The action moves faster, requiring better eye-hand co-ordination."

"Yeah, nothing I can't handle."

"What level are you on?"

Thomas never looks up and continues playing. "Seven."

"Seven out of ten, not bad. I'll bet you're having trouble finding the enchanted sword that will take you to the Kingdom of Incense, where you'll have to slay the demon dogs to find the coveted key forged out of mystical, elvish, petrified wood."

Thomas hits pause on his game. He looks up at Kris. "What do you know about it?" Thomas is impressed by this old gent's video-gaming knowledge, but he is not going to let that be known.

"I know enough about it to get to level eight. Then nine. Then ten." He gives Thomas a coy smile.

"How do you know so much about it?"

"Oh, I know a thing or two or three about toys, er, I mean, personal entertainment devices." Kris changes his voice to a deeper, more serious tone, knowing Thomas would argue that the video game is not a toy.

"So, where's the sword?"

"Well, I'm not going to take the pleasure and personal satisfaction of finding it yourself away from you. I'll give you a hint, though: Sometimes things are in plain sight, right in front of you. You don't see it, or believe that it's there, therefore making it more complicated than it is."

"Great, thanks for nothing." Thomas turns off the pause button and goes back to playing the game.

Kris asks, "Did you enjoy seeing the aurora borealis?"

"It was okay. Like Conductor Maggie said, it's just a bunch of space particles hitting earth's atmosphere and turning into different-colored gases. Not a big deal."

"That's where you and I differ, Master Thomas. Just because we understand how God created something makes it no less a miracle and beautiful, just like knowing how the manufacturer made that video game makes it no less enjoyable to play."

"I don't believe in miracles, I don't believe in fairytales, and I don't believe in anything science can't prove. If I can't see it, I don't believe it."

"So we have a doubting Thomas here, eh? Well, you're not the first, and you won't be the last. You're a science guy? Me too! I love science! Science is humankind learning to understand God's creation looooong after God created it! People who were scientists, physicists, physicians, inventors, biologists, chemists, and so on who helped form modern-day science were men and women of faith believing in things they could not see, such as Nicholas Copernicus. Good name, Nicholas, eh?" Kristopher chuckled. "There's Sir Francis Bacon, who is credited with helping establish the scientific method of inquiry based on experimentation and inductive reasoning. There's Johannes Kepler, Hildegard of Bingen, Galileo Galilei, Rene Descartes, Blaise Pascal, Sir Isaac Newton, Robert Boyle, Michael Faraday—"

"Okay, okay, I get it," Thomas interjects. "Lots of science people who believed without seeing."

Kris continues, "Maria Gaetana Agnesi, Gregor Mendel, William Kelvin, Max Planck, Mary Anning and so on. Even today, there are many believing scientists asking God to reveal His creation to them. Albert Einstein said, 'I want to know how God created this world. I am not interested in this or that phenomenon, in the spectrum of this or that element. I want to know His thoughts. The rest are details.'"

Thomas pauses his game. "Einstein said that?"

"Yes. Science without God is like music without a composer. Art without an artist. It's there, but it has no soul."

"Okay, so lots of famous scientists believe in God and things they can't see. So what's your point?"

"That video game you're playing has electric currents running through it. If you open up the cover and look at the details inside, you can see the battery, the circuits, the connections, but can you see the electric current?"

"No."

"No, but you *believe* there's an electric current because you are using the power of the electric current surging through that device. Did that device randomly form on a rock somewhere, or did an intelligent designer think of that video game idea and create it?"

"Someone smart invented it."

"Yes, someone smart, highly intelligent, who has never seen an electric current, invented it. Have you ever seen the electric current in your home that powers your television, microwave, lights, hair dryer, refrigerator, and so on?"

"No."

"No, because you cannot see it, but you can see the effects or the power of the electric current. You have personal experience of the power of the electric current. Have you ever seen a microwave?"

"No."

"No, but you see the results of microwaves heating up food for your basic need of hunger. Have you ever seen a radio wave?"

"No."

"No, but you hear the results of radio waves communicating to you. Have you ever seen a satellite beam?"

"No."

"No, but you've seen the results of a satellite beam projecting images to a television while orbiting the earth from outer space giving you visions to see. Correct?"

"Yes."

"So my point, my dear doubting Thomas, is that you already believe all the time without seeing, and you didn't even realize it. And when you believe without having to see, a whole new invisible world is opened up to you! We cannot see electric currents or microwaves or sonar or radar or wind, but yet we believe in them and we interact with them, they are real. Their power helps us in many ways; they provide for our basic needs and wants in many ways. Fortunately, for us, there are people that believe without seeing who give us these wonderful inventions. Things we cannot see give us power, meet our basic human needs, communicate with us, and give us visions. Like God does, eh?"

"I don't know much about God. My mom talks a lot about Him, and she has us go to church with her, but I don't listen. It's boring."

"You believe in electricity, microwaves, radio waves, satellite beams, radar, sonar, and so many other things you cannot see, but they all had creators, so why not believe in *the* Creator, an intelligent designer that created everything you see *and* don't see? You're aware we live in a three-dimensional world. You could say electricity, gravity, sonar, and other invisible entities are in a fourth dimension. A dimension that is real but cannot be seen. I believe there is a spiritual dimension, a fourth, or fifth dimension if you will, that we can interact with. I do every day. Your mother believes in it, too, and interacts with it every day. People all over the world believe in a god. Most believe in a spiritual god, but even the people who say they don't believe in the one God, like you, actually do believe in *a* god. You are your own person, right?" Thomas nods.

"You'll believe what you want, when you want, and how you want, right?"

Thomas nods again.

"The person who makes the rules we live by is the person who is god to us. You've made up your own rules, so you've set yourself up to be your own god and you're full of pride, thinking you know it all and that you don't need God. God opposes the proud, but gives grace to the humble. Are you omnipotent, omniscient, and omnipresent?"

"I don't know what those words mean, but I have a strong suspicion you're gonna tell me I'm not any of those things."

"You're correct, you're not any of those things. They mean all-powerful, all-knowing, and everywhere at the same time; so that being-your-own-god deal? Good luck with that. Sadly, there's too many self-gods running around making up their own rules as they go. Me, I'd rather put my faith in Someone who knows me better than I know myself. He's full of love, kindness, peace, patience, encouragement, acceptance, forgiveness, grace, mercy, and *so* much more. That's who I hang out with every minute of the day and our relationship is glorious! Doesn't that sound like Someone you want to be around?"

Thomas sits back in his seat. "Kinda sounds like my mom, but cooler because He invented everything."

"Many people said the same thing you said: 'I don't believe what I don't see.' They were closed-minded to even the possibility of something existing that they could not see. But, thankfully, there are people who have faith, who believe without seeing, and a lot of those men and women have changed the world, pursuing science and bringing us wonderful inventions. But even more importantly, these same people have faith in God and are given so much more than we can ever imagine and hope for—love, kindness, peace, patience, and so on—the true meanings of Christmas. The true meanings of life. Just because you don't see God doesn't mean He is not real. You may not believe in Him, but He believes in you. God reveals Himself to those who have faith and believe without seeing. After they take that step of faith, they do see God—not in the way you're thinking, but in God's way. Faith is the assurance of things hoped for, the conviction of things not seen. Have I given you food for thought?"

"Yeah, food for thought. It would be tastier food and a miracle I would believe in if you show me how to find the enchanted sword now."

"Oh yeah? That's an easy miracle, and I'll do whatever it takes to help you believe. You're in the Hall of Cross, correct?"

Thomas replies, "That's where the Yellow Wizard said the enchanted sword would be."

"There are three doors in the hall, but you cannot enter any until you find the enchanted sword because it also acts as a key to unlock the correct door. There's a sign over the three doors that says, '**No trespassing or be cursed forever**.' A sword, also shaped like a cross, can take a life just as a cross took Jesus' life. However, a sword can be a saving instrument as well; used to defend and save lives, just as Jesus dying on the cross has spiritually defended and saved all the lives of those who believe in Him. We know the sword is real, but it is enchanted, which usually means it was cast under a spell and cannot be seen unless you look at it differently. Is there anything on that sign right in front of you that you see with your own eyes that looks like a sword and or a cross?" Thomas scans the written words. "Oh, I see it!" He moves his warrior character to the sign. He reaches out and grabs the **t** in "**trespassing**," and it magically transforms into the sword he has been looking for. "Yes! It IS a miracle! It was real, and it was right in front of my eyes the whole time, but I didn't see it, so I didn't believe it was there. Interesting."

"Imagine how that works," Kris says, enjoying watching Thomas' eyes become open to possibilities.

Commotion happens at their train compartment door. Mary walks in with Joe, Laura, and Wayne. "There you two are! We were wondering what happened to you both. What are you doing here? Why weren't you enjoying the last of the amazing northern lights?"

"Oh, we're just talking video games, science, deep theology about God and faith, seeing without believing, believing without seeing, and the true Spirit of Christmas," responds Kris.

"Whoa, some deep stuff," Mary is impressed.

Conductor Maggie pops into the cabin, "Hi ho, all, were the northern lights amazing or what?" Everyone gleefully agrees. "Excellent, we aim to please around here. Oh, and the fun never stops on this train, look what we have here." Maggie steps out the cabin door and comes back in rolling a cart with six delicious-looking, fancy drinks in giant mugs with whipped cream covering the tops.

Everyone in the cabin lets out one long, "Mmmmm."

"This is Kris' special holiday hot chocolate! It's made with real chocolate and real milk heated to the perfect temperature. Once poured into the mug, one candy cane is added to infuse a hint of peppermint. Then a layer of miniature marshmallows is placed on top with several dollops of freshly made, vanilla whipped cream. There's more! Then it's all topped with chocolate shavings to complete the yumminess. The marshmallows become melt-in-your-mouth goodness as they float over your tongue and down your throat on a wave of chocolate rush. Mm, mm, mm!"

Maggie hands the drinks out. "Enjoy, and I'll see you soon." A chatter of appreciation rises during her swift exit.

Having a sip, Mary gets some whipped cream on her nose. "Wow, Kris, this is amazing. This is your special recipe?"

"Yes, indeed, I created it a *long* time ago, and it's always been a favorite of everyone who's tried it."

Mary is not the only one with whipped cream on her nose. It is hard to avoid with the cream piled high and the delicious taste drawing one in to down more each time.

As the kids are in their own world enjoying this addictive beverage, Kris reaches into his left vest pocket and leans over to Joe and Mary to whisper. Mary and Joe lean in to listen, and Kris whispers, "One last secret ingredient, special only for those of us with more refined tastes." He pulls out a little shaker of spice and nonchalantly sprinkles it on top of their drinks, speckling the white cream and chocolate shavings with tiny flakes of red, brown, and black. "Nutmeg, with a few other secret exotic spice ingredients that will lift your spirits."

Joe and Mary both take in deep breaths of the added aroma and close their eyes and smile as the flavors transport them to a place somewhere in their minds that they have not connected with in a long time. Wherever it is, it feels like home.

Everyone settles back into their seats, and for several moments there is quiet satisfaction as *all* their senses take in this new, tasty, sweet addiction. The glorious cup is a sight-to-behold. Its aromas are to die for. The feeling of the creamy liquid passing over their lips, into their mouths, over their tongues, and down their throats is blissful. Of course, the taste is out of this world! And the sounds of sipping, slurping, smacking, swallowing, and, yes, even a little burping are heard among them. Pure enjoyment!

Wayne is the youngest, but he is the first to finish. He is a bit out of breath but wears a look of satisfaction only a five-year-old can make. He has a dot of whipped cream on his nose, and he emits a burp, followed by an, "Excuse me." As he catches his breath, he wastes no time. "Please tell more of Nicholas' story! What happened that almost ended Nicholas' giving and his life?"

"Well, Wayne, I am glad you're interested in the story. Is everyone settled and ready for me to continue?"

All nod in agreement, and Laura says to Kris in between sips, "I'm still being patient."

Kris smiles, finishes his last sip, and wipes his mouth. "Well, then, let's begin. First, let me fill you in on some things that happened to Nicholas before that fateful time that almost ended his giving and his life."

## Devotion

Thomas on the train had doubts, and Thomas in the Bible had doubts. Thomas in the Bible did not believe the other disciples when they told him Jesus had risen from the grave. He said he would not believe unless he saw Jesus with his own eyes. Through locked doors, Jesus appeared to Thomas and said, "Put your finger in the holes in my hands, put your hand in my side." He continued, "Stop doubting and believe." Thomas said to him, "My Lord and my God!" Then Jesus told him, "Because you have seen me, you have believed; blessed are those who have not seen and yet have believed."

Jesus is the Way, therefore, when we stay close to Him He will guide us to the answers for our questions and He will keep us on the right path in life. We need to be still, know that He is God, practice being in His presence regularly, and follow Him.

Jesus is the Truth and He is bigger than our doubts and questions. Doubts are only a concern when we use them to keep God at a distance. He wants intimacy with us and will help us with any questions that stand in our way.

**Questions to consider:** Do I have my doubts? If so, it's okay. What are they and am I allowing them to stop me from asking, seeking, and knocking?

*"Jesus answered, "I am the way and the truth and the life. No one comes to the Father except through me." John 14:6*

*"But he should ask in faith, not doubting, for the one who doubts is like a wave of the sea that is driven and tossed about by the wind." James 1:6*

*"Jesus said to him, "'If you can?' Everything is possible to one who has faith.' Then the boy's father cried out, 'I do believe, help my unbelief!'" Mark 9:23-24*

*"The Advocate, the holy Spirit that the Father will send in my name—he will teach you everything and remind you of all that I told you. Peace I leave with you; my peace I give to you. Not as the world gives do I give it to you. Do not let your hearts be troubled or afraid." John 14:26-27*

**Prayer:** "Heavenly Father, please strengthen my faith. And where I have my doubts, help me entrust them to You. Help me overcome my unbelief. Thank You. Amen."

# 15
# Let the Adventures Begin!

NICHOLAS HAD GROWN up with his parents doing business at the docks in Patara, where ships had traveled from near and far. He knew quite a few of the sailors, captains, and owners that came and went, but he knew the one captain whose ship he wanted to work on more than any other. Captain Omar's ship. Captain Omar was from Africa and he had done business with Nicholas' parents his whole life. Omar, knowing Nicholas had a sweet tooth, would bring sweets from all over the world to let him try, but that's not the reason why he wanted to be with Captain Omar, though it is a good reason!

Nicholas wanted to be on Omar's ship because Omar had sailors from all around the Mediterranean Sea who spoke different languages from near and far, which was helpful when they went into ports in different countries. Nicholas loved to learn from people different from him, and about different cultures and languages, so he could not think of a better ship.

Nicholas had gone with Falon to the docks several weeks before he planned to leave, when he knew Captain Omar and his ship, *The Queen of Africa*, would be back at port. Captain Omar hired Nicholas without hesitation because he knew Nicholas was intelligent and hardworking. Omar and the crew welcomed Nicholas with open arms. This arrangement made Falon, Tana, and Bishop Nicholas happy, too, because they knew Omar and his crew. They were confident Omar would watch over Nicholas and treat him like family. Some of the other crewmembers were brothers Pol and Aindriú from Ireland, Mathias from France, Marcus from Spain, Lukas from Bavaria, Yahya from Syria, and Pietro from Italy.

Nicholas jumped right in and learned all the jobs on the ship quickly. He enjoyed hard work and already had calloused hands and feet before he boarded the ship from working hard back home. He had the respect of the men before he started, but when they saw how quickly he learned, how hard he worked, and how skilled he had become, they could not help but be amazed. He lifted the spirits of all on the ship from his jolly nature! They understood why God had called him to be a priest because even at his young age, his knowledge and understanding of scripture were way beyond that of all of them put together.

Israel was the ultimate destination that Nicholas wanted to visit, but he was a working man now, so he had to go where the ship went. Nicholas accepted this course and enjoyed the journey of different sites and ports they visited along the way, including Athens, Rome, Cyrene, Alexandria, and, eventually, Caesarea, a port city in Israel. Working on the ship was hard work, but to visit all those ports and see all those cities was worth every drop of shed sweat and aching muscles.

Between ports, they would be out to sea for weeks. It did not matter if Nicholas was working or not for he was in constant conversation with his shipmates, learning about their backgrounds, their cultures, and their languages. They discussed religion and their relationships with Jesus.

There were times when Nicholas would find a quiet corner on the ship for scripture reading and meditation, prayer in different postures before the Lord, and personal reflection. He sat remembering his parents, or holding the mistletoe and thinking of Wren and praying for her and her family. These quiet moments were needed and appreciated as much as the social interactions he enjoyed so much. The quiet times with God invigorated him and gave him strength.

Some of Nicholas' other favorite times were sitting with Captain Omar and others on the deck at night. Captain Omar taught Nicholas how sailors used the locations of particular stars, especially those of the constellation Ursa Major, the bear, to orient and navigate the ship in the correct direction. They marveled at the star-filled sky and were in awe of God's grand design of the universe. The Heavens proclaimed the glory of God and the skies displayed His artistry.

Nicholas would share God's word in prayer, to the men's delight:

"You are the Lord, You alone. You have made Heaven, the Heaven of heavens, with their host, the earth and all that is on it, the seas and all that is in them; and You preserve all of them; and the host of Heaven worships You... For Your invisible attributes, namely, Your eternal power and divine nature, have been clearly perceived since the creation of the world in the things that have been made. So humankind is without excuse... You, Lord, laid the foundation of the earth in the beginning, and the heavens are the work of Your hands... As we look not to the things that are seen but to the things that are unseen. For the things that are seen are transient, but the things that are unseen are eternal... In the beginning, God created the heavens and the earth. The earth was without form and void, and darkness was over the face of the deep. And the Spirit of God was hovering over the face of the waters."

These biblical words were poetry and spiritual food to the people who heard them.

After many months of traveling, the time came when Captain Omar announced that their next port of call would be Caesarea. Next stop, Israel! Nicholas was so excited that he could hardly sleep that night, but in the little sleep he received, Nicholas had a dream that a storm would put their ship and all on board in great peril. When he awoke in the morning, he warned Captain Omar and the sailors that a severe storm was coming, but said, "God will protect us." Almost immediately, the sky darkened and strong winds roared around the ship. The wind and waves made it impossible to keep the ship under control. Even with lowered sails, the sailors feared for their very lives as the ship was tossed about. They begged Nicholas to pray for safety.

Captain Omar commanded one sailor, Aindriú, who was one of their most nimble and experienced men, to climb the main mast to tighten the ropes so the mast did not break in half and come crashing onto the deck. In the wind and rain and the ship heaving back and forth, Aindriú's mission was successful. However, as he was coming back down, the sailor lost his grip about twenty feet high and tragically fell to the deck, landing head first, and died.

Nicholas had been praying, and the storm finally quieted, relieving the sailors. However, their comfort was dampened by grief over the death of their shipmate, Aindriú, Pol's brother. Nicholas, saddened, prayed over Aindriú's lifeless body, interceding and petitioning God for mercy and deliverance. Moments later, a miracle! A revived Aindriú took a breath as if he were only waking from a deep sleep. Aindriú had no sign of injury and to his brother's and the whole ship's sheer delight, Aindriú was miraculously healed! That day there was much to rejoice about, and the ship's arrival to the Holy Land three days later was filled with more reverence and awe than was anticipated. Praise be to God!

This port call was different from all the others. It was bittersweet because Nicholas had grown close to his shipmates, Captain Omar, and the paid passengers. He had witnessed miracles, and he had enjoyed seeing the different countries and sites, but now Nicholas' time on the ship was to end. This was his main destination, to be on pilgrimage in Israel, the Holy Land. He did not know how long he would be here, but he did know his time on the ship had ended.

It was déjà vu for Nicholas because though it had been over half a year, it still seemed like yesterday that tears had flowed when saying goodbye to Noll, Tana, Falon, and Shimmel back on the dock in Patara. Here he was again, tears flowing, saying his goodbyes to Captain Omar, Aindriú, Lukas, Marcus, Mathias, Pietro, Pol and Yahya and the many others he had had the honor of getting to know. He would miss them and they would miss him.

When packing, he had his bundle of scrolls, his walking staff, an extra set of clothes, a little food, and some wages in his pocket. Sadly, Nicholas discovered he had lost the mistletoe Wren had given him. He thought it must have happened during the storm. Nicholas felt the Lord tell him that he would always have a special place in his heart for his dear Wren, but that His will for her was in a different direction than it was for Nicholas. It was now time for Nicholas to let the past go and focus on God's presence in the present. Nicholas left his sea family and started walking inland. He was on his way. His pilgrimage had begun.

When Nicholas visited Israel, he lived in a small cave in Beit Jala overlooking Bethlehem, the birthplace of Jesus. Nicholas embarked on his pilgrimage to the holy places, walking where Jesus had walked. He visited the Sea of Galilee, where the majority of Jesus' miracles had taken place; Golgotha, also known as Calvary, a site immediately outside Jerusalem's walls where Jesus was crucified; the Garden Tomb area where Jesus was buried and rose on the third day; and many other holy sites.

Nicholas spent most of his time studying, praying, and talking with the most knowledgeable scholars he could find.

It was a powerful time of learning and growing in faith for Nicholas—so much so that Nicholas' pilgrimage ended up lasting over five years. It was then that he began hearing the Holy Spirit in his prayers, calling him back to Lycia, where he was to continue doing the Lord's work. He had treasured his time in the Holy Land living the life of a monk, but by this time, he was excited to return home and minister to his people.

Nicholas jumped for joy when he first saw the docks of his homeland fast approaching while still aboard the ship. All he could think about was starting his life of ministry. When he docked at the port in Patara, he went straight to his uncle and gave himself to begin his training for the priesthood immediately.

He had left six years earlier, having only just reached adulthood. Now he returned as a man, still strong, wiry, and nimble, but his frame had filled out with about thirty more pounds of muscle. He now wore a beard—not the peach fuzz it had been before. His voice was deeper than remembered. Though he looked older and more mature, he still had that hop in his step, the gift of hearty laughter, and a generous heart for others. Bishop Nicholas was so glad to see his nephew and they talked for hours about the younger man's adventures. They exchanged stories about the Holy Land—Bishop Nicholas had taken his own pilgrimage to Israel as a young man as well.

Nicholas wanted to see Noll and his family, but he knew they would be coming to the city in a matter of time on business, so he would wait. He sent a messenger with word of his return and his wish to see them upon their next city visit. His uncle shared with him that not much had changed for Noll and family. Noll had followed in Falon's footsteps and became a well-thought-of businessman and local leader. Kari and Dax too, had taken on more and more duties and responsibilities in their family's businesses.

The bishop indicated that Patara was growing and more outsiders were moving in, due in part to Emperor Diocletian helping bring back some stability to the Roman Empire economically, politically, and militarily. Diocletian had managed to stay healthy and alive. He had formed enough alliances with rivals to have avoided assassination so far. He had been good for the Roman Empire, but there was still unease among Christians because of his known dislike for them. It was felt that if the empire continued to regain its strength, glory, and prosperity, then the persecution of Christians would increase.

This led Bishop Nicholas to get serious with Nicholas about his desire to become a priest. He warned that if things continued in this way, the persecution of Christians, especially of the leaders and clergy, would be dangerous for all. Imprisonment, torture, and death were all possibilities. Nicholas did not have to consider this for a second. His immediate response was, "The Lord is my light and my salvation—whom shall I fear? The Lord is the stronghold of my life—of whom shall I be afraid? ... For God did not give us a spirit of cowardice, but rather of power and love and self-discipline."

This response was no surprise to the bishop. He was proud of the young man Nicholas had become.

"And now I'll bet you're wondering what happened to Wren, eh?" Kris asks on the train. "Well, Wren ended up getting mar—"

Kris sees the expression of immense sadness on Laura's face as she sits in Mary's arms.

He feels Joe and Mary shooting darts at him with their eyes. "Oh, well, she moved away from home and moved to the big city, and at this part of the story she ended up getting mar . . . mariner, a mariner roommate. A roommate who sailed the sea."

"Mr. Kris," Laura says, stone-faced and sad. "I get it. Wren married another man. I don't like it, but I get it. I'm still patient. I know things are going to work out some way, somehow for Wren and Nicholas. I don't know how, but I have faith."

Kris nods and is impressed with her maturity.

She asks, "Did she marry a good man?"

"Yes, Laura, he's a good man who loves the Lord and is from a good family who loves the Lord."

"What kind of job does he have?"

"His family is in shipping. They own a small ship, and he is on his way to being the captain of his own ship someday."

"Is he nice?"

"Yes, he's a very nice man."

"Okay, thanks."

"Are you okay?" he inquires.

"Yes, like I said, I'm being patient. I have faith and I know how this story ends, so I'm just waiting for you to get there."

"Okay then, shall I continue?"

"Please do."

Kris nods and continues.

*Two days later . . .*

Noll, Falon, Tana, Kari, Dax, John, and Leila visited Nicholas in the city and enjoyed a warm reunion, catching up on the past six years. Noll sported a beard himself, and Nicholas was amazed at how Kari, Dax, John, and Leila had grown. It felt as if it were just yesterday when Kari and Dax had been tiny tots running around playing famous Roman wrestlers, hurting whomever got in their way, and John and Leila had been just learning to walk and talk. Nicholas felt good to be back in Patara again, near his home, and the Mikros clan were happy to have him back with them once again.

They spent hours enjoying a good meal together while listening as Nicholas shared his adventures—his time aboard the ship and his pilgrimage to Israel. The Mikroses shared stories of their own and news from back home, including that of Wren and her sisters. Wren was married, and Kyra and Kalista both were betrothed, all to good men from good families who loved the Lord. It was hard for Nicholas to hear about Wren, but he was genuinely happy for her and her sisters. Noll, knowing this news would hurt, surprised Nicholas by bringing Shimmel to help lessen the sting and try take his mind off it. Nicholas was so elated and thankful he could hardly speak!

While Noll and his family tended to some business, Nicholas took Shimmel for a ride to see what had changed in the city he had visited often as a child. Later that afternoon, he met up with the Mikroses and they all said their goodbyes, acknowledging that they had been blessed to have that time together and were thankful for each other. The next day, Nicholas would begin his training for the priesthood, which would be intensive. He and Noll agreed to meet up at least once a month and spend some time enjoying each other's company, "iron sharpening iron."

Nicholas lived in the church with his uncle and the other clergy. He was the only candidate at that time, so he got all the help he needed to learn to be a competent and effective priest. The number one duty of a priest was to share the love of God and the word of God. One way this was done was by spending time performing the Seven Sacraments. The Seven Sacraments were religious ceremonies regarded as visible signs, or symbols of inward and spiritually divine grace, which revealed the Lord Jesus and through which His divine life and love were communicated.

All the sacraments were entrusted to the church to be celebrated in faith within and for the community of believers, to express visibly what God was doing invisibly. The Seven Sacraments were baptism, communion, confirmation, penance, anointing of the sick, matrimony, and holy orders, the order of hierarchy including deacons, priests, and bishops. All believers are to fulfill Jesus' Great Commission—to go forth into the world and preach the gospel and make disciples of all nations. All are to be ambassadors of God's Kingdom. As it is read in the scroll of Peter, "But you are 'a chosen race, a royal priesthood, a holy nation, a people of his own, so that you may announce the praises' of him who called you out of darkness into his wonderful light."

Nicholas' duties as a priest would be plentiful and demanding, but incredibly rewarding. The vast majority of priests lived happy, fulfilling lives. They loved the people they served, and, in turn, their parishioners loved them. Nicholas would guide, unite, and encourage his parishioners in holiness. He would celebrate mass by preaching the gospel, other duties included hearing confessions, feeding the poor, visiting prisons, visiting orphanages, and advocating for justice. He would counsel people going through difficult times, visit the sick and anoint them for healing, perform funerals, and pray daily for the people of God and those who had yet to believe.

This job was made for Nicholas—or maybe it could be said that Nicholas was made for this job. Nicholas fit being a priest like a snug, cozy glove fits on a hand. A match literally and figuratively made in Heaven. He loved everything he had to do, but his favorite part was being out with the people, especially children, and ministering to the sick, the needy, and the suffering. That was where he felt he made the biggest difference in people's lives. That was where his heart lay.

Nicholas had a love for learning and he soaked up everything taught him about the priesthood, like a sponge. He finished his training in just over a year when he was ordained. The sacrament required a bishop along with other priests to perform the ceremony. For Nicholas, his ordination was extra special for having his uncle administer the sacrament of holy orders for him. It was a glorious accomplishment!

Nicholas did not miss a beat. After his ordination and he was now officially a priest, he kept on with his priestly duties, except now he was more independent and did not require any formal guidance. He would usually have some free time in the mornings, and that was when he would go about visiting the sick, needy, and suffering. He enjoyed being out with the people in general, especially playing with children, with whom Jesus had had a special connection.

A well-recorded story of Jesus told of how people brought little children to Jesus so that He would place His hands on them for prayer and anointing, but the disciples rebuked them. When Jesus saw this, He was indignant. He said to them, "Let the little children come to me, and do not hinder them, for the Kingdom of God belongs to such as these."

Another time, Jesus set a child before the disciples and took the boy in His arms. He said to them, "Whoever receives one child like this in my name receives me; and whoever receives me does not receive me, but Him who sent me." God has a special place in His heart for children. Nicholas did as well and was very protective of them. Woe be to anyone who harms a child, for they will incur their consequences in due time.

Nicholas, as many priests did, would refer to his parishioners as his spiritual children, following the apostles' biblical example of referring to members of their flock as "my son," "my daughter," or "my child," thus taking on the role of spiritual fathers. Therefore, it became customary to call priests "father." Father Nicholas' bond with the people was as strong as any being that he was so well-loved.

## Devotion

On the ship, Nicholas would retreat to a corner of the ship for private time with God. For five years, Nicholas retreated to Israel to learn and grow spiritually. Many people today go on weekend retreats to rejuvenate spiritually, mentally, physically, and emotionally. Jesus withdrew from life and ministry to be alone with the Father and pray. Jesus' solitude and silence is a major theme in the Gospels.

Jesus' solitude, or retreating, if you will, is how he began his ministry. It's how he made important decisions, dealt with the demands of his ministry, cared for his soul, prepared for his death on the cross, and went more deeply into his love-relationship with his Abba Father. Jesus modeled this for his disciples and for us.

Loving others, taking care of ourselves, being joyful always, praying continually, and being thankful in all circumstances takes spiritual, mental, physical, and emotional energy. It can be draining. The purpose of a retreat, or what many call a quiet time, is to get away from the busyness of life to give full, undivided attention to our Father in Heaven, and to meditate on His Word and be in His holy, peace-filled presence.

There's a saying—BUSY means Being Under Satan's Yoke. The enemy wants our busyness to draw us away from God to hurt our relationship with Him. A retreat, or quiet time, allows God to fill us up again with Himself, His power, His glory, and the fruits of His Holy Spirit: love, joy, peace, patience, kindness, goodness, faithfulness, gentleness, and self-control. When we are filled up, then we can pour into those around us. We retreat to rejuvenate to advance His Kingdom.

**Question to consider:** Am I retreating to rejuvenate to advance spiritually, mentally, physically, and emotionally, regularly? At least daily?

*"But seek first the kingdom of God and his righteousness, and all these things will be given you besides." Matthew 6:33*

*"Your word is a lamp for my feet and a light for my path." Psalm 119:105*

*"Thus faith comes from what is heard, and what is heard comes through the word of Christ." Romans 10:17*

*"Draw near to God, and he will draw near to you. Cleanse your hands, you sinners, and purify your hearts, you of two minds." James 4:8*

**Prayer:** "Heavenly Father, please help me make it a practice to regularly rest in Your holy presence daily, read and meditate on Your Word, and bask in Your glory not just every day, but continually through my day, no matter where I am or what I'm doing. Thank You. Amen."

# 16
# The Marketplace

DECEMBER 10 READING

*15 days until Christmas*

NICHOLAS BEGAN THIS day as he did all his others. He got up before the dawn and walked to the beach by the sea with his bag of scrolls over his shoulder to read and meditate on. He prayed in different postures before the Lord, as had been done by many of God's people for many millennia before him. He loved watching the miracle of the sun rising over the Mediterranean Sea every morning, with the glory of daylight touching his face and illuminating the land, just as God's glory and light touched his soul and illuminated his being, continuing to heal and transform him in his Christian walk with the Lord. *Ahh, no better way to start the day*, Nicholas thought.

He then walked along the coast to the docks and prayed traveling mercies over the sailors and ships that were leaving port that morning. He walked through the back alleys of the bars helping those who overindulged the night before to get home safely, and prayed for their healing from addiction. He thanked every Roman soldier he saw for keeping order in and around the city and to have a nice day. At the orphanage, he taught the older children reading by using his scrolls and having them memorize scripture. He helped the women who ran the orphanage feed the babies, and he pretended to be a jungle animal, such as a tiger or monkey, playfully chasing the children around when they were on their break from chores. He loved their giggles and they loved his ho, ho, ho's.

As he was preparing to take leave, Nicholas and the women heard arguing in one of the rooms and found two brothers ready to punch each other. Nicholas grabbed the boys by the scruff of their necks just in time as they started swinging and separated them.

"What have we here, what's going on?" demanded Nicholas.

The first boy, Abe, replied, "Caleb said we're trash, and all the kids here are trash, because our parents threw us away and no one wants us either. I told him we're not trash and to take it back. He wouldn't take it back and said, 'Shut up, trash.' So I was about to shut him up with my fist when you walked in."

"Is this true Caleb?"

"Yes."

"Now boys, I know the wounds on your souls are fresh from your parents abandoning you recently. We'll be counseling you and praying regularly for your wounds to be healed and for your parents to be healed of their troubles. This is a perfect example of how hurt people, hurt people. Caleb, you have hurt feelings from the rejection of your parents, so you're calling your brother, yourself, and all the others here a bad name. And Abe, your brother is hurting your feelings, so you want to hurt him for hurting you. Am I right?"

Both boys nodded their heads.

"You're new here and you've had difficult lives. You're not familiar with Christian ways of love, forgiveness, and repentance, we have to teach you these ways, and we will. But for now, I want you to listen up, and I want everyone here to listen up!"

Nicholas looked at all the children and workers who had now gathered around to see what was happening.

He said, "I don't ever want to hear anyone ever call someone a bad name here. Violence doesn't solve hurts and problems. Calling someone a mean name is violent language trying to hurt and damage another human being. Inappropriate! We focus on the truth, God's truth! His truth says that regardless of what another imperfect, sinful, hurting human being does or says to us, including our parents, that Jesus loves us. God loves you and I love you, too, and that's the truth, the whole truth, and nothing but the truth! Do you understand?!"

Everyone looked at him with mouths open, in shock, not too many have ever seen Nicholas speak so sternly.

"I said, do you understand?!

A clamor of yeses arise in the room.

"And if anyone tells you differently, you don't do anything, you just tell them 'I don't care what you say, God loves me, Father Nicholas loves me, all these ladies love me, and that's all that matters!' If they a problem with that, then you tell them to go take it up with Father Nicholas! Do you understand?!"

A chorus of yeses!

"Whaaat?!"

"YESSS!" They shouted.

Nicholas stretched out his arms. "Hugs."

The excited children bull rush him to give and get hugs. The women workers stood in their places jolted by Nicholas' firm, but loving tone.

Looking at them, Nicholas firmly repeats. "Huuugs." The women gladly join in the hug-fest.

Nicholas responds to all, "Ho, ho, hooo, I love you all so much, you are so wonderful, ho, ho hooo!"


Nicholas met Noll for one of their monthly lunches at the town square not far from the water's edge. The square regularly held a farmers' market selling all kinds of fruits, vegetables, and other goods. This was where people like Noll's family would bring their crops and goods for barter and sales. Likewise, the sailors, like his former shipmates, would bring their exotic products from overseas.

It was an exciting place to meet, filled with energy. Many things happened to awaken the senses as townspeople bargained, bartered, and sold their wares. There was always lots to see and smell. The scents of fruits, vegetables, baked breads, and spices wafted to all in the vicinity. Nicholas enjoyed the whole scene and he loved to see and meet people from all over. Due to his role in the city as a priest now, he was more widely known than ever, and people enjoyed seeing him and experiencing his jolly disposition. Nicholas was always joy-filled. His selfless giving, while taking nothing in return, earned Nicholas widespread respect from people of many diverse backgrounds.

Occasionally, if the Holy Spirit moved him, Nicholas would gather some empty fruit boxes and stand in the middle of the square, sharing a teaching that God would put on his heart. Nicholas may have been a bit small in stature, but he had a booming voice. He was second-to-none at storytelling. When Nicholas spoke, people listened. He poured his heart out to the people in the city, helping anyone and everyone in need when he could; thus, the people enjoyed listening to him share whatever was on his heart, whenever he wanted, however he wanted. Nicholas was well-respected and well loved by all. Well, by almost all.

There was the exception of Emperor Diocletian. He despised Nicholas for his Christian beliefs and because he was so-loved by the people. It did not help that occasionally Nicholas and the emperor crossed paths around the city. If moved, Nicholas would take the opportunity to share some of God's truth within earshot of Diocletian. This day was no exception.

Nicholas and Noll had just finished a lively discussion about a trend that was happening in the region among Christians. There were some folks preaching a prosperity gospel, also called a health and wealth gospel, involving the belief that a problem free life was the will of God for all Christians. If a person had enough faith and gave enough donations to the church, his or her health and material wealth would increase and they would have few, if any, struggles in this life. This is inaccurate because though scripture was clear Christians had access to many of God's blessings, there was never any indication that Christians would live problem-free.

Emperor Diocletian, Prisca, and Valeria had just stopped near the market, scanning market stands to decide which to visit, when Nicholas felt moved to share with the people. He gathered several empty fruit boxes near the splashing fountain, stepped up, and began, "The promise of life enhancement!" His blaring voice caught the attention of those standing nearby, who quickly quieted. In a matter of a minute, the town square was silent and all eyes were on Nicholas. He continued, "The promise of life enhancement . . ."

Before Nicholas could proceed further, an unfamiliar man from the crowd interrupted. He was a learned man from another land, dressed in noble clothes. He mocked, "Priest, do not waste our time with your lies! I've traveled all around the world. I've had many discussions with people from every religion and philosophy you can imagine. I've read all their scrolls, including your Christian scrolls. I am a teacher of politicians, business leaders, philosophers, and scholars. One thing I have learned is that everyone has their own truth, therefore everyone's so-called truth equates to this: there is NO truth!"

Nicholas, always one for a robust discussion, gently responded, "Well, my good sir, is that *true*?"

"Yes, of course it's true. There is no *one* truth!" The crowd chuckled, and the man realized he had contradicted himself. He retorted, "You mock me? How dare you!"

"No, sir, I only asked a question and you answered it quite perfectly. Thank you."

"You think I'm wrong? That is another point I have learned through my studies and experiences; there is no right or wrong in this world!"

"Yes, sir, you're either *right* or *wrong* about that."

"There's no being wrong about that. I am right that there is no right or wrong!" Again the crowd laughed. This man became furious. He tried once more to put this little God-believing priest in his place. "You do not understand what I am saying. I'm trying to tell you there are no absolutes in this world. Nothing is absolute!"

"And now I have to ask you this, my dear sir. Are you *absolutely* sure about that?"

"Yes, I am absolutely positive there are no absolutes in this world." At this point, the crowd was done with this gentleman, and with laughs and jeers, there were calls for him to be quiet and let the priest continue.

The stranger stormed off angrily, mumbling, "Idiots, you're all idiots."

Nicholas embraced these times of being challenged because he would use these experiences to grow deeper in knowledge and wisdom. The challengers were usually smart, but not very wise. Nicholas was knowledgeable, but, more importantly, he asked God for wisdom as King Solomon did. As a wise person, Nicholas recognized he did not know everything, which brought him humility. As a child, he had learned to be wiser than wise by, not only learning from his own mistakes, but also by learning from others' mistakes.

He did not become angry with these so-called experts or critics. He felt compassion for them because they were searching, which is a good thing. Our human design is to search for Truth by a Creator who intended for us to search for Him and find our significance in Him. Sadly, these lost souls were searching for love, acceptance, and significance in all the wrong places.

The person who makes the rules we live by is the person who is god to us—many people live by their own rules, therefore, they make themselves out to be god. They try to find significance within themselves or false idols in such things as money, status, pleasure, power, material possessions, or other people. Many of these people were scroll smart. They read a lot and knew many facts, but it seemed to end there. The God-given gift of intelligence they have, they use to reject God and His existence. There *is* truth—God's Truth. There *is* right and wrong and absolutes in this world, and God created them with our best interest in mind. Truly, a wise person will embrace God's instruction to have honorable judgment and action in his or her life.

Nicholas publicly thanked the man for sharing his interesting thoughts, and then continued, "The promise of life enhancement. The promise of unending happiness with no troubles. That God is a genie in the sky waiting to give you whatever you want, whenever you want. That is what some of you are teaching, and that is what some of you are hearing and believing. Tis' true, believing in Jesus will surely enhance your life, and your after-life as a matter-of-fact, however, the teaching that believing in Jesus will give you a problem-free life is indeed, false."

He cups his hands behind his ears to signal to listen closely. "My children please have ears to hear, Jesus told the parable, 'The kingdom of Heaven is like a merchant looking for fine pearls. When he found one of great value, he went away and sold everything he had and bought it.' Jesus' first lesson here is that nothing is more valuable than God's Kingdom. Whoever understands this will pursue it like there is nothing better. Jesus' second lesson is that nothing will cost you more. The merchant sold everything. *But*, and it's a big but—my brother Noll here doesn't like big 'buts,' but he's going to like this one—*but*, the merchant knew that he was getting something more valuable than anything else. Anything! So it was worth everything he had. Amen?" People from the crowd, including a smiling Noll, cheered.

"God wants your whole heart. Commitment to God should be greater than everything. You have to surrender your life to gain life. And Jesus' third lesson was to go all in for the Kingdom. The greatest Treasure, in the greatest Kingdom, is the King Himself." Nicholas looked in Diocletian's direction. "And I'm not talking about any earthly king or kingdom! The apostle Paul said everything in this world is a pile of garbage, actually dog poop, compared to the Kingdom of God and God Himself. Jesus is the prize! When we recognize the worth of God the Father, Jesus, the Holy

Spirit, and His Kingdom, guess what we get? Humility, which leads to joy. Joy that surpasses all understanding. This is the good news! Yes, this is why the merchant sold all he had for that one pearl, to have it in his presence. True joy comes by being mindful of God's presence and living in God's presence every moment of the day. When you learn how to live in God's presence in the present moment every moment, then you can experience joy in palaces, in prisons . . . anywhere! Anytime! Good news!"

The crowd showered Nicholas with Amens.

"However, do not be deceived. Now back to the teaching about life enhancement. Becoming a believer in Christ does not make us immune to life's trials and tribulations. Trials are guaranteed, but God wants to use our trials for our own good. Trials reveal what is in our hearts. Like squeezing an orange, something *will* come out. Will it be something good to taste or something rotten? Goliath was a big problem for the Israelites. He squeezed and brought out fear in King Saul and his army's hearts. But, in young David's heart, Goliath squeezed out childlike trust in God. What do trials squeeze out in your heart? Trials remind us we need God. Trials refocus us from material things to spiritual things. Trials develop our trust muscles in God. Trials can reinforce God's strength in our weakness, for He is bigger than any trial or Goliath we'll ever face. Trials realign our perspectives from the temporal to the eternal. Are you hearing me?" A roar of Amens were heard.

"This earth is not our home. Heaven is our home if we believe, thus giving us hope. We have hope now, in the present, because we can have intimate relationship with our Heavenly Father in the present moment. He said He will never leave us nor forsake us, and He will walk through trials with us and bring us joy amidst our trials in His presence. We have hope for the future because the home God has awaiting us, is heavenly. Rejoice in hope, be patient in tribulation, be constant in prayer. 'For I know the plans I have for you,' declares the Lord, 'plans for good and not for evil, to give you a future and a hope. Then you will call on Me, come, and pray to Me, and I will listen to you. You will seek Me and find Me when you seek Me with all your heart.' Good news, people, we have joy and peace in believing because we know the righteousness of Christ is going to deliver us from the wrath that is to come, thus giving us hope. Jesus said, 'I have told you these things, so that in me you may have peace. In this world, you will have trouble. But take heart! I have overcome the world.' Amen!" A chorus of "Amen!" rang out.

"Peace be with you!" Father Nicholas stepped down and people surrounded him thanking him and asking questions about his teaching.

Noll joyfully looked on. He loved to see people hungry for truth, and he loved to see his dear friend do what he loved. The market slowly went back to business.

On the outskirts of the square, in a well-ordained carriage surrounded by soldiers, sat the emperor, his wife, and his daughter. Diocletian declared, "Drivel. That man rambles on and makes no sense, and the people just eat up whatever he says. Ridiculous."

Prisca, who enjoyed hearing Nicholas, quoted the scroll of Job to herself about her husband: "Great men are not always wise; neither do the aged understand judgment."

"Speak up, wife. I cannot hear you when you speak softly next to the noise of the market. What did you say?"

"My husband, how is it that Nicholas has nothing, yet seems filled with contentment and joy? You have all. You are emperor of the greatest empire on earth, king of the greatest earthly kingdom, if you will, yet you seem filled with discontentment and anger."

"I am a man of great responsibility. Many people depend on me for many things. I deal with serious matters daily, including life and death issues. There is no time for contentment. Happy times are a luxury I cannot afford."

"You rule the entire Roman Empire. If you cannot afford it, who can?" Prisca inquired, a bit incredulous.

Diocletian shook his head in annoyance and scoffed.

Prisca inquired further, "Do you think it is possible to have joy, to find peace, in spite of our circumstances?"

"I imagine it possible. I have not found it."

Valeria listened quietly. She reflected back on that day years ago when she had met Nicholas and he had spoken of having the secret to contentment. At that time, if he had said what the secret was, she had not understood it. Now, as she related that time long ago to Jesus' parable about the merchant and the pearl, it dawned on her what the secret was. Nicholas had an in-person relationship with the Heavenly Father, thus giving him joy. He had Jesus' righteousness; salvation was his, giving him hope for eternal glory with the Father, Son, and Holy Spirit forever. His faith in Christ saved him and gives him hope through the good times and bad times. Without hesitation, her revelation blurted out of her mouth before she could stop it. "His presence and hope!"

Diocletian and Prisca were startled, both turned and looked at their daughter. "What did you say, dear?" Prisca inquired. If it were only Prisca in the carriage, Valeria would talk freely because they had many conversations about Christianity, scriptures, God, and Nicholas. With her father there, she wished she had not said anything at all. What made Valeria's predicament even worse was that she had been married to Galerius, one of Diocletian's soldiers, who was rising quickly through the ranks. With Galerius being Diocletian's son-in-law, it was destined for him to be a co-ruler someday, and her new husband was as anti-Christian as her father.

What Valeria wanted to say was that joy and contentment in any circumstance, good or bad, rich or poor, is in the practice of basking in God's presence. Enjoying the hope that is in Him in the present, and in the hope that is in Him in the time that is to come. Instead, she fibbed, "Um, his presents and hope. I find joy and contentment in my husband's *presents* he gives me from his long journeys and I have *hope* he returns to me soon." Whew, she dodged an arrow on that one. Then the urge to share Truth was too great and a sudden surge of boldness was too powerful to resist. "But I liked what Nicholas said about the pearl—"

"Silence!" commanded Diocletian. "I do not want to hear anything that dirty little speck Nicholas has to say, or anything any Christian has to say, especially about God or Jesus or any of it! I and your husband Galerius forbid you to talk with Christians ever, do you hear me?"

"Yes, Father." Valeria and Prisca looked at each other, reminded that they needed to keep their readings of Christian writings, and their growing faith, between themselves only. How could they both be married to men who hated the very thing that they were discovering brings them peace, guidance, and hope? Sadly, Valeria's father forced her to marry Galerius for political reasons. There was no choice.

### <u>Devotion</u>

Jesus was born in a humble manger a few miles away from a luxurious palace, called the Herodian, built by the Roman emperor King Herod, ruler of the greatest kingdom on earth at the time. By all appearances, it looked like Herod had all the power and glory, and Jesus had none. Thousands of years later, Herod and his kingdom are gone, dust in the wind. Yet Jesus the Messiah, Lord of Heaven and earth, triumphed over death and evil. His life, death, and resurrection have influenced billions of lives as the King of kings and Lord of lords. Jesus is alive and His Kingdom has no end!

Three hundred years after the birth of Jesus, we have a humble, faithful follower of Jesus, named Nicholas, whose life mission was only to share the gospel, the good news, of Jesus. The gospel of Nicholas/Santa Claus, IS, the good news, the message, of Jesus.

Nicholas lived in the shadow of the Roman emperor Diocletian, ruler of the greatest kingdom on earth at the time. Nicholas' only claim to fame was being a humble servant of the Lord, and through his sacrificial giving and living, history connected him with that humble baby born in the manger, Jesus, who has the True Power and Glory. Almost two millennia later, there are thousands of St. Nicholas churches pointing people to God around the world and millions of people know of St. Nicholas, otherwise known as Santa Claus. What about Diocletian? He and his kingdom are gone, dust in the wind, like Herod's. God's Kingdom reigns!

**Questions to consider:** Whose kingdom am I living for? An earthly kingdom that will pass away with its leaders? Or God's Kingdom, which will last for eternity with its triumphant King of kings?

*"But seek first the kingdom of God and his righteousness, and all these things will be given you besides." Matthew 6:33*

*"Asked by the Pharisees when the kingdom of God would come, he said in reply, 'The coming of the kingdom of God cannot be observed, and no one will announce, 'Look, here it is,' or, 'There it is.' For behold, the kingdom of God is among you.'" Luke 17:20-21*

*"This is the time of fulfillment. The kingdom of God is at hand. Repent, and believe in the gospel." Mark 1:15*

*"In the lifetime of those kings the God of heaven will set up a kingdom that shall never be destroyed or delivered up to another people; rather, it shall break in pieces all these kingdoms and put an end to them, and it shall stand forever."*
*Daniel 2:44*

*"This, then, is how you should pray: 'Our Father in heaven, hallowed be your name, your kingdom come, your will be done, on earth as it is in heaven.'"*
*Matthew 6:9-10*

*"For the kingdom of God is not a matter of eating and drinking, but of righteousness, peace and joy in the Holy Spirit," Romans 14:17*

**Prayer:** "Heavenly Father, please help me to pursue your Kingdom that lasts forever over any earthly kingdom. Thank You. Amen."

# 17
# Troubled Times

DECEMBER 11 READING

*14 days until Christmas*

NICHOLAS EXCUSED HIMSELF from the crowd to walk with Noll to his wagon and say goodbye. The two were discussing the day's events when they turned the corner and Noll stopped in midsentence. He stared straight ahead with his mouth gaping open as if he had seen something his eyes could not believe.

As they moved slowly forward, Nicholas scanned the crowd, trying to see what had stunned his friend. Ahead on his left, Kari and Dax stood near their wagon—nothing unusual there. In front of him, there were many stands—business as usual. Ahead on his right, his former shipmates, Pol and Aindriú, were shopping. What was Noll looking at that had provoked this look of awe? Was it a dessert cart, a piece of art, or a rare fruit?

"What do you see, Noll?"

Noll silently gazed ahead. As the two friends continued to move forward, Nicholas continued scanning, and he finally caught a set of emerald green eyes staring their way. They were attached to a Noll-sized, attractive, redheaded young woman standing between two market booths. In her hands was a basket of fresh produce. She was as mesmerized by Noll as he was of her, and when they came to the open area, Nicholas stopped. He stood back to watch as Noll continued moving closer to the object of his attraction.

Noll beamed as he stopped in front of her. "Hello."

"Hello," she replied.

"Lewk, a rainbow!" Pol yelled in his Irish accent, pointing up to the sky.

Aindriú enthusiastically answered, "I see it, brutha. Let's go find us the leprechaun's pot o' gold at the end of the rainbow!" They both dropped the small crates of produce they were carrying and ran to their horses. They mounted their steeds, making a ruckus, galloping by. The crowd watched, except for Noll and his mysterious woman, who were both enamored. Pol saw Kari and Dax up ahead standing in the middle of the road watching Noll.

"Lewk, leprechauns!" Pol and Aindriú scooped up Kari and Dax, laying the twins on their stomachs across the horses' manes. "This is our lucky day. These leprechauns will help us find their gold!" Before Nicholas could react, the siblings were out of sight.

Nicholas, overwhelmed by the sudden activity, grabbed Noll by his arm. "Noll, we have to go save your brother and sister!"

"Oh, hi, Nicholas. Nicholas, this is Glikia. Glikia, this is Nicholas."

Glikia smiled and curtsied, "Hello, Nicholas."

"Um, hello, it's nice to meet you, Glikia. Um, I'm sorry to interrupt, but Noll, we have to go rescue your siblings. Did you see what just happened?"

"No, was it Kari and Dax?"

"Yes!"

"Then whatever just happened, either they deserve whatever they get or they can get themselves out of it." Noll and Glikia continued to gaze at each other, ignoring Nicholas.

Noll said to Glikia, "So where were you saying your clan is from?"

Nicholas figured Noll was useless at this point. He ran over to the Mikroses' wagon parked nearby and commandeered it for his Kari and Dax rescue mission. He knew Pol and Aindriú well and did not think they would purposely hurt Kari and Dax. However, they often became so fixated on an idea that impulsivity took them over and reason went out the window.

Nicholas slowly set out on his mission. He could not go very fast because the wagon was loaded down with boxes of goods from the day's business. He was hoping to catch up to them before anything bad happened. A short while later, Nicholas approached the area where the rainbow seemed to end. Faint pleas for help came from behind some trees off the road. He parked the wagon, leaped out, and bounded his way in the direction of the yelps. As soon as he arrived at the tree line, he saw Pol and Aindriú tied up by ropes and hanging upside down from two different trees.

"Nicholas! Oh, thank heaven you found us. Help us!" Pol whimpered loudly.

"Are you two okay?"

"We will be, once you've gotten us down," Pol said.

Nicholas helped free Pol and Aindriú by cutting the ropes around their feet first, lowering them to the ground, then freeing their hands.

"Are Kari and Dax okay?"

Aindriú responded, "If those are the names of the two little leprechauns, then what do you think? We're the ones tied up here."

"Okay, good. I'm glad everyone is okay."

"Aye, them some angry little leprechauns. I learned you don't mess with a leprechaun's pot o' gold, that's for sure."

"Aye, agreed," said Pol, "but maybe we made a mistake and those were elves."

"Leprechauns, elves, whatever they are, they're angry, scary little creatures."

"Aye brutha, you got that right."

Several years later, as the Roman Empire stabilized and regained its power and glory, Bishop Nicholas' prediction came true. Emperor Diocletian and his co-ruler, Maximian, to whom Diocletian gave power to help make his rule more effective, declared themselves the individual sons of the Roman gods. Diocletian claimed to be the son of the chief Roman deity, the king of all the gods, Jupiter, also known as Jove (the Greek equivalent of Zeus), god of the sky and thunder. Maximian claimed to be the son of Hercules, son of Jupiter who had great strength and many adventures.

By connecting themselves with the gods—Diocletian adopting the title Jovianus and Maximian adopting the title Herculius—it was meant to heighten their statuses even more and set them apart from the world around them. No previous emperor had ever gone so far. Shortly thereafter, Diocletian commanded all the citizens of the Roman Empire to worship him as a god, and the people were to kneel before him and kiss the hem of his robe.

Unlike most religions in the Roman Empire, Christianity required its followers to renounce all other gods. Christians refused to join pagan celebrations. Therefore, they were unable to participate in much of public life. This caused non-Christians, including those in the Roman government, to fear that the Christians were angering the Roman gods, threatening the peace and prosperity of the empire.

Due to persecution, many Christians chose to worship in private. The perception of their "secret" religious practices generated rumors that Christians were guilty of incest because they called each other "brothers" and "sisters in the Lord." And guilty of cannibalism due to practicing Holy Communion—Jesus' decree to eat bread as His body in remembrance of His broken body, and drink wine as Jesus' blood in remembrance of His shed blood, which He allowed to happen as the sacrificial Lamb of God for the atonement of humankind's sins. All this resulted in even more persecution.

Christians believed in one God only, so their consciences would not allow them to obey the emperor's order. Angered by the Christians' steadfast beliefs, Diocletian warned the Christians that they would be imprisoned. A series of more broad and organized persecutions of Christians emerged when the emperors decreed that Christians' refusal angered the gods and caused many of the empire's military, political, and economic troubles. Orders required all residents to give sacrifices to appease the gods or be punished. Jews were exempt as long as they paid a Jewish tax.

Some of Diocletian's brutal acts toward Christians included removing the tongue of the deacon Romanus of Caesarea for defying the order of the courts and interrupting official sacrifices. Romanus went to prison, where the famous and feared fighting champion, Sandor the Great, executed him.

After that, a fire destroyed part of Diocletian's imperial palace. Galerius, Valeria's husband and a senior military leader, convinced Diocletian that the culprits were Christians, conspirators who had plotted with the eunuchs of the palace. After conducting an investigation, they found no responsible party. Executions by Sandor followed anyway and he executed the palace eunuchs Dorotheus and Gorgonius.

Sandor tortured many Christians that worked in Diocletian's palace, including Peter Cubicularius, Diocletian's butler. Sandor stripped him, raised him high and scourged him, then poured salt and vinegar into his wounds. Then he slowly boiled Peter over an open flame. Sandor's executions continued when he decapitated six other individuals, including the Bishop Anthimus.

This was the same Sandor the Great who had been the people's beloved fighter, known for his grace and mercy. No one knew what, but something had happened in Sandor's life to make him retire from professional wrestling and gladiator fighting and request to be a Roman torturer and executioner. Being a champion fighter, he found favor with Diocletian, who granted Sandor anything he asked for, including his request for this new and evil line of work: master executioner. At one time, people believed Sandor to be a Christian, but now his reputation was for preferring Christians as his victims.

Diocletian razed the newly built church at Nicomedia, and he burned its scriptures. He also seized the prized treasures for the government coffers. The next day, Diocletian published his first edict against the Christians. The edict ordered the destruction of Christian scriptures and places of worship across the empire and prohibited Christians from assembling for worship. More edicts followed, arresting all Christian clergy and throwing them in prison, releasing them only if they had made sacrifices to the Roman gods.

### Devotion

During Nicholas' lifetime, persecution for being a Christian was part of the culture. Today, in certain parts of the world, persecution continues; however, in the western world overall, we are fortunate to have freedom of religion.

**Questions to consider:** How do I fare today as a Christian representing Christ to the world? Am I embracing my freedom (if I have it)?

*"... but sanctify Christ as Lord in your hearts. Always be ready to give an explanation to anyone who asks you for a reason for your hope ..." 1 Peter 3:15*

*"Now Jesus did many other signs in the presence of his disciples that are not written in this book. But these are written that you may come to believe that Jesus is the Messiah, the Son of God, and that through this belief you may have life in his name." John 20:30-31*

*"The Lord does not delay his promise, as some regard "delay," but he is patient with you, not wishing that any should perish but that all should come to repentance." 2 Peter 3:9*

**Prayer:** "Heavenly Father, please help me get to know You so well that I'll love you more than anything, and I'll have so much faith in You that I won't care what anyone says or thinks about me or does to me. That I'll be free, through You, to be whom You mold me to be. Thank You. Amen."

# 18
# Arrested Like No Other

DECEMBER 12 READING

*13 days until Christmas*

THE CLERGY IN Patara knew it was not a matter of *if*, but *when*, the Roman soldiers would come to arrest Nicholas, his uncle the bishop, and the other clergy members who refused to worship Emperor Diocletian. Patara was an important port city, and Diocletian and Prisca had a small palace in Patara, so armies of Roman soldiers were already in place. Diocletian and his advisors were very aware of the popularity of Nicholas among the citizens in Patara, as well as his notoriety in Rome and elsewhere because of the church sharing news about his good works. Diocletian wanted to make an example of Nicholas, but at the same time, they knew that if they killed him, there would be a major uprising. They could not kill him, but they could do anything and everything *but* kill him. Who should do the job, but the famous Sandor.

Soldiers were on guard throughout the city day and night, waiting for the command to round up the Christian clergy and squash any sign of an uprising against Roman authority. Nicholas and his brethren did not venture out much. They spent most of their time in their church praying—praying for God's will to be done; for their parishioners, friends, and families; for each other and themselves; and even for their enemies, the Roman leaders and soldiers, as God's word called them to do.

Finally, one fateful morning, fifty Roman soldiers arrived at the church, entered its doorway, and arrested Nicholas, his uncle, and the other priests who were still there. Prior to this, Bishop Nicholas had tried to send away all his priests, including Nicholas. Over half of the priests took him up on his offer and tried to escape persecution by going back to their hometowns or to other countries to share God's love. However, this small contingent felt God was telling them to stay and trusted in Him for whatever happened. Nicholas was one of them.

The bishop and his priests did not fight. They left their church peacefully to be escorted to the prison on the edge of the city. There was nothing to take, no belongings to keep, only the clothes on their back. When the giant church doors were opened and the flood of sunlight shone into the sanctuary where they were praying, they blew out all the candles and walked quietly and willingly out the door and into the bright light. They squinted as their eyes adjusted to the brightness. Bishop Nicholas led the procession with Nicholas bringing up the rear. Nicholas noted before he stepped outside that the street and city were eerily quiet. He did not know what to make of it.

As he continued to slowly shuffle along behind the other clergy, he looked up at the beautiful blue sky and noticed three tiny figures on the roof ledge of the building across the street from the church. He knew right away that Noll, Kari, and Dax had come to see him one last time. He was already at peace with going to prison for his faith. God's peace that surpassed all understanding overcame him, but knowing his good friends were nearby warmed his heart even more.

As he paused and looked down the steps to begin his descent, he saw Bishop Nicholas and all his clergy brothers looking up at him with a look of horror in their eyes. Nicholas extended his pause to try to understand why everyone stopped, and then he saw everyone turning their gazes from him to a massive figure in front of them. Sandor!

Nicholas had never seen Sandor in person. He had only heard the stories of the living legend and remembered the descriptions of him. He knew who this behemoth of a man was standing there, a head taller than the tallest Roman soldier, with shoulders twice as wide as any soldier's he'd ever seen. He had chiseled, bulky muscles from neck to feet and was dressed in Roman soldier garb. However, he wore an executioner's mask and held a long, leather whip.

Images of Deacon Romanus, Bishop Anthimus, and Peter Cubicularius came flooding into his mind. This was not to be a processional walk, a ceremonial march to prison, after all. It was a death march to execution—Nicholas' execution. Nicholas' quiet calm turned into fear. A lump formed in his throat, his stomach churned, and he could hardly swallow, but then he had a fleeting thought. A moment of pain, even excruciatingly unfathomable pain, would make dying and being with sweet Jesus in Heaven all the sweeter when his body took its last breath and his spirit ascended to the heavenly realm. Fear knocked at the door. Faith answered. No one was there. A peace and calm came back over him.

Sandor called in a slow, deep, gravelly voice, "Nicholaaas."

Before Nicholas could respond, Bishop Nicholas stepped into the road. "I am Nicholas!"

Sandor took two steps toward the bishop, long steps compared to anyone else, and stared down at the bishop. Before anyone could take another breath, Sandor backhanded the brave but unsuspecting bishop, sending him flailing in the air. Sandor knocked the bishop out cold. No one took a breath so as not to draw attention to himself.

His uncle was in God's hands at this point. He did not know if his uncle was dead or alive, but Nicholas knew Sandor was there for him. In hopes of sparing the others, Nicholas had to step up and give Sandor what he wanted. Before Sandor could do or say anything else, Nicholas stepped forward and down the stairs to where his uncle had just stood.

"I am Nicholas, son of Theophanes."

"Get down on your knees and sing praise to your god Jovianus."

"There is only one true God, and his name is Je—"

Sandor swung his log-sized right leg around, sweeping Nicholas' feet from under him, sending him straight to the ground. He landed on his left side with a loud thud, knocking the wind out of him, leaving him gasping for breath. He glanced over at his uncle, thinking they would both be with Jesus soon. Sandor grabbed Nicholas by his hair, picked him up, and propped him on his knees. Nicholas slowly regained his breath and held his side, grimacing in pain.

Sandor commanded again, "Sing praise to your god Jovianus!"

"He's not my—"

Sandor kicked Nicholas in the chest, sending him flying into the legs of his brethren behind him. They stepped back, feeling helpless. They wanted to help, but they knew they would be killed immediately if they tried. Nicholas groaned, again having the wind knocked out of him, again trying to catch his breath. His chest and side throbbed. He rolled around, writhing in pain and gasping for air.

Nicholas saw something move to his left. It was his uncle. He was alive! Nicholas thought of the story of David taking on Goliath. He remembered his two little warrior friends on the rooftop that could take out this Goliath with their slingshots. However, that was not God's plan this day, as it was for David. Nicholas accepted that this suffering was God's will for him.

Sandor lifted Nicholas by his hair and stood him on his feet to face the direction of the prison. "Walk."

Nicholas started to stumble forward, weak in the legs. After a few steps, he heard an ear-splitting CRACK! and felt a sharp pain in his back that felt like a hundred bee stings all at once. He fell forward to the ground and glanced back to see Sandor bringing his whip back over his shoulder, then send it flying at him a second time. Before Nicholas could react, there was another CRACK! and pain seared through the back of his right leg. The agony propelled his body to jump up as if he had sat on a hornet's nest. He limped forward and reached to feel the back of his leg. Not only had the whip ripped through his well-known red robe with white trim, but it also had ripped through his undergarment and torn a stripe of flesh. He could feel clothing sticking to his body with blood.

Nicholas found himself the leader of a sick parade with Sandor following close behind, sending his whip Nicholas' way. Sometimes he hit him and sometimes purposely not, like a cat toying with its prey, occasionally clawing or biting it before a slow, cruel death. Sandor toyed with Nicholas. Each time Nicholas heard the *CRACK!* he flinched, not knowing if a searing pain would follow.

Behind Sandor, having to watch the horrific display before them, were Bishop Nicholas and the other clergy. Bishop Nicholas swayed, unstable on his two legs. He had a blackened eye and a throbbing headache, but he was able to walk on his own. It was torture for him to see his beloved nephew be a whipping post.

Following behind the clergy were Roman soldiers making sure everyone stayed close and kept moving. Few citizens stood outside. Most hid inside their homes, looking out windows to see the drama that had visited their fair city. There had been excitement when the word of this living legend, Sandor, was visiting. None of them could wait to see this man of lore in person, but that excitement grew dim quickly when word spread that he was in Patara to torture their favorite citizen. Up above, following along on the rooftop ledges, were three tiny, nimble figures who felt powerless as their friend suffered below.

The demented procession passed by the Thalassa Pub, where Nicholas' former shipmates witnessed the brutality passing by. They had to restrain Aindriú from trying to help because this man of God had saved his life once. He owed it to Nicholas to try to save him. His brother, his captain, and the others would not allow it. Captain Omar said, "This is not our fight today. We are to live to fight another day. How did Nicholas teach us to fight?"

Pol knelt and clasped his hands together. All the crewmembers knelt with him; others joined them in the bar, and they all offered prayers to God. "Have mercy on Nicholas." "Spare Nicholas' life." "Comfort Nicholas." "Deliver him from this evil."

Not far from this scene was Wren in her home on her knees fighting for Nicholas as well. Outside in the streets the procession moved toward the prison. The soldiers and Sandor found the eerie quiet of the streets odd. In most towns and cities, when they gathered Christian clergy, there were citizens lined along the streets and hanging out windows, cheering for scenes such as this. They would spit on the Christians, curse them, and wish judgment upon them. They would pray for their Roman gods to pour out their wrath on these rebels. But not this day in Patara. The soldiers did not enjoy this experience as much as they had in the past.

Sandor noted the different experience, but continued his torment of Nicholas. He would crack his whip and Nicholas would flinch at the sound and keep walking. Sandor would crack his whip again, striking Nicholas, who would grimace and stumble to the ground in pain. Sandor would kick Nicholas, sending him rolling down the road. Sandor would pick him up by his hair, prop him back on his feet, and command him to walk. Then the whole cycle of abuse would start over again with the whip, the kicks, the punches, and the curses. Sandor knew the right amount of pain to inflict so as not to disable or kill him.

Nicholas did his best to master his body to keep moving. All the while, he asked God, if it was not His will to rescue Nicholas this day, then what was His will? In the midst of his affliction, it came to him what God's will was in this situation, as in all things good and bad: "Love Me. Love others. Rejoice always, pray without ceasing, give thanks in all circumstances, for this is the will of God for you in Christ Jesus." This day was no different, and God's will was no different this day. In Nicholas' pain and affliction, he prayed to God, he thanked God for this torment, and he took joy in his suffering, pain, and affliction . . . as best he could, under the circumstances, with the help of the Holy Spirit.

Finally, when Nicholas doubted whether his body could take any more, they arrived at the courtyard in front of the prison. With one last kick from Sandor, Nicholas flew battered, bruised, and bloodied to the ground. His once-beautiful robe was in tatters. Nicholas had enough sense left, while he crumbled to the ground, to make out other clergy members from other parts of the region arrested as well. Roman soldiers surrounded them all.

He caught a glimpse of Father Absalom. Nicholas was in the center of a big circle of clergy and soldiers with Sandor standing over him. Sandor lifted Nicholas by his dirt-stained and bloody hair and propped him on his knees. He commanded, "Praise the name of your god, Diocletian."

Nicholas could barely speak but uttered, "Jesus is my Sav—"

Sandor kicked Nicholas in the stomach, doubling him over, and said, "Apparently he's not your savior today, but Diocletian can be." He pulled Nicholas up again and shouted into his face, "Worship your God Diocletian now, and you will be saved!"

"No," Nicholas panted.

Sandor punched him in the stomach, sending him back to the ground.

Nicholas writhed in pain, desperately trying to catch his breath. When he was able to do so, out of his delirium, he showed some sense of emotion for the first time. He summoned enough strength to make it back to his knees on his own, and, with wild eyes, he yelled at his executioner, "That all you got?!"

Shocked, everyone, even hardened soldiers, all braced for what was to come. Sandor's face grew red with anger that had not yet appeared up to this point, and he grabbed Nicholas by his head. With his left hand, he raised Nicholas off the ground with his outstretched tree limb of an arm to eye level. He drew his right arm back, way back, as if drawing back an arrow, then he let his massive brick of a fist fly directly into Nicholas' face, smashing his nose. Blood splattered in all directions, knocking Nicholas into next week.

## Devotion

We pray that none of us will ever experience what Nicholas experienced. However, there are Christians in the world today who do suffer in Jesus' name and are being martyred. Cultures change, social norms shift, and many believe that the times are changing to where the attack on Christianity is increasing in subtle and not-so-subtle ways all over the world, including in western society.

**Questions to consider:** How would I do experiencing severe persecution and/or torture in the name of Jesus?

*"But rejoice to the extent that you share in the sufferings of Christ, so that when his glory is revealed you may also rejoice exultantly. If you are insulted for the name of Christ, blessed are you, for the Spirit of glory and of God rests upon you. But let no one among you be made to suffer as a murderer, a thief, an evildoer, or as an intriguer. But whoever is made to suffer as a Christian should not be ashamed but glorify God because of the name."*
*1 Peter 4:13-16*

*"Blessed are you when they insult you and persecute you and utter every kind of evil against you falsely because of me. Rejoice and be glad, for your reward will be great in heaven. Thus they persecuted the prophets who were before you." Matthew 5:11-12*

*"Whoever finds his life will lose it, and whoever loses his life for my sake will find it." Matthew 10:39*

**Prayer:** "Heavenly Father, I pray that if I ever face persecution for my belief in You, whether in great or small ways, that You will strengthen me to endure it with Your Holy Spirit. That by Your grace, You will give me the resolve to love my persecutors as You did on the cross when You said, 'Forgive them, for they know not what they do.' Thank You. Amen."

## 19
# Bloom Where You're Planted

"COME TO THE light, Nicholas. Nicholas, come to the light."

Nicholas' eyes focused on a light at the end of the tunnel. Yes! All the pain he had gone through had ended, and he would now be in glory for all eternity with God! The dot of life was over, and the line of eternity had begun! Glory! *Except for one thing*, he thought to himself. He still felt excruciating pain all over his body.

"Come to the light, Nicholas. Nicholas, come to the light," his uncle beckoned.

Slowly, Nicholas became aware that he was not dead and was not in Heaven. Rather, his eyes slowly focused on the prison cell. The light came from a small window above, and his uncle and Father Absalom watched over him. He could only groan in pain. It hurt to breathe.

"There you are my nephew. You're alive! Welcome back!"

Father Absalom trickled some water into Nicholas' mouth, which took a bit of the dryness away, but even the water hurt his mouth. It hurt to swallow. Everything hurt.

Father Absalom greeted him, "Hello there, my son. We weren't sure if you were going to make it for a while. It's a miracle you're alive!"

Nicholas struggled to talk. His voice was hoarse. "I thought I'd died and was going to Heaven. I see I'm back in hell."

175

The bishop shared, "My nephew, what you just went through was no doubt hellish, hell on earth truly. I can't imagine your physical pain and suffering. For all of us believers on earth, thankfully, this is the closest we'll ever get to hell. And, sadly, for those who do not believe, this is the closest they'll ever get to Heaven."

"Yes, uncle."

They helped Nicholas to a sitting position so he could get a better look at his surroundings. Bishop Nicholas had to ask his nephew, "'That all you got?' Really? Where did that come from?"

Nicholas shook his head, unable to recall what his uncle was talking about.

"You don't remember saying that to Sandor? 'That all you got?' That precipitated him rearranging your face—particularly your nose!"

"No," Nicholas said, and they chuckled. Nicholas shook his head in disbelief. "I have no idea where that came from." Then he groaned as he touched his now-broken and crooked nose. Several broken ribs, a broken left arm, and bruises, not to mention the more than thirty whip lacerations of varying sizes all over his body, accompanied it. His beloved long red robe with white trim was now tattered and stained with blood and dirt. It was a blessing that Sandor and the soldiers had not taken the robe before the whipping, because the heavy fabric had helped minimize the damage. It had even stopped the bleeding in most spots. Otherwise, Nicholas would have bled to death.

Nicholas took in the scene around him. He saw eleven small cells, each with a little window up high to enable one to see the sky but not much else. Each cell contained three prisoners, and Nicholas recognized all of them as Christian brothers and fellow clergymen from around the region. They began pouring blessings upon Nicholas with words of encouragement, quotes from scriptures, and praises to God for their brother Nicholas being alive.

A few minutes later, some noise came from the steps, and everyone grew silent. Two Roman guards began giving three pieces of bread and one bowl of water to each cell. No one spoke. Nicholas' cell was the last one, and when the two soldiers looked in and saw Nicholas sitting up, alive, they grew excited. They looked around and quieted.

One whispered, "Hello, Father Nicholas. So glad you're alive. My name is Argus."

The other guard whispered, "Me too. Well not 'me too' that I'm Argus, I'm not Argus. I'm Baruch, pronounced Baruch. But I'm glad you're alive as well. It's a true miracle you're alive! Whew, you took a beating and you look like hell."

"You don't tell the father that he looks like hell. What are you thinking? That's rude," said Argus.

"Well, he does look like hell, don't you think?" Baruch retorted.

"Well, yes, he does, but you don't say that to him. Have some manners and tell him he looks, uh, alive and well."

"But that would be lying, and lying is the ninth commandment. He is alive, that's true. But he doesn't look well; that's a lie because he really looks like hell. Hey, that rhymes!"

Argus ignored his partner. "Father Nicholas, we are so honored to have you on our cell block. We met you years ago. We helped you load your wagon one time, and you said you wished you had something to give us for our kindness. Then you said you had something better than money or a gift, you had knowledge for us, and you taught us the Ten Commandments with hand signs. You were very kind to us even though we were Roman soldiers, which opened us to your Christian beliefs. My favorite commandment is the eighth commandment." He raised four fingers on each hand and tucked his thumbs under. He looked through his fingers and said, "Hey, I stole. That's bad. That breaks God's eighth commandment of 'do not steal.' If you steal, you go to jail, and now look at me. I'm in jail now looking through the jail bars." He chuckled to himself.

"Oh no. Argus, look." Baruch pointed to the prison bars they were looking through and they both panicked, thinking they were in a cell and forgetting they were the guards outside it.

"Oh no, we're in jail? How did this happen? Is this for me stealing and eating your honey cake yesterday at lunch?" Argus unknowingly confessed.

"Is that what happened to my honey cake? My mom made that for me. That's my favorite. I waited all morning to eat that at lunch." Baruch, who was a bit bigger, grabbed Argus by the neck and said, "I'm going to kill—"

"Ahem," interrupted Father Absalom.

Both men stopped and looked in the direction of Father Absalom, Nicholas, and Bishop Nicholas, who were all staring at them with perplexed looks on their faces.

"Sixth commandment," Bishop Nicholas said.

Baruch let go of Argus because he needed both hands to do the hand sign that would help him remember what the sixth commandment was.

He put five fingers up on one hand and his index finger up on the other. "Hmm, oh yeah. 'Do not murder.'" He started to use his lone index finger as a sword cutting down the other five fingers.

"Yeah, you can't kill me," said Argus.

Baruch, still killing his five fingers with the sixth, said, "Okay, I won't kill you. I'll just torture you because I hate you for eating my honey cake." He changed his index finger weapon from a sword to a whip and started whipping his other five fingers and making the sound of a tiny whip crack. "Hey, that's like what Sandor did to Father Nicholas." He giggled but stopped quickly when he looked up and saw everyone looking at him with anger and shock on their faces. "Sorry, too soon?" he asked Nicholas.

Nicholas had fresh wounds all over his face and body, and he was in more pain than he ever imagined. "Way too soon."

"Sorry."

"I can't believe you just did that," Argus said to Baruch. "You're so insensitive."

"I said I'm sorry. That's more than you. You didn't apologize for eating my honey cake. I hate you."

"Ahem."

Both guards eyed Bishop Nicholas, who said, "What did *Jesus* say about the sixth commandment?"

Baruch and Argus searched the shallow recesses of their minds. Baruch found the answer first. "Jesus said, 'You have heard it said, do not murder, but I tell you do not have hate in your heart or you will be judged.'" Baruch gasped at the revelation. He said to Argus, "I'm sorry for breaking the sixth commandment and murdering you by having hate in my heart for you eating my honey cake."

"I forgive you," Argus responded with satisfaction. Bishop Nicholas gave Argus a look indicating he should have something to say as well. "Oh, and Baruch, I'm sorry for breaking the eighth and ninth commandments of stealing your honey cake and then lying to you that I had not seen it."

"I accept your apology."

"Okay, well, shall we get back to work before the new boss finds us?"

"Yes, let's, he scares me. Oh, and here's your bread and water. Enjoy." Baruch set three pieces of bread and the bowl of water on the floor in the cell before they both scurried away.

"New boss?" Nicholas asked when they had gone.

"Yes, well, we have some bad news, then more bad news, and then some good news for you," his uncle responded.

"Let me have it, in that order."

"The first bad news is that Sandor requested to be the new warden of this prison, and what Sandor wants, Sandor gets."

"I'll get to share the love of Jesus with him. Excellent."

"Yes, you do that." The bishop smiled with a smile that said, *I think the injury to your head is worse than we thought.*

Father Absalom continued, "The second bad news is that, physically, you are a mess, and it's going to take you a long time to heal. The good news is you'll have plenty of time on your hands to heal because we're not going anywhere anytime soon. God has us planted here. So let us bloom."

In the prison, between all the imprisoned clergymen in their cellblock, they pretty much had the whole collection of Christian scrolls and letters memorized, from Genesis to Revelation. There was plenty of teaching, memorizing, and ministering to each other spiritually. Having a band of brothers with whom to go through this ordeal with was enormously helpful because when some were having bouts of discouragement, there always were others to lift them up in spirit and prayer. All men had their moments of discouragement now and again.

Daily prayers included something like this from the scroll of Lamentations: "Heavenly Father, thank You for Your great love which will keep us from being consumed by discouragement, bitterness, or hopelessness. Thank You for Your mercy and compassion, which is fresh and new every morning. When we feel as though all peace and joy are lost, remind us that You are worth waiting for and that You are good to those who put their hope in You."

Nicholas gradually healed as best he could. It was a slow process because of the lack of nutrition, but he made progress and healed with a slightly crooked nose and many scars with which to remember his traumatic arrest. He and his fellow prisoners strived to bloom where planted, living out God's simple will of loving God, loving others, being joyful always, praying continually, and being thankful in all circumstances through the guidance of the Holy Spirit. Nicholas did not get to share the love of Jesus with any non-Christian prisoners because there were few, if any. To make room for all the Christians in the prisons around the empire, the government had released most all the prisoners, including murderers, thieves, and other wrongdoers.

Nicholas did not get to share the love of Jesus with Sandor, either, like he had hoped because he rarely saw the new warden. Nicholas would occasionally hunger to share the good news with nonbelievers and at times, the Holy Spirit filled him so much so that he would shout out his little window to the city so anyone within earshot might hear his preaching.

When he did this sometimes Nicholas would have enough energy to jump up to the window and hold himself steady using the window's bars. Usually he was too weak due to injuries and malnutrition, so Bishop Nicholas and Father Absalom would allow themselves to be used as stepping stools for Nicholas to reach the window.

His sermons were short-lived because Sandor lived at the prison, and when he heard Nicholas, he would sprint up the stairs and fly into the cell. He would grab Nicholas by the scruff of his neck and it never ended well for Nicholas. Sandor would beat him and throw him into solitary confinement, otherwise known as the dungeon, where there was no light. Nicholas would remain alone for weeks, sometimes months. You would think he would learn his lesson, but he wouldn't, he couldn't. The Holy Spirit would sweep him away, and he never had any regrets.


Argus and Baruch, though not the sharpest tools in the shed, were blessings from God. They were sympathetic toward Christians. Young believers themselves in their hearts, they could not be outspoken because of their positions as Roman guards. They were rough around the edges, having come from tough upbringings, but they had childlike faith and big hearts, and they were very desirous of learning all that they could about God.

They were unable to show favoritism to the men in their cellblock because Sandor ran a tight prison. Even though he did not visit the cellblocks much, he monitored all the food and water the guards brought and made sure it was the bare minimum, just barely enough to keep the prisoners alive. Though Argus and Baruch were not able to minister to their captives' physical needs, they did unwittingly provide entertainment to the clergymen. Sometimes they operated with no filters and would have colorful conversations within earshot of the prisoners.

In one such situation, it was a warm and beautiful spring day, shortly after the Resurrection Day Mass celebration, also called Easter—the second spring Nicholas and the clergy had spent in prison. Argus and Baruch were standing in the front doorway, which was only a few blocks from the main marketplace. It was clear that Sandor was not around because Argus, Baruch, and some of the other guards appeared to be in a relaxed state. As they stood there enjoying the sunshine on their faces, they took pleasure in watching the people come and go and commenting on this or that passerby.

The prisoners, starved for life outside their enclosed, bleak brick walls, were as quiet as mice to hear what these two guards were unknowingly reporting to their prisoners. Standing in the open doorway allowed a warm breeze to act as a vacuum, blowing fresh air throughout the prison all the way up to the top floor—seven stories up and out the individual jail cells' tiny windows. The breeze brought blessed freshness and warmth to the brisk, barren prison after a long, cold winter. It helped remove some of the stench from the grisly conditions in which they lived. The breeze also acted as a sound enhancer, amplifying Argus and Baruch's conversation throughout the prison for all to hear.

The front door where they stood was about thirty meters from the road in front of them. "A lot of people out and about today," Baruch announced. "There must be multiple ships docking and unloading lots of goods for this many people to be heading down to the marketplace."

"Aye," Argus replied, "we won't have a break until later this afternoon. I hope there's some good stuff left by the time we get there."

"Agreed. I want to pick up some flour and honey for my mother to make my favorite honey cakes. I'll be sure not to bring any to work so you're not tempted to steal them, breaking the eighth commandment, again. Ha!"

"Or you could be nice and bring some to share, rather than be greedy and keep it all to yourself," Argus said. "I think food is an idol in your life, breaking the second commandment: 'Have no false idols before God.' Ha!"

"Ouch, you might be right. I do love food. It is a big temptation for me. Do you really think I put food before God?"

"I don't know, maybe sometimes." Something caught Argus' eye on the road. "Good God, Jesus, Mary, and Joseph! Christ almighty!" Baruch quickly looked in the direction where Argus was looking to see what had elicited such a reaction. He spied an attractive woman with dark hair, red lips, and a red, form-fitting tunic walking along the road. "Talk about temptation! Whoa! I'd like to, huh?" They watched a man come up alongside her, and she appeared happy to see him. They locked arms, and she gave his shoulder a kiss. They passed in front of the prison, heading toward the market.

"Oh, man, I know that guy. His name is Kopanos. What a jerk. I hate that guy. That's his wife? That isn't right. Oh man, I'd love to steal her away from him. I'd show her some lovin'. I'd like to—"

"Whoa, whoa, whoa!" Baruch's face registered shock. "Holy moly, do you hear yourself?"

"What?" Argus responded, clearly annoyed by the interruption to his thoughts.

"Argus, do you hear yourself? Oh my gosh, how many commandments did you just break?"

"What are you talking about? I don't know. What'd I say?"

Baruch's eyes grew wide as he counted on his fingers. "I don't believe it. I think you just broke all Ten Commandments in about ten seconds! That has to be a record! I think I should move away from you, so I don't get mistakenly struck by lightning. I don't want to be guilty by association." Baruch took a couple of steps away from Argus toward the road.

Argus looked afraid. "Help me, what did I say? How did I break all Ten Commandments, and how'd I do it that fast?"

Baruch held up his right index finger. "Number one, 'I am the Lord thy God.' You can have only one God. God's number one. Jesus said to love God with all your heart, soul, mind, and strength. Where was your mind just now? Where was your heart?"

"Let's see. I was looking at that woman, then the guy, then the two of them and, oh no, my mind was in a dark place. A really, really dark place, so my heart was right there with it."

"Number two," Baruch continued, holding up two fingers. "Two gods is one god too many. 'Thou shalt have no other gods before me.' Talk about idols! Okay, I may struggle with food as an idol, putting food and gluttony before God at times, but you have the same problem with women, putting your lust for them before God."

"No, I don't! Do I? I don't think so. Maybe? I do think about women maybe *way* more than I should! Or not." Argus wore a face of denial.

"Number three," Baruch held up his three middle fingers, forming the shape of a W, "Words. Watch your words. 'Thou shalt not take the name of the Lord thy God in vain.' You didn't just use the Lord's name in an insulting manner; you used his whole family's names in vain!"

Argus was trying to remember. "What'd I say?"

"I'm not going to repeat it, but you mentioned the Father, the Son, his mother, his stepfather, and then the son again, and not in a nice context!"

"Oh my gosh. I didn't even realize it. I've been hanging out down by the docks way too much lately. All that salty language, oy." He was angry with himself.

Baruch held up four fingers and had his thumb tucked-down, moving it and making snore sounds as if it were sleeping or resting. "Number four: 'Remember the Sabbath; keep it holy.' It's a day for rest and set aside for the Lord. What's today?"

"Oh no! It's Sunday!" Argus tried to bargain. "But wait, Jesus was Jewish, and He celebrated the Sabbath on Saturday. Ha!"

"Are you Jewish, Argus?"

"I can be."

"But you're not, and let's be real, do you really keep any days holy and set aside for God and for rest?"

"I will, starting now."

"Commandment five," Baruch held up his right hand with all five fingers pointing upward like someone in a Roman court taking an oath, "'Honor thy father and thy mother.' Did your parents teach you better than to act that way?"

Convicted, Argus responded faintly and with genuine sadness, "Yes."

"Commandment six."

"Okay, how about we quit while I'm behind?"

"Commandment six," Baruch held up five fingers on one hand and one finger on the other, using the one finger as a sword to cut down the five fingers, "'Thou shalt not kill.' Okay, you didn't murder Kopanos, but what was in your heart, and what does Jesus say about this?"

"'I hate the jerk,' and Jesus says if I harbor hate in my heart, it's equivalent to murder. Okay, I get your point. I accept that I've fallen short and made poor choices and that I need to confess my sin, ask for forgiveness, and repent. You don't need to go any further."

183

"Sure, I do. We're going for the record here, breaking all Ten Commandments in one shot!" Argus was dejected and shook his head; his friend was on a mission and there was no stopping him. He'd gone through the stages of grieving his sin with shock, denial, anger, bargaining, depression, and finally acceptance. He became exhausted quickly.

"Commandment seven!" Baruch held up five fingers on one hand and two on the other. He laid flat the hand with five fingers and walked the two fingers on top of it while humming a wedding song, as if the two fingers were a man and woman taking wedding vows. "Or . . ." he said. Then he changed that motion of the two fingers to represent a woman walking seductively. "'Thou shalt not commit adultery.' She's married, and you're not. So she would be committing adultery, and you would be committing fornication, having sex outside marriage. But even more, Jesus said if you look with lust upon a woman, then you've committed adultery in your heart."

Argus did not say anything at this point; there was no arguing number seven. He stood solemnly, waiting for the exposition of his sins to end.

Holding four fingers up on each hand and looking through them as if behind bars in prison, Baruch went on, "Commandment eight, 'Thou shalt not steal.' You did in your heart and you even used the word steal—'I'd love to steal her away from him' were your exact words. Commandment nine." Baruch held five fingers on one hand and four on the other with the five whispering about the four. "'Thou shalt not bear false witness against thy neighbor.'"

Argus jumped back into the conversation. "Aha! I did not lie about anything. If anything, I was *too* truthful about everything. Ha!"

"You said the guy was a jerk."

"He is!"

"Well, I met the guy before, and I thought he was nice."

"Oh, come on, the guy walked by me and said aloud for all to hear, 'Hey, do you smell that? Pee-yew! Smells like the prison just walked in!' Then he looked at me and said, 'Oh, the pee *is* you.' That's not nice. He's a jerk."

"Well, I have had a different experience with him. So let's use the THINK test here. T: Is it True? Is what you say true or gossip? In this case, we have had different experiences with one man, so it could be gossip. H: Is it Helpful? Was sharing this information helpful to me?"

"It should be."

"No, it wasn't. I: Is it Inspiring? I don't feel inspired. N: Is it Necessary? No, it was not necessary, even if it was true in your experience. It wasn't necessary. K: And is it Kind? Even if it was true in your experience and he was not kind, were you being kind in return? No, it was not kind."

"If I practiced that kind of THINKing, then I'd probably have very little to say," Argus said annoyed.

"That's a grand idea!" Without giving Argus time to respond, Baruch held up all ten fingers. "Commandment ten." He turned his hands flat and started motioning his fingers as if to say, *Gimme, gimme, gimme.*

"'Thou shalt not covet thy neighbor's house; thy neighbor's wife; thy neighbor's belongings.' Greed and discontentment. Check!" He motioned, making a big checkmark in the air. "Yes, folks, we have a record. You broke all Ten Commandments in ten seconds. If the Ten Commandments are supposed to be a mirror reflecting the sin in our lives, you just shattered the mirror!" Baruch gestured with his hands to represent a mirror shattering. "Hence why we need a Savior."

Argus was completely frightened now. "Oh my gosh. I set a horrible record, and it was so easy. I must have a demon. I must be demon possessed." Baruch stepped even farther away from Argus as if he were a leper. Argus continued, "I have to go to church and find a priest and go to confession and get circumcised!"

"I think you mean exorcised."

"That too! I have to get to a church! Oh no, we burned all the churches down! I have to find a priest! Oh no, we killed or locked all the priests away. What am I going to do? I need to find a priest! Where can I find a priest?"

At this question, the prison full of priests listening in on this conversation shook their heads in disbelief, thinking: *Did he really just ask that?*

Baruch helped his partner. He pointed inside the doorway to the prison. Argus received the epiphany and his face lit up. He sprinted into the doorway to find the first priests he could, exclaiming, "Thank you, Lord!"

"Lord, help him." From that day forward, due to feeling bad for Argus and recognizing his own sin of gluttony, Baruch would share his mother's homemade honey cakes with Argus whenever he had some.

## Devotion

Father Absalom mentioned blooming where they are planted. The word *bloom* conjures up images of beauty, radiance, a glow, freshness, opening, and maturing. Can Father Absalom, Nicholas, Bishop Nicholas, and the others really bloom in a dark, dank prison? Have you ever been in a place you did not want to be, such as an unhappy workplace, family, school, class, etc.? Imagine radiating, glowing, and bringing freshness and beauty to whatever negative place you have imagined. We all have probably felt stuck in unhappy situations at some point in our lives, and we all would have liked to have had someone come and bloom in that situation to make it better.

**Questions to consider:** What if I am the one called to bloom where I am, where I'm planted? Can I do it? If not, why? What do I have to do in my life to bloom?

*"Do nothing out of selfishness or out of vain glory; rather, humbly regard others as more important than yourselves, each looking out not for his own interests, but also everyone for those interests of others."*
*Philippians 2:3-4*

*"Do to others as you would have them do to you." Luke 6:31*

*"He has shown you, O mortal, what is good. And what does the Lord require of you? To act justly and to love mercy and to walk humbly with your God."*
*Micah 6:8*

**Prayer:** "Heavenly Father, thank You for the times I have been around someone who blooms and who has made me feel good. I pray that You will help me bloom where I'm planted, in whatever situation I'm in. Thank You. Amen."

# 20
# 𝕸𝖎𝖐𝖗𝖔𝖘 𝕸𝖎𝖑𝖎𝖊𝖚

BELIEVERS OUTSIDE THE prison in Patara still tried to live life as normally as possible. They still held joyous occasions, such as that of the wedding of Noll and Glikia. They were married about a year after the clergy members went to prison, and it was a quieter celebration than those to which the Mikroses were accustomed. In the past, a big event such as a wedding could last for days, with music, dancing, eating, drinking, and making merry. In these days and times, it did not feel appropriate, and they did not want to bring any attention to themselves. Though they still had these special occasions, they were few, far between, and very low-key.

Overall, life in Patara had a more stifling atmosphere. Business went on as usual. It was a central port city with a lot of trade and commerce, but because the government had locked up the clergy who were a benefit to society—ministering to the poor and lifting up the spirits of people in general—poverty became worse than ever. The poor became easy targets and were used and abused. This led to many turning to crime themselves and adding to the troubles of society.

This was in addition to all the criminals who were released from prison to make room for the Christian clergy. They ran loose, causing the Roman army to double their troops in the region in an effort to minimize the rising crime and violence. At times, it was difficult to distinguish who was worse, the criminals or the Roman army. The soldiers would be overly aggressive and punitive in their daily interactions with all citizens in general.

These negative changes made the Mikroses take special precautions. Small in stature, peaceful, and passive, the Mikros family members were vulnerable. Some changes included going to town in teams of ten or more for safety, and they now placed their money in a secret compartment in their wagon to keep it safe. On occasion, intruders would steal from the Mikroses' barns, flocks, and homes while the families were working. Sadly, the Mikros clan suspected some of their neighbors were the intruders, or at least informants to criminals about their properties and schedules.

Their troubles at their homeland lessened as time went on because their area started to get a reputation for being dangerous to outsiders. City dwellers came to know the forest between Patara and the Mikros country-side lands as the "dark woods." When in town, Falon and Noll occasionally heard someone talking about the dark woods and asked their friends and business associates about the rumor. They were told stories of some city folk going to the Mikros area with bad intentions, and when traveling through the woods, invisible forces attacked them including being pelted with rocks, shot with darts, caught in booby traps, or followed by scary, unknown noises.

It was said that not everyone who had gone up there to pillage had returned or been heard from again. The Mikroses did not know how the rumors started, though some in the inner circle of their clan suspected Kari and Dax had something to do with it. If the twins did, they never said so. Regardless, the Mikroses were thankful.

Overall, this was an unfortunate situation for the Mikros clan because they were always a friendly and helpful people to all with whom they came into contact. These incidents caused them to become more suspicious and reclusive. The times had been slowly changing for the Mikroses for quite a while, even before the imprisonment of the clergy. Back in the days before commerce had caused the growth of the city over the last decade, the Mikros clan had been well known, well liked, and well respected across the region. That had lessened with the influx of new people; a lot of them knew each other from whence they had come and chose to do business with each other. Since the imprisonment of the clergy, the level of respect for one's fellow man, especially for the Mikros family, had declined at a rapid rate.

One day in the city, several weeks before what would be the fifth Christmas on which the clergy would be imprisoned, Noll and his team traveled to pick up different shipments from the docks. One of the most exotic spices in the world, saffron, was late to be delivered. Enormous numbers of flowers were required to produce a small quantity of the large, red stigmas used for the saffron spice. It came from an autumn-flowering crocus with reddish-purple flowers. This spice had many uses for the Mikroses, including medicinal ones, and some of the older Mikroses were in need of these cures.

The Mikros team bided its time with tasks and returned in the afternoon to see if the ship had arrived. It grew later and still no ship. As they were readying to leave, a dock watchman spotted the boat they were waiting for on the horizon. Noll made the executive decision to send the nine others off with the wagons to get home by dark, and he would wait for the ship to come in and get the box of stigmas. He had his horse, his black beauty named Vida, and the box would be small enough for him to carry while riding. He and Vida had completed this trip hundreds of times, so he could ride quickly to catch up to the wagons in order for them to all arrive home before dark.

The team hesitated, but they knew if anyone could make up for lost time and handle himself in a crisis, it would be Noll. The ship had trouble docking and unloading, dusk set in by the time Noll received the box and started riding home. Eyes watched him. The Mikroses, instead of blending in due to their small statures, stood out.

In the business world of Patara, the Mikros clan was seen as a threat, and it didn't help that they were Christians. Rumors spread that many of the earlier thefts, intrusions, and violations that had occurred on the Mikroses' lands were threats and intimidation tactics from other businesses. After "unknown forces" in the Mikros woods had curbed those incidences, the dislike for the family had grown even more. When they were off their land and in the city, they were subject to prejudice, persecution, and mockery. These easily recognizable little people drew a lot of stares and attention due to being Christians, but even more, due to who they were as business competitors.

Noll was barely out of town before a band of men along the road gave chase. Noll and Vida evaded them for a while and Vida fought a few off valiantly, however, there were too many and eventually Noll was knocked off his steed and subdued. It was a brutal attack, and Noll was left for dead.

Vida escaped and while making his way home he met the Mikros team who had already been home, dropped their goods off, and started doubling back to meet Noll. Seeing Vida without Noll confirmed their worst fear.

They found Noll quickly and tended to his wounds. He was unconscious, his breath was shallow, and he was bleeding in many places. They stopped the bleeding, secured his broken limbs, the obvious ones, and bathed him in prayer until they were able to place him on a wagon filled with hay to return home. No one thought Noll was going to live through the night, and there was no priest available to give last rites. Father Absalom was in prison, but there were many godly Mikros men capable of conducting the sacrament of last rites when needed. Regardless, all the Mikroses and their friendly neighbors prayed for Noll unceasingly. Glikia cried and prayed endlessly, never leaving Noll's side.

Two days later, Noll regained consciousness. He required intensive care and was not out of danger yet. He was awake, and that was a good sign and a good start to recovery.

Days later, Falon and the other Mikros leaders met, prayed, and came to the tough decision to relocate their society to a new area. They knew going south, east, and west were not options because all lands were overpopulated. This left only north as an option, and they voted unanimously to have Kari and Dax scout the area. Their skills with navigation and experiences with adventure had prepared them for the journey. They had been farther north than any other Mikros and were adept at traveling light, swift, and far, all the while being stealth and safe. The twins would leave at the end of winter when the north's cold season was ending and spring thaw was beginning.

Kari and Dax were excited about their newly assigned mission and planned for their big exploration. Kari started working with their horses, putting them on a training regimen to prepare them for the long journey. She also gathered Roman maps to plan their trek. Dax helped; however, he had some other things in mind as well.

One day, Falon discovered Dax doing something unexpected. As Falon was walking by the barn, he glanced in and saw Dax painting. He clearly saw the colors red and white, but the whole scene was not very clear to him, so he went in. Dax was sitting down with Nicholas' walking staff. He was painting red and white stripes up and around the shaft (yes, you guessed it, like a candy cane). The top part, the crook, was unfinished. Falon gave Dax a confused look. Dax paused his painting and gave Falon a confused look in return. Falon scratched his head. "What, may I ask, are you doing with, and to, Nicholas' walking staff?"

"Yes, you may ask. What I am doing *with* it is I want to use it. Nicholas won't need it any time soon; he's in prison, hello! And it's a fine walking stick that I can use on Kari's and my journey north. What I am doing *to* it is I'm painting it."

"And why are you painting it that way and with those colors?"

"We will be traveling far north, most likely being in snow, so the red will be easy to see and I won't lose it. In case I get lost or buried in an avalanche, it'll be easier to find me. And I chose this design because I think it is neat. It's an optical illusion. Look, when I turn it, it looks like the staff is moving up and it really isn't." Dax twirled the staff. It did look like it was moving up, yet was not. Falon was still confused about this project of Dax's. He started to say something, but then he realized Dax was in a trance watching his optical illusion and seemed to have forgotten that Falon was there. Falon determined it was not worth discussing any further. Experience told him he wouldn't get anywhere anyway, so he left Dax to his own little optical illusion world.

### Devotion

Noll was doing a good thing, waiting for the ship to get the spice needed to make medicine for the sick and elderly in his clan, but then something bad happened to him. Why do bad things happen to good people or to someone doing something good? Has this happened to you?

A simple answer is that we live in a fallen, imperfect world with imperfect people who have free will to do good or evil. Another simple answer, though unsatisfactory to some, is, "We don't know, but God does. He's God. We can ask, but it doesn't mean He will give us an answer. Or He won't give us the answer we're looking for." This is where trust comes in.

Dig into God's Word and find answers. There are many Christian books written on the subject, read one or more of those books. There are many wise Christian leaders to seek counsel. Ask, seek, knock. For any questions we have.

**Questions to consider:** Is understanding why bad things happen to everyone, including someone who I consider a good person, something I am struggling with? If it is, why don't I research the Christian answers? Am I willing to go to the Lord to ask? Am I willing to seek counsel from wise leaders? If I have any other questions or concerns, am I asking God?

*"But I say to you, love your enemies, and pray for those who persecute you, that you may be children of your heavenly Father, for he makes his sun rise on the bad and the good, and causes rain to fall on the just and the unjust."*
*Matthew 5:44-45*

*"And we know that in all things God works for the good of those who love him, who have been called according to his purpose."* Romans 8:28

*"Consider it all joy, my brothers, when you encounter various trials, for you know that the testing of your faith produces perseverance."* James 1:2-3

*"Blessed is the man who perseveres in temptation, for when he has been proved he will receive the crown of life that he promised to those who love him."* James 1:12

**Prayer:** "Heavenly Father, help me trust You no matter what happens to me in this world, good or bad, right or wrong. You are the same yesterday, today, and forever, and no matter how unpredictable this world may be, You are the Rock I stand on; You care for me in my time of need. Thank You. Amen."

# 21
# ⚙n the 𝕭rink

MORE THAN FIVE years had passed since Emperor Diocletian had thrown all the Christian clergy into jail for their Christian beliefs and burned all the churches. It was a dark time. Sadness was everywhere because the love, joy, and peace of the Lord had been suppressed from the land. It had been a while since any word had come from inside the prison. There had been no word from the clergy, nor any word from Nicholas via the window, as he had spent most of his time in the dungeon as of late. Greatly needed were their words of hope and encouragement, but silence and hopelessness had filled the land.

Inside the prison, years of starvation, thirst, and abuse had finally taken their toll on the prisoners. This included Nicholas, who had taken more than his fair share of punishment to deflect attention from older prisoners such as his uncle and Father Absalom. Their weakness had overtaken them. They had nothing left to give. They were at the stage of waiting to die, waiting for the Lord to come and carry them home into His glory. Considered lucky were the ones the Lord took.

Returned from solitary confinement after two months, Nicholas had nothing left. His spirit and flesh were both too weak to go on. He was ready for the Lord to bring him home. He was ready for his dot of life to end and for the line of his eternity to begin. Nicholas curled into the fetal position in the corner of his cell, farthest from the window, to try to keep warm. There was a severe chill in the air, so much so that his breath was visible. His clothes were tattered, barely hanging on to his emaciated body.

His once beautiful, red dress robe with white trim was now unrecognizable. He had not the strength to stand anymore, let alone sit up or eat.

It was Christmas Eve; the fifth Christmas Eve the clergy had spent in prison. Normally, the prisoners would be joyful, prayerful, and thankful in spite of their circumstances. Christmas was an event—God coming to earth as a babe. Christmas was a message—God desiring to renew a personal relationship with His creation again. And Christmas was a person—Jesus. That first Christmas, when Jesus was born, was not merry: The government was overbearing. Imposed taxes on the people caused financial burden. Traveling a long journey was inconvenient. Inhospitable people were unwilling to help Mary in a strange city, leaving her no choice but to give birth in a filthy barn with no comforts.

The original Christmas featured difficult circumstances, but Christmas was not about circumstances. It was about an event with a message and the person of Jesus. Here in prison, it could not be any bleaker. The lack of nourishment and water, the lack of exercise, and the excess of unsanitary conditions led to many deaths. The clergy were plagued with dysentery—severe diarrhea with blood, fever, and abdominal pains. The stench was unbearable. Feces, urine, vomit, blood, and the occasional rotting corpse imposed their rank odors into one's nostrils.

It was a dark night and heavy clouds blocked the light of the moon. It was Christmas Eve, but no one in the prison realized it. Throughout the city, no one sang; there were no jubilant festivities, no joyous activities, no merry well-wishes, no midnight Christ-Masses to attend. A cloud of darkness and sadness had filled the land. A haze of despair and hopelessness consumed Nicholas. He was dying.

Nicholas had hardly slept a wink in days, possibly weeks, but this evening, exhaustion took over his body. The darkness and stillness in the room were stifling. Death knocked at his door. He coughed three distinct coughs and then he fell into a deep, comatose state.

Nicholas appeared in a bright room. It was a room in God's house. There were no walls, no boundaries—only bright white everywhere the eyes could see. He wore a simple white linen robe from his shoulders to his ankles. His feet were bare. He was in the good health as before he went to prison.

"Nicholas," a man said.

Nicholas froze. "Yes, Lord." He could not see anyone, but he knew it was his Heavenly Father, God. He did not know what to do. Should he fall prostrate on his face in holy worship or run and jump into His arms for a loving embrace? Since he could not see Him, he automatically fell on his face.

"Do not be afraid."

"Yes, Lord."

"You have been a good and faithful servant."

"Thank you, Lord. I know I fall short of your glory, but I know Jesus' holy blood makes me new in Your eyes. Daily being in Your presence and surrendering to Your Holy Spirit leads me."

"There are some who say believing in me is a crutch. What say you?"

Nicholas overcame the fear of the Lord by feeling the peace of His presence. He lifted his face off the ground and stayed on his knees. "O Lord, You are way more than a crutch to me. For without You, I can do nothing. I could not even limp my way into Heaven; therefore, You are my stretcher that carries me through my days and nights."

Nicholas then laid on his back, legs straight down, and arms stretched out to his sides as if on a comfortable stretcher. A stretcher appeared under him, raising him off the ground. He felt light, carrying no burdens, no weight, no stress, and no pressure. He felt overwhelmingly free and weightless as he had never felt before.

"In the world, dependency on me is seen as immaturity. But in my Kingdom, dependency on Me is a prime measure of maturity. You have matured well my son."

"By your grace my Lord."

"My peace I give unto you. I give you endless rest."

"Thank You, my merciful Lord."

Nicholas basked in the glory of God and felt a refreshing sensation he had never felt before. The stretcher disappeared, and Nicholas found himself sitting next to Jesus.

Jesus looked into Nicholas' eyes. "Accept your weariness because I know your journey has been difficult, my son. I am sorry for your pain and loss. Know that your weakness and weariness draws me closer to you because it stirs my compassion and desire to help you. Allow my power to rest on you, for when you are weak, I am strong for you. I am always with you. I am all you need."

Realizing that Jesus knew his pain he had suffered, a wave of emotion overcame Nicholas, and he began to cry as if he were a little boy again.

Jesus hugged Nicholas and pulled him close; Nicholas wrapped his arms around Jesus' waist and rested his head on Jesus' chest, hearing the Lord's soothing heartbeat. Jesus held Nicholas and softly stroked his hair as Nicholas continued to shed tears of pain and joy. It felt as if Nicholas were a little child again in the loving arms of his mother or father, being comforted. As good as that was as a child, the comfort and joy Jesus brought him was amazingly more.

Jesus occasionally whispered, "I am Emmanuel. God with you, always." This brought Nicholas even more joy. He had no gauge of how much time had passed in this way, and he did not care. He was with Jesus Himself, who is not bound by the restraints of time. Nicholas could focus only on the present moment—not what had happened in the past or about what would happen going forward. He simply savored the present joy in his heart for as long as he possibly could.

Though he never wanted this time to end, Nicholas eventually felt prompted to ask a question before he became too accustomed to this euphoric state.

"Oh, my Master, may I ask You a question?"

"Yes, my son. You know as a child of mine you may ask me any question, anytime, anywhere."

"You mentioned giving me 'endless rest.' Have I died? Is this Heaven?"

"You have not died. This is only a taste of Heaven. Your time on earth is not up yet. I have more work for you to do. The calling I have for you will touch many generations to come."

"Yes, my Lord. Thank You for this moment."

Jesus put his hands on Nicholas' face and stared with eyes of warmth into Nicholas' own eyes. "You are welcome, my child. I love you so much." Jesus kissed Nicholas on the forehead and Nicholas closed his eyes. When he opened them, Jesus was gone and Nicholas was back on the stretcher. Though he was by himself once again, he still felt utterly free and weightless.

Then Nicholas heard the Lord's voice. "My son, are you rejuvenated?"

"Yes, I've never felt better, my Lord."

"Good. Are ready for your next steps with Me?"

"Yes."

"Tell me my greatest commandment."

"To love You with all my heart, mind, soul, and strength." Nicholas, with his right index finger, drew a vertical line in the air indicating a vertical relationship between himself on earth and the Lord in the Heavens. The sign he drew in the air resembled the number one—the greatest commandment.

"And Lord," he continued, filled with the Holy Spirit and feeling intoxicated with joy, "You also added to that, 'Love your neighbor as you love yourself.' So we are to love our neighbors, and we are to love ourselves as well, and we love ourselves by being in an intimate relationship with You. And when we're in a personal, intimate relationship with You, then it doesn't feel like a *command* to love You. Rather, it becomes a natural response to *want* to love You and be with You all the time because You are so amazing. And when we receive Your love, then it becomes a natural response to love others." Nicholas then made a horizontal line in the air, going from left to right, indicating the horizontal relationship we are to have with others while on earth.

"Good, Nicholas. Now, what do those signs make when you put them together?"

"Oh, Heavenly Father, it is Your holy cross!"

"Yes, Nicholas. The cross is a symbol of My gospel, My good news, that I want you and all believers to share with the world about my birth, life, death, and resurrection. My gospel is your gospel, the gospel of Nicholas. I want you to continue preaching the gospel of the cross and the forgiveness of sins and the freedom it brings, throughout all my creation, so that all who hear the good news will believe and become my children. If they believe, then they are my sons and daughters, joining my royal family. I want all to believe. Faith cometh by hearing, and hearing by the word of God. Spread my Word, Nicholas."

"Yes, Abba Father, Your will be done, not mine. I am Your obedient servant here to surrender to You, to Your will, and to Your Holy Spirit. It is my joy to preach Your gospel! Your Good News *is* my good news."

"Before I came into the world as a babe, there was separation between me and my creation. This separation broke my heart. I desired fellowship as I'd once had in the garden with Adam and Eve. To make fellowship possible again required an unblemished holy lamb, set apart, to be slain to cover people's sins and take away the punishment that sinful man deserves, which is death. The wages of sin are death."

The stretcher beneath Nicholas morphed into a giant, torturous cross, and his outstretched arms and legs now tied to the massive beams. Fear gripped Nicholas.

"Here is My reminder Nicholas. All people fall short of the glory of God. My nature is holy, so I can have only that, which is holy, in my presence in My Heaven. You are a fallen man living in a fallen world, and in a court of law, justice is served and you are sentenced to death."

At those words, giant spikes appeared above each of Nicholas' wrists and feet, and then a large hammer appeared above each of the spikes, ready to slam the spikes into the cross beams through Nicholas' flesh and bones. Nicholas' brow started sweating. He opened his eyes wide, glancing at the spikes, all the while trying to look straight up.

"You and all humans are in need of a Redeemer, someone to pay your fine, pay the price of your sins. You are in need of *the* Lamb of God to be slain for your sins and the sins of the whole world, so that we may have the intimate father-child relationship that I so cherish. For I so loved the world that I gave my one and only Son, that whosoever believeth in Him shall not perish but have eternal life. For I did not send my Son into the world to condemn the world, but to save the world through Him. Do you believe in me, Nicholas?"

Frightened, Nicholas tried to keep his focus on the Lord, nervously trying not to glance at the spikes ready to puncture his limbs. He cried out, "Yes, Lord. I believe! I believe in You! I believe You are one God, the Father almighty, maker of Heaven and earth, of all things visible and invisible. I believe You are the one Lord Jesus Christ, the only begotten son of God, born of the Father before all ages. God from God, Light from Light, true God from true God, begotten, not made, being one with the Father; through You all things are made. For us and for our salvation, You came down from Heaven, and by the power of the Holy Spirit, You were born of the Virgin Mary and became man. For our sake, You were crucified; You suffered, died, and were buried, and You rose again on the third day in accordance with the Scriptures. You ascended into Heaven and are seated at the right hand of the Father. You will come again in glory to judge the living and the dead, and Your Kingdom will have no end. I believe You are the one Holy Spirit, the Lord, the giver of life, who proceeds from the Father and the Son, who with the Father and the Son is adored and glorified and who has spoken through the prophets. I believe in one, holy, catholic and apostolic church. I confess one baptism for the forgiveness of sins, and I look forward to the resurrection of the dead and the life of the world to come. Oh, Lord, have mercy on my soul!"

A thunderous boom jolted Nicholas and a flash of lightning blinded him, he found himself standing at the side of the cross. Jesus, brutally bloodied and battered, was now nailed to the cross. The heavy spikes pierced His body into the hardened wood.

"I took this thorny crown stabbing my scalp because I hate sin that separates you from Me," Jesus said to him. "I was brutally beaten by fist after fist because I hate sin. I was cursed, mocked, and spat upon because I hate sin. I was whipped with leather and bone and metal tearing the flesh off my body because I hate sin. I was tortured and nailed to this cross because I hate sin. As the sacrificial Lamb of God, I bled my holy blood to death because I hate sin. I hate sin because sin separates you from Me. But, Nicholas, I love sinners, and I want to die on the cross for your sins, taking your punishment, making this cross the bridge allowing for you, and all who believe in Me, to be in relationship with Me again—a personal, intimate, loving, forgiving, redeeming relationship with Me forever. That's the good news of the cross I want you to share, Nicholas, along with my victorious resurrection."

"Yes, my Lord, great news indeed!"

"You believe, Nicholas. Therefore, this gift of eternal life is given to you, along with my dunamis resurrection power of the Holy Spirit to live a life of victory on this earth. Like with any gift, it has to be accepted; it has to be received, embraced. A transaction has to take place. The receiving transaction requires repentance and faith. Repentance, turning *away* from sin, but more importantly turning *to* Me. And faith, trusting and believing that I am who I say I am, your Savior, Lord, and Servant-King. I know you believe, Nicholas, therefore, salvation and my dunamis resurrection power of the Holy Spirit is yours."

The cross slowly lifted up from where it lay on the ground to standing straight up in the air, then suddenly it dropped a few feet into a hole in the ground with a thunderous slam, jolting Jesus' tortured and bound body abruptly, His face grimacing with shocking pain. Nicholas fell to his knees, overcome with emotion. He was distraught over the sight of his Lord and Savior bloodied and nailed to the cross for his sins, but he was humbled and indebted to his Savior for taking his place on the cross, paying his fine, taking his punishment. Nicholas knew that it should be him nailed to the cross—that it should be all of us nailed to that cross. Jesus was delivered over to death for our sins and was raised to life for our justification. Nicholas cried tears of joy, and praise flowed from his lips. "That should be me! Thank You Jesus, thank You Lord, praise You God! I repent, I turn to You, I trust in You! I believe, I believe . . ."

He knelt, hunched over, tears pouring down his face, rocking back and forth, overwhelmed by joy and relief, hailing, "I believe, Father, thank You Jesus, thank You Holy Spirit, I repent, I trust, I believe." Nicholas slowly became aware of his stark reality. He realized he was coming out of his vision and was back in prison in his emaciated, dying body. He didn't care. He *did not care*! He was filled with joy as if he had died and been brought back to life with new eyes and a fresh purpose. This time, his spirit was willing and his flesh did not have a choice. As Nicholas became more and more aware, he looked around his cell and saw Uncle Nicholas and Father Absalom huddled together with fear and trepidation in their eyes. They were unsure whether Nicholas had been filled with the Holy Ghost or if he had gone mad.

## Devotion

Nicholas was dying in prison, and he was ready to give up. He was done with his miserable circumstances and couldn't take it anymore. He was ready to check out for good. Being human, we've all been there. Sometimes our circumstances are unbearable. Even tragic and horrific.

On that first Christmas, there were tough circumstances for Joseph and a pregnant Mary. They were forced by the government to travel on hot, dusty roads for miles and miles and days and days. They had to pay major taxes and travel expenses to return to Joseph's place of birth only to arrive and have no grace extended to them and be forced to sleep in a dirty, smelly barn with filthy animals all around.

Today in the western world births happen in clean, sterile hospitals, but it wasn't so on that night long ago. After being dirty, sweaty, and smelly with tangled hair and no make-up, giving messy, painful birth in a barn,

Mary had to place her baby, who, oh yeah, is the prophesied Son of God, in a manger—an animal's stinky, saliva-tainted, empty water trough. Then in her condition, she had to entertain numerous unexpected and unknown visitors, an army of sheepherders. Do you think that's how Mary planned the birth of the Son of God? Talk about a bad day.

The original Christmas featured difficult circumstances, but in spite of those circumstances, the reality is that it was actually a glorious day! The first Christmas was not about circumstances. It was an event, with a message, and the person of Jesus.

**Questions to consider:** When I am in horrible circumstances, am I focused on my horrible circumstances and ready to give up, or am I focused on historical events, God's Word, and the presence of my Heavenly Father, Jesus, and the Holy Spirit providing comfort, guidance, and reminders of their goodness?

*"Do not fear: I am with you; do not be anxious: I am your God. I will strengthen you, I will help you, I will uphold you with my victorious right hand."*
*Isaiah 41:10*

*"For thus said the Lord God, the Holy One of Israel: By waiting and by calm you shall be saved, in quiet and in trust shall be your strength." Isaiah 30:15*

*"The Lord is at hand. Do not worry about anything, but in everything by prayer and supplication with thanksgiving let your requests be made known to God. And the peace of God, which surpasses all understanding, will guard your hearts and your minds in Christ Jesus." Philippians 4:6*

**Prayer:** "Heavenly Father, thank You for the gift of baby Jesus given in tough circumstances. This reminds me that my focus should not be on my circumstances, but on You, who is journeying with me in my circumstances. I'm not alone and there is always hope in You. Thank You! Amen."

# 22
# Unseen Battle

NICHOLAS GRINNED FROM ear to ear, "Ho, ho, hooo!" And then, just as quickly, a serious look spread across his face: he was a man given a revelation and a serious mission from God. With his change of emotion, like a flip of a switch, he had the makings of a madman. This holy man was only mad for God. He wiped the tears from his face with the tatters of a sleeve. The moon broke through the clouds and shone into the cell. Nicholas stared into the moonlight, his eyes twinkling.

He spoke to God aloud in words from Psalm 7: "In You, Lord, I have taken refuge; let me never be put to shame. For You are my rock and my fortress. Deliver me, my God, from the hand of the wicked, from the grasp of those who are evil and cruel. For You have been my hope, sovereign Lord, my confidence since my youth. You are my strong refuge. My mouth is filled with Your praise, declaring Your splendor all day long. For my enemies speak against me; those who wait to kill me conspire together. They say, 'God has forsaken him; pursue him and seize him, for no one will rescue him.' As for me, I will always have hope; I will praise You more and more. My mouth will tell of Your righteous deeds, of Your saving acts all day long. Since my youth, God, You have taught me, and to this day I declare Your marvelous deeds. Even when I am old and gray, do not forsake me, my God, till I declare Your power to the next generations, Your mighty acts to all who are to come."

Nicholas summoned the energy to stand and leaned forward to gain momentum toward the window. Bishop Nicholas and Father Absalom had seen that look on Nicholas' face before, and they started moving toward the window on all fours, readying themselves to be stepping-stones to the outside world. Nicholas continued without missing a beat; he grew louder as he got closer.

"Your righteousness, God, reaches to the Heavens. You who have done great things. Who is like you, God? Though You have made me see troubles, many and bitter, You will restore my life again. From the depths of the earth, You will again bring me up."

He stepped onto his brethren's backs and grabbed hold of the bars, pushing his face out the window. The last line became a loud crescendo for the entire kingdom to hear with his deep, booming voice: "You will increase my honor and comfort me once more. My lips will shout for joy when I sing praise to You—I whom You have delivered. My tongue will tell of Your righteous acts all day long, for those who wanted to harm me have been put to shame and confusion."

He immediately burst into song on this hallowed Christmas Eve. The rumor had spread that Nicholas had died, and many were starting to believe the rumor to be true, until now. This was the first the kingdom had heard from Nicholas in more than one-third of a year.

*"Hark! The herald angels sing, 'Glory to the new born King! Peace on earth, and mercy mild, God and sinners reconciled.'"*

Across the city in a large bedroom on the top floor of a palace—an equivalent height to the prison cell in which Nicholas lived—lay Emperor Diocletian and his wife, Prisca, in their plush royal bed. Diocletian lay on his side facing the window, as he drifted to sleep, he started to hear a noise in the distance. His mind awakened and focused. It dawned on him what he was hearing—singing. Then with a groan, he realized who was singing across the kingdom for all to hear: Nicholas. "Uuuugh. I hate that man," he mumbled loud enough for Prisca to hear. Diocletian unexpectedly coughed three distinct, sickly coughs. Prisca lay facing the opposite way, away from the window, but she heard the singing as well. If Diocletian could see her, he would see his wife's face glowing with a bright, wide grin as she listened to Nicholas sing.

*"Joyful, all ye nations rise, Join the triumph of the skies; With th' angelic host proclaim, 'Christ is born in Bethlehem!' Hark! the herald angels sing, 'Glory to the newborn King!'"*

In an adorned room down the hall from the royal couple was their daughter, Valeria. She rested in bed underneath the covers. By candlelight, she read from the scroll of Matthew. Her husband, Galerius, was off in a foreign land leading an army into battle; he would not approve, but he was not here. She read, "An angel of the Lord appeared to Joseph in a dream saying, 'Joseph, son of David, do not be afraid to take Mary as your wife; for the Child who has been conceived in her is of the Holy Spirit; She will bear a son, and you shall call his name Jesus, for he shall save his people from their sins.'" When hearing the sounds coming from her window, she recognized Nicholas' voice. A smile came to her face and an "Amen" to her lips.

*"Christ, by highest Heav'n adored; Christ the everlasting Lord; Late in time, behold Him come, Offspring of a virgin's womb. Veiled in flesh the Godhead see; Hail th' incarnate Deity, Pleased with us in flesh to dwell, Jesus our Emmanuel. Hark! the herald angels sing, 'Glory to the newborn King!'"*

In the Thalassa Pub near the docks, Captain Omar, Aindriú, Lukas, Marcus, Mathias, Pietro, Pol and Yahya sat at a table, silent, sullen, and staring into their drinks. Yahya was the first to hear something come from the open doorway. He noticed several people outside the door gathered together and looking upward. He slowly rose and walked to the door. The others noticed that he looked as if he were high up on a ship's mast, looking and listening through the fog with his keen senses, searching for something important. Intrigued, they followed him outside. They immediately knew exactly what was happening. Sweet relief overcame them all, and they expressed it with hugs and pats on each other's backs.

Lukas whispered, "Well, Merry Christ-Mass."

Aindriú, in his Irish accent, replied, "Yes, Merry Christmas."

Lukas tried to correct him. "Merry Christ-Mass."

"That's what I said," Aindriú emphasized, "Merry Christmas."

Lukas went with it. "Merry Christmas!" They laughed and embraced. "And a Mighty Christmas to all."

*"Hail the heav'nly Prince of Peace! Hail the Sun of Righteousness! Light and life to all He brings, Ris'n with healing in His wings. Mild He lays His glory by, Born that man no more may die; Born to raise the sons of earth, Born to give them second birth. Hark! the herald angels sing, 'Glory to the newborn King!'"*

In another part of town, Wren darned a stocking by the fireplace. She heard the singing and quickly recognized the voice. She grinned and sighed, "Thank You, sweet Jesus. Oh, thank You, God." While pausing from her task, an idea came to mind. She sprang from her chair with a purpose. She hurried across the room, opened a big trunk and started sifting through different fabrics until she found the one she wanted. She threw it across a nearby table and started to take measurements. The stocking would have to wait. She had a new task in mind, a joy-filled task!

*"Come, Desire of nations, come, Fix in us Thy humble home; Rise, the woman's conqu'ring Seed, Bruise in us the serpent's head. Now display Thy saving pow'r, Ruined nature now restore; Now in mystic union join Thine to ours, and ours to Thine. Hark! the herald angels sing, 'Glory to the newborn King!'"*

Outside the city limits in the countryside stood a beautifully built two-story home on a hill with a city view above the trees. Kari and Dax sat on the roof. Where else would these two be, late at night, on Christmas Eve? Kari played a hymn on a lyre and Dax sat next to her, carving a little wooden sleigh. Kari heard something in the far-off distance and stopped playing, she cupped one hand behind her ear to catch the sound. Dax sat up to listen. As the sound became clearer, they looked at each other and excitedly kicked and karate-chopped the air as if fighting invisible forces.

On the floor below, Glikia helped Noll get into his nightgown and sleeping cap because his body was too battered, bruised, and broken to do so alone. They stood at the window staring at the city toward where they heard his best friend singing. Glikia held Noll from behind with her arms wrapped around his waist and her chin resting on his shoulder. With his hands on top of hers, with smiles of relief on their faces, and tears of joy welled up in their eyes, they listened to the sweet voice resounding.

Down on the first floor, Falon and Tana cuddled in a big chair next to the fire, enjoying Kari's playing from above. When she stopped, they tuned in to the joyful song from the city prison and held hands, joyous, with faces raised toward heaven. They glorified God in a heavenly tongue.

Though there were sad times in the land, it was still a holy night. Christians still remembered the reason for the season, in spite of feeling the melancholy. In that moment, there was still peace and joy for those who believed. However, in the spirit world, in that region, the struggle was not against flesh and blood, but against the rulers, authorities, and powers of this dark world and the spiritual forces of evil in the heavenly realms. An unseen battle was raging and the momentum was shifting for the glory of God.

*"Adam's likeness, Lord, efface, Stamp Thine image in its place: Second Adam from above, Reinstate us in Thy love. Let us Thee, though lost, regain, Thee, the Life, the inner man: Oh, to all Thyself impart, Formed in each believing heart. Hark! the herald angels sing, 'Glory to the newborn King!'"*

Normally, by this time, Sandor would have heard Nicholas and sprinted up to his cell with the angry giant pummeling Nicholas as much as he could get away with. He would beat him to the brink of death, and then drag him to the dungeon to lock him away. But this time was different from the others. Instead of having the energy and enraged resolve he usually had, Sandor quietly arrived at Nicholas' floor, his face holding no emotion; he seemed drained. Why? Maybe he was tired of repeating this same scenario over and over again, and it had lost its luster. Maybe the perverse joy he received from hurting this little man of God had waned. Maybe he was just tired.

Nicholas' human step-stools, Bishop Nicholas and Father Absalom, grew wide-eyed with fear for their beloved Nicholas when they saw the giant standing at their cell door. Nicholas, now finished with his song, released the bars and stepped off their backs. Due to weakness, he stumbled, and with his legs too frail to hold him any longer, he fell to his knees.

Argus and Baruch arrived to the scene. They grimaced, waiting for the bloodbath to begin. They wondered if they would be brave enough to step in this time and stop Sandor before he killed Nicholas. Surely, this was the last straw and Nicholas was doomed.

Sandor unlocked the door and slowly swung it open, making a long, eerie creak. All the men in all the cells watched with fear in their eyes. Sandor did not step inside the cell this time; rather, he stood in the entryway and uttered the word, "Come." He had no expression on his face or in his tone. Sandor seemed numb.

Nicholas, exhausted from his brief Holy Spirit-filled moment of strength, attempted to stand, but his emaciated body gave way, and he fell flat on his stomach. His face hit the cold slab floor. Sandor slowly walked over and loomed over Nicholas. Baruch summoned enough bravery to step toward Sandor and stop him from swinging one massive blow with his rock-like fist to Nicholas' head, crushing his skull and ending his life.

But Argus stopped Baruch and they watched.

Sandor slowly bent over, and with his giant right hand, grabbed a fistful of Nicholas' filthy, torn clothes and lifted him up like a ragdoll. He cradled the little man of God in his arms. He walked out the cell door, closed it, and locked it. He walked past Argus and Baruch, headed down the hallway, and descended the stairs toward the dungeon.

Argus and Baruch looked at each other, confused. They looked at Bishop Nicholas and Father Absalom, who had bewilderment on their faces. They all thought, for sure, just like every other time, Sandor would give Nicholas a beating to the brink of death. This time, though, they expected there would not be a brink, but only death. Bishop Nicholas motioned for these two faith-filled guards to follow. They turned and placed a safe distance between them and Sandor— close enough to see what happened, but not close enough to be discovered.

In the dungeon, all the rooms were empty. Nicholas was the only customer. Sandor walked past a couple rooms and turned into a dark, dank, musty cell. He gently lay Nicholas on his back, all skin and bones. Nicholas managed to roll onto his side, too exhausted to lift his head. As Sandor stepped outside and locked the door, God gave Nicholas a revelation into this giant warrior's wounded soul.

Nicholas whispered, "The plague."

The big man, sure of what he had heard, questioned nonetheless. Tiredly, he asked, "What?"

Nicholas, louder but hoarse, repeated, "The plague. I lost my parents when I was young to the plague."

Sandor was unspeaking. A painful, repressed memory returned to him. Images of his wife and children, lost to the plague, came to the forefront of his thoughts.

"Anger and bitterness take captive those who harbor them. They are the result of unforgiveness, including unforgiveness toward God. Unforgiveness is like drinking poison, waiting for the other person to die. It is futile."

"Why do you speak this to me?"

"I am captive from the outside, but am free on the inside. You are free from the outside, but you are captive on the inside. Jesus came to set us free. I want to see you freed. A poison is killing you. Forgive."

"It is not in me to forgive. I will die of poisoning."

"Would you be willing to, maybe, someday, sometime, forgive?"

"Maybe. But if I were to be willing, I do not know how. I am too far gone. I've done too much evil to go back."

"It's never too late. There's nothing you've done that Jesus' blood cannot cover. Nothing. I can help."

"No. I cannot talk to you in here. All of you who preach and teach of this cure for poisoning are locked away, or dead."

"We're not all locked up. I know someone you can talk to." Nicholas let out a soft, "Ho, ho, hooo."

And with the last bit of energy he had for the night, he whispered something that only Sandor could hear.

## Devotion

In the Roman Empire, including Patara, was an unseen spiritual battle being waged. The battle was for the citizens' unseen souls—their minds, wills, and emotions. And within each person was a battle with pain and struggles and unseen fleshly desires. There is always more going on in this world than meets the eye, just as there is always more going on within an individual than meets the eye. We are called to recognize pain in our own lives and pain in others to allow the Great Physician to heal us, and others.

**Questions to consider:** How well am I doing at taking control of my worldly, stinking thinking, capturing my thoughts of hurt, pain, anger, bitterness, unforgivingness, etc.? And how well am I doing at giving them to God, and allowing Him to renew my mind and wash my brain, so that I will embrace His holy thoughts and walk in victory?

*"Finally, brothers, whatever is true, whatever is honorable, whatever is just, whatever is pure, whatever is lovely, whatever is gracious, if there is any excellence and if there is anything worthy of praise, think about these things. Keep on doing what you have learned and received and heard and seen in me. Then the God of peace will be with you." Philippians 4:8-9*

*"I urge you therefore, brothers, by the mercies of God, to offer your bodies as a living sacrifice, holy and pleasing to God, your spiritual worship. Do not conform yourselves to this age but be transformed by the renewal of your mind, that you may discern what is the will of God, what is good and pleasing and perfect." Romans 12:1-2*

**Prayer:** "Heavenly Father, thank You for fighting for my soul. You want to win my mind, will, and emotions for eternity. Forgive me, because I know there are many times that I don't help You with that battle. Instead of pursuing You and Your love, I'm out pursuing worldly, ungodly, unholy things and hurting my soul with unhealthy behaviors and thoughts through my senses with ungodly things that I choose to watch, hear, ingest, smell, touch, and do. Help me to no longer conform to the patterns of this world, but be transformed by the renewing of my mind in You. In this culture, *brainwashing* has a negative connotation because evil has used it to hurt people. But Lord, I need You to wash my brain clean of all the hurt, pain, filth, and negativity that I have been subjected to, or subjected myself to, in my life. Wash my brain, Lord, of all the filth and replace it with true, noble, just, pure, lovely, admirable, virtuous, and praiseworthy thoughts centered on Your Truth. Thank You. Amen."

# 23
# New Beginnings

IT WAS CHRISTMAS DAY, and all across Patara there was a buzz in the air that had not been around for years. Nicholas was alive and had sung praises to the Lord from his prison cell window! The hope-filled energy caught fire and spread fast. This event was a reminder that pain did not mean God had turned His back on us; pain is a sign that we live in a broken world, but we are never alone. *"Behold, the virgin shall be with child and bear a son, and they shall name him Emmanuel, which means 'God is with us.'"* Humankind was not formed to live this life alone, but rather we were created for dependency upon God. The person in pain and the person not in pain are the same. They are both dependent on God; it is just that one is more aware of it than the other.

At the docks, Captain Omar, Pol, Aindriú, and the others excitedly told those who were arriving to Patara what they had witnessed the prior evening and what the birth of Jesus meant to them.

The farmers, ranchers, shepherds, and workers from Nicholas' hometown in the countryside all rejoiced at the news of Nicholas being alive. Amara and her family organized a Christ Mass of their own for all in the area since they were much safer to do so, distanced from Roman rule outside the city.

Nicholas' congregation in Patara, who had gone underground due to persecution, met in peoples' homes and celebrated private Christ Masses

211

throughout the city. Quiet rejoicing was abundant; a celebration of Jesus' birth had not been so sweet in years.

The Mikros clan had a quiet Christ Mass celebration that morn. That afternoon, Falon, Kari, and Dax weeded the field and turned the soil. Noll sat nearby getting some fresh air and sun as he recovered. Working hard near the side of the road, they did not notice a giant figure on a gigantic horse approaching them. Falon shuddered when a shadow enveloped him and he looked up and saw whom it was. His reaction immediately caught Noll, Kari, and Dax's attention. When they looked up to see this fierce threat in front of them, Kari and Dax went into fight mode and stepped in front of Falon. Kari held a machete and Dax held a pickax. Noll did his best to stand up, holding a sickle. Sandor wore a blank look on his face. He looked down upon the four unsettled, but brave Mikroses, and inquired in a flat tone, "I'm looking for Falon of the Mikros clan."

Falon responded, "'Tis I." He bravely stepped forward to be in line with his three children.

Sandor dismounted his monstrous horse and stood on the side of the road, towering over the guarded foursome in front of him. Noll, Kari, and Dax huddled closer to Falon and raised farm tools, ready for a fight to protect their father.

Sandor's face filled with emotion, and his demeanor softened. He looked sad, lost, and a bit frightened, which was difficult to believe possible for this mountain of a man. He was a warrior champion of the people, a battle-born veteran fighter, the Roman Empire's executioner, and a sadistic torturer of Christians and anyone he legally could torment. Nevertheless, in his vulnerable state, he trembled.

"Nicholas has sent me."

Falon recognized the situation for what it was and saw a broken man before him. He reached out to Kari and Dax's weapons and lightly pushed them down. Noll saw and followed suit, letting down his guard. Dax and Kari complied hesitantly. Falon gave Sandor a friendly smile and gently invited him. "Come, my son. Come inside."


A short time later, Sandor sat in Falon and Tana's home, his head bowed, with tears dripping off his chin onto his lap. Falon, Noll, Dax, and John laid their hands on Sandor and prayed with him and over him for salvation, deliverance, and inner healing. He was bigger than the four of them combined. Tana, Kari, Glikia, and Leila stood in the background, praying over all the men with hands lifted high, praising God: "Glory, Lord, glory!"

Over the next few months, time passed quickly with much happening everywhere. Kari and Dax traveled to explore the far North Country for a new homeland for the Mikros clan. The clan felt the Lord leading them to start over in a new land. And Wren continued to sew and work on her clothing project that she had begun on Christmas Eve.

Sandor met occasionally with Empress Prisca, receiving advisement on matters of the prison. Valeria would sit in on these discussions. Around this same time, Nicholas, Bishop Nicholas, Father Absalom, and all prisoners started receiving larger rations of bread and water, giving them a bit more nourishment.

Sandor was still present at the prison, but he traveled more frequently out of town. Now things at the prison were a bit different. Instead of Sandor watching Argus and Baruch's every move and striking fear in the hearts of all the guards as well as all the prisoners, Sandor became more hands-on when he was there. They worked to make prison less miserable. It was not sterile—that would take emptying the prison out and doing a serious overhaul—but the living conditions were better suited for human inhabitants.

Sandor sometimes even helped Argus and Baruch with food and water distribution. They had quiet, friendly conversations all together. Argus and Baruch taught Sandor the Ten Commandments with the hand signs. Baruch even shared his mother's honey cakes with the big man.


Kari and Dax traveled far north, days beyond when they had last seen people. As Dax had predicted, it was cold and snow was on the ground, but signs of spring thaw were evident. One day, while scouting the area, the twins met a clan they had never seen before. They were a small nation of family-oriented people like the Mikroses. They lived off the land and cared for it greatly. Though Kari, Dax, and their new friends spoke two different languages, they were kindred in spirit and peacefulness.

When meeting the clan's chief, Amuruq, Dax, out of curiosity, drew a big, half circle in the snow with the bottom of Nicholas' now, red-and-white-striped staff. Amuruq looked at Dax, then at Kari, then at the half circle. He stepped forward and put his hand out for Dax's staff. Dax handed it to Amuruq, he looked the staff up and down and gave Dax a nod of approval.

Dax looked at Kari with a smug face, Kari rolled her eyes. Amuruq used the tip of the staff and drew a half circle, connecting one end of it and completing the snow design to look like a fish, the secret symbol called the Ichthus that Christians use to identify each other. It meant, "Jesus Christ, Son of God, and Savior." Upon finishing the drawing, they discovered they were Christian family and rejoiced together.

The Mikroses became good friends with Amuruq and his clan, who took Kari and Dax in as their own. Bringing the twins into their village, they had a festive feast, exchanged gifts, and made a pact with one another. Kari and Dax spent time learning the ways of their new friends and how to live off the land by ice fishing, building igloos, and making warm clothing that they had never seen before. Kari and Dax felt their Mikros leaders would approve of this location—the place they had been seeking.

Emperor Diocletian's Christmas Eve coughs were the beginning of a chronic illness and his health continued to deteriorate. Seen less and less by the public, Diocletian kept within his palace at all times. At one point, it was reported Diocletian had died. Rumors alleged that Diocletian's death was being kept a secret until his daughter's husband, Galerius, could come to assume power. The city was sent into mourning from which it was only reclaimed by official public declarations of his survival. When Diocletian reappeared in public on March 1, he was emaciated and barely recognizable. Galerius arrived in the city later in March with plans to force Diocletian to step down and fill the imperial office with men who were submissive to his will. Through coercion and threats, he eventually convinced Diocletian to comply with his plan. Galerius had done the same to Co-Emperor Maximian.

On the first day of May, Diocletian called an assembly of his generals, troops, and representatives from distant legions. They met at the same hill where Diocletian had been proclaimed emperor. With tears in his eyes in front of a statue of Jupiter, his patron deity, Diocletian addressed the crowd. He told them of his weakness, his need for rest, and his will to resign. He declared he needed to pass the duty of emperor to someone stronger, Galerius. Diocletian thus became the first Roman emperor to abdicate voluntarily his title. He retired to his homeland, Dalmatia, on the shores of the Adriatic Sea. Prisca stayed with her daughter, by then called

Galeria Valeria, and her son-in-law, the new Roman emperor, Galerius, in Thessalonica.

Diocletian's edicts were ultimately unsuccessful. Non-Christians, called pagans, were generally sympathetic to the persecuted Christians because they realized that the Christians' basic tenets of loving their God, loving others, and making a positive difference in their society were a good thing and that, as a whole, they were good people and not a threat. The persecution was no longer popular with the general Roman population. Overall, the martyrs' sufferings strengthened the resolve of their fellow Christians. Though Galerius did not officially discontinue Diocletian's edicts against Christians until before his death years later, he did recognize the edicts' ineffectiveness and proclaimed the release of all Christians across the empire.

It was in August, three months after Diocletian stepped down, when it was finally clear that Diocletian would not be returning. It was then that the Christian prisoners began to gain freedom. That day in Patara, when the clergymen filed out of the prison for the first time in almost six years, there was celebration in the streets. Sandor had left Patara on official business; however, Argus, Baruch, and all the guards stood by the doorway as they discharged their many prisoners. Many Christian brothers, sisters, and families stood outside in the courtyard, waiting to take their loved ones home and take care of them.

The mistreatment of the prisoners was well-documented and well-known by citizens, but this would be the first time the public would see for themselves the damage done to these unfortunate and innocent prisoners. Even though conditions had somewhat improved over the last months of their captivity, the years of abuse was still evident on their malnourished and gaunt bodies. The prisoners staggered feebly out the door and into the courtyard. Though this was a happy day, it was still painful to see this previously life-filled, healthy group of men come out weak and unrecognizable. They were filthy, smelly, moving skeletons. What was left of their clothes hung by threads onto their wasted frames. In spite of all this, there were many cheers of "Thank you, God!" "Glory to you, Lord!" "All praise and honor to you, Abba Father!"

Once they had found the clergy members they were looking for, friends and families' joyful greetings quickly turned to caretaking measures. They covered the newly freed prisoners with blankets and gently escorted them to wagons that would carry them home to receive aid and begin the recovery process. Falon, Tana, Noll, Glikia, Kari, Dax, John, and Leila were there for Nicholas. Amara, her husband, and her family members were there for Father Absalom. Many of Bishop Nicholas' parishioners from the city were there to care for him. There was concern that Roman authorities might change their minds about releasing the prisoners, so everyone left as quickly as possible.

In a matter of minutes, the guards were the only ones left standing in the courtyard. Without Sandor there to give them orders, they were a bit lost and uncomfortable standing around not knowing what to do next. Argus and Baruch eventually took charge and had them file back into the prison.

### Devotion

The dark season of imprisonment was long, almost six years, but Nicholas, his uncle, Father Absalom, and many others persevered and were blessed to survive. The ones that did not survive were blessed to go Home. Just as the weather has different seasons, so does life, and this was one long season everyone was glad to see end.

Are you in a rough season now? There is a saying that either you're just coming out of a rough season, or you're in the thick of a rough season, or, if you're not in a rough season now, it's only a matter of time before you will be.

**Questions to consider:** If I am in a rough season now, how am I handling it? If I am in a good season right now, am I being thankful, and am I establishing good habits with the Lord while times are good, to help me persevere and bloom when times are rough?

*"The Advocate, the holy Spirit that the Father will send in my name—he will teach you everything and remind you of all that I told you. Peace I leave with you; my peace I give to you. Not as the world gives do I give it to you. Do not let your hearts be troubled or afraid." John 14:26-27*

*"Trust in the Lord with all your heart, on your own intelligence do not rely;*
*In all your ways be mindful of him, and he will make straight your paths."*
*Proverbs 3:5-6*

*"… but he said to me, 'My grace is sufficient for you, for power is made*
*perfect in weakness.' I will rather boast most gladly of my weaknesses, in order*
*that the power of Christ may dwell with me. Therefore, I am content with*
*weaknesses, insults, hardships, persecutions, and constraints, for the sake of*
*Christ; for when I am weak, then I am strong." 2 Corinthians 12:9-10*

*"Rejoice in the Lord always. I shall say it again: rejoice! Your kindness should*
*be known to all. The Lord is near. Have no anxiety at all, but in everything,*
*by prayer and petition, with thanksgiving, make your requests known to God.*
*Then the peace of God that surpasses all understanding will guard your hearts*
*and minds in Christ Jesus." Philippians 4:4-7*

**Prayer:** "Heavenly Father, I thank You for the good times. And contrary to worldly thinking, I also thank You for the difficult times, so that You may do a wondrous work in me. Help me in good times and bad times establish good habits in You, loving myself by practicing daily being in Your presence, loving You, loving others, and being joyful, prayerful, and thankful in all circumstances to persevere and bloom. Help me experience Your perfect love that casts out all fear. Thank You. Amen."

# 24
# Let the Healing Begin

IT WAS A quiet ride home for Nicholas while he lay in the hay of Noll's wagon, looking up at all his dear friends' faces. It was like a dream, a glorious daydream! He rotated, seeing first a friendly face and then the blue sky, and then he closed his eyes, enjoying the warmth of the sun on his face. He repeated this cycle over and over again. Everyone basked in the moment without speaking. Tana did not waste any time. She brought a bowl of her special chicken-vegetable-herb broth, and during the ride, she helped Nicholas take occasional sips to begin nourishing him. "This will help your body heal and put some meat on your bones, my son. We'll get you fattened back up in no time." He could hear her speak, but everything was still a bit foggy to him.

Though no one said so aloud, everyone thought Nicholas looked woeful. He was pitiful. The strong, jolly, energetic, enthusiastic man they had always known to be so full of life, now looked like the living dead. His once-rosy cheeks were now pallid with protruding bones. His once-nicely groomed beard and hair were now a scraggly bird's nest. His once-straight nose was now crooked. A layer of prison filth coated his skin. What was left of his clothes, which at one time had been so distinctive, were now unrecognizable. He stank of urine, feces, and other unidentifiable rank. His long fingernails and toenails were chipped and broken. He was a miserable sight, and everyone's heart broke for him.

Nicholas had no words to describe the joy in his heart. He could only grin sweetly and peacefully with the knowledge that he was going to be all right. As Jesus was born and called Immanuel, God is with us; God had been with Nicholas in prison, and God was with him now. Nicholas was at peace with the world. He fell asleep into a mini-hibernation. Later, he would not remember arriving at the Mikroses' home, nor that they bathed him in warm, soapy water and groomed his hair, beard, and nails; nor that they fed him and hydrated him.

It was as if he had not slept in years and was making up for lost time. Thanks to the Mikroses' special herbs and remedies, Nicholas' body went into a coma-like, deep, peaceful rest to maximize its healing process. It didn't hurt, either, that he slept on a comfortable feather bed, which felt as if he were floating on a cloud in the heavens above, and no longer on the bare, cold, hard, rock prison floor. It was four days before he was fully conscious again and had his wits about him.

Though his full recovery would still be a long road, with the help of special herbs and remedies, when he became coherent again Nicholas felt one hundred percent better than he had just days before. As he tuned in to his surroundings he noticed he was in a living room next to the fireplace. He could breathe clearly and actually smelled the flowers on the table near him. What a sweet, sweet scent! Nothing had smelled so sweetly in years.

He was clean, groomed, and wearing a soft, fresh white robe.

For the first time in years, his skin did not hurt. He noticed special ointment rubbed into his wounds and scars, and all over his body, rejuvenating him. He still had aches and pains in his joints and muscles, but he felt them much less now, and some of that pain and stiffness had to do more with lying still for days. Once he moved, warming his muscles up a bit, that would help. Overall, he had not felt nearly this good since that fateful day of his arrest many years before. That day seemed like another lifetime ago.

Tana and Glikia were working in the kitchen when Tana glanced over and saw Nicholas awake. Excitedly, she sent Glikia to tell everyone Nicholas was up. She moved toward him and gave him a kiss on his forehead, saying, "My boy, welcome home! It's so good to see you!"

Nicholas beamed, "Thank you, Tana. You are an angel from heaven come to my side. Thank you for your love."

Tana helped Nicholas into a seated position and went back to cooking as all the others trickled in to see him. It was a joyous reunion with lots of chattering as they told each other tales from their years of life in prison and at home. Nicholas was so happy about the marriage of Noll and Glikia, and she was just as sweet as could be, a gentle-natured woman who was able to hold her own in conversation and wit. She was exactly the mate Noll needed to keep him from flying too high on himself. She was also filled with love and tenderness at the same time—a nice balance of personality. She fit right in with the Mikros clan.

They helped Nicholas move to a chair at the table. He moved as if he were a hundred years old, but he made it. They talked of taking him for a short walk outside after dinner to start loosening him up. Falon led the family in saying grace and blessing their meal. They all thanked God for bringing Nicholas back to them. They had not enjoyed such Christian fellowship together for years, and it was marvelous!

Tana served Nicholas more of her special broth, and that seemed to take the edge off what pain he still felt and it greatly relaxed him. He was certain it was filled with special Mikros herbs for pain relief and healing. His taste buds loved every sip. The others ate a thicker, heartier version of the soup with the actual chicken and vegetables. Nicholas' stomach still needed time to adjust to normal food.

During dinner, the conversation turned to the subject of Sandor's visit to their home. The visit had nearly scared the life out of them, but it turned out to be one of the most special moments they had over the many years. They led Sandor in prayer, repentance, and faith in Jesus. Nicholas laughed, trying to picture this giant man, a trained killer, sitting in the little Mikros home. How had he gotten through the door?

"Ho, ho, hooo," Nicholas chuckled, so pleased that Sandor had become a Christian. Through his limited contact with Sandor after that last Christmas Eve, he had noticed a change for the better and heard through Argus and Baruch about the hunger Sandor had developed for learning more about God.

Kari asked Nicholas what had kept him going. There was the indwelling of the Holy Spirit, of course, but was there something he had prayed for, said, or done that had been his lifeline while enduring the hardship?

Nicholas took his last sip of broth. "There were lots of things such as praying and enjoying fellowship with the other clergy prisoners that helped, and knowing you all on the outside were praying for us helped as well. Thank you for your faithful prayers. We had hope in things to come.

We reflected on Jesus. I'm thankful for having been in the habit of daily practices of being in God's presence and receiving His peace. I was also in the habit of being in God's will, of loving God, loving others, being joyful always, praying continually, and being thankful in all circumstances. By having those habits in good times and bad before prison, it was just part of my way of life in that lengthy bad time." He paused for a moment to rest and reflect.

He then added, "You know what, though? One particular scripture spoke to my spirit as much as any other that helped me endure. In Revelation: 'And they overcame him, Satan, by the blood of the Lamb, and by the word of their testimony; and they loved not their lives unto the death.' Jesus' blood conquered Satan, His holy, precious deity blood. So I prayed His blood over everyone and me as much as I could.

Secondly, Satan is conquered when we speak God's word and our testimonies aloud as often as we can, and I did especially when locked in the dungeon.

Lastly, I think many people leave this off, but it is as important as doing the first two. I do not love my life unto the death. Before prison, in prison, and even now, I am not afraid to die because my life is not my own; it is God's to do with as He pleases. As much as I love life, people, giving, and ministering, I do not love my life unto death. God can take me any second and I am good with it. Taking my life is His prerogative. I belong to Him. Jesus bought me for a price, and by having this in mind, Satan has no power over me. He can torture and kill this carcass that my spirit is living in, but my spirit will live on. I am not an eternal body with a decaying soul. I am an eternal soul in a decaying body. My spirit and soul will live on long after this body turns back to dust. Knowing this helped me endure."

"Amen," everyone said around the table. There was a moment of silence as everyone reflected on this heavy truth for themselves.

Noll got up from the table with a cane and used it to limp over to a shelf. He retrieved peppermint for the tea. Nicholas became cognizant of Noll's limp for the first time as his friend sat back down. Nicholas inquired about it. Noll did not want to tell what happened. Nicholas looked around the table.

"What's wrong? Why the hesitancy?"

Noll finally answered. "A short time before last Christmas, I was returning from the city, and I was attacked and beaten. They left me for dead.

Unconscious, I had broken ribs, a broken arm, a broken leg, and many contusions and lacerations. Watching you on the day you were arrested made me feel left out. It looked like so much fun I thought I'd give it a try myself." He chuckled, trying to lighten the mood. "Yeah, well, it wasn't as fun as it looked. The good news is, I've mended well, and this leg is the last to heal."

Glikia interjected, "It doesn't help that he won't sit still long enough to let it heal properly."

Nicholas sympathized. "Oh, my brother, I am so sorry to hear this. If there is anything I can do, please let me know."

Tana chimed in, "Yes, Nicholas, there is something you can do. You can have him for a healing partner, and you two can entertain each other while you both take it easy and heal properly. I know you, Nicholas, and you both are cut from the same fabric—with boundless energy that you cannot deny. So you'll be good for each other for the next two or three months, okay, you two?" She sternly looked at both Noll and Nicholas.

"Yes, ma'am," they responded in unison as best friends sometimes do.

Glikia smirked with satisfaction.

Falon sensed this was a good time to continue some serious conversation. "Nicholas, we, meaning the Mikros clan, have some changes happening that you should know about."

"Yes?" Nicholas felt there was more bad news, so he braced himself.

"As you know, Patara and the surrounding region have been slowly transforming for years, but while you have been in prison, the rate of change has been exponential, with the growth of trade and commerce bringing in thousands of new people to the area. It did not help that Diocletian released the violent criminal population back into the public during this time, while locking up spiritual and community leaders like yourself, who helped keep peace. The growth has not been favorable to us, and what happened to Noll was, sadly, inevitable. This is why Noll and Glikia have not built their own home. We have to live together for safety in numbers. We have suffered and been persecuted for being Christians, but also because there is resentment by the new business community. They use cutthroat business tactics, literally and figuratively. In addition, being peaceful people we are natural targets for bullying. So the religious, business, and personal attacks have grown, and we would rather not have to raise our families in a hostile environment, with no relief in sight."

"So what does this mean for you and your clan?" responded Nicholas.

"The leaders of the clan from around the region met after Noll's attack. That was the final straw. We all committed it to prayer and we all received a unified answer from the Holy Spirit. Move."

"To where?"

"North. Way north. At the end of this last winter, Kari and Dax scouted a territory far north from here, several weeks' journey, which has many possibilities. We've had several scout teams visit there since, to confirm the location, including one team that Mr. Wilderness over there," Falon looked at Noll, who gave an embarrassed smile, "sneaked off with. That long journey certainly didn't help his leg mend. Anyway, that's the big news. We will have some Mikros communities strategically located between here and our new land to continue with trade and commerce, and we'll still have businesses here. We'll just be doing business from afar while creating new business and ministry opportunities in new parts of the world. We're looking at expanding upward and outward rather than just being in one spot. God is taking us out of our comfort zone—well, what was *once* our comfort zone—and is now in a way forcing us to be more mission-minded. We're expanding our horizons from a northern location that will allow us to reach out to more people more easily around the world. We're sad in ways, but overall we feel good about this. You know how God likes us to be in a place of dependency on Him, and we *will* be, like never before. That's okay because there's no better place to be than in His will, amen?"

Nicholas' sadness was obvious on his face, and he felt as if Sandor had just punched him in his gut and knocked the wind out of him. He summoned the energy and gave Falon an "amen." He pondered for a moment and said, "'Our Father, who is in Heaven, honored be Thy name. Thy Kingdom come, Thy will be done, on earth as it is in Heaven.' Yes, this is a good thing. Change is not always what we want, but if it's what God wants for His Kingdom, then it's all good. His will be done. In prison, we would talk about blooming where we're planted, letting God shine His light through us into dark places, being the salt of the earth, the flavoring of God so that the world may taste and see that He and His ways are good. Yes, this is a good thing. Sad for me because I will see you all less, but good for the world and the Kingdom of God. What's your timeline?"

Noll answered, "We plan to systematically plant our satellite communities along the journey all the way up to our new land through next summer and make the final big move next fall."

Nicholas did the math in his head. Excitedly, he remarked, "That's a year before you all leave! That's wonderful! Excellent!"

This good news immediately lifted Nicholas' spirit just as, many years previous, his own similar good news had lifted everyone's spirits when he had announced he would stay around for a year before leaving for the priesthood. He had a year of the Mikroses around, which would allow all of them to slowly transition into the next phase of their lives. Their world as they knew it with each other was not going to end tomorrow like Nicholas had imagined.

They finished eating dinner and sat around the table having a more casual conversation. Kari excused herself to retrieve something and to change to go for a ride on her horse after dinner. As they relaxed, something in the corner caught Nicholas' eye. It appeared to be a red and white stick. As his eyes focused more, it dawned on him. "Is that my father's walking staff?"

The room grew silent. All heads turned simultaneously to look at the staff. Everyone knew this was something that Dax would have to reconcile with Nicholas at some point.

Dax slowly slid his chair back and walked over to the staff. He brought it to Nicholas. "Uhhh, what do you think? Do you like it?"

Nicholas did not respond immediately. He stared at it with his eyes squinting and his mouth open. He'd never seen anything quite like it before, and all he could think was, *Why?*

Dax explained. "Look, it's real easy to spot, even far away. And, hey, check this out." He put the bottom on the floor, and started to twirl it, creating the design's optical illusion.

Nicholas was still quiet, looking, looking, looking. He asked to hold it and examined it further, turning it upside down and all around. There was nervous tension in the room—everyone knew how special Nicholas' walking staff was to him because it belonged to his father.

Finally, he spoke. "Well, Dax, this is very interesting for sure." Nicholas was thoughtful in his words. He always tried to find the positive in everything. "First, we start with the staff itself, a noble tool that has much Biblical meaning. Jesus was called the Good Shepherd, we are His flock, and a shepherd's staff is used to guide sheep, to provide security to them and to help reign in lost sheep. Shepherds were some of the first to find out about Jesus' birth and visit Him at his manger. Hmm." Nicholas turned the staff upside down. "Now, it looks like a fisherman's hook. Jesus was a fisher of men and called His disciples to be fishers of men, as He calls us to be today. It also looks like the letter *J* for Jesus."

Nicholas turned it right side up and looked at it again, pondering. "Stripes. Isaiah 53: 'But he was pierced for our rebellion, crushed for our sins. He was beaten so we could be whole. He was whipped so that by his *stripes* we are healed.' I received stripes from a whipping, but mine are only scars. Jesus' stripes are for healing, our healing. Yes, stripes, red and white stripes. Red for the blood Jesus shed. Jesus' holy, precious blood. He is the ultimate sacrificial Lamb of God who takes away the sin of the world. When we admit we're sinners, ask for forgiveness for our sins, repent from our sins and turn to Him, surrender our lives to Him, and accept His gift of salvation, then we activate in the spiritual realm His holy blood that washes away our sins and makes us white and pure as snow. Or, in this case, as white as the stripes on this staff."

There was a pause in the room. It was so good to have Nicholas back, a man who could see God's hand in most any situation, including the funny-looking painted design on his walking staff.

Dax took a proud, deep breath after Nicholas' affirming validation. He exclaimed, "Yes, my thoughts exactly! It was like you were reading my mind!"

To which Noll responded, "Whatever." Everyone had a little laugh at Dax's expense, but he was a good sport.

Dax said to Nicholas, "Great, so you like it and want to keep it like that?"

To which Nicholas quickly responded, "No."

"Huh?"

"No. Sorry, Dax. Please return my father's staff to its original state." Everyone snickered. "Thank you anyway, but no."

Kari walked in carrying a figurine about the height of a large foot, which she had carved herself. It was beautiful, exquisitely detailed, and quickly recognizable as the likeness of Nicholas in his red dress robe. She set it on the table in front of Nicholas, and his face lit up. He loved the professionalism of the work of art itself, but he was taken aback a little that it looked like him. It was a little embarrassing, not to mention there was one detail that stood out like a sore thumb.

Kari said, "A welcome home gift for you. Welcome home, Nicholas!"

"Thank you so much, Kari! It's embarrassing seeing myself created in art, but it is beautiful! None surpasses your talent. Thank you so much!" He reached up and gave her a hug.

Kari beamed. Nicholas was very grateful. However, he tried not to notice and acknowledge the one very distinctive component. His figurine held a walking staff painted like Dax's version with red and white stripes. She had missed the conversation with Dax.

"Sorry, sis, Nicholas doesn't like the design on his walking staff. I have to change it back."

"Good. It doesn't look like a walking staff anyway; it looks like a funny-looking cane."

Dax sneered.

Nicholas, trying to be gracious, said, "As interesting a design as it is, I prefer its original state."

Kari picked the removable little staff up and said, "No worries, I'll just make a new one." She handed it to Dax. "You can keep this one as a souvenir, brother."

Dax threw it on the table, disappointed.

Noll, sipping his peppermint tea, picked it up and gave it a good look. He commented as he studied the miniature, striped staff, "It must be my sweet tooth ready for dessert because it kind of looks like something sweet one would eat. A little cane made out of candy? Is that the case or is it just me?"

Dax and Kari looked perplexed and responded in unison, "It's just you."

Kari started to leave for an after-dinner ride when Nicholas noticed for the first time her unusual clothes. Before she exited, Nicholas asked her what she was wearing and why.

"Oh," Kari said excitedly, getting to show off her new garb, "we learned how to make these clothes up north. They're called trousers. First of all, they are warmer than tunics. You don't have the big open draft coming up from below. Second, they are much more conducive for fighting. For instance, you can do a high sidekick, *kee-yihhh!*" She proceeded to demonstrate a high sidekick, putting her foot into the side of Dax's head and sending him flying across the room. No one flinched at this scene or ran to Dax's aid because they had seen this show a thousand times with these two. She continued while holding her foot high in the air. "And see? Good flexibility while not exposing your privates for the entire world to see." She dropped her leg. "And third, these trousers are perfect for horseback riding. Again, no hiking up the tunic before getting on a horse. It's great!"

Dax added groggily but enthusiastically, as he stumbled into a chair, "And you know how we like to clean chimneys? Well, these trousers make it way easier for climbing onto roofs and going up and down chimneys, too!" He was too into the conversation to think about retaliation towards Kari.

As much as these twins marched to their own beat and did some strange things, this idea made a lot of sense to Nicholas. Though the trousers were a bit odd looking, he touted, "I like these trousers. I think they have good utility! I'm not one for fighting, but they would be good for riding, climbing, and cooler weather for sure! I may be interested in having a pair for myself someday."

Kari responded, "Excellent, we will set you up!"

### Devotion

After the season of Christian persecution, the Mikros clan had to make some difficult decisions about the persecution they continued to experience, with God's guidance of course. Even though they tried to love others and live in peace with all people, not all people reciprocated. As Christians, we are called to be in right relationships with others, and put in the hard work to make right relationships and keep them healthy, but sometimes some people don't change or won't change and the relationship becomes toxic.

As humans, we can be creatures of habit and we desire life to be somewhat predictable. Some people though, for various reasons, will take this so far as to stay in unhealthy and maybe even dangerous relationships and situations because they are familiar, or predictable, to them. They stay in an unhealthy situation rather than seek wise counsel, and if need be, take the risk to leave what is unhealthy to pursue healthier lives and relationships.

**Questions to consider:** How do I handle making tough decisions, particularly with difficult relationships? How can I help myself make decisions that are going to benefit me spiritually, mentally, physically, emotionally, sexually, and financially? Do I seek guidance from God regularly? Do I have trustworthy, Christian counsel in my life that I can consult with?

*"But if any of you lacks wisdom, he should ask God who gives to all generously and ungrudgingly, and he will be given it." James 1:5*

*"For where jealousy and selfish ambition exist, there is disorder and every foul practice. But the wisdom from above is first of all pure, then peaceable, gentle, compliant, full of mercy and good fruits, without inconstancy or insincerity. And the fruit of righteousness is sown in peace for those who cultivate peace." James 3:16-18*

*"Do not fear: I am with you; do not be anxious: I am your God. I will strengthen you, I will help you, I will uphold you with my victorious right hand." Isaiah 41:10*

**Prayer:** "Heavenly Father, please give me the courage to take an honest look at my life and open my eyes to what and whom I'm allowing in my life that is healthy and unhealthy for me. Help me seek You for Your divine care and guidance and give me ears to hear and eyes to see what You're telling me and showing me. Help me have healthy boundaries in my relationships. Help me also have trustworthy, wise Christian counsel in my life as a resource. And, after receiving guidance and knowing what I need to do or not do, please give me the courage to do it. Thank You. Amen."

# 25
# Redeeming Goodbye

ON A BEAUTIFUL, late summer afternoon in September, the Mikros family sat out front enjoying the day when they saw a large figure on an even larger horse come up the road toward the house. Having had him visit several times in recent months for inner healing and prayer sessions, they recognized it was Sandor right away. However, this was the first time they had seen him since the clergy were released, and Nicholas only knew Sandor from within the prison walls, so this was a bit unsettling for him. He was not sure what to feel. As Sandor approached the house, Nicholas stood up with his still-colorful staff along with Falon, Noll, Kari, and Dax. They sensed Nicholas' trepidation and thought it best to stand with him in case the big man had some ill intentions.

Sandor stopped his enormous horse in front of the group and dismounted, landing with a loud thud and sending a cloud of dust up from his feet. He took two steps forward and put his hand on his sword handle. He slowly pulled it from its leather scabbard. Nicholas and the Mikroses braced for a worst-case scenario. Sandor, staring Nicholas in the eyes, put the tip of his sword in the dirt in front of him and slowly drew a half circle.

With some relief, Nicholas accepted the invitation and stepped forward. With his staff, he finished the drawing of the Ichthus. Sandor smiled and said in his deep and powerful voice, but with a gentle tone, "Greetings in the name of our Lord Jesus Christ, my fellow brothers and sisters in the Lord." Oh, sweet relief! There was a group exhale. "I'm just messing with you. I've still got it." He laughed at his purposely-intense arrival joke. They laughed along, but out of nervousness and alleviated fear.

Nicholas gathered his composure. "To what do we owe the honor of your visit, Sandor? Now that I know you're not here to kill us, I'm happy to see you! Ho, ho, hoo! Please come sit down and join us for a fresh cup of cider!"

"Thank you," Sandor responded. "I will partake, but my visit is to be short, as I am leaving for Rome."

Everyone sat down. Instead of Tana pouring Sandor a mug of cider from a re-filled pitcher, she gave him the whole pitcher because he is so big. He gave her a smile and a hug.

"Yes. Because of my newfound faith and internal freedom, I have prayed for God's will. He told me to get out of the business of fighting, killing, and torturing."

"That's *niiice*," Nicholas said, trying to sound sincere, though some sarcasm leaked out.

"Yes, it is. I have made contact with someone whom I understand is a mutual acquaintance of ours. Do you remember being a teenager and having a chance encounter with Constantine?"

"Yes I do, of course I remember him. He is royalty. I'm surprised he remembers me!"

"I had heard he was sympathetic to Christians and, as he is a rising emperor, I felt God prompting me to reach out to him. He obliged, and we met. That's where I was when you were released from prison. I asked him what his stance was with Christianity, and he told me of a chance encounter with an interesting little character that he'd had one day in this province."

"I'm not that little."

"He said this little vagabond named Nicholas helped them get their wheel repaired, and when you spoke in conversation, you spoke of God in ways that made him pause. He decided to rethink how he viewed Christians and be open to their theology."

"I'm not that little."

"He said the little man's act of kindness, all with a smile and a positive attitude, struck him as funny but touched his cold heart."

"I'm not that little."

"Anyway, Constantine and I connected on a personal level as well as a spiritual level, and he extended an invitation for me to be on his staff as a personal advisor. He is still asking, seeking, and knocking about his faith, as you said to do that day of your meeting, but he felt that maybe God could use me in his life in some way. I told him that I no longer want to be involved in violence, and he told me he would honor that."

Falon, Noll, and the others congratulated Sandor and gave praises to God for what He was doing in this big man's life.

Now that the sting of being called "little" had passed, Nicholas added to the congratulations and praises. Sandor took a big gulp of his cider. "Ahhh, Mikros cider is the best! Salud!" Everyone cheered him and he finished his drink. "So, now I am here to tell you all, thank you for your prayers, your love, your fellowship, and your unconditional acceptance. Thank you from the bottom of my forgiven heart."

Falon responded, "It has been our pleasure, my son. And here's to you and all you will do for the Kingdom of God. Salud." All toasted and as they finished their drinks, Nicholas, under his breath, quickly added to the toast, "And thank you for not killing us."

Sandor finished his drink, stood, and everyone rose with him to say their goodbyes. He released the belt holding his scabbard and sword, and it dropped to the ground with a giant boom. "I no longer need or want this. I would like to offer it to your family to do with as you wish. This is a gesture of my commitment to giving up my old life, and a token of my appreciation for all you have done for me." Kari and Dax drooled at the thought of holding the most famous sword from the most famous gladiator in the land! It took everything in them to refrain from attacking it while Sandor was still there.

Sandor walked to his horse, let loose a box, and brought it over to Nicholas. He handed it to him and kneeled. Tears welled up in his eyes. "For you, my brother. I cannot say enough times how sorry I am for all the horrible things I did to you. I know that in your heart you have forgiven me over and over to our Father; that's the kind of man you are. But I now, personally, ask for your forgiveness. If you are willing, I need to hear it from you."

"I forgive you, my brother."

"Thank you." He choked back tears, but a few trickled. Nicholas set the box down and hugged the giant man. After the embrace, Sandor wiped the tears, stood, and went around giving everyone goodbye hugs.

Before he mounted his horse, he turned back toward Nicholas and said, "And for the record, Nicholas, in my scroll, there is nothing little about you. In fact, you are the biggest, toughest, and strongest man I have ever met. And I'll make sure Constantine, and anyone I ever talk with about you, knows it."

Nicholas beamed. "Thank you. That's one of the nicest things anyone has ever said to me." They smiled at each other with admiration.

Nicholas glanced down at the box and asked, "Oh, shall I open this now?"

Sandor got on his horse and nodded. "If you wish. Nicholas, as God redeems us, I think you too are good at taking something once used for evil, and turning it into something for good. I think you will do the same with this."

Nicholas opened the box. His eyes grew wide and his legs grew weak. He was not sure what to make of the gift. It evoked all kinds of emotions in him, all bad ones.

Kari and Dax urged Nicholas to show everyone.

Nicholas reached in and removed Sandor's giant whip, the one he had used to torture Nicholas and many others. He composed himself and responded to Sandor, "Thank you. I will find a *good* use for it."

Sandor smiled. "Blessings to all of you."

"And blessings to you," the group responded. Sandor turned his horse and rode away.

Kari and Dax ran over to the massive sword and it took both of them to pick it up. They scurried off with it like two dogs who had found a giant bone and could not wait to go enjoy it.

Everyone shook their heads as they watched the twins scurry away. Nicholas examined his new whip. He was quiet, thinking about that fateful day when he had felt the end of the whip repeatedly. He shuddered at the thought of cracking the whip and hearing the sound. Everyone watched him to see what he would do. He announced, "God redeems people. I think God can redeem this whip. I think I have a new driving whip, that when cracked, will communicate to my team of beasts to take me to do good works." At that, he cocked his arm back, and, whipping the end, he made it fly backward and then forward into the air. *CRACK!*

What a difference two months made! In two months, with Nicholas and Noll committed to keeping each other accountable for getting proper rest, eating healthy, and doing proper stretching and exercising, Noll was completely healed and doing well. Nicholas, though still not one hundred percent, was eating anything and everything he desired. He gained plenty of healthy weight, and the color in his face and rosy cheeks reappeared. He felt wonderful. He resembled his old self but needed to give it a little more time of stretching and exercise to get his full agility and strength back.

On a beautiful October day, as they walked laps around the property, they stopped to look at two unique animals Kari and Dax had brought back from their journey north. They were young male and female animals with antlers, called reindeer. They were beautiful creatures, and the family was raising them to learn more about them and to breed and train them for labor for when they moved north. They were docile and very intelligent animals. They were in the same corral as Shimmel, Vida, and Aria, to have fatherly and motherly role models. They liked Nicholas, as all animals did, and came up to him and Noll. The men fed them apples and continued their conversation.

"You know, Noll, of course I missed many things while in prison, but do you know what I missed as much as, if not more than, anything?"

"What?"

"Giving people gifts and making them feel good. When I gave away my inheritance that was one of the happiest times of my life! After I became a priest and went around ministering to people, I did not have much, but the little I was able to give, especially to children, brought me joy. It was only a little here and there, but everyone would appreciate it. I love making people smile and feel good in the knowledge that I've thought of them with a little gift, letting them know that in remembrance of God's gift to us in Jesus, I am giving a humble gift to them."

"You will again. You'll be back at it in no time."

"Yes, but, unfortunately, with being a priest, I don't make much money, not nearly enough to give gifts as I would like. I think of the amazing gift God gave us in Jesus, and I cannot help but ooze the desire to give and bless others as God has blessed me. How can I scratch this itch? Even if it's only occasional?"

"Follow me." Noll walked around the animal corral and headed toward the front doors of the barn. Nicholas followed behind, still walking a bit slowly with a limp. For stability, he used his colorful walking staff, which Dax still had not refurbished to its original state. Dax said his special paint remover was on back order.

Noll stopped in front of the barn doors, and when Nicholas caught up, Noll asked, "Maybe you can help us get rid of these?" He swung the barn doors open, and as the late afternoon sunlight flooded the entrance, Nicholas saw thousands of little wooden figurines. There were sailors, farmers, ranchers, shepherds, Roman soldiers, and all kinds of animals. He also saw toy wagons, sleighs, plows, chariots, and boats, in addition to miniature furniture, and so much more! What stood out more than even the toys was miniature manger scenes that made Nicholas' heart glow. Seeing Nicholas' reaction to it all, Noll may as well have swung open the gates of Heaven because Nicholas lit up as if he was at a Christ-Mass!

"Noll, you have just made me the happiest man in the world! Just the thought of having the privilege of giving away your and your Mikros family's amazing creations brings joy to my heart! Oh, thank you so very much!"

"Let's just say, over the last five years, we Mikroses have literally and figuratively been whittling the time away."

"Yes, you have. You have all been very, very busy in your workshops! Ho, ho, hooo! Ho, ho, hooooo!"

"Any thoughts on when and how you would want to distribute the gifts?"

"Hmmm. This will take some planning. I know I would like to do it all at the same time, somehow, some way, so everyone gets a gift at the same time to be fair. Moreover, I would need some help, of course. As for when? I think I have an idea. There is one day that stands above all others to represent the season of gift giving like no other. A special, holy day."


That evening during dinner, Nicholas and Noll shared with the family what they envisioned doing with the toy carvings stockpiled in the barn. Nicholas and Noll had similar toys to play with as young children and they had loved them! They narrowed the plan to give the gifts only to children because children enjoy playing with toys much more than adults. The gift to parents would be to see their children receive toys they enjoyed so much, and toys helped entertain their children while the parents did chores and had adult time. Noll's family was excited about the plans, including *how* the toy distribution would happen, and especially *when* the distribution would occur. It brought joy to everyone's heart thinking about the big event!

After dinner, while enjoying bread pudding with hot green tea, Tana shared, "Well, since we are all in the spirit of giving, we have a gift for you, Nicholas." She went to a chest in the corner and opened it.

"Oh, you don't have to give me a gift. All of you *are* the best gifts God can give me."

Tana pulled out a handsome, brand-new red robe with white trim like the one he had cherished many years before. Nicholas' eyes lit up! Not only did he feel thanksgiving in his heart, but also he felt a wave of nostalgia overtake him. All the wonderful memories the robe held for him rushed back.

The robe originally had been a gift of love from his parents for his confirmation. He had worn it on the *The Queen of Africa* ship during the cool evenings when he and his shipmates would sit on the deck looking at the star-filled sky. In Israel, he had used his robe as a blanket on chilly nights and as a pillow on warm ones. He remembered how it had felt when he jumped onto Shimmel and the back of the robe swung behind him like a cape and gracefully draped over the back of his horse. When he would gallop away, it would flap in the wind, making him feel like a hero off to save a damsel in distress. And he remembered when he was with Wren the last time he laid his eyes upon her, and he held her snuggled tight inside that robe. She gave him that special smile that was hard to describe, but he had only seen her give him that special smile. Ah, so many wonderful memories came from a simple robe.

"Oh, joy! Thank you so much. You went way above and beyond! It's beautiful, and it brings me so many wonderful memories!" Tana helped him slide his arms into the sleeves, and he fully wrapped himself in it as if cloaking himself in a blanket of love. "I don't know how I could thank you."

"You don't have to thank us," Tana said. "Thank Wren. She made it for you."

Nicholas was stunned. He stared straight ahead, looking at nothing as his mind fell into deep thought. "Then I will have to thank her sometime. I will write her a note." Nicholas sat back down, his eyes a bit glazed, thinking about Wren. He was touched by her kind gesture, and by the thought that the wonderful robe he was now wearing, she made with her own hands. Her hands had touched the fabric that was now touching him and blanketing his body. He felt as if her arms were wrapped around him.

Nicholas still did not have any words to say. Everyone watched him enjoy his new robe, which made him resemble his old self more than ever.

"Nicholas, we have a team going to town tomorrow," Falon spoke up. "You're well enough now. How about you go along for a ride? It will be good for you to have a change of scenery and start seeing the parishioners you love so much. They would love to see you as well. When we're in town, we always have people asking us about how you're doing. It will be good for you to start seeing people and being seen again. You can see your uncle. He's doing well. Last time we were in town, two prison guards recognized us and said they would like you to stop by the prison and see them. We thought that strange, but I can only imagine having a prison full of clergy is going to have a positive impact on a guard. One would hope anyway. They seemed excited at the thought of seeing you, so it appears to be fruit of you blooming where you were planted and having a positive effect on these two men."

Nicholas pondered the idea for a moment as he transitioned his mind away from Wren. "Yes, I would like that. I *am* ready. I would like that very much."

"Great! Then we will also take you to see Wren. You can thank her in person."

"Huh?!" Nicholas was flustered. What would he say? How would he act? It had been so long, and she had a family. "No, I will send her a note. I'm sure she is very preoccupied as a mother and wife taking care of her children and husband. I wouldn't want to disturb them. I'll send a thank you note."

"Don't you know?" Tana inquired.

"Know what?"

"Nicholas. Wren is a widow," revealed Tana.

"What?"

"Wren is a widow. During the fourth year of the clergy imprisonment, the ship her husband was on was in a storm off the coast of England. A giant wave flung the boat into rocks. It sank in the frigid waters and all lives were tragically lost. His body was one of the few recovered."

Nicholas was in shock. "Oh my, how sad. Sincerely. How tragic. I am so sorry to hear that. How traumatic for Wren. And her children? I don't even know, does she have children?"

"Three daughters; the eldest just turned six. Yes, it was devastating. He was a good man. There were many good men lost that day. Wren has done well; she mourned for the first year and is in the process of moving forward. Because of the dowry gift, she had been able to marry an established man from an established family, so she is well-taken care of financially. She and her children are doing well, overall."

"That's good. How are they all doing emotionally? I feel the children's pain of losing a parent."

"They have a lot of family support. Madelyn lived with them for a while to help. Brodin passed away during the second year of the clergy imprisonment. The drinking finally caught up to him. He went out drinking one night, passed out in an alley, and never woke up. Very sad as well."

"Oh my, poor Madelyn. That poor family."

Noll reflected, "They have had their share of tragedy, but they have also had a lot of support. They are all doing as well as can be expected in these circumstances. As you know, Madelyn and Wren are strong women of faith, and they have the Lord as their refuge. They also have had support from Kyla and Kalista and their families, in addition to their church family of believers who have come alongside them all and helped when needed. We've visited them when able, and they've visited us when they wanted to get out of the city and come back home. They've stayed with us a few times. They truly are remarkable women."

"That's good. I still don't know about visiting her. I will travel with the team, visit my uncle and the prison, and see how my strength is doing at that time. I appreciate the offer. I agree with you that I am ready to start getting out and into the public again. I cannot thank all of you enough for all you have done for me over these last months. All of you are angels sent from Heaven."

### Devotion

Sandor, as with all Christians, was redeemed by the Lord. He then passed his whip on to Nicholas to redeem it. To redeem means to reclaim something for a price, to make it valuable or important again. A simple example is that back in the day, empty soda bottles could be redeemed for five cents each. The bottle itself was worthless, trash, but the bottle company saw value in it, so they were willing to pay a price to get bottles back.

Kids used to search neighborhoods high and low to find bottles to redeem so they could get money to buy candy. The bottle company gave value to something that did not appear to have any.

When we were dead in our sins, we were useless empty bottles that were trash, but God saw value in us, so He redeemed us by giving his own Son's life to get us back, to save us from the trash heap and inevitable destruction. By giving Jesus' life, God gave our lives value. In this sin-plagued world, we gain value by doing, by performing, or by pleasing other people, all for naught. The Bible says we all fall short of the glory of God, so there is nothing we can do to save ourselves from the trash heap on our own. Therefore, God did it for us. Something is only as valuable as someone is willing to pay for it. God valued us so much He paid for us with His own Son's life. That is how much God loves us.

**Questions to consider:** Do I recognize how much God loves me? Do I take it for granted? Do I need to reflect on it deeper and more often?

*"In him we have redemption by his blood, the forgiveness of transgressions, in accord with the riches of his grace that he lavished upon us." Ephesians 1:7-8*

*"Christ ransomed us from the curse of the law by becoming a curse for us, for it is written, 'Cursed be everyone who hangs on a tree,' that the blessing of Abraham might be extended to the Gentiles through Christ Jesus, so that we might receive the promise of the Spirit through faith." Galations 3:13-14*

*"… realizing that you were ransomed from your futile conduct, handed on by your ancestors, not with perishable things like silver or gold, but with the precious blood of Christ as of a spotless unblemished lamb." 1 Peter 1:18-19*

*"… for, if you confess with your mouth that Jesus is Lord and believe in your heart that God raised him from the dead, you will be saved. For one believes with the heart and so is justified, and one confesses with the mouth and so is saved." Romans 10:9-10*

*"For our sake he made him to be sin who did not know sin, so that we might become the righteousness of God in him." 2 Corinthians 5:21*

**Prayer:** "Heavenly Father, there have been times in my life that I have felt worthless. Please forgive me for trying to find my worth based on what other imperfect human beings think of me, or even about what I have thought about myself. You are the only source I am to seek my worth from, and You love me so much that You gave Your only Son so that I shall not perish, but have eternal life with You in Heaven. Help me to reject the lies of this world and the enemy, and help me to meditate on Your truth daily. I am not an accident and I am not worthless. I am here by Your grand design, and I have purpose and I am so valued, loved, and cherished by You! Help me comprehend that more and more every day. Thank You! Amen."

# 26
# Hope

"WELL," LAURA SAYS mournfully, wrapped in Joe's arms, "I'm very sorry to hear Wren's husband died, especially so young, and with children. I wouldn't want to lose my mom or dad."

"Yes, my lady. So true," says Kris.

"I feel sad for the girls."

"Yes, my lady. It's tragic any time a child loses a parent, or a parent loses a child, any time, but especially when young."

Mary softly adds, "If there is a moral to this story, honey, it's that there is hope for believers because as believers we know that we will see our loved ones again in Heaven, with no sadness and pain."

"Like when Nicholas lost his parents when he was young, and his father said that we cannot take our earthly treasures to Heaven, except for our loved ones who believe." Laura reflects.

Mary is so proud of her daughter. "Yes, Laura, yes."

"And I'm sure Wren's daughters will become believers someday. It sounds like they have a lot of support around them. And now they will have Nicholas in their life, and who wouldn't want Santa Claus in their life?"

"Exactly," affirms Kris.

Joe, a bit emotional himself. "Laura I've heard your mom say all things work for the good of those who love God. Now, I think I understand what she means by that, and I believe it. Good will come from this sad situation, honey, okay?"

"Yes. It's sad, but I know it's going to get better. Hopefully sooner than later." Laura looks at Kris pleading with her eyes.

"Yes, my lady," Kris reassures her with a gentle, understanding smile.


*The next morning . . .*

Nicholas set out with four teams of Mikroses driving four wagons loaded with goods for the business of trading, selling, and bartering. Falon, Noll, Kari, and Dax were among members of one team, and Nicholas rode on their wagon. Though nervous about the possibility of seeing Wren, he was immensely excited at riding into the city and seeing people again. He wore his new robe, identical to his old robe. Everywhere the wagon went, people recognized him and waved and shouted best wishes to Nicholas. His heart warmed at the outpouring of support he received.

The first stop was his uncle. The wagon dropped Nicholas off and left to do business; it would return in several hours. Nicholas and his uncle embraced when they saw each other and shared tears of God's grace and mercy. They had survived the persecution, and now they gave thanks to the many of their clergy brethren who had not survived but were with their Heavenly Father. *Praise be to God!* They gave God glory and shared their recovery stories—both men were looking mostly like their old selves again, though both a bit more aged due to the difficult conditions they survived, but they were thankful.

They also talked business, and the bishop shared that he would be calling a meeting for all of the clergy in the region to plan rebuilding churches and ministering to the people again. First, they would need to determine what clergy members were still alive and were able to serve, and also who still felt called to service. News slowly trickled in from the different regions, and word was that the bishop of Myra had died during the persecution. This was an important position to be filled soon because; similar to Uncle Nicholas' position in Patara, Myra was another port city that had far-reaching implications for ministering God's love.

After a time, Noll's wagon picked Nicholas up for the next stop, the prison. Argus, Baruch, and the other guards were delighted to have Nicholas back and enjoyed catching up. Argus and Baruch had grown so much in their faith. Having listened to all the clergy over the years reciting scripture to each other, teaching each other, and memorizing scripture together, they were now well-versed in the Christian scrolls. A fire was lit in their hearts as they came to trust Jesus, and they had grown much in their faith, so much so that they both want to enter the priesthood. Nicholas was elated at the idea, and the timing could not have been more perfect with the great need to replace clergy. Their time served in the Roman guard was ending, and Nicholas urged that when they finished, they should see him. He would help them take their next steps in becoming clergymen.

Argus and Baruch were interim co-leaders of the prison, appointed by Sandor before he left, until the Roman government could find a new warden for the prison. Nicholas suggested that if one of the two men had a passion for the prisoners, maybe they could petition Sandor to allow one of them to be the new warden, and they could continue the positive changes they had made to the system. Both Argus and Baruch were excited at the idea and said they would commit it to prayer. Argus thought that would be something he would be interested in doing.

Argus and Baruch invited Nicholas in to minister to the current prisoners. Real criminals of all sorts repopulated the prison again. Ministering to the prisoners brought joy to Nicholas' heart and refueled his passion to reach the lost, lonely, and destitute. The three men visited each floor, giving words of God's encouragement and praying for the men. The stench was gone after the walls and floors were sanitized.

The once dank, hostile building had a lighter, more hopeful feeling, an atmosphere more apt for rehabilitation and personal change than the filthy, unfriendly, and uninhabitable one it had been during Nicholas' time. This was due to some of the changes implemented by Sandor before he left, with the help of Argus and Baruch.

Nicholas' time at the prison was fruitful and joy-filled, but it was also draining physically, mentally, and emotionally. When Noll and the team picked Nicholas up, they took him to one of the smaller, quieter markets and bought some lunch. They found Nicholas' favorite candy from Egypt, which was made of dates, cinnamon, cardamom seeds, walnuts, almonds, and honey.

They rested while they ate, and Nicholas shared information about his conversations with his uncle, Argus, and Baruch, of which Noll and the team were very interested to hear. Having rested and eaten, Nicholas announced that he was feeling rejuvenated and was ready for the next activity on the agenda, whenever they were. Noll reported that they had some last business to attend to that afternoon down by the docks, and they would drop Nicholas off to his last visit for the day: Wren's house.

Instantly, a lump formed in Nicholas' throat, and the feeling of butterflies fluttered around in his stomach. "Um, I'm not sure about that. I'm a bit tired, um, and I don't want to arrive unannounced. That would be rude."

"You just announced that you were rejuvenated," Dax reminded Nicholas.

"Yeah, and you said you were ready for the next activity, which for you is seeing Wren," added Kari.

"We sent a message to Wren, and she responded she'd be ready for you," Noll said.

"Oh," said Nicholas.

Noll continued, "And you said you're ready when we are, and we're all ready, right?" Everyone responded positively, and they all climbed back into the wagons or onto their horses to prepare to leave. Nicholas stood there for a moment, but when he realized it was all of them against him, he reluctantly climbed into the wagon. As soon as he sat down, they were off.

It was a short ride as it was only a few minutes away. Wren lived between the market and the docks, a quick, simple stop on the way. With her husband having been in shipping, it made sense they lived near the water. The wagon stopped in front of her house, called a townhouse, which was connected to several other homes as was normal in the crowded city.

Nicholas sat there for a moment, not moving until Noll pointed to which door was Wren's, taking away Nicholas' last excuse. He now knew where he was going. He slowly and gingerly climbed out of the wagon and landed with both feet on the ground. He felt as weak-kneed as he looked, so he reached into the wagon for his walking stick, which he had not used yet that day. As he walked to the steps in front of Wren's door, the staff helped stable him. The staff was a security blanket in an uncomfortable situation. Quite frankly, he was scared to death to see Wren, and he didn't know how he was going to react.

Before he knew it, the wagon left, with the team waving and smiling at Nicholas as they moved farther away. They loved seeing their good friend, who was normally a strong, confident, bold man of God, become nervous and timid at the thought of being in the presence of a certain woman. They had all known that there had always been something more to Nicholas and Wren's relationship than either of them would ever admit.

Before the wagon got too far, Dax appeared out of nowhere, leaped up the few steps, gave Wren's door several loud, quick knocks, and jogged away. He gave Nicholas a wink as he went. There was no escaping the situation. Before he could give Dax a displeased look, he heard the pitter-patter of little footsteps inside the house, and the door swung open. Three little angels' stared at him and asked if he was their mother's childhood friend. Before he could gather his wits about him, Wren appeared in the doorway.

"Nicholas! Come in, come in. It's so wonderful to see you!" Wren motioned in, and she and the children backed away from the entrance to allow him room to enter.

"You look busy. I can come back another time."

"Don't be silly. We've been waiting for you. Come in." Nicholas stepped into Wren's home. He did not know what to say. Her beauty astounded him. She gave him a big hug, and the touch of her embrace, the warmth of her smile, the sound of her voice, the glow in her eyes, and the smell of her hair awakened all his senses. His mind was flooded with sunny memories from days long past and helped ease his nerves. Wren introduced him to her children, three girls just as Wren's parents had had, ages six, four, and two.

They were all sweet natured like Wren and were equally beautiful, with her same brown hair and blue eyes. They were little Wrens. Nicholas sat in a chair at the table while she finished preparing some hot, spiced apple cider. The girls took to Nicholas, sitting on his lap, playing with his beard, and they giggled when they heard him laugh. He was elated to be with children again and he could not hold back his "Ho, ho, hooo!"

Wren finished making the cider and brought two adult-sized cups for her and Nicholas and three smaller cups for the children, which she placed at a kid-sized table near the fireplace. She blew on the small cups to make sure the drinks would not burn the children's mouths, and then she had them sit while mother and her old friend caught up. The girls were compliant and excited for warm cider and freshly baked sweet cakes as Wren sat at the big table with Nicholas. He had calmed down by now and felt welcomed and at home with Wren and her children.

"Wren, your daughters are so beautiful, just like their mother."

Wren blushed. "Thank you. They're wonderful, true gifts from God."

"Yes, they are. I'm not sure how to say this . . . I wish not to bring up any sad memories . . . but my sincere condolences to you for your loss. I just learned about it last night, what a horrible tragedy. I am so, so sorry."

"Thank you. I know you are sincere."

"I only heard good things about him. I heard he was a good man from a good family who loved the Lord."

"Yes. He was a good husband and father. Looking back, those dowry gifts from a generous donor saved my life and my sisters' lives. We could never repay that donor for what he, or she, did for us. We are forever indebted to that person for the kind act of love given us."

"I'm sure that donor would say that what we are is God's gift to us, and what we make of ourselves is our gift to God. It looks like you have taken what God has given you and made a beautiful, godly family. You have a beautiful home and life for you and your children. Knowing you, my dear Wren, you have always loved all you meet and are a blessing to all. I'm sure it is no different now."

"Thank you. You're too kind." They looked into each other's eyes long enough to feel slight embarrassment.

Wren broke eye contact and looked away, noticing Nicholas' walking staff. She paused and asked, "What happened?"

"Dax happened."

"Ah," she responded, "enough said."

They snickered together, and then Wren's oldest daughter asked if they could play with Nicholas' "funny cane." Nicholas obliged, and the girls took the staff into the next room where they played shepherds and animals. Little girl giggles could be heard throughout the house, and it brought a smile to Nicholas' face.

"Nicholas," Wren said, "I heard that you and many of the clergy members were on the brink of death when you were released. I thankfully didn't see you then, it would have broken my heart to see you in that condition, but I have to say that you look wonderful! And you have a new nose with character."

Nicholas chuckled. "Yes, a souvenir of the beating I took from the greatest warrior of all time. Lucky me."

"I like it. Makes you look tough. And you're getting a bit of gray in your beard."

"Gee, thanks for noticing!" Nicholas responded sarcastically as he stroked his beard.

"I like it! A lot! It makes you look distinguished. You've always been handsome, but now the gray makes you *dashingly* handsome."

"Hmm. Okay, well, I'll trust you're telling me the truth. I'll take dashingly handsome."

"You know me, I'm not an ear-tickler; I'm telling the truth."

"Oh my joy!" Nicholas exclaimed as a revelation hit him!

"What?!" said Wren, surprised at Nicholas' sudden burst of emotion.

"I am so sorry; it's so rude of me. But speaking of you being a blessing and being kind, thank you *so* much for this handsome and exquisite robe!" He stood to display it, spinning around. "I am so sorry I didn't say something sooner. I love it! Your kind act touched me in so many ways. You have no idea how wonderful you made me feel last night when they gave it to me, especially when Tana told me you had made it. Thank you, thank you!"

"You are so welcome. I'm glad you like it, and it looks like it fits you well."

"It fits me perfectly." Now that the nervous tension was gone, these lifelong friends chatted away as they had when they were younger; catching up on each other's lives and what God had taught them. They started back at the last time they had seen each other, under the mistletoe at Wren's home. Nicholas shared the Mikros' plan to relocate and Bishop Nicholas' plan for the next steps of the clergy. They had a meaningful time together and Nicholas played with her three daughters and told them stories, which, of course, they loved.

Alas, several hours had passed quickly, and the time for Nicholas to leave arrived. Wren and Nicholas agreed to meet monthly to enjoy each other's company and were thankful that they had been able to renew their friendship. Noll and the team picked Nicholas up and journeyed home. Nicholas was tired, but he could not have asked for a better day. A joyous day for sure!

## Devotion

Nicholas had friends and family that were precious to him. The Mikros clan, his uncle, his guards who became friends, and dear Wren, are some we've heard about. God was clearly in the center of those relationships.

Over the course of our lives, there will be people who come and go. Some will return, some won't. Some we'll miss, and some we won't. Sometimes we're the ones who leave. Sometimes we may return, sometimes not. Sometimes we'll be missed, sometimes maybe not. And then there are people who are with us for our lifetimes, and we are with them.

There is a saying that "people come into our lives for a reason, a season, or a lifetime. When you know which one it is, you will know what to do with that person." Regardless of which one it is, God calls us to love, and we do that by having Him at the center of all our relationships.

**Questions to consider:** Is there a person or people on my mind right now more than others? At this point in time, are these people here for a reason, a season, or a lifetime? Am I having nice thoughts or not-so-nice thoughts about them? Am I blessing them and praying for them regardless? It's a good habit to get into, to bless and pray for someone when they pop into your mind. They may need blessings and prayers at that moment. If I pop into someone's mind in a nice thought, or even in a not-so-nice thought, would I like that person to bless me and pray for me? Do I have God at the center of my relationships?

*"Put on then, as God's chosen ones, holy and beloved, heartfelt compassion, kindness, humility, gentleness, and patience, bearing with one another and forgiving one another, if one has a grievance against another; as the Lord has forgiven you, so must you also do. And over all these put on love, that is, the bond of perfection." Colossians 3:12-14*

*"And let the peace of Christ control your hearts, the peace into which you were also called in one body. And be thankful. Let the word of Christ dwell in you richly, as in all wisdom you teach and admonish one another, singing psalms, hymns, and spiritual songs with gratitude in your hearts to God. And whatever you do, in word or in deed, do everything in the name of the Lord Jesus, giving thanks to God the Father through him."*
*Colossians 3:15-17*

**Prayer:** "Heavenly Father, thank You for everyone You have brought into my life over my lifetime. Regardless of the reason, good or bad, You can teach me something from my experiences with them. Help me to have a teachable heart and mind. If I only knew them for a season, then help me bless them as they go, or bless them as I leave. And if I know them for a lifetime, may we have You in the center of our relationship, filled with Your love, grace, peace, patience, mercy, forgiveness, and encouragement for each other. Thank You. Amen."

# 27
# The New Bishop

NOVEMBER BROUGHT THE crucial meeting of clergy that Bishop Nicholas had organized. Approximately one hundred clergy members attended, and it was productive. Some church leaders from Rome, the central location of the Christian church, attended the gathering. They shared that the church in Rome would be able to help with the rebuilding process, but the local church would have to elicit additional financial support and labor. All were in agreement with this, and there was much encouragement among all in attendance. A spiritual awakening occurred among the clergy.

Since the meeting was in Patara, Nicholas had Argus and Baruch attend so he could introduce them and have the leaders discuss how best to recruit and train new clergy under the difficult circumstances. Some good ideas came about to help interested men such as Argus and Baruch. The two men had prayed about what God would want of them, and Argus felt led to do as Nicholas suggested and sought to become the new prison warden.

Argus gave it to God and sent a message to Sandor inquiring about the possibility. Sandor consulted with the rising emperor, Constantine, and both agreed that Argus would be a good fit. Argus would go to Rome to get more training on how to run a prison for the Roman Empire, and the church leaders in Rome said they would also do some training with Argus to prepare him for ministry as well. He would then be able to combine all he had learned to be an effective warden, not just for the prison and the empire, but also for the Kingdom of God. Argus was very excited to have all these doors opening for him and felt God's hand was in it all.

While Argus was away in Rome, Baruch would continue as interim warden while being trained under Bishop Nicholas and Father Nicholas for the priesthood. After Argus returned and Baruch's training was complete, then the church would determine where God was leading him to live and serve in the ministry. Nicholas was pleased with the opportunities that had arisen and he felt God's anointing on the events that had occurred.

After the meeting, all who had gathered from near and far went back to their homes with renewed energy and a strategy to rebuild. The contingency from Myra had many of their questions answered. However, the question of who would be their new bishop was left unanswered. They were instructed to go back home and pray. Bishop Nicholas understood their struggles and recognized the great need for assistance. They arranged for Nicholas to visit Myra with a team of Mikros builders to provide support for a short time, until they chose a new bishop.

A week later, Nicholas and the Mikros contingent journeyed the day and a half trip by wagon to Myra. They were almost there when darkness fell. Not being familiar with the area, they felt it safer to stop for the night and arrive in the morning rather than traveling in the darkness in unfamiliar territory with possible unknown dangers.

They broke camp early the next morning and arrived at the temporary building used as the church. When Nicholas arrived, he opened the doors and, much to his surprise, all the clergy in Myra were there praying. All bowed heads lifted and looked with great curiosity. The bright morning sunlight shone in the doorway behind him, blinding the clergy from seeing who their early visitor was.

As he stepped into the room further, people recognized Nicholas and whispered his name until a great clamor arose to greet him. They thanked God for answering their prayers. Nicholas was confused and asked what prayer was being answered, and they shared with him that God had told them to pray all night and that the first person to walk through their door in the morning would be their new bishop, the bishop of Myra. Nicholas was surprised and greatly honored. He said during his time there that he would pray about it for confirmation from God, and he also sent word back to his uncle to pray about it as well, because he and the church leaders in Rome would have the final say.

The Mikros team members that joined Nicholas were builders and craftsmen, so they helped the clergy clear the rubble from their burned down church. They salvaged what could be re-used and started building the foundation for their new church. The clergy members were so thankful for the assistance. When the time came for Nicholas and the team to return to Patara, the clergy were eager to hear what Nicholas sensed from the Holy Spirit. Nicholas said he felt the Lord leading him to accept the position of bishop in Myra, but he wanted to hear what his uncle and the church leaders heard from God.

The message from his uncle arrived that morning, and in front of everyone, he opened the scroll with the bishop's emblem on it. It had one word written upon it: "Yea." Celebration erupted! Nicholas was to be the new bishop of Myra, and the clergy members there could not have been happier.

Nicholas explained that he would travel home first to take care of personal matters and spend Christ's birthday, which was a month away, with his family, friends, and congregation. Then he would return after the New Year to begin his duties in Myra on a part-time basis, spending two weeks in Myra and two weeks in Patara until the following fall. Nicholas wanted to be part time until after the Mikros migrated north, then he would perform his duties full time in Myra. The clergy thought that reasonable; they knew Nicholas had many ties to Patara, and it was only fair to allow him to arrange his affairs in the period of time he felt appropriate. Nicholas was grateful to them for their understanding.


News spread quickly. Everyone from Lycia to Rome heard the news. When Nicholas returned to Patara, he stopped by Wren's to inform her personally. She took it well, as well as could be expected, and was glad to hear that he would still be in Patara two weeks every month and that they would still have their monthly get-togethers.

She shared some news of her own as well. Falon, Tana, Noll, and Glikia had been talking with her about their relocation to the north, and she had felt a strange stirring from within, urging her to go also. She had already been contemplating moving back to the country because the city life was not for her; she did not want to raise her girls there as it had become more crowded and dangerous, especially without her daughters' father. Wren shared her thoughts with the Mikros clan, and they said she had always felt like a part of their family, and she felt the same, so she and her daughters would be more than welcome to move with them.

Wren mentioned the possible move to her mother, Madelyn, and the older woman said that this would be something she would be interested in doing as well. The thought of living among the Mikros clan felt right for both of them. For Wren, the idea of surrounding her daughters with the God-centered living and loving people of the Mikros clan was a perfect scenario.

Kalista and Kyla were married with their own families and living in other parts of the region, so she rarely saw them. She also rarely saw her in-laws because they were busy with their shipping business. In addition, seeing Wren and the girls was a sad and difficult reminder for them of losing their son, so Wren was feeling like God was slowly releasing her of any ties to the region. Her last tie was to Nicholas, and with him being a priest and now becoming a bishop and moving to Myra, that seemed to be the final answer for her. She no longer felt a connection keeping her in Patara.

Nicholas was sad to hear that Wren would be gone as well as the Mikros clan in a matter of time, but he understood her viewpoint. Though sad for himself, he thought it wonderful for Wren, her daughters, and Madelyn. He had in his mind that he would make every effort to visit them up north as often as he could.

When Nicholas returned home to the Mikroses' house, they had already heard the news from the team members who had joined Nicholas in Myra. They were happy for him, but there was a solemn feeling as well. He would be phasing out of their lives again. They all agreed that change was not always easy, but if it was God's will, then it was good. They all felt their plans were in God's hands.

## Devotion

Lots of changes are happening for Nicholas and his work, social, and family systems that include Wren, the Mikroses, Argus and Baruch, and his Christian church family. In life, change is inevitable. One thing in life that does not change is God. God is the same yesterday, today, and tomorrow.

Thankfully! He is the one constant we have. He is the center of Nicholas' different systems, and as believers, they all have God to focus on, center them, and help them navigate the change.

**Questions to consider:** Is God the center of my social, family, work, and other systems in my life? When change happens that takes me out of my comfort zone, am I focusing on God? Am I letting Him center me and help me navigate change in a healthy manner that's good for me and those around me?

*"Jesus Christ is the same yesterday and today and forever." Hebrews 13:8*

*"Your word is a lamp for my feet, a light for my path." Psalm 119:105*

*"Trust in the Lord with all your heart, on your own intelligence do not rely; In all your ways be mindful of him, and he will make straight your paths." Proverbs 3:5-6*

*"I command you: be strong and steadfast! Do not fear nor be dismayed, for the Lord, your God, is with you wherever you go." Joshua 1:9*

**Prayer:** "God, give me grace to accept with serenity the things that cannot be changed, Courage to change the things which should be changed, and the Wisdom to distinguish the one from the other." (Original Serenity Prayer portion by Reinhold Niebuhr)

# 28
# The Big Event

AFTER A COUPLE somber days of mentally adjusting to the new changes ahead for all of them, Nicholas and the Mikros clan all snapped out of their pity party when Wren and her daughters visited for the day. Having little children around with their endless energy, natural curiosity, and playfulness, this lifted the spirits of everyone and reminded them of their big plan, the big gift-giving extravaganza!

What was the night they chose to bear gifts to all the good boys and girls who believe? What better night than the eve of Jesus' birthday! The plan was to leave toys by fireplaces hidden in or under stockings and shoes, so when the children woke up, they would find the gifts on the day God gave us His own greatest gift, His son, Jesus Christ the Lord. Amen!

After Wren's visit, the preparation work began. The whole Mikros clan helped scout the region for homes in which children lived and map out the best route to take. They would start at midnight and finish before sunup. They scouted by day and continued carving toys in the evenings all the way up to Christmas Eve.

Kari, Dax, and Wren surprised Nicholas with his very own pair of trousers, and, even better, they matched his red robe with white trim. Kari and Dax solicited Wren's help, since she was an amazing tailor and already had the same fabric. She happily agreed. Additionally, she made Nicholas a pair of warm, black leather boots that were as soft as anything Nicholas had ever worn. They were extra quiet for walking on rooftops, they had excellent grip on the bottom to prevent against slipping, and they were snug so he could feel the surfaces. They were perfect, and Nicholas was so thankful for these gifts. They were ready!

When Christmas Eve arrived, Nicholas was running late due to trying to figure out how to wear his new clothes. Kari and Dax, very time-oriented people, were growing impatient. They had even invented sundials to wear on their wrists to help tell the time wherever they were during the day. Finally, Nicholas arrived at the barn and stopped to discuss with Noll how the reindeer would pull the wagon. Kari walked by and yelled in an annoyed tone, "Talk does not cook rice!" Then she walked away.

Nicholas looked at Noll and asked what that meant.

"That's Kari's way of saying hurry up."

Then Dax walked by, and, looking just as annoyed as Kari, he pointed to his sundial and walked away.

Nicholas looked at Noll, confused because it was almost midnight. There was no sun. "Why was Dax pointing to his sundial?"

Noll shrugged his shoulders. "I have no idea. Maybe it's a moondial at night."

Nicholas petted the two reindeer pulling his wagon. They were quieter than horses since their hooves were softer and they were calmer than horses, so it made sense to use them. He gave them each a carrot and said, "Okay, Dasher and Dancer, let's have some fun. Ho, ho, hoo!"

Nicholas boarded the wagon; he had Sandor's whip in hand. He had his special bag in which he had carried his scrolls all these years. It was now was filled with toys, and he had extra toys stuffed into nooks and crannies of the wagon. With a slight crack of his whip signaling the reindeer, they were off!

Noll, Kari, and Dax organized all the toys according to house and route in numerous wagons in the barn. Of course, every home would get their very own manger scene to display and remind them of the Reason for the Season. Throughout the night, they planned to meet Nicholas in strategic locations and exchange his empty wagon with one full of toys. When arriving at the marked house, Nicholas would fill his special bag with the well-organized gifts for that home. He would sneak in an open window, if there were one. If not, then he would nimbly bound up to the roof in his new trousers and soft leather boots, via a ladder on the wagon, then climb down the chimney, deliver the presents, and then back up the chimney, back to the wagon and off to the next house.

But (and it's a giant, colossal BUT!) something very unexpected happened that night that even amazed Nicholas. He found he *never* had to refill his special bag! The bag would continually fill with presents, but not just any random presents—the gifts that matched each house. These were the same gifts the Mikros family had labeled and organized. It was a Christmas MIRACLE!

When Jesus had compassion for the multitudes of people who followed Him and grew hungry, Jesus took five loaves of bread and two fish, and He looked up to Heaven and gave thanks. The food in the baskets multiplied to feed more than five thousand men, in addition to all the women and children!

Likewise, it appeared God had compassion for Nicholas and the Mikroses, who followed Him and grew hungry to use their gifts and talents to bless others. It seemed by using a sack that had held God's miraculous Word for many years, and doing this kind act to honor a Holy Day, that God gave them a Christmas Eve miracle! Praise be to God!

If one had happened to be awake during the night and were in the right place at the right time, a faint "ho, ho, hoo" could be heard. Nicholas could not contain the joy welling up inside him. He would occasionally burst out in laughter, thinking of the miracle God had given to him while doing what he loved most—giving to others!

The night went smooth and quickly. Back at the house, Noll, Kari, and Dax discovered something special was happening as well because when they went out to the barn to gather the toy-filled wagons to deliver to Nicholas, they discovered the barn was empty! Completely and utterly empty! They knew God's hand was behind it. Somehow, some way, God was doing something special. They did not know what exactly, but they knew.

That morning of Christ's birthday, when the sun was rising, Nicholas arrived back at the house. Over a big hearty breakfast, he confirmed to the whole family the Christmas miracle they had discerned earlier that morning in the empty barn. They rejoiced and gave God glory! Glory be to God, Hosanna in the highest! After a time of praise and worship, Nicholas, Noll,

Glikia, Kari, and Dax rode in one wagon into town, while Falon, Tana, John, and Leila rode in a second wagon. They could not wait to see what was happening. When they arrived, what did their wondering eyes see?

Everywhere they went, they saw children in front of their homes playing with little toy sailors, farmers, ranchers, shepherds, and soldiers. There were toy farm animals, wild animals, horses, and even reindeer. There were toy wagons, chariots, and ships. There were yo-yos and building blocks, too! Everywhere, they saw their toys being played with they saw happy children and happy parents through and through, all thankful to God. People wished Nicholas and the Mikroses a very Merry Christmas and a Mighty Christmas as they rode by, and no one knew it was they, who were responsible for the gifts, success! Glory to God!

"Oh, joy!" exclaimed Nicholas, probably for every single child he saw. There were many "Oh, joys!" that day!

At lunchtime, they stopped by Wren's house where she and Madelyn had prepared lunch for all of them. They shared with them the Christmas miracle and rejoiced. They gave God glory all over again. They ate and watched Wren's three daughters play with their toys, and, of course, Nicholas was down on the floor playing right along with them. "Oh, joy!"

They left after lunch, taking Wren, Madelyn and the girls with them. They picked up Bishop Nicholas, who had finished conducting Christ-Masses that morning for all the city parishioners. They picked up Argus and Baruch, who had conducted a Christ-Mass for each floor in the prison that morning.

That afternoon, they all gathered out in the country at Nicholas' old family home. All the other Mikros families, Father Absalom, and Amara and her family were already there preparing the Christmas feast. Captain Omar, brothers Pol and Aindriú, Lukas, Marcus, Mathias, Pietro, and Yahya were there as well, surprising Nicholas with a visit! They all rejoiced and celebrated a Christ-Mass, giving thanks for the Reason for the Season, for the true meaning of Christmas, to God for the ultimate gift in Jesus. After the mass and singing happy birthday to Jesus, blessing the food and giving thanks, the feast began! It was a glorious day!

Over the following months, there was much excitement and buzz as everyone slowly transitioned into their new lives. Nicholas started his part-time bishop duties in Myra every two weeks per month, and he spent the other two weeks per month being a part of the Mikroses' planning, ministering with Bishop Nicholas in Patara, and spending time with Wren and her girls.

The Mikroses were sending teams of people to plant encampments along the way, about a day's ride apart from each other for points of rest while traveling between the north and south. They also had a team at their new settlement in the north, living with Amuruq and his clan, and learning their ways of adapting to the cold. They learned how to cope with snowy winters and the warmer summer months. They built homes, barns, and workshops like those to which they were accustomed for their businesses and crafts. They were ready to make toys!

The Mikroses still owned their lands and lucrative businesses around Patara, but they took in non-Mikros people who fit the culture, such as Amara and her husband, to manage their properties and businesses. The Mikroses paid well. They were fair landowners and excellent trainers, so this was a blessing to their workers giving them more responsibilities and more pay. This allowed families like Amara's to be able to raise their standard of giving, which brought them joy.

Spring came and went, and then summer came and went. By September, the majority of the Mikros clan had emigrated north, and the day came when the last of the bunch would leave. Falon, Tana, John, and Leila rode in one packed wagon. Noll and Glikia rode another packed wagon with Vida tied along. Kari and Dax rode their horses. The last few other Mikros clan families had their wagons, and, lastly, the new bishop of Myra, Nicholas, drove the final packed wagon with Wren by his side, along with her three daughters and Madelyn. Shimmel and Aria were tied to their wagon to follow along.

With a crack of his redeemed whip, Nicholas signaled to all in the caravan to begin their trek north to their new homeland. Nicholas took a short leave of absence from Myra to join them on the journey and be a part of this momentous occasion, to learn the route and all the Mikroses' stops along the way, and to see their new home. Then, riding Shimmel, he would return to minister full time to the people of Myra and those traveling through.

Nicholas kept his promise and visited up north as often as he could. Alternately, the Mikroses made toys and sent regular wagon shipments south to Nicholas. They helped him organize and store them to give away to all the good boys and girls who believe, every year, on Christmas Eve.

## Devotion

Nicholas and the Mikros clan loved to give! Giving is not just giving a present, it can also involve giving thought, time, energy, skills, talents, and resources. There can be a lot involved in giving. So as much as they would receive joy from giving, it was not always easy. At times it felt like a labor of love that required sacrifice, all for the benefit of making those who received their gifts happy. The more thankful the gift receivers, the more joy-filled the gift givers.

In general, all of us enjoy giving and receiving! It's fun to give and make someone happy! And it's fun to be thought of and be made happy receiving a gift! Amen?!

**Questions to consider:** Am I giving my time, energy, skills, talents, and resources to others, especially to those less fortunate than me? When I give, am I a cheerful giver? When I receive, am I a thankful receiver?

*"Each must do as already determined, without sadness or compulsion, for God loves a cheerful giver." 2 Corinthians 9:7*

*"Whoever gives benefits will be amply enriched, and whoever refreshes others will be refreshed." Proverbs 11:25*

*"Give and gifts will be given to you; a good measure, packed together, shaken down, and overflowing, will be poured into your lap. For the measure with which you measure will in return be measured out to you." Luke 6:38*

*"You are being enriched in every way for all generosity, which through us produces thanksgiving to God." 2 Corinthians 9:11*

**Prayer:** "Heavenly Father, help me recognize all You give to me, and help me have a thankful heart and mind. And, as You are generous and give freely to me, help me recognize all I have is from You, causing me to turn around and be generous and give freely to those around me. And to those who bless me with gifts, help me be ever so grateful. Thank You. Amen."

## 29
# Do You Believe?

"AS TIME WENT ON," Kris finishes, "Nicholas obeyed Jesus' Great Commission to 'Go into all the world and preach the gospel to all creation.' Jesus' gospel is the gospel of St. Nicholas, the gospel of Santa Claus. It is the Biblical gospel of Matthew, Mark, Luke, and John and all those who believe in Jesus and who continue to share it all over the world. Nicholas and the Mikros clan worked year round and limited the gift-giving travel to just one day of the year—that being the eve of one of the holiest days of the year, Christmas, which was symbolic of giving as much as any holy day, or, as we say today, holiday."

"Arrival to North Town, five minutes, five minutes!" Conductor Maggie's voice announces throughout the train. They hear the sound of train pistons releasing steam and feel the train slowing down.

Wayne, unfazed by the announcement, says, "I don't understand. You said Nicholas went back to Myra, but Santa Claus lives at the North Pole."

"Good observation, Wayne. Of course, there is more to the story. Nicholas went on to do many great things, but as we all get older, we transition into other phases of life. Some people retire, some people change careers, some people travel. There were even rumors that Nicholas had died, if you could believe that. Humbug!"

Laura announces, "I got this, Mr. Kris. I know exactly what happened next. We're finally to the good part of the story." She turns to Wayne. "This is what happened. Nicholas went back to Myra and did more great things as a bishop. Meanwhile, he made many, *many* visits to the north, which is actually the North Pole, seeing Noll and everyone, but, most importantly, seeing and courting *Wreeen*."

"What's courting?" Wayne asks.

"That's the old-fashioned way of saying making Wren his *girrrlfrieeend*." Wayne makes an ew-girls-have-cooties face.

Laura continues, absorbed in her own story, sounding more like a teenager than nine years old, "So after Nicholas did this traveling back and forth deal for a long while, eventually God called him into a new full-time ministry of being Santa Claus. So, he retired from being a bishop and moved to the North Pole full time. He joined in the business of toy making with the Mikros clan, who tradition now calls elves. Now every Christmas Eve Santa travels the world delivering toys to all the good boys and girls who believe in Jesus. And, finally, this is what we've *all* been waiting for! Nicholas finally marries the beautiful Wren, his long-lost childhood love! And living happily ever after, they are the Santa and Mrs. Claus we all know and love today!" Laura takes a big, satisfied breath and exhales, smiling.

Wayne says, "Ohhh, okay."

Kris, Joe, and Mary, a little in awe of Laura's ending to the story, all look at each other with nothing to add, change, or delete. They shrug their shoulders; it sounds good to them.

Kris turns to Laura and says, "Miss Laura, I couldn't have said it any better myself. Well done, bravo!" He gives her a wink.

Thomas rolls his eyes. "Whatever."

Wayne asks, "Hey, how does the poem end?"

No one is sure what Wayne is talking about, and then it dawns on Kris. He starts:

*'Twas the night before Christmas, when all through the house*
*Not a creature was stirring, not even a mouse;*
*The stockings were hung by the chimney with care, In hopes that . . .*

All together, including Wayne this time, chime in, "St. Nicholas would soon be there!"

*The children were nestled all snug in their beds;*
*While visions of sugar plums danced in their heads;*
*And mamma in her 'kerchief, and I in my cap,*
*Had just settled our brains for a long winter's nap.*
*When out on the lawn there arose such a clatter,*
*I sprang from the bed to see what was the matter.*
*Away to the window I flew like a flash,*
*Tore open the shutters and threw up the sash.*

*The moon on the breast of the new-fallen snow,*
*Gave the luster of midday to objects below,*
*When, what to my wandering eyes should appear,*
*But a miniature sleigh, and eight tiny reindeer,*
*With a little old driver, so lively and quick,*
*I knew in a moment he must be . . .*

All together, they exclaim, "St. Nick!"

"One minute! One minute!" Conductor Maggie's voice is heard in the aisle outside their compartment doorway.

Kris tells Wayne, "Your father will read it to you before bed tonight. Okay?" Wayne nods. Kris looks at Joe, and Joe gives Wayne a thumbs up.

Conductor Maggie appears. "Well, everyone, the wonderful train engineer, who happens to be my wonderful husband, Jeb, and I hope you had a wonderful trip with us!" Everyone cheers.

"Maggie," Kris says, "thank you so much for your hospitality. Do you and Jeb have any special plans for Christmas?"

"Kristopher, I'm looking forward to clearing the train and finishing up work for the evening to go home with my hubby and cuddle for an evening nap together with our kids in front of the fire. Then we'll awake later tonight to go enjoy a worshipful, midnight Christmas Eve service at church worshipping God, then back to bed, to wake up in the morning to see what Santa brought for our precious little kiddos under the Christmas tree. We'll spend the rest of the day relaxing, eating and celebrating Jesus' birthday with them."

Kris stands and gives her a strong hug. "That sounds wonderful! God bless you, my dear, and Jeb, and your lovely children! Merry Christmas!"

"Thank you, Kris. Merry Christmas to you, and the missus!"

Before Maggie steps out, Joe says, "Thank you, Conductor Maggie, for the wonderful train ride!"

"We had an amazing time," Mary adds, "and you were so kind and helpful. Thank you!"

Joe turns to the kids. "Kids?"

Thomas, Laura, and Wayne offer together, "Thank youuu!"

"You're so welcome, and we'll do it again in a few days when we go south and take you back home. Make sure you leave milk and cookies out for Santa tonight, and leave some oats and carrots out for his reindeer, too." Wayne and Laura nod their heads excitedly. Thomas gives her a courtesy smile. "Merry Christmas everyone!" She waves and walks out of the compartment, and they hear her as she moves toward the next train car. "Ho, ho, hooo! We have arrived, so now it's time for you to leave. Quickly. Merry Christmas!"

People shuffle down the aisle and down the stairs to exit the train. Kris turns to the family and abruptly says, "I need to run out and make sure my helpers are here. I will see you before you leave." Then he was gone.

Joe and Mary look at each other, surprised by Kris' sudden departure. Then, noticing the hustle and bustle, Joe says to everyone, "Let's go, hurry up! Grandma and Grandpa are waiting for us!" He grabs some luggage and packages, jumps in the aisle, and heads for the exit.

Mary looks at the kids next. "Hurry up!" Then she departs.

Laura quips to the boys, "Hurry up!" and is gone.

Thomas breaks the cycle. Instead of barking at Wayne, he picks his big suitcase up with one hand, a big wrapped present in the other, and he steps aside in the aisle. He lets his little brother, carrying his own suitcase and a present, go ahead of him.

"Thanks, my brother from another mother," Wayne says.

"You can't say that to me. It doesn't work."

"Why not?"

"Because we have the same mother."

"Oh, okay then. Thanks, my brother from the same mother."

Thomas shakes his head. "Whatever." They both walk down the aisle to exit the train.

Outside the train, the daylight is winding down as the sun drops behind the snow-covered, tree-lined hills. Dusk is slowly settling in. The train has only ten-passenger cars total and a few storage-only cars at the back.

Kris is outside, toward the rear of the train, near the last car directing about twenty helpers as they unload boxes, packages, groceries, and Christmas wrapping paper in the developing shadows.

The helpers are small and nimble, well organized, and choreographed, and they are moving swiftly as if they have done this a thousand times before. Like ants carrying their goods, they have a line going back and forth from the train storage cars to the tree line, disappearing into the woods and then coming back again. With the train station at the front of the train and all the passengers gathering in the front being picked up by their rides for their next destinations, these stealthy workers blend into the shadows unnoticed.

Joe and Mary find Mary's parents who are around Kris' age. They are standing next to a big blue vehicle that has three rows of seats and its back doors open, awaiting luggage. Everyone shares holiday greetings, hugs, and kisses. The air is cold and snow flurries linger after a newly fallen bed of snow has covered the countryside. There is plenty of bustling around as luggage is loaded into cars. Kris wanders up to the family gathering to say his goodbyes.

"Well, Joe and Mary, it has been a pleasure traveling with you."

Mary responds, "Oh, Kris, you have to meet my parents!" Excitedly, she pulls him behind the vehicle where her parents are. "Mom, Dad, this is Kris. He was our wonderful traveling companion who made our trip the best! He truly made it the train ride of our lives!"

Kris reaches out his arms and gives Mary's mother a big hug. "Oh, Evelyn, I've heard so much about you. Merry Christmas!"

"Well, thank you," Evelyn says, "and a very Merry Christmas to you, Kris! So nice to meet you!"

Mary, Evelyn, and Joe go back to loading the car and chatting busily as Kris turns to greet Mary's father. He reaches out his hand for a handshake and says, "Merry Christmas, Regis!"

"Thank you, Merry Christmas to you, Kris." Regis gives a firm handshake and is friendly, but a bit reserved.

Kris says encouragingly, "You have a beautiful family here. Enjoy them this holiday season!"

"I will thank you. By God's grace, we're blessed to have them visit. Life's short, and for some of us life's even shorter, so we'll enjoy it while we can." Regis' face has some sadness in it as he rubs his chest where his heart is.

Kris sees this and, with compassion on his face and hope in his voice, he says, "From what I can see, you've instilled love in your daughter, and you've taught her the ways of our Lord." He touches Regis' chest with his hand. "You're a good man with a *good* heart." At "good heart", Kris gives a firm pat to Regis' chest. The sadness on Regis' face slowly gives way to a smile. It feels good to smile again, it's been a while for him. He does not know what just happened and is at a loss for words, however, he feels good.

"God is good, amen?"

"Amen," Regis affirms.

"Do you believe?"

"Yes, I'm a believer."

"Good, me too." He gives Regis a wink. "I'm sorry to hurry off, Regis, but I must finish my goodbyes and be on my way. A long, busy night ahead for me. Merry Christmas to you!"

Regis, feeling very thankful to have met this new acquaintance, replies, "Yes, Merry Christmas! Thank you!" What he is so thankful for, he is not sure, but he knows he feels blessed for something special in that moment.

With a nod, Kris is off to say more goodbyes.

Regis finds himself putting his hand on his chest; it feels better or it's his imagination. He has peace about it, either way. He feels the Spirit of Christmas stirring inside him, and it feels awesome!

Kris finds Mary around the corner of the vehicle and hugs her. She tears up and is not sure why. She is taken aback by the sudden surge of emotion and is a bit embarrassed.

Kris reassures her, "It's okay. It's good. Tears are healing, and these are tears of joy. Know that your many faithful prayers all these years have been heard. Yes?" She nods. "Even during those dry seasons when you thought you were talking to a wall, you were being heard and cared for. Your patience and trust and prayers are beginning to bear fruit, okay?"

She nods. "Yes, thank you."

"God's telling you, 'Mary, well done, good and faithful servant.'"

At that, Mary's tears flow even more; those words minister to her spirit like she has never experienced before. She feels validated in a way she never has. They are the exact words she needed to hear in that exact moment. "Do you believe?" he asks.

"Yes, I believe. Thank you, Kris."

"You are more than just a believer, you're a disciple, soon to be an apostle making disciples of your family spreading to the nations."

She kisses Kris on the cheek and steps away to compose herself before she loses total control of her tears. She wants to do so, but not at that moment or place. She is filled with peace and joy.

Joe notices Mary step away from Kris and comes over. "Is Mare okay?" he asks.

"She's more than okay." He smiles.

"Good. This may sound weird, but thank you, Kris, for the roller coaster ride of emotions you took us on. Happy, sad, mad, holy moly, I'm emotionally drained! It looks like my wife will be, too." He smiles, shaking his head in dismay, and then he chuckles aloud. It was the ride of his life, and he's all wiped out but still functioning on an adrenaline rush. He embraces Kris with a bear hug and says, sincerely, "Thank you, for everything."

Kris asks, "Do you believe now?"

"Thanks to you. Also, thanks to the love, patience, and, I'm sure, lots of prayers of an amazing wife. By the amazing grace of a gracious God who saved a wretch like me, I believe. 'I once was lost but now am found, 'twas blind, but now I see.' Yes, Kris. I believe."

"Oh, joy! Mighty Christmas, Joe."

"Mighty Christmas, Kris."

Joe turns around going back to helping Regis organize the luggage and packages to fit securely in the big vehicle. The four adults excitedly chatter away.

## Devotion

This family trusted Kris on the train. There were times when they were not sure where he was taking them on their journey with Nicholas' story, but they did their best to hang in there with him and be patient and trust that things were going to end well.

God wants to be with us in the train compartment of our lives. He wants us to trust Him, hang in there with Him, and be patient. He wants to be involved in our transformation, but this requires us to trust Him. Unfortunately, many of us have trust issues and have had them maybe going back as far as our childhoods. We have difficulty trusting others, trusting ourselves, and even trusting God.

Have you ever done one of those trust falls where you fold your arms, close your eyes, and fall backward, requiring you to trust the two people standing behind you to catch you? You have to trust they will catch your full weight. Do you get a little anxious just thinking about it?

**Questions to consider:** Am I putting my full trust in God? Will I allow the fullness of who I am, what I carry, and what I'm struggling with to fall spiritually into God's arms?

**Answer:** Whether we live like it or not, God can catch and take on the full weight of our lives. God is so committed to us, God loves us so much, God is so mindful of us that He tells us, yes, we can bring on the full weight of ourselves, our marriages, single lives, health, finances, career, brokenness, unresolved issues, and anything else weighing heavy on us. We can let the whole weight of our lives fall into the grace, love, peace, truth, wisdom, and power of the spiritual arms of God.

*"The eternal God is your refuge, and underneath are the everlasting arms."*
*Deuteronomy 33:27*

*"Sovereign Lord, you are God! Your covenant is trustworthy, and you have promised these good things to your servant." 2 Samuel 7:28*

*"May the God of hope fill you with all joy and peace as you trust in him, so that you may overflow with hope by the power of the Holy Spirit."*
*Romans 15:13*

*"Come to me, all you who are weary and burdened, and I will give you rest. Take my yoke upon you and learn from me, for I am gentle and humble in heart, and you will find rest for your souls. For my yoke is easy and my burden is light." Matthew 11:28-30*

**Prayer:** "Heavenly Father, help me put my full trust in You, for who I am, what I'm carrying, and what I'm struggling with. Heal me from past hurts that interfere with my ability to fully trust You, others, and myself. Thank You. Amen."

# 30
# 𝔄 𝔅ig 𝔑ight

KRIS WALKS AROUND to the other side of the vehicle and finds Laura and Wayne throwing snowballs. He calls out, "Miss Laura! Master Wayne!"

They drop their snowballs and run to hug him. He sits down on a bench, and each child takes a seat on one of his knees. Thomas is leaning against the train while the adults pack the vehicle. He watches Kris and his siblings, with the woods in the background. The scene seems vaguely familiar for some reason.

Movement toward the back of the train catches his attention, piquing his curiosity, but Kris and his siblings keep drawing Thomas' attention back as he listens. Thomas misses witnessing one of Kris' male helpers jumping out of the train, leading with his elbow, and pile driving an unsuspecting female helper, laying her out. He scurries away with an armful of packages. She is dazed, but manages to gather herself and stagger back to work.

Kris asks Laura and Wayne, "So what did you learn about the true story of Santa Claus and Christmas?"

Laura starts, "We learned that Santa Claus is St. Nick, whose real name is Nicholas."

"We learned that he really loves God," Wayne contributes.

"We learned that he wants us all to remember Jesus is the real reason for Christmas," Laura says.

"Christmas is Jesus' birthday."

"That Jesus is God on earth telling us how much He loves us and how He wants us to live."

Wayne adds, "We are to be thankful for everything we get. And to be thankful for the Gift-Giver more than the gift."

Laura finishes, "And Jesus is the greatest Gift ever. And believing in Jesus is the best Gift we could ever give ourselves."

Kris is amazed. "Wow, I think you are two of the smartest children in the world! Do you believe, Laura?"

She answers, "Yes, I believe in Jesus."

"Do you believe, Wayne?"

"Yes, I believe in Jesus," the boy says earnestly.

"Don't ever stop believing, and you'll always have the miracle of Christmas in your heart. Okay?"

"Okay," they say together, as brothers and sisters sometimes do.

"Will we ever see you again?" Laura asks.

"That's a great question. As you are my sister from another mister in the Lord and as my brother from another mother in the Lord, it's not goodbye. It's 'see you later,' right?" They nod.

"So, I don't know when later will be; it could be on earth, it could be in Heaven, but it sure will be wonderful when later arrives." They smile and nod in agreement.

"Merry Christmas, Miss Laura. Merry Christmas, Master Wayne!"

"Merry Christmas, Kris!"

He hugs them both and they hop off his lap. They go back to throwing snowballs. Laura says, "I'm Kari the Killerrr!" as she whizzes a snowball by Wayne's head.

"Ha!" says Wayne, "I'm Dax the Destroyerrr!" flinging a snowball back at her.

Kris begins to walk toward the train to board and notices Thomas standing there. "Well, Master Thomas, it has been an honor traveling with you."

"It's nice to have met you, sir."

"Please don't be too smart for your own good, okay?"

Thomas chuckles. "I'll try not to be."

"Intellect is a gift from God, and I think God has given you an abundance. What you are is God's gift to you, what you make of yourself is your gift to God. Sadly, for many so-called intellectuals, this asset has become a stumbling block to knowing the Truth and being saved. Some people need some proof. Sadly, for some others, proof is never enough. Have I at least given you some food for thought about God, Jesus, the Holy Spirit? About Christmas, St. Nicholas, and Santa Claus?"

"Yes, you have me questioning a few things."

"Ah, questioning is good! Questioning is asking. It's seeking. It's knocking. Jesus says, 'Ask and it will be given to you; seek and you will find; knock and the door will be opened to you.'"

"Just like Nicholas got Empress Prisca, Valeria, and the future Emperor Constantine to do."

"Exactly! And if you are open to possibilities, Master Thomas, then possibilities are possible."

Kris smiles and shakes Thomas' hand. "Merry Christmas, Master Thomas."

"Merry Christ . . . Mass, Mr. Kris."

Kris smiles even bigger and points to Thomas, saying, "Oh, joy! I like it!" Thomas opens his hand to find seven chocolate gold coins. Now *he* smiles widely. Kris requests as he steps away, "Please share with your family, okay?" Thomas gives an affirming nod. "Keep your eyes open to the possibilities, Master Thomas, keep your eyes open and watch for the simple answer to be right in front of you!"

Behind them, another scene unfolds in the shadows. The female helper baits the male to jump again, but this time she steps aside, leaving the flying male with only the hard frozen ground to break his fall, landing flat on his back. He groans and lies there for a moment, doing a body check to see if he is all right. He rises but is hunching over in pain.

At this point, there are very few people left at the train station. Regis, Evelyn, Joe, and Mary are wrapping up their conversations while waiting for the kids to say their goodbyes to Kris. Kris announces loudly, "I forgot one last item on the train. Merry Christmas to all, and to all a good night!" Everyone shouts Merry Christmas greetings and waves to him as Kris bounds back onto the train.

Thomas immediately jumps in the back third-row seat and finds himself drawn to Kris as his siblings were when they first met him. Thomas watches Kris as he boards the train and then appears in the train compartment they shared. He picks up a forgotten, wrapped package from under the seat and tucks it under his arm, but then instead of coming back out the same way to the front of the train, Kris surprisingly walks toward the back of the train to exit. He leaps down the stairs, off the train, and starts heading straight toward the woods.

By now, Regis is in the driver's seat, Evelyn is in the front passenger seat, and Thomas and Wayne are in the back-row seat. Wayne looks out the window and sees the little blue-eyed, blonde girl he met on the train sitting in a nearby car looking at him. She smiles and gives him a thumbs-up. Wayne smiles and gives a thumbs-up back to her as her car pulls away. He checks his pocket to see if the chocolate gold coin she secretly gave him is still there. It is. He smiles as he thinks about being more thankful for the cute, little gift-giver, than he is for the gift, wishing he could have gotten to know her more.

Mary, who had to brush snow off Laura and Wayne before they got into the vehicle, is now waiting her turn to enter while Laura climbs into her seat in the middle row. Laura is excited to get to grandma and grandpa's house and yells, "Let's go! Talk does not cook rice!"

Kris is halfway across the small snow-covered field between the train and the woods when he hears Laura's loud command. He chuckles. He looks over in time to see and hear Joe say, in a very loud voice for all to hear, "Hold on, hold on! We still have the most precious cargo left to load!"

Mary, thinking everything was loaded, turns around to see what Joe is talking about and before she can ask, Joe scoops her up in his strong arms and twirls her around in a circle. He looks deeply into her eyes and says, "You." Mary melts into Joe's arms. He gives her a sweet kiss on the lips.

Evelyn and Laura say, "Awww."

Wayne says, "Ew."

Kris smiles approvingly and exclaims to himself, "Well done, my good man, well done."

*Then what does Thomas' wandering eyes see?*
*A scene so incredible he cannot believe! Or can he?*

*As he watches Kris walk toward the dark wood,*
*a torchlight flares up, lighting an opening, where Kris has now stopped and stood.*

*Kris miraculously transforms from a goateed man in a pinstriped suit, to a*
*white-bearded gent in a majestic red robe, and on each foot, a black boot.*

*In his red hat, it's difficult to refute,*
*he is Santa Claus!*

*Thomas dares not to blink. Before entering the woods,*
*Kris, Santa, or St. Nick, whoever he is, gives Thomas a wink!*

*But wait! This jolly ol' gent is not alone!*

*Suddenly, more and more torches light up with glee, from the edge of the*
*woods through the trees as far as the eyes can see.*

*People of small stature dash and dart about,*
*tending to four giant sleighs, four reindeer each, of which they go in and out.*

*As they are preparing to make way,*
*Thomas' mouth drops wide open, exclaiming, "I believe, I must say."*

Joe gently places Mary in her seat, closes her door, and runs around to the other side to get in.

Thomas is in a state of disbelief. He says more loudly, "I believe."

Joe looks back, puzzled at the revelation-filled look on Thomas' face. "Great son, I'm happy for you. What do you believe?"

"I believe!" is all Thomas can say, looking back and seeing St. Nick waving goodbye to him as he takes leave.

Joe has no clue what is going on, so he looks at Mary and Mary looks at him. They both shrug their shoulders, not knowing what has gotten into their eldest son.

Evelyn turns around in the front passenger seat and says, "That man you met on the train, Kris, there's something very familiar about him, a good familiar. I feel like I know him from somewhere. I wonder who he is."

Thomas raises his voice and points out the window to the lit-up woods, still able to see Santa and his helpers walking to their sleighs. "I believe!"

Everyone looks at Thomas, wondering what in the world he is talking about, but no one looks to where he's pointing.

Regis chimes in, "Yes, Kris seems familiar to me, too. A gentle, friendly spirit is he." Regis smiles and touches his chest. "A real blessing to have met."

Mary ponders aloud for a moment, "Hmm, we talked about you a little with Kris, but now that I think about it, I don't remember any of us mentioning your names. Yet he called you both by name. How strange." Joe shrugs his shoulders.

Regis concludes, "It's a mystery how—"

"I believe!" Thomas interrupts to exclaim one more time and emphatically points to the woods. This time everyone looks out the window to see what he's pointing at, but now the woods are dark, nothing to see. Thomas sits back with the realization that what he just saw was for his eyes and his eyes only.

Everyone turns their attention from Thomas back to Regis, who finishes his thought. "It's a mystery how he knew our names, but what a jolly ol' gent is he."

Everyone smiles and nods to agree.

Regis faces forward and turns the car key, a Christmas song fills the vehicle as the engine starts. Everyone is feeling the Spirit of Christmas and excitedly joins in to sing with the radio as they pull away from the train station:

*Deck the halls with boughs of holly*
*Fa-la-la-la-la, la-la-la-la*
*'Tis the season to be jolly*
*Fa-la-la-la-la, la-la-la-la*

*In the woods . . .*

Nicholas asks Noll, "Is everything ready for tonight? Are the reindeer resting? Have they had their special miracle food?"

"We have everything ready," Noll says, "and we have all this covered, so you can hurry home and enjoy some delicious fare. You have some time to rest before your long journey begins tonight!"

"Hmm, something delicious and *someone* deeelicious is waiting for me? A pertty little birdy? Ho, ho, hoo."

Noll rolls his eyes. "Yes."

"Oh, joy!" Nicholas becomes like a little kid looking forward to getting an extra special something on Christmas Eve. "Well, then, we'd better get going, and fast!"

Nicholas steps onto the sleigh, takes his whip to drive, and before he can sit down, Noll says, "I said we have you covered." He gives a whistle. Suddenly, a white stallion appears out of the woods and trots up to Nicholas, shimmering like an angel in the moonlight. He stands beside Nicholas like a loyal soldier reporting for duty. Seeing his beautiful horse arrive unexpectedly warms Nicholas' heart and makes him excited at the same time, because he so loves to ride.

Nicholas gives Noll a smile, the kind given to someone who brings you a pleasant surprise at just the right time. Nicholas hands Noll his well-used whip and quickly boards his trusty steed. He moves his horse close to Noll, who is now standing on the fully packed sleigh by himself. Nicholas extends his hand to shake Noll's.

Noll reaches out his hand in return for a firm handshake, and Nicholas looks endearingly at him. "Thank you, my . . ." Noll grimaces, bracing himself, for he knows his friend's misguided attempt at humor is coming next, "brother . . . from another mother!"

Noll is taken aback by Nicholas' moment of brotherly love. He gives a contented nod of approval as they release their grip. Nicholas readies his steed to ride north to home. "You are welcome," Noll tells his friend. And then, as if he's waited a very long time for this opportunity, Noll satisfyingly continues, "My *sister* from another mister! Hahahahahahaha!"

Nicholas, knowing he walked right into that by allowing himself a moment of sentimentality, is not surprised his old friend took the opportunity to pounce. Heartily he laughs. "Hohohohohoooo!" At that, he pulls his horse's reigns to head up the trail and gives a giddyup with his heels. "Away Shimmel!" Off Nicholas rides, swiftly toward his northernmost home, all the while declaring aloud, "You're no saint, Nooooll, you're nooo saint! Ho, ho, ho! Ho, ho, hooo!"

Noll watches his lifetime friend and brother in the Lord slowly disappear as dusk falls heavily upon them. He says to himself aloud, "But you are, my friend. Saint Nicholas, you are." He smiles and reflects for a moment on the centuries of wonderful memories.

Kari bounds up and squeezes into the sleigh. It is completely full of boxes, bags, and goods. She looks at Noll, who has a goofy grin on his face and asks if he is okay. Noll becomes aware of his surroundings and realizes his is the last sleigh to depart. He replies to her, "Yes, I feel phenomenal. It's Christmas Eve." In his best singing voice he chimes, "Tis the season to be jooolly!"

Kari responds, "Aaaaamen. Yeah. Okay, we'd better go, lots to do. Don't want to be late!" She motions with her hands for him to move forward quickly while looking around, as if she wants to get *away* from there more than get *to* somewhere.

"Do we have everyone?"

Kari hurriedly looks around. "Um, yeah, looks like it. Let's get a move on! Talk does not cook rice! Chop, chop! *Schnell, schnell! Andale andale, arriba arriba!*" At that, trusting his little sister and now in a hurry himself, Noll cracks the whip, and his four reindeer reply, quickly taking off at a steady pace.

Seconds later, Dax comes walking out of the woods carrying a bag of Christmas wrapping paper with his left arm and fixing his belt with his right hand. When he looks up, he is stunned to find the sleigh gone. Looking around, he sees it driving off into the distance.

Leaping and bounding, he starts after the sleigh as quickly as he can, yelling, "Wait for me!" Fortunately, for him, he happens to be one of the fastest Mikroses around, and he soon catches up to the sleigh enough for Noll to hear his faint pleas to stop. Noll does not stop, but he slows down enough to allow Dax to get a hand up into the sleigh. Huffing and puffing, Dax squeezes into a spot and catches his breath.

Dax is very irritated and looks across the bench seat at Kari. "I am *so* gonna put your name on the naughty list when we get home. Just you wait. I hope you like coal. Again!"

Kari looks at Dax with a *paybacks-suck-don't-they* look while rubbing her sore neck. Then she puts on the most angelic and innocent expression she can muster and apologetically says, in a not-very-genuine-sounding manner, "Sor-ry! My bad." She bats her eyelashes to evoke a sympathetic response, at which Dax and Noll look at each other, rolling their eyes. They respond in unison, as brothers sometimes do, "Whatever." All three siblings are amused with their antics.

Noll, feeling the love and the Spirit of the season, looks at Dax and wishes him, "Merry Christmas, my brother." and then to Kari, "Merry Christmas, my sister." Kari and Dax look at him and respond in unison, as twins often do, "Merry Christmas, Noooll!"

Looking at each other, they are pleased with the sounds of their voices and think themselves clever. Without missing a beat, they sing "No-o-ell, N-o-ell, No-o-ell, N-o-ell . . ." One star shines more brightly than all the others in the sky, the full moon lights up the star-filled heavens illuminating the earthly countryside blanketed by freshly fallen snow. Noll joins in and all three Mikroses sing a loud and proud crescendo, for the final, but most holy of lyrics, "Born is the Ki-ing of I-israeeel!"

**Merry Christmas!**

# Epilogue

SIX YEARS AFTER the Christian clergy were released from prison, in AD 311, both Emperor Diocletian and Emperor Galerius died. The cause of Galerius' death in May was an unknown disease he contracted at the age of fifty-one. Depressed by his long-term illness, Diocletian was reported to have committed suicide in December of that year at the age of sixty-six. Co-Emperor Licinius was entrusted with the care of Prisca and her daughter, Valeria, but when Licinius wanted to take all their assets, the mother and daughter fled from Licinius to his co-emperor, Maximinus.

After a short time, Maximinus proposed marriage to Valeria. He was rumored to have been more interested in her wealth and the prestige he would gain by marrying the widow of the emperor, than he was in Valeria as a person. She refused his hand, and Maximinus reacted by having her arrested. He confined her and her mother in Syria and confiscated their properties. The mother and daughter escaped, hiding in city after city in disguise for approximately fifteen months. They were finally caught and taken to a square in the Greek city of Salonika and beheaded. The bodies of Valeria and Prisca were thrown into the sea. They were both later canonized as Christian saints.

The Roman emperors who reigned after Diocletian either had difficulty trying to implement edicts against Christians, or they chose not to apply the later edicts, leaving Christians unharmed. Prior, at the urging of Valeria and Prisca, Galerius had rescinded the edicts, announcing that the persecution had failed to bring Christians back to traditional religion.

Emperor Constantine conquered Licinius and gained total rule of the empire. He would rule the empire alone. He reversed the edicts completely and returned all confiscated property to Christians. Under Constantine's rule, Christianity would become the empire's preferred religion.

In AD 325, Emperor Constantine convened the Council of Nicaea, the first ecumenical council, and many different Christian churches participated. More than three hundred bishops came from all over the Christian world to discuss the nature of the Holy Trinity. Nicholas was one of the bishops invited, and the Council of Nicaea agreed with many of Nicholas' views. The work of the council produced the Nicene Creed, which to this day many Christians around the whole world repeat weekly standing together, united, to confirm what they believe.

It also established the theology of the Holy Trinity and the yearly date for Easter. Easter falls on the first Sunday after the Full Moon date, based on mathematical calculations, that falls on or after March 21. If the Full Moon is on a Sunday, Easter is celebrated on the following Sunday.

## *A Visit from St. Nicholas*

### *By Clement Clarke Moore*

'Twas the night before Christmas, when all through the house
Not a creature was stirring, not even a mouse;
The stockings were hung by the chimney with care,
In hopes that St. Nicholas soon would be there;
The children were nestled all snug in their beds;
While visions of sugarplums danced in their heads;
And mamma in her 'kerchief, and I in my cap,
Had just settled our brains for a long winter's nap,
When out on the lawn there arose such a clatter,
I sprang from my bed to see what was the matter.
Away to the window I flew like a flash,
Tore open the shutters and threw up the sash.
The moon on the breast of the new-fallen snow,
Gave a lustre of midday to objects below,
When what to my wondering eyes did appear,
But a miniature sleigh and eight tiny reindeer,
With a little old driver so lively and quick,
I knew in a moment he must be St. Nick.
More rapid than eagles his coursers they came,
And he whistled, and shouted, and called them by name:
"Now, Dasher! now, Dancer! now Prancer and Vixen!
On, Comet! on, Cupid! on, Donner and Blitzen!
To the top of the porch! to the top of the wall!
Now dash away! dash away! dash away all!"
As leaves that before the wild hurricane fly,
When they meet with an obstacle, mount to the sky;
So up to the housetop the coursers they flew
With the sleigh full of toys, and St. Nicholas too—
And then, in a twinkling, I heard on the roof
The prancing and pawing of each little hoof.
As I drew in my head, and was turning around,
Down the chimney St. Nicholas came with a bound.
He was dressed all in fur, from his head to his foot,

*And his clothes were all tarnished with ashes and soot;*
*A bundle of toys he had flung on his back,*
*And he looked like a peddler just opening his pack.*
*His eyes—how they twinkled! his dimples, how merry!*
*His cheeks were like roses, his nose like a cherry!*
*His droll little mouth was drawn up like a bow,*
*And the beard on his chin was as white as the snow;*
*The stump of a pipe he held tight in his teeth,*
*And the smoke, it encircled his head like a wreath;*
*He had a broad face and a little round belly*
*That shook when he laughed, like a bowl full of jelly.*
*He was chubby and plump, a right jolly old elf,*
*And I laughed when I saw him, in spite of myself;*
*A wink of his eye and a twist of his head*
*Soon gave me to know I had nothing to dread;*
*He spoke not a word, but went straight to his work,*
*And filled all the stockings; then turned with a jerk,*
*And laying his finger aside of his nose,*
*And giving a nod, up the chimney he rose;*
*He sprang to his sleigh, to his team gave a whistle,*
*And away they all flew like the down of a thistle.*
*But I heard him exclaim, ere he drove out of sight—*
*"Happy Christmas to all, and to all a good night!"*

## *O Holy Night*

*Lyrics: Placide Cappeau 1847; Music: Adolphe Charles Adama 1847*

*O holy night, the stars are brightly shining,*
*It is the night of the dear Saviour's birth;*
*Long lay the world in sin and error pining,*
*'Till he appeared and the soul felt its worth.*
*A thrill of hope the weary world rejoices,*
*For yonder breaks a new and glorious morn;*

*Chorus*
*Fall on your knees, Oh hear the angel voices!*
*O night divine! O night when Christ was born.*
*O night, O holy night, O night divine.*

*Led by the light of Faith serenely beaming;*
*With glowing hearts by his cradle we stand:*
*So, led by light of a star sweetly gleaming,*
*Here come the wise men from Orient land,*
*The King of Kings lay thus in lowly manger,*
*In all our trials born to be our friend;*

*Chorus*
*He knows our need, To our weakness no stranger!*
*Behold your King! Before Him lowly bend!*
*Behold your King! your King! before him bend!*

*Truly He taught us to love one another;*
*His law is Love and His gospel is Peace;*
*Chains shall he break, for the slave is our brother,*
*And in his name all oppression shall cease,*
*Sweet hymns of joy in grateful Chorus raise we;*
*Let all within us praise his Holy name!*

*Chorus*
*Christ is the Lord, then ever! ever praise we!*
*His pow'r and glory, evermore proclaim!*
*His pow'r and glory, evermore proclaim!*

# References

All references to and quotes from New American Bible Revised Edition (NABRE) scripture come from Biblegateway.com.

**Chapter 1**
- Poem "A Visit from St. Nicholas" by Clement Clarke Moore (or possibly Henry Livingston, Jr.) found in *The Random House Book of Poetry for Children* (Random House Inc., 1983), as referenced by Poetry Foundation at https://www. poetryfoundation.org/poems/43171/a-visit-from-st-nicholas.

- Historical background on Nicholas found at St. Nicholas Center at http://www.stnicholascenter.org/pages/who-is-st-nicholas/ and on Wikipedia at https://en.wikipedia.org/wiki/Saint_Nicholas.

- Nicholas' name definition from Behind the Name at https://www. behindthename.com/name/nicholas.

**Chapter 2**
- History about the shepherd's staff found in the book *A Shepherd Looks at Psalm 23*, by W. Phillip Keller (Zondervan, 1970).

- The "dot and line analogy" and "tithes and offerings" information from *The Treasure Principle*, by Randy Alcorn (Multnomah Books, 2017).

- The information about "loving God, loving others, and loving ourselves righteously" found in the book *Secrets of God's Armor*, by Gil Stieglitz (Principles to Live By, 2015).

- The explanation about hell from *Biggest Question* video by Todd Friel, featuring Kirk Cameron.

- Wishing a "Mighty Christmas" found in the book *Defeating Scrooge*, by Renae Baker (Morway Media, 2018).

**Chapter 3**

- The "raising standard of giving versus the standard of living" information from *The Treasure Principle*, by Randy Alcorn (Multnomah Books, 2017).

- Information about horse named Shimmel from St. Nicholas Center at http://www.stnicholascenter.org/pages/who-travels-with-st-nicholas/.

**Chapter 4**

- The quote "What's right isn't always popular . . . ," is by Albert Einstein.

- Hughmongous and Nigerian Terror: Both names are in the public domain, confirmed with United States Patent and Trademark Office (USPTO) website search and phone call—Reference Number 1602882438.

**Chapter 5**

- "Love God, Love Others, Make a Difference" motto provided by LifeChurch Reno Pastor Dave Pretlove.

**Chapter 7**

- Information about last rites from United States Conference of Catholic Bishops at http://www.usccb.org/prayer-and-worship/bereavement-and-funerals/overview-of-catholic-funeral-rites.cfm.

**Chapter 8**

- Information about Confirmation found at Catholic Online, https://www.catholic.org/prayers/prayer.php?p=1653.

**Chapter 9**

- The quote "What you are is God's gift to you. What you become is your gift to God," is by Hans Urs von Balthasar.

- The quote "Outside the will of God, there's nothing I want. Inside the will of God, there's nothing I fear," is by A.W. Tozer.

- Information from "I Pick You" drawn from Bayside Church's *Refuel* video, featuring Pastor Curt Harlow, July 18, 2018.

**Chapter 11**

- Information from the book *Hurt People Hurt People: Hope and Healing for Yourself and Your Relationships,* by Dr. Sandra D. Wilson (Discovery House, 2001).

**Chapter 13**

- Northern Lights Information from "Northern Lights shine on" by Adrian Bridge, March 2013, *The Telegraph,* https://www.telegraph.co.uk/travel/news/Northern-Lights-shine-on/.

**Chapter 14**

- Information about Christian female scientists drawn from "Christian Women in Science, Technology, and Engineering," by Alice C. Linsley, September 2013, *The American Scientific Affiliation,* https://network.asa3.org/blogpost/999882/169929/Christian-Women-in-Science-Technology-and-Engineering.

- Information about famous scientists who believed in God taken from Evidence for God, http://www.godandscience.org/apologetics/sciencefaith.html.

- The quote "The person who makes the rules we live by is the person who is God to us," from the book *Hurt People Hurt People: Hope and Healing for Yourself and Your Relationships,* by Dr. Sandra D. Wilson (Discovery House, 2001).

- The quote "Jesus is the truth. He is bigger than our doubts and questions," from the book *Give Me an Answer,* by Cliffe Knechtle (InterVarsity Press, 1986).

**Chapter 15**

- "All seven sacraments were instituted by Christ and were entrusted to the Church to be celebrated in faith within and for the community of believers. The rituals and prayers by which a sacrament is celebrated serve to express visibly what God is doing invisibly," from For Your Marriage, http://www.foryourmarriage.org/marriage-as-sacrament/.

- Information about Jesus and solitude from the article "Jesus' Solitude and Silence" by Bill Gaultiere at Soul Shepherding, https://www.soulshepherding.org/jesus-solitude-and-silence/.

## Chapter 16

- Information from the great pearl sermon "A Bargain at Any Price," by Pastor Tom Chism, LifeChurch Reno.

- The quote "The God-given gift of intelligence they have, they use to reject God and His existence," from the book *Jesus Calling: Enjoying Peace in His Presence* by Sarah Young (Thomas Nelson, Special and Revised edition, 2004).

- Information about the Herodian from the video series *Life and Ministry of the Messiah Video Study: Learning the Faith of Jesus,* by Ray Vander Laan, 2009.

## Chapter 17

- History of Diocletian from *Encyclopædia Britannica* at https://www.britannica.com/biography/Diocletian.

## Chapter 18

- The quote "Fear knocked at the door. Faith answered. No one was there." By unknown, English Proverb.

## Chapter 20

- The reference to "Christmas was an event . . . a message . . .a person" comes from "Surviving the Holidays," a video presented by DivorceCare, a ministry of Church Initiative, at https://www. divorcecare.org/holidays.

## Chapter 21

- The quote "I could not even limp my way into heaven; therefore, you are my stretcher that carries me through my days and nights," is taken from a Rally in the Valley sermon by Pastor Dave Johnston.

- The passage that reads, "I believe You are one God, the Father almighty, maker of Heaven and earth, of all things visible and invisible . . ." is from the Nicene Creed, by the First Council of Nicaea in 325AD.

- The references to hating sin, but loving sinners, and a transaction that must take place are drawn from the *Biggest Question* video by Todd Friel, featuring Kirk Cameron.

## Chapter 22

- Lyrics from the song "Hark the Herald Angels Sing," by Charles Wesley, 1739.

- The reference to lack of forgiveness being like drinking poison and expecting the other person to die is said to come from a variety of sources. Anne Lamott wrote, "Not forgiving is like drinking rat poison and then waiting for the rat to die," in her book *Traveling Mercies: Some Thoughts on Faith*. Others credit Malachy McCourt, who wrote, "Resentment is like taking poison and waiting for the other person to die."

## Chapter 23

- "This event was a reminder that pain did not mean God had turned His back on us; pain is a sign that we live in a broken world, but we are never alone" is attributed to "Surviving the Holidays," a video presented by DivorceCare, a ministry of Church Initiative, at https://www.divorcecare.org/holidays.

- Information about reasons to be hopeful comes from article "Christmas: A Reason for Hope" by DivorceCare, a ministry of Church Initiative, at https://www.divorcecare.org/holidays/help-center/christmas.

## Chapter 27

- Reference to the original Serenity Prayer by Reinhold Niebuhr, as discussed in "History and the Author of the Original Serenity Prayer" by Dr. Ron L. Adams, October 2014, https://www.linkedin.com/pulse/20141029035141-319167549-history-andthe-author-of-the-original-serenity-prayer/.

## Chapter 28

- Lyrics from the song "Amazing Grace," by John Newton, 1779.

## Chapter 29

- Reference to the "trust fall" drawn from *Letting our "Trust Fall" into God's Arms*, video from Bayside Church, featuring Pastor Efrem Smith, July 2018.

## Chapter 30

- Lyrics from "Deck the Halls," traditional Welsh carol written by Thomas Oliphant, 1862.

- Lyrics from "The First Noel," in its current form, was first published in *Carols Ancient and Modern* (1823) and *Gilbert and Sandys Carols* (1833), both of which were edited by William Sandys and arranged, edited, and with extra lyrics written by Davies Gilbert for *Hymns and Carols of God*. Information provided by Wikipedia at https://en.wikipedia.org/wiki/The_First_Noel.

# About the Author

Wayne Van Der Wal grew up inside the beltway of Washington, D.C., in Falls Church, Virginia (with times in Michigan, Pennsylvania, Wyoming). He moved to the Reno/Lake Tahoe area of Nevada when he was 20 and never left.

His diverse leadership and speaking experience spans over thirty years of leading various ministries, including Bible Studies, College Ministry, DivorceCare, Jail Ministry, Inner-City Ministry, Men's Ministry, and Youth Group.

His professional work experience extends almost three decades, and includes being a School Psychologist (Ed.S.), School Counselor (M.A.), President of his State Association, and having a B.A. in Social Psychology.

His ultimate joys are the love of God, sermons, worship, and talking with anyone who wants to talk about God. He also enjoys beaches, vineyards/wineries, traveling, running, and watching movies. His two children were part of the inspiration for writing *The Gospel of Santa Claus* by giving him a desire to illuminate and celebrate the true meaning of Christmas with all.

To contact Wayne A. Van Der Wal, please complete the contact form at TheGospelofSantaClaus.com.